FOREIGN AFFAIRS

Sun-kissed seductions...

Idyllic interludes...

The world's most eligible men!

Dreaming of a foreign affair? Then, look no further! We've brought together the best and sexiest men the world has to offer, the most exciting, exotic locations and the most powerful, passionate stories.

This month, in *Greek Grooms*, we bring back two best-selling novels by Lynne Graham and Michelle Reid in which gorgeous Greek tycoons have marriage on their minds. But it's only the beginning...each month in **Foreign Affairs** you can be swept away to a new location — and indulge in a little passion in the sun!

Look out for some Parisian-style proposals in

FRENCH KISS

by

Catherine George & Helen Brooks

coming next month!

LYNNE GRAHAM

Lynne Graham was born in Northern Ireland and has been a keen Mills & Boon® reader since her teens. She's happily married, with an understanding husband who has learned to cook since she started to write! Her five children keep her on her toes. When time allows, Lynne is a keen gardener.

Don't miss Lynne Graham's *Rafaello's Mistress* in Modern Romance™, November 2001!

MICHELLE REID

Michelle Reid grew up on the southern edges of Manchester, the youngest in a family of five lively children. But now she lives in the beautiful county of Cheshire with her busy executive husband and two grown-up daughters. She loves reading, the ballet, and playing tennis when she gets the chance. She hates cooking, cleaning, and despises ironing! Sleep she can do without and produces some of her best written work during the early hours of the morning.

Look out for *The Bellini Bride* by Michelle Reid in Modern Romance™, November 2001!

greek grooms

LYNNE GRAHAM & MICHELLE REID

PASSION IN THE MEDITERRANEAN SUN!

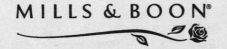

MILLS & BOON®

*MILLS & BOON and MILLS & BOON with the Rose Device
are registered trademarks of the publisher.
Harlequin Mills & Boon Limited,
Eton House, 18-24 Paradise Road, Richmond, Surrey, TW9 1SR*

Greek Grooms © Harlequin Enterprises II B.V., 2001

Married to a Mistress and *The Price of a Bride*
were first published in Great Britain by
Harlequin Mills & Boon Limited in separate single volumes.

Married to a Mistress © Lynne Graham 1998
The Price of a Bride © Michelle Reid 1998

ISBN 0 263 83180 9

126-1001

*Printed and bound in Spain
by Litografía Rosés S.A., Barcelona*

greek grooms

MARRIED TO A MISTRESS

LYNNE GRAHAM

CHAPTER ONE

'AND since Leland has given me power of attorney over his affairs, I shall trail that little tramp through the courts and *ruin* her!' Jennifer Coulter announced with vindictive satisfaction.

Angelos Petronides surveyed his late mother's English stepsister with no more than polite attention, his distaste concealed, his brilliant black eyes expressionless. Nobody would ever have guessed that within the last sixty seconds Jennifer had made his day by putting him in possession of information he would've paid a considerable amount to gain. Maxie Kendall, the model dubbed the Ice Queen by the press, the one and only woman who had ever given Angelos a sleepless night, was in debt...

'Leland spent a fortune on her too!' As she stalked his vast and impressive London office, Jennifer exuded seething resentment. 'You should see the bills I've uncovered...you wouldn't *believe* what it cost to keep that little trollop in designer clothes!'

'A mistress expects a decent wardrobe...and Maxie Kendall is ambitious. I imagine she took Leland for everything she could get.' Angelos stoked the flames of his visitor's outrage without a flicker of conscience.

Unlike most who had witnessed the breakup of the Coulter marriage three years earlier, he had never suffered from the misapprehension that Leland had deserted a whiter than white wife. Nor was he impressed by Jennifer's pleas of penury. The middle-aged blonde had been born wealthy and would die even wealthier, and her miserly habits were a frequent source of malicious amusement in London society.

5

'All that money gone for good,' Jennifer recounted tight-mouthed. 'And *now* I find out that the little tart got this huge loan off Leland as well—'

Imperceptibly, Angelos had tensed again. Trollop, tart? Jennifer had no class, no discretion. A mistress was a necessity to a red-blooded male, but a whore wasn't. However, Leland *had* broken the rules. An intelligent man did not leave his wife to set up home with his mistress. No Greek male would ever have been that stupid, Angelos reflected with innate superiority. Leland Coulter had made a fool of himself and he had embarrassed his entire family.

'But you have regained what you said you wanted most,' he slotted into the flood of Jennifer's financial recriminations. 'You have your husband back.'

The dry reminder made the older woman flush and then her mouth twisted again. 'Oh, yes, I got him back after his heart attack, so weak he's going to be recuperating for months! That bitch deserted him at the hospital…did I tell you that? Simply told the doctor to contact his wife and walked back out again, cool as a cucumber. Well, I *need* that money now, and whatever it takes I intend to get it off her. I've already had a lawyer's letter sent to her—'

'Jennifer…with Leland laid low, you have many more important concerns. And I assure you that Leland would not be impressed by the spectacle of his wife driving his former mistress into the bankruptcy court.' From below lush black lashes, Angelos watched the blonde stiffen as she belatedly considered that angle. 'Allow *me* to deal with this matter. I will assume responsibility for the loan and reimburse you.'

Jennifer's jaw slackened in shock. 'You…you *will*?'

'Are we not family?' Angelos chided in his deep, dark, accented drawl.

Slowly, very slowly, Jennifer nodded, fascinated against her will. Those incredible black eyes looked almost warm, and since warmth was not a character trait she had ever associated with Angelos Petronides before she was thrown off balance.

The head of the Petronides clan, and regarded with immense respect by every member, Angelos was ruthless, remorseless and coldly self-sufficient. He was also fabulously wealthy, flamboyantly unpredictable and frighteningly powerful. He scared people; he scared people just by strolling into a room. When Leland had walked out on his marriage, Angelos had silenced Jennifer's martyred sobs with one sardonic and deeply unsympathetic glance. Somehow Angelos had discovered that *her* infidelity had come first. Chagrined by that galling awareness, Jennifer had avoided him ever since...

Only the greater fear of what might happen to Leland's international chain of highly profitable casinos under her own inexpert guidance had driven her to approach Angelos for practical advice and assistance. Indeed, just at the moment Jennifer could not quite comprehend *how* she had been led into revealing her plans to destroy Maxie Kendall.

'You'll make her pay...?' Jennifer prompted drymouthed.

'My methods are my own,' Angelos murmured without apology, making it clear that the matter of the loan was no longer her province.

That hard, strikingly handsome face wore an expression that now chilled Jennifer. But she was triumphant. Clearly family ties, even distant ones, meant more to Angelos than she had ever dreamt. That little trollop would suffer; that was *all* Jennifer wanted.

When he was alone again, Angelos did something he had never been known to do before. He shattered his secretary by telling her to hold all his calls. He lounged indolently back in his leather chair in apparent contemplation of the panoramic view of the City of London. But his eyes were distant. No more cold showers. A sensual smile slowly formed on his well-shaped mouth. No more lonely nights. His smile flashed to unholy brilliance. The Ice Queen was *his*. After a three-year-long waiting game, she was finally to become *his*.

Mercenary and outwardly cold as she was…exquisite, though, indeed so breathtakingly beautiful that even Angelos, jaded and often bored connoisseur that he considered himself to be, had been stunned the first time he saw Maxie Kendall in the flesh. She looked like the Sleeping Beauty of popular fable. Untouchable, *untouched*… A grim laugh escaped Angelos. What nonsensical imagery the mind could serve up! She had been the mistress of a man old enough to be her grandfather for the past three years. There was nothing remotely innocent about the lady.

But for all that he would not use the loan like a battering ram. He would be a gentleman. He would be subtle. He would rescue her from her monetary embarrassments, earn her gratitude and ultimately inspire her loyalty as Leland had never contrived to do. She would not be cold with *him*. And, in reward, he would cocoon her in luxury, set the jewel of her perfection to a fitting frame and fulfil her every want and need. She would never have to work again. What more could any rational woman want?

Blissfully unaware of the detailed plans being formed on her behalf, Maxie climbed out of the cab she had caught from the train station. Every movement fluid with long-limbed natural grace, her spectacular trademark mane of golden hair blowing in the breeze, she straightened to her full five feet eleven inches and stared at her late godmother's home. Gilbourne was an elegant Georgian house set in wonderful grounds.

As she approached the front door her heart ached and she blinked back tears. The day she had made her first public appearance in Leland's company, her godmother, Nancy Leeward, had written to tell her that she would no longer be a welcome visitor here. But four months ago her godmother had come to see her in London. There had been a reconciliation of sorts, only Nancy hadn't said she was ill, hadn't given so much as a hint—nor had Maxie received word of her death until *after* the funeral.

So somehow it seemed all wrong to be showing up now for a reading of Nancy's last will and testament…and, worst of all, to be nourishing desperate prayers that at the last her godmother had somehow found it within her heart to forgive her for a lifestyle she had deemed scandalous.

In her slim envelope bag Maxie already carried a letter which had blown her every hope of future freedom to smithereens. It had arrived only that morning. And it had reminded her of a debt she had naively assumed would be written off when Leland severed their relationship and let her go. He had already taken three irreplaceable years of her life, and she had poured every penny she earned as a model into repaying what she could of that loan.

Hadn't that been enough to satisfy him? Right now she was homeless and broke and lurid publicity had severely curtailed her employment prospects. Leland had been vain and monumentally self-centred but he had never been cruel and he was certainly not poor. Why was he doing this to her? Couldn't he even have given her time to get back on her feet again before pressing her for payment?

The housekeeper answered the door before Maxie could reach for the bellpush. Her plump face was stiff with disapproval. 'Miss Kendall.' It was the coldest of welcomes. 'Miss Johnson and Miss Fielding are waiting in the drawing-room. Mrs Leeward's solicitor, Mr Hartley, should be here soon.'

'Thank you…no, there's no need to show me the way; I remember it well.'

Within several feet of the drawing-room, however, not yet ready to face the other two women and frankly nervous of the reception she might receive from one of them, Maxie paused at the window which overlooked the rose garden that had been Nancy Leeward's pride and joy. Her memory slid back to hazily recalled summer afternoon tea parties for three little girls. Maxine, Darcy and Polly, each of them on their very best behaviour for Nancy, who had never had a child of her own, had had pre-war values and expectations of her goddaughters.

Of the three, Maxie had always been the odd one out. Both Darcy and Polly came from comfortable backgrounds. They had always been smartly dressed when they came to stay at Gilbourne but Maxie had never had anything decent to wear, and every year, without fail, Nancy had taken Maxie shopping for clothes. How shocked her godmother would've been had she ever learned that Maxie's father had usually sold those expensive garments the minute his daughter got home again...

Her late mother, Gwen, had once been Nancy's companion—a paid employee but for all that Nancy had always talked of her as a friend. Her godmother, however, had thoroughly disliked the man her companion and friend had chosen to marry.

Weak, selfish, unreliable... Russ Kendall was, unfortunately, all of those things, but he was also the only parent Maxie had ever known and Maxie was loyal. Her father had brought her up alone, loving her to the best of his ability. That she had never been able to trust him to behave himself around a woman as wealthy as Nancy Leeward had just been a cross Maxie had had to bear.

Every time Russ Kendall had brought his daughter to Gilbourne to visit he had overstayed his welcome, striving to butter her godmother up with compliments before trying to borrow money from her, impervious to the chill of the older woman's distaste. Maxie had always been filled with guilty relief when her father departed again. Only then had she been able to relax and enjoy herself.

'I thought I heard a car but I must've been mistaken. I wish Maxie would come...I'm looking forward to seeing her again,' a female voice said quite clearly.

Maxie twisted in surprise to survey the drawing-room door, only now registering that it was ajar. That had been Polly's voice, soft and gentle, just like Polly herself.

'That's one thrill I could live without,' a second female voice responded tartly. 'Maxie, the living doll—'

'She can't help being beautiful, Darcy.'

Outside the door, Maxie had frozen, unnerved by the biting hostility she had heard in Darcy's cuttingly well-bred voice. So Darcy *still* hadn't managed to forgive her, and yet what had destroyed their friendship three years earlier had been in no way Maxie's fault. Darcy had been jilted at the altar. Her bridegroom had waited until the eleventh hour to confess that he had fallen in love with one of her bridesmaids. That bridesmaid, entirely innocent of the smallest instant of flirtation *with* or indeed interest *in* the bridegroom, had unfortunately been Maxie.

'Does that somehow excuse her for stealing someone else's husband?'

'I don't think any of us get to choose *who* we fall in love with,' Polly stressed with a surprising amount of emotion. 'And Maxie must be devastated now that he's gone back to his wife.'

'If Maxie ever falls in love, it won't be with an ancient old bloke like that,' Darcy scorned. 'She wouldn't have looked twice at Leland Coulter if he hadn't been loaded! Surely you haven't forgotten what her father was like? Greed is in Maxie's bloodstream. Don't you remember the way Russ was always trying to touch poor Nancy for a loan?'

'I remember how much his behaviour embarrassed and upset Maxie,' Polly responded tautly, her dismay at the other woman's attitude audible.

In the awful pool of silence that followed Maxie wrapped her arms round herself. She felt gutted, totally gutted. So nothing had changed. Darcy was stubborn and never admitted herself in the wrong. Maxie had, however, hoped that time would've lessened the other woman's antagonism to the point where they could at least make peace.

'She *is* stunningly beautiful. Who can really blame her for taking advantage of that?' Darcy breathed in a grudging effort at placation. 'But then what else has Maxie got? I never did think she had much in the way of brains—'

'How can you say that, Darcy? Maxie is severely dyslexic,' Polly reminded her companion reproachfully.

Maxie lost all her natural colour, cringing at even this whispered reference to her biggest secret.

The tense silence in the drawing-room lingered.

'And in spite of that she's so wonderfully famous now,' Polly sighed.

'Well, if your idea of fame is playing Goldilocks in shampoo commercials, I suppose she is,' Darcy shot back crushingly.

Unfreezing, Maxie tiptoed back down the corridor and then walked with brisk, firm steps back again. She pushed wide the door with a light smile pasted to her unwittingly pale face.

'Maxie!' Polly carolled, and rose rather awkwardly to her feet.

Halfway towards her, Maxie stopped dead. Tiny dark-haired Polly was pregnant.

'When did you get married?' Maxie demanded with a grin.

Polly turned brick-red. 'I didn't...I mean, I'm *not*...'

Maxie was stunned. Polly had been raised by a fire-breathing puritanical father. The teenager Maxie recalled had been wonderfully kind and caring, but also extremely prim and proper as a result. Horribly aware that she had embarrassed Polly, she forced a laugh. 'So what?' she said lightly.

'I'm afraid the event of a child without a husband is not something as easily shrugged off in Polly's world as in yours.' Darcy stood by the window, her boyishly short auburn hair catching fire from the light behind her, aggressive green eyes challenging on the point.

Maxie stiffened at the reminder that Darcy had a child of her own but she refused to rise to that bait. Poor Polly looked strained enough as it was. 'Polly knows what I meant—'

'Does she—?' Darcy began.

'I feel dizzy!' Polly announced with startling abruptness.

Instantly Darcy stopped glaring at Maxie and both women anxiously converged on the tiny brunette. Maxie was the more efficient helper. Gently easing Polly down into the nearest armchair, she fetched a footstool because the smaller woman's ankles looked painfully swollen. Then, noting the untouched tea trolley nearby, she poured Polly a cup of tea and urged her to eat a digestive biscuit.

'Do you think you should see a doctor?' Darcy asked ruefully. 'I suppose I was lucky. I was never ill when I was expecting Zia.'

'What do you think, Polly?' Maxie prompted.

'I'm fine…saw one yesterday,' Polly muttered. 'I'm just tired.'

At that point, a middle-aged man in a dark suit was shown in with great ceremony by the housekeeper. Introducing himself as Edward Hartley, their godmother's solicitor, he took a seat, politely turned down the offer of refreshment and briskly extracted a document from his briefcase.

'Before I commence the reading of the will, I feel that I should warn you all beforehand that the respective monies will only be advanced *if* the strict conditions laid down by my late client are met—'

'Put that in English,' Darcy interrupted impatiently.

Mr Hartley removed his spectacles with a faint sigh. 'I assume that you are all aware that Mrs Leeward enjoyed a very happy but tragically brief marriage when she was in her twenties, and that the premature death of her husband was a lifelong source of sorrow and regret to her.'

'Yes,' Polly confirmed warmly. 'Our godmother often talked to us about Robbie.'

'He died in a car crash six months after they married,' Maxie continued ruefully. 'As time went on he became pretty much a saint in her memory. She used to talk to us about marriage as if it was some kind of Holy Grail and a woman's only hope of happiness.'

'Before her death, Mrs Leeward made it her business to visit each one of you. After completing those visits, she altered her will,' Edward Hartley informed them in a tone of wry regret. 'I advised her that the conditions of inheritance she chose to include might be very difficult, if not impossible for any one of you to fulfil. However, Mrs Leeward was a lady who knew her own mind, and she had made her decision.'

Maxie was holding her breath, her bemused gaze skimming over the faces of her companions. Polly wore an expression of blank exhaustion but Darcy, never able to hide her feelings, now looked worried sick.

In the pin-dropping silence, the solicitor began to read the will. Nancy Leeward had left her entire and extremely substantial estate evenly divided between her three goddaughters on condition that each of them married within a year and remained married for a minimum of six months. Only then would they qualify to inherit a portion of the estate. In the event of any one of them failing to meet the terms of the will, that person's share would revert to the Crown.

By the time the older man had finished speaking, Maxie was in shock. Every scrap of colour had drained from her face. She had hoped, she had *prayed* that she might be released from the burden of debt that had almost destroyed her life. And now she had learnt that, like everything else over the past twenty-two years, from the death of her mother when she was a toddler to her father's compulsive gambling addiction, nothing was going to be that easy.

A jagged laugh broke from Darcy. 'You've just got to be kidding,' she said incredulously.

'There's no chance of me fulfilling those conditions,' Polly confided chokily, glancing at her swollen stomach and looking away again with open embarrassment.

'Nor I...' Maxie admitted flatly, her attention resting on Polly and her heart sinking for her. She should have guessed there would be no supportive male in the picture. Trusting, sweet-natured Polly had obviously been seduced and dumped.

Darcy shot Maxie an exasperated look. 'They'll be queuing up for you, Maxie—'

'With my colourful reputation?'

Darcy flushed. 'All any one of us requires is a man and a wedding ring. Personally speaking, I'll only attract either by advertising and offering a share of the proceeds as a bribe!'

'While I am sure that that is a purely facetious comment, made, as it were, in the heat of the moment, I must point out that the discovery of any such artificial arrangement would automatically disqualify you from inheriting any part of your godmother's estate,' Edward Hartley asserted with extreme gravity

'You may say our godmother knew her own mind...but I *think*...well, I'd better not say what I think,' Darcy gritted, respect for a much loved godmother evidently haltering her abrasive tongue.

Simultaneously, a shaken little laugh of reluctant appreciation was dredged from Maxie. *She* was not in the dark. The reasoning behind Nancy Leeward's will was as clear as daylight to her. Within recent months their godmother had visited each one of them...and what a severe disappointment they must all have been.

She had found Maxie apparently living in sin with an older married man. She had discovered that Polly was well on the road to becoming an unmarried mother. And Darcy? Maxie's stomach twisted with guilt. Some months after that day of cruel humiliation in the church, Darcy had given birth to a baby. Was it any wonder that the redhead had been a vehement man-hater ever since?

'It's such a shame that your godmother tied her estate up like that,' Maxie's friend, Liz, lamented the following afternoon as the two women discussed the solicitor's letter which had bluntly demanded the immediate settlement of Leland Coulter's loan. 'If she hadn't, all your problems would've been solved.'

'Maybe I should have told Nancy the real reason why I was living in Leland's house…but I couldn't have stood her thinking that I was expecting *her* to buy me out of trouble. It wouldn't have been fair to put her in that position either. She really did detest my father.' Maxie gave a fatalistic shrug. She had suffered too many disappointments in life to waste time crying over spilt milk.

'Well, what you need now is some good legal advice. You were only nineteen when you signed that loan agreement and you were under tremendous pressure. You were genuinely afraid for your father's life.' Liz's freckled face below her mop of greying sandy hair looked hopeful. 'Surely that *has* to make a difference?'

From the other side of the kitchen table, casually clad in faded jeans and a loose shirt, Maxie studied the friend who had without question taken her in off the street and freely offered her a bed for as long as she needed it. Liz Blake was the only person she trusted with her secrets. Liz, bless her heart, had never been influenced by the looks that so often made other women hostile or uneasy in Maxie's company. Blind from birth and fiercely independent, Liz made a comfortable living as a potter and enjoyed a wide and varied social circle.

'I signed what I signed and it did get Dad off the hook,' Maxie reminded her.

'Some thanks you got for your sacrifice.'

'Dad's never asked me for money since—'

'Maxie…you haven't *seen* him for three years,' Liz pointed out grimly.

Maxie tensed. 'Because he's ashamed, Liz. He feels guilty around me now.'

Liz frowned as her guide dog, Bounce, a glossy black

Labrador, sprang up and nudged his head against her knee. 'I wonder who that is coming to the door. I'm not expecting anyone…and nobody outside the mail redirection service and that modelling agency of yours is supposed to know you're here!'

By the time the doorbell actually went, Liz was already in the hall moving to answer it. A couple of minutes later she reappeared in the doorway. 'You have a visitor…foreign, male, very tall, very attractive voice. He also says he's a very good friend of yours—'

'Of mine?' Maxie queried with a perplexed frown.

Liz shook her head. 'He *has* to be a good friend to have worked out where you're hiding out. And Bounce gave him the all-over suspicious sniff routine and passed him with honours so I put him in the lounge. Look, I'll be in the studio, Maxie. I need to finish off that order before I leave tomorrow.'

Maxie wondered who on earth had managed to find her. The press? Oh, dear heaven, had Liz trustingly invited some sneaky journalist in? Taut with tension, she hurried down the hall into the lounge.

One step into that small cosy room, she stopped dead as if she had run into a brick wall without warning. Smash, *crash*, her mind screamed as she took a sudden instinctive backward step, shock engulfing her in rolling waves of disorientation.

'Maxie…how are you?' Angelos Petronides purred as he calmly extended a lean brown hand in conventional greeting.

Maxie gaped as if a boa constrictor had risen in front of her, her heart thumping at manic speed and banging in her eardrums. A very good friend. Had Liz misheard him?

'Mr Petronides—?'

'Angelos, please,' he countered with a very slight smile.

Maxie blinked. She had never seen him smile before. She had been in this arrogant male's company half a dozen times over the past three years and this was the very first time he had deigned to verbally acknowledge that she lived and breathed. In her presence he had talked around her as if she wasn't there, switching to Greek if she made any attempt to enter the conversation, and on three separate occasions, evidently responding to his request, Leland had sent her home early in a taxi.

With rock-solid assurance, Angelos let his hand drop again. Amusement at her stupefied state flashed openly in his brilliant black eyes.

Maxie stiffened. 'I'm afraid I can't imagine what could bring you here…or indeed how you found me—'

'Were you ever lost?' Angelos enquired with husky innuendo while he ran heavily lidded heated dark eyes over her lithe, slender frame with extraordinarily insulting thoroughness. 'I suspect that you know very well why I am here.'

Her fair skin burning, Maxie's sapphire blue eyes shuttered. 'I haven't the slightest idea—'

'You are now a free woman.'

This is not happening to me, a little voice screeched in the back of Maxie's mind. She folded her arms, saw those terrifyingly shrewd eyes read her defensive body language and lowered her arms again, fighting not to coil her straining fingers into fists.

One unguarded moment almost six months ago… Was that all it had taken to encourage him? He had caught her watching him and instantaneously, as if that momentary abstraction of hers had been a blatant invitation, he had reacted with a lightning flash look of primitive male sexual hunger. A split second later he had turned away again, but that shatteringly unexpected response of his had shaken Maxie inside out.

She had told herself she had imagined it. She had almost cherished this arrogant Greek tycoon's indifference to her as a woman. OK, so possibly, once or twice, his ability to behave as if she was invisible had irritated and humiliated her, but then she had seen some excuse for his behaviour.

Unlike Leland, Angelos Petronides would never be guilty of a need to show off a woman like a prize poodle at what was supposed to be a business meeting.

'And now that you *are* free, I want you in my life,' Angelos informed her with the supreme confident cool of a male who had never been refused anything he wanted by a woman. Not a male primed for rejection, not a male who had even contemplated that as a remote possibility. His attitude spoke volumes for his opinion of her morals.

And at that mortifying awareness Maxie trembled, her usual deadpan, wonderful and absolute control beginning to fray round the edges. 'You really believe that you can just walk in here and *tell* me—?'

'Yes,' Angelos cut in with measured impatience. 'Don't be coy. You have no need to play such games with me. I have not been unaware of your interest in me.'

Her very knees wobbled with rage, a rage such as Maxie had never known before. He had the subtlety of a sledgehammer, the blazing self-image of a sun god. The very first time she had seen Angelos Petronides she *had* had a struggle to stop staring. Lethally attractive men were few and far between; fiercely intelligent and lethally attractive men were even fewer. And the natural brute power Angelos radiated like an aura of intimidation executed its own fatal fascination.

He had filled her with intense curiosity but that was *all*. Maxie had never learnt what it was like to actually want a man. She didn't like most men; she didn't trust them. What man had ever seen her as an individual with emotions and thoughts that might be worth a moment's attention? What man had ever seen her as anything more than a glamorous one-dimensional trophy to hang on his arm and boast about?

As a teenager, Maxie had always been disillusioned, angered or frankly repelled long before she could reach the stage of reciprocating male interest. And now Angelos Petronides had just proved himself the same as the rest of the common herd. What she couldn't understand was why she should be feeling a fierce, embittered stab of stark disappointment.

'You're trembling...why don't you sit down?' Angelos switched into full domineering mode with the polished ease of a duck taking to water and drew up an armchair for her occupancy. When she failed to move, the black eyes beneath those utterly enviable long inky lashes rested on her in irritated reproof. 'You have shadows under your eyes. You have lost weight. You should be taking better care of yourself.'

She would *not* lose her temper; she would tie herself in knots before she exposed her outrage and he recognised her humiliation. How dared he...how *dared* he land on Liz's doorstep and announce his lustful intentions and behave as if he was awaiting a round of applause? If she spread herself across the carpet at his feet in gratitude, he would no doubt happily take it in his stride.

'Your interest in my wellbeing is unwelcome and unnecessary, Mr Petronides,' Maxie countered not quite levelly, and she sat down because she was honestly afraid that if she didn't she might give way to temptation and slap him across that insolent mouth so hard she would bruise her fingers.

He sank down opposite her, which was an instant relief because even when she was standing he towered over her. That was an unusual sensation for a woman as tall as Maxie, and one that with him in the starring role she found irrationally belittling.

For such a big, powerfully built man, however, he moved with the lightness and ease of an athlete. He was as dark as she was fair...quite staggeringly good-looking. Spectacular cheekbones, a strong, thin-bladed nose, the wide mouth of a sensualist. But it was those extraordinary eyes which held and compelled and lent such blazing definition to his fantastic bone structure. And there was not a soupçon of softness or real emotion in that hard, assessing gaze.

'Leland's wife was planning to take you to court over that loan,' Angelos Petronides delivered smoothly into the thumping silence.

Maxie's spine jerked rigid, eyes flying wide in shock as she gasped, 'How did you find out about the loan?'

Angelos angled a broad, muscular shoulder in a light, dismissive shrug, as if they were enjoying a light and casual conversation. 'It's not important. Jennifer will *not* take you to court. I have settled the loan on your behalf.'

Slowly, her muscles strangely unwilling to do her bidding, Maxie leant forward. 'Say that again,' she invited shakily, because she couldn't believe he had said what he had just said.

Angelos Petronides regarded her with glittering black unfathomable eyes. 'I will not hold that debt over you, Maxie. My intervention was a gesture of good faith alone.'

'G-good *faith*…?' Maxie stammered helplessly, her voice rising to shrillness in spite of her every effort to control it.

'What else could it be?' Angelos shifted a graceful hand in eloquent emphasis, his brilliant gaze absorbing the raw incredulity and shock which had blown a giant smoking crater in the Ice Queen's famed façade of cool. 'What man worthy of the name would seek to blackmail a woman into his bed?'

CHAPTER TWO

MAXIE leapt upright, her beautiful face a flushed mask of fury. 'Do you think I am a complete fool?' she shouted at him so loudly her voice cracked.

Unhurriedly, Angelos Petronides shifted his incredibly long legs and fluidly unfolded to his full height again, his complete control mocking her loss of temper. 'With regard to some of your past decisions in life...how frank am I allowed to be?'

Maxie sucked in oxygen as if she was drowning, clamped a hand to her already opening mouth and spun at speed away from him. She was shattered that he had smashed her self-discipline. As noise filtered through the open window she became dimly aware of the shouts of children playing football somewhere outside, but their voices were like sounds impinging from another world.

'You don't need to apologise,' Angelos drawled in a mocking undertone. 'I've seen your temper many times before. You go pale and you stiffen. Every time Leland put so much as a finger on you in public, I witnessed your struggle not to shrug him off. It must have been fun in the bedroom...'

Maxie's slender backbone quivered. Her fingernails flexed like claws longing to make contact with human flesh. She wanted to *kill* him. But she couldn't even trust herself to speak, and was all the more agitated by the simple fact that she had never felt such rage before and honestly didn't know how to cope with it.

'But then, it was always evident to me that Leland's biggest thrill was trotting you out in public at every possible opportunity. ''Look at me, I have a blonde twice as tall as

22

me and a third of my age,"' Angelos mused with earthy amusement. 'I suspect he might not have demanded intimate entertainment that often. He wasn't a young man…'

'And you are…without doubt…the most offensive, objectionable man I have ever met!' Maxie launched with her back still rigidly turned to him.

'I am a taste you will acquire. After all, you *need* someone like me.' A pair of strong hands settled without warning on her slim shoulders and exerted sufficient pressure to swivel her back round to face him.

'I need someone like you like I need a hole in the head!' Maxie railed back at him rawly as she tore herself free of that controlling hold. 'And keep your hands off me…I don't like being pawed!'

'Why are you so angry? I *had* to tell you about the loan,' Angelos pointed out calmly. 'I was aware that the Coulters' lawyer had already been in touch. Naturally, I wanted to set your mind at rest.'

The reminder of the debt that had simply been transferred acted like a drenching flood of cold water on Maxie's overheated emotions. Her angry flush was replaced by waxen pallor. Her body turned cold and weak and shaky and she studied the worn carpet at his feet. 'You've bought yourself a pup. I can't settle that loan…and right now I haven't even got enough to make a payment on it,' she framed sickly.

'Why do you get yourself so worked up about nothing?' Angelos released an extravagant sigh. 'Sit down before you fall down. Haven't I already given you my assurance that I have no intention of holding that former debt over your head in any way? But, in passing, may I ask what you needed that loan for?'

'I got into a real financial mess, that's all,' she muttered evasively, protecting her father as she always did, conscious of the derisive distaste such weakness roused in other, stronger men. And, drained by her outbursts and ashamed of them, she found herself settling back down into the chair again.

For the very first time she was genuinely scared of Angelos Petronides. He owned a piece of her, just as Leland once had, but he would be expecting infinitely more than a charade in return. She wasn't taken in by his reassurances, or by that roughly gentle intonation she had never dreamt he might possess. In the space of ten minutes he had reduced her to a babbling, screeching wreck and, for now, he was merely content to have made his domineering presence felt.

'Money is not a subject I discuss with women,' Angelos told her quietly. 'It is most definitely not a subject I ever wish to discuss with you again.'

Angelos Petronides, billionaire and benevolence personified? Maxie shuddered with disbelief. Did he ever read his own publicity? She had sat in on business meetings chaired by him, truly unforgettable experiences. The King and his terrified minions, who behaved as if at any moment he might snap and shout, 'Off with their heads!' Grown men perspired and stammered with nerves in his presence, cowered when he shot down their suggestions, went into cold panic if he frowned. He did not suffer fools gladly.

He had a brilliant mind, but that superior intellect had made him inherently devious and manipulative. He controlled the people around him. In comparison, Leland Coulter had been harmless. Maxie had *coped* with Leland. And Leland, give him his due, had never tried to pose as her only friend in a hostile world. But over her now loomed a six-foot-four-inch giant threat without a conscience.

'I know where you're coming from,' Maxie heard herself admit out loud as she lifted her beautiful head again.

Angelos gazed down at her with steady black eyes. 'Then why all the histrionics?'

Maxie gulped, disconcerted to feel that awful surge of temper rise again. With that admission she had expected to make him wary, force him to ease back. About the last reaction she had expected was his cool acknowledgement that she was intelligent enough to recognise his tactics for what they were. The iron hand in the velvet glove.

'Have dinner with me tonight,' Angelos suggested smoothly. 'We can talk then. You need some time to think things over.'

'I need no time whatsoever.' Maxie stared back up into those astonishingly dark and impenetrable eyes and suffered the oddest light-headed sensation, as if the floor had shifted beneath her. Her lashes fluttered, a slight bemused frown line drawing her fine brows together as she shook her head slightly, long golden hair thick as skein on skein of silk rippling round her shoulders. 'I will not be your mistress.'

'I haven't asked yet.'

A cynical laugh was torn from Maxie as she rose restively to her feet again. 'You don't need to be that specific. I certainly didn't imagine you were planning to offer me anything more respectable. And, no, I do *not* intend to discuss this any further,' she asserted tightly, carefully focusing on a point to the left of him, the tip of her tongue stealing out to moisten her dry lower lip in a swift defensive motion. 'So either you are a good loser or a bad loser, Mr Petronides…I imagine I'll find out which soon enough—'

'I do not lose,' Angelos breathed in a roughened undertone. 'I am also very persistent. If you make yourself a challenge, I will resent the waste of time demanded by pursuit but, like any red-blooded male, I will undoubtedly want you even more.'

Without even knowing why, Maxie shivered. There was the most curious buzz in the atmosphere, sending tiny little warning pulses of alarm through her tautening length. Her unsettled and bemused eyes swerved involuntarily back to him and locked into the ferocious hold of his compelling scrutiny.

'I will also become angry with you,' Angelos forecast, shifting soundlessly closer, his husky drawl thickening and lowering in pitch to a mesmeric level of intimacy. 'You made Leland jump through no hoops…why should I? And I would treat you *so* much better than he did. I know what a woman likes. I know what makes a woman of your nature feel secure and appreciated, what makes her happy, content, *satisfied*…'

Like a child drawn too close to a blazing fire in spite of all warnings, Maxie was transfixed. She could feel her own heartbeat accelerating, the blood surging rich and vibrantly alive through her veins. A kind of craving, an almost terrifying upswell of excitement potently and powerfully new to her gripped her.

'A-Angelos…?' she whispered, feeling dizzy and disorientated.

He reached out and drew her to him without once breaking that spellbinding appraisal. 'How easily you can say my name…'

And she said it again, like a supplicant eager to please.

Those stunning eyes of his blazed gold as a hot sun with satisfaction. She trembled, legs no longer dependable supports beneath her, and yet in all her life she had never been more shockingly aware of her own body. Her braless breasts were swelling beneath the denim shirt she wore, the tender nipples suddenly tightening to thrust with aching sensitivity against the rough grain of the fabric.

There was a sudden enormous jarring thud on the windowpane behind her. Startled, Maxie almost jumped a foot in the air, and even Angelos flinched.

'Relax…a football hit the window,' he groaned in apparent disbelief as he raised his dark, imperious head. 'It is now being retrieved by two grubby little boys.'

But Maxie wasn't listening. She had been plunged into sudden appalled confusion by the discovery that Angelos Petronides had both arms loosely linked round her and had come within treacherous inches of kissing her. Even worse, she realised, every fibre of her yearning body had been longing desperately for that kiss.

Jerking back abruptly from the proximity of his lean,

muscular frame, Maxie pressed shaking hands against her hot, flushed cheeks. 'Get out of here and don't ever come back!'

Angelos grated something guttural in Greek, stood his ground and dealt her a hard, challenging look. 'What's the matter with you?'

And what remained of Maxie's self-respect drained away as she recognised his genuine bewilderment. Dear heaven, she had encouraged him. She had been straining up to him, mindlessly eager for his lovemaking, paralysed to the spot with excitement and longing, and he knew it too. And did his body feel as hers did now? Deprived, aching... As she registered such unfamiliar, intimate thoughts, Maxie realised just how out of control she was.

'I don't have to explain myself to you,' she gabbled in near panic as she rushed past him out into the hall to pull open the front door. 'I want you to leave and I don't want you to come back. In fact I'll put the dog on you if you ever come here again!'

In a demonstration of disturbing volatility, Angelos vented a sudden appreciative laugh, the sound rich and deep and earthy. His quality of dark implacability vanished under the onslaught of that amusement. Maxie stared. The sheer charisma of that wolfish grin took her by surprise.

'The dog's more likely to lick me to death...and you?' An ebullient ebony brow elevated as he watched the hot colour climb in her perplexed face.

'Leave!' The word erupted from Maxie, so desperate was she to silence him.

'And *you*?' Angelos repeated with steady emphasis. 'For some strange reason, what just happened between us, which on my level was nothing at all, unnerved you, scared you...embarrassed you...'

As he listed his impressions Maxie watched him with a sick, sinking sensation in her stomach, for never before had she been so easily read, and never before had a man made her feel like a specimen on a slide under a microscope.

'Now why should honest hunger provoke shame?' Angelos asked softly. 'Why not pleasure?'

'Pleasure?'

'I do not presume to know your every thought…as yet,' Angelos qualified with precision. His brilliant eyes intent, he strolled indolently back into the fresh air. 'But surely when ambition and desire unite, you should be pleased?'

He left her with that offensive suggestion, striding down the path and out to the pavement where a uniformed chauffeur waited beside a long, dark limousine. The two wide-eyed and decidedly grubby little boys, one of whom was clutching the football, were trying without success to talk to the po-faced chauffeur. She watched as Angelos paused to exchange a laughing word with them, bending to their level with disconcerting ease. Disturbed by her own fascination, she slammed shut the door on her view.

He would be back; she knew that. She couldn't explain how but she knew it as surely as she knew that dawn came around every morning. Feeling curiously like someone suffering from concussion, she wandered aimlessly back down into the kitchen and was surprised to find Liz sitting there, her kindly face anxious.

'Bounce started whining behind the studio door. He must've heard you shouting. I came back into the house but naturally I didn't intrude when I realised it was just an argument,' Liz confided ruefully. 'Unfortunately, before I retreated again, I heard rather more than I felt comfortable hearing. You're a wretched dog, Bounce…your grovelling greeting to Angelos Petronides affected my judgement!'

'So you realised who my visitor was—?'

'Not initially, but my goodness I should've done!' Liz exclaimed feelingly. 'You've talked about Angelos Petronides *so* often—'

'Have I?' Maxie breathed with shaken unease, her cheeks burning.

Liz smiled. 'All the time you were criticising him and

complaining about his behaviour, I could sense how attracted you were to him...'

A hoarse laugh erupted from Maxie's dry throat. 'I wish you'd warned me. It hit me smack in the face when I wasn't prepared for it. Stupid, wretched chemistry, and I never even realised... I feel such an idiot now!' Eyes prickling with tears of reaction, she studied the table, struggling to reinstate her usual control. 'And I've got the most banging headache s-starting up...'

'Of course you have,' Liz murmured soothingly. 'I've never heard you yelling at the top of your voice before.'

'But then I have never hated anyone so much in my life as I hate Angelos Petronides,' Maxie confessed shakily. 'I. wanted to kill him, Liz...I really wanted to kill him! Now I'm in debt to *him* instead of Leland—'

'I did hear him say that you didn't have to worry about that.'

Maxie's eyes flashed 'If it takes me until I'm ninety, I'll pay him back every penny!'

'He may have hurt your pride, Maxie...but he was most emphatic about not wanting repayment. He sounded sincere to me, and surely you have to give him some credit for his generosity whether you choose to regard it as a debt or otherwise?' Liz reasoned with an air of frowning confusion. 'The man has to be *seriously* interested in you to make such a big gesture on your behalf—'

'Liz—' Maxie broke in with a pained half-smile.

'Do you think he might turn out to be the marrying kind?' the older woman continued with a sudden teasing smile.

That outrageous question made Maxie's jaw drop. 'Liz, for heaven's sake...are you nuts?' she gasped. 'What put that in your mind?'

'Your godmother's will—'

'Oh, that...forget that, Liz. That's yesterday's news. Believe me when I say that Angelos Petronides was not thinking along the lines of anything as...well, anything as lasting as marriage.' Mindful of her audience, Maxie chose her words carefully and suppressed a sigh over the older woman's romantic imagination. 'He is not romantically interested in me. He is not that sort of man. He's hard, he's icy cold—'

'He didn't sound cold on my doorstep…he sounded downright *keen*! You'd be surprised how much I can pick up from the nuances in a voice.'

Liz was rather innocent in some ways. Maxie really didn't want to get down to basics and spell out just how a big, powerful tycoon like Angelos Petronides regarded her. As a social inferior, a beautiful body, a target object to acquire for his sexual enjoyment, a *live* toy. Maxie shrank with revulsion and hated him all over again. 'Liz…he would be offended by the very suggestion that he would even consider a normal relationship with a woman who's been another man's mistress—'

'But you haven't *been* another man's mistress!'

Maxie ignored that point. After the horrendous publicity she had enjoyed, nobody would ever believe that now. 'To be blunt, Liz…all Angelos wants is to get me into bed!'

'Oh…' Liz breathed, and blushed until all her freckles merged. 'Oh, dear, no…you don't want to get mixed up with a man like that.'

Maxie lay in bed that night, listening to the distant sound of the traffic. She couldn't forgive herself for being attracted to a male like Angelos Petronides. It was impossible that she could *like* anything about him. 'A woman of your nature,' he had said. His one little slip. Wanton, available, already accustomed to trading her body in return for a luxurious lifestyle. That was what he had meant. Her heart ached and she felt as if she was bleeding inside. How had she ever sunk to the level where she had a reputation like that?

When Maxie had first been chosen as the image to launch a new range of haircare products, she had been a complete unknown and only eighteen years old. Although she had never had the slightest desire to be a model, she had let her father persuade her to give it a try and had swiftly found herself earning what had then seemed like enormous amounts of money.

However, once the novelty had worn off, she had loathed the backbiting pressure and superficiality of the modelling circuit. She had saved like mad and had planned to find another way to make a living.

But all the time, in the background of her life, her father had continued to gamble. Relying on her income as a safety net, he had, without her knowledge, begun playing for higher and higher stakes. To be fair, Leland's casino manager had cut off Russ Kendall's credit line the minute he'd suspected the older man was in over his head. Maxie had met Leland Coulter for the first time the day she settled her father's outstanding tab at his casino.

'You won't change the man, Maxie,' he had told her then. 'If he was starving, he would risk his last fiver on a bet. He has to be the one who wants to change.'

After that humiliating episode her father had made her so many promises. He had sworn blind that he would never gamble again but inevitably he had broken his word. And, barred from the reputable casinos, he had gone dangerously down-market to play high-rolling poker games in smoky back rooms with the kind of tough men who would happily break his fingers if he didn't pay his dues on time. That was when Maxie's life had come completely unstuck...

Having got himself into serious debt, and learning to his dismay that his daughter had no savings left after his previous demands, Russ had been very badly beaten up. He had lost a kidney. In his hospital bed, he had sobbed with shame and terror in her arms. He had been warned that if he didn't come up with the money he owed, he would be crippled the next time.

Distraught, Maxie had gone to Leland Coulter for advice. And Leland had offered her an arrangement. He would pay off her father's gambling debts and allow her to repay him at her leisure on condition that she moved in with him. He had been very honest about what he wanted. Not sex, he had insisted. No, what Leland had craved most had been the ego-boosting pleasure of being seen to possess a beautiful young woman, who would preside over his dinner table, act as his hostess, entertain his friends and always be available to accompany him wherever he went.

It hadn't seemed so much to ask. Nobody else had been prepared to loan her that amount of money. And she had been so agonisingly grateful that her father was safe from further harm. She hadn't seen the trap she was walking into. She hadn't even been aware that Leland was a married man until the headlines had hit the tabloids and taken her reputation away overnight. She had borne the blame for the breakup of his marriage.

'Jennifer and I split up because *she* had an affair,' Leland had admitted grudgingly when Maxie had roundly objected to the anomalous situation he had put her in. 'But this way, with you by my side, I don't feel like a fool…all right?'

And she had felt sorry for him then, right through the protracted and very public battle he and his wife had had over alimony and property. Jennifer and Leland had fought each other every inch of their slow path to the divorce court, yet a week before the hearing, when Leland had had a heart attack, the only woman he had been able to think about when he was convinced that he was at his last gasp had, most tellingly, been his estranged wife. 'Go away, leave me alone… I need Jennifer here… I don't want her seeing you with me now!' he had cried in pathetic masculine panic.

And that had hurt. In a crazy way she had grown rather fond of Leland, even of his silly showing-off and quirky little vanities. Not a bad man, just a selfish one, like all the men she had ever known, and she hoped he was happy now that he was back with his Jennifer. But he had used her not only to soothe his wounded vanity but also, and less forgivably, she recognised now, as a weapon with which to

punish his unfaithful wife. And Maxie could not forget that,
or forgive herself for the blind naivety that had allowed it
to happen in the first place. Never, ever again, she swore,
would she be *used*...

Early the next morning, Maxie helped Liz pack. Her friend
was heading off to stay with friends in Devon. The fact that
her house wouldn't be left empty during her absence was
a source of great relief to Liz. The previous year her home
had been burgled and her studio vandalised while she was
away.

As soon as she had seen the older woman off, Maxie
spent an hour slapping on make-up like war-paint and
dressing up in style. Angelos Petronides needed a lesson
and Maxie was determined to give it to him.

Mid-morning, she pawned the one piece of valuable jew-
ellery she owned. She had been eleven when she'd found
the Victorian bracelet buried in a box of cheap costume
beads which had belonged to her mother. She had cried,
guessing why the bracelet had been so well concealed. Even
in the three short years of her marriage, her poor mother
had doubtless learnt the hard way that when her husband
was short of money he would sell anything he could get
his hands on. Afterwards, Russ would be terribly sorry and
ashamed, but by then it would be too late and the treasured
possession would be gone. So Maxie had kept the bracelet
hidden too.

And now it hurt so much to surrender that bracelet. It
felt like a betrayal of the mother she could barely remember. But she desperately needed the cash and she had nothing else to offer. Angelos Petronides *had* to be shown that
he hadn't bought her or any rights over her by settling
Leland's loan. The sacrifice of her mother's bracelet, temporarily or otherwise, simply hardened Maxie's angry, bitter resolve.

Half an hour later, she strolled out of the lift on to the
top floor of the skyscraper that housed the London head-

quarters of the vast Petronides organisation. She spared the receptionist barely a glance. She knew how to get attention.

'I want to see Angelos,' she announced.

'Miss...Miss Kendall?' The brunette was already on her feet, eyes opened wide in recognition: in a bold scarlet dress that caressed every curve, her spectacular hair rippling in a sheet of gold to her waist, and heels that elevated her to well over six feet, Maxie was extremely noticeable.

'I know where his office is.' Maxie breezed on down the corridor, the brunette darting after her with an incoherent gasp of dismay.

She flung wide his office door when she got there. Infuriatingly, it was empty. She headed for the boardroom, indifferent to the squawking receptionist, whose frantic pursuit had attracted the attention of another two secretarial staff.

Bingo! Maxie strolled through the boardroom's double doors. An entire room full of men in business suits swivelled at her abrupt entry and then gaped. Maxie wasn't looking at them. Her entire attention was for Angelos Petronides, already rising from his chair at the head of the long polished table, his expression of outrage shimmering in an instant into shocking impassivity. But she took strength from the stunned quality that had briefly lit those fierce black eyes of his.

'I want to see you now,' Maxie told him, sapphire-blue eyes firing a challenge.

'You could wait in Mr Petronides's office, just through here, Miss Kendall.' The quiet female intervention came from the slim older woman who had already rushed to cast invitingly wide the door which connected with her employer's office.

'Sorry, I don't want to wait,' Maxie delivered.

A blazing look of dark, simmering fury betrayed Angelos. It was the reaction of a male who had never before been subjected to a public scene. Maxie smiled sweetly. He couldn't touch her because she had nothing to lose. No money, no current employment, nothing but her pride and her wits. He should've thought of that angle. And, no matter what it took, she intended to make Angelos pay for the state he had put her in the day before.

In one wrathful stride, Angelos reached her side and closed a forceful hand round her narrow wrist. Maxie let out a squeal as if he had hurt her. Startled, he dropped her wrist again. In receipt of a derisive, unimpressed glance that would've made a lesser woman cringe, Maxie noted without surprise that Angelos was a quick study.

'Thank you,' she said, and meant it, and she strolled through to his big, luxurious office like a little lamb because now she knew he was coming too.

'Unexpected visitors with unpredictable behaviour are so enervating…don't you think?' Maxie trilled as she fell still by the side of his impressive desk.

Angelos swore in Greek, studying her with seething black eyes full of intimidation. 'You crazy—' His wide mouth hardened as he bit back the rest of that verbal assault with the greatest of visible difficulty. 'What the hell are you playing at?' he growled like a grizzly bear instead.

'I'm not playing, I'm *paying*!' With a flourish, Maxie opened her fingers above his desk and let drop the crushed banknotes in her hand. 'Something on account towards the loan. I can't be bought like a tin of beans off a supermarket shelf!'

'How dare you interrupt a business meeting?' Angelos launched at her full throttle. 'How *dare* you make a scene like that in my boardroom?'

Maxie tensed. She had never heard a man that angry. She had never seen a male with so dark a complexion look that pale. Nor had she ever faced a pair of eyes that slashed like bloodthirsty razors into her.

'You asked for it,' she informed him grittily. 'You embarrassed me yesterday. You made me feel *this* big…' With her thumb and her forefinger she gave him a literal demonstration. 'You made me feel powerless and this is pay-back time. You picked on the wrong woman!'

'Is this really the Ice Queen I'm dealing with?' Angelos responded very, very drily.

'You'd burn the ice off the North Pole!' Maxie sizzled back at him, wondering why he had now gone so still, why his naturally vibrant skin tone was recovering colour, indeed why he didn't appear to be in a rage any more.

'Do you suffer from a split personality?'

'Did you really think you *knew* me just because you were in the same room with me a handful of times?' Maxie flung her head back and was dumbstruck by the manner in which his narrowed gaze instantly clung to her cascading mane of hair, and then roved on down the rest of her with unconcealed appreciation. It struck her that Angelos Petronides was so convinced that he was an innately superior being and so oversexed that he couldn't take a woman seriously for five minutes.

Brilliant black eyes swooped up to meet hers again. 'No way did you ever behave like this around Leland—'

'My relationship with him is none of your business,' Maxie asserted with spirit. 'But, believe me, nobody has ever insulted me as much as you did yesterday.'

'I find that very hard to believe.'

Involuntarily, Maxie flinched.

Immensely tall and powerful in his superbly tailored silver-grey suit, Angelos watched her, not an informative glimmer of any emotion showing now on that lean, strong, hard-boned face. 'Since when has it been an insult for a man to admit that he wants a woman?' he demanded with derision.

'You frightened the life out of me telling me you'd paid off that loan…you put me under pressure, then you tried to move in for the kill like the cold, calculating womaniser you are!' Maxie bit out not quite levelly, and, spinning on her heel, she started towards the door.

'All exits are locked. You're trapped for the moment,' Angelos delivered softly.

Maxie didn't believe him until she had tried and failed to open the door. Then she hissed furiously, 'Open this door!'

'Why should I?' Angelos enquired, choosing that exact same moment to lounge indolently back against the edge of his desk, so cool, calm and confident that Maxie wanted to rip him to pieces. 'Presumably you came here to entertain me…and, although I have no tolerance for tantrums, you *do* look magnificent in that dress, and naturally I would like to know why I'm receiving this melodramatic response to my proposition.'

In one flying motion, Maxie spun back. 'So you admit that that's what it was?'

'I want you. It's only a matter of time until I get what I want,' Angelos imparted very quietly in the deadly stillness.

Maxie shivered. 'When the soft soap doesn't work, weigh in with the threats—'

'That *wasn't* a threat. I don't threaten women,' Angelos growled with a feral flash of white teeth. 'No woman has ever come to my bed under threat!'

Nobody could feign that much outrage. He was an Alpha male and not one modestly given to underestimating his own attractions. But then, he had it *all*, she conceded bitterly. Incredible looks and sex appeal, more money than he could spend in a lifetime and a level of intelligence that scorched and challenged.

Maxie shot him a look of violent loathing. 'You think you're so special, don't you? You thought I'd be flattered, ready to snatch at whatever you felt like offering…but you're no different from any of the other men who have lusted after me,' she countered with harsh clarity. 'And I've had plenty of practice dealing with your sort. I've looked like this since I was fourteen—'

'I'm grateful you grew up before our paths crossed,' Angelos breathed with deflating amusement.

At that outrageous comment, something inside Maxie just cracked wide open, and she rounded on him like a tigress. 'I shouldn't have had to cope with harassment at that age. Do you think I don't *know* that I'm no more real to a guy like you than a blow-up sex doll?' she condemned with raw, stinging contempt. 'Well, I've got news for you, Mr Petronides...I am not available to be any man's live toy. You want a toy, you go to a store and buy yourself a railway set!'

'I thought you'd respect the upfront approach,' Angelos confided thoughtfully. 'But then I could never have guessed that behind the front you put on in public you suffer from such low self-esteem...'

Utterly thrown by that response, and with a horrendous suspicion that this confrontation was going badly wrong shrilling through her, Maxie suddenly felt foolish.

'Don't be ridiculous...of course I don't,' she argued with ragged stress. 'But, whatever mistakes I've made, I have no intention of repeating them. Now, I've told you how I feel, so open that blasted door and let me out of here!'

Angelos surveyed her with burning intensity, dense lashes low on penetrating black eyes. 'If only it were that easy...'

But this time when Maxie's perspiring fingers closed round the handle the door sprang open, and she didn't stalk like a prowling queen of the jungle on her exit, she simply fled, every nerve in her too hot body jangling with aftershock.

CHAPTER THREE

WHAT had possessed her, what on *earth* had possessed her? Maxie asked herself feverishly over and over again as she walked. The rain came heavily—long, lazy June days of sunshine finally giving way to an unseasonal torrent which drenched her to the skin within minutes. Since she was too warm, and her temples still pounded with frantic tension, she welcomed that cooling rain.

Something had gone wildly off the rails in that office. Angelos had prevented her quick exit. He had withstood everything she threw at him with provocative poise. In fact, just like yesterday, the more out of control she had got, the calmer and more focused he had become. And he zipped from black fury to outrageous cool at spectacular and quite unnerving speed.

Melodramatic, yes, Maxie acknowledged. She had been. Inexplicably, she had gone off the deep end and hurled recriminations that she had never intended to voice. And, like the shrewd operator he was, Angelos Petronides had trained those terrifyingly astute eyes on her while she recklessly exposed private, personal feelings of bitter pain and insecurity.

It was stress which had done this to her. Leland's heart attack, the sudden resulting upheaval in her own life, the dreadful publicity, her godmother's death. The pressure had got to her and blown her wide open in front of a male who zeroed in on any weakness like a predator. Low self-esteem…she did *not* suffer from low self-esteem!

A limousine drew up several yards ahead of her in the quiet side-street she was traversing. Alighting in one fluid movement, Angelos ran exasperated eyes over her sodden appearance and grated, 'Get in out of the rain, you foolish woman…don't you even know to take shelter when it's wet?'

Swallowing hard on that in-your-face onslaught, Maxie pushed shaking fingers through the wet strands of hair clinging to her brow and answered him with a blistering look of charged defiance. 'Go drop yourself down a drain!'

'Will you scream assault if I just throw you in the car?' Angelos demanded with raw impatience.

A kind of madness powered Maxie then, adrenaline racing through her. She squared up to him, scarlet dress plastered to her fantastic body, the stretchy hemline riding up on her long, fabulous legs. She dared him with her furious eyes and her attitude and watched his powerful hands clench into fists of self-restraint—because of course he was far too clever to make a risky move like that.

'Why are you following me?' she breathed.

'I'm not into railway sets…too slow, too quiet,' Angelos confessed.

'I'm not into egocentric dominating men who think they know everything better than me!' Maxie slung back at him, watching his luxuriant ebony hair begin to curl in the steady rain, glistening crystalline drops running down his hard cheekbones. And she thought crazily, He's getting wet for me, and she liked that idea.

'If this is my cue to say I might change…sorry, no can do. I am what I am,' Angelos Petronides spelt out.

Stupid not to take a lift when she could have one, Maxie decided on the spur of the moment, particularly when she was beginning to feel cold and uncomfortable in her wet clothing. Sidestepping him, enjoying the awareness that she was rather surprising him, she climbed into the limousine.

The big car purred away from the kerb.

'I decided to make you angry because I want you to leave me alone,' Maxie told him truthfully.

LYNNE GRAHAM 41

'Then why didn't you stay away from me? Why did you get into this car?' Angelos countered with lethal precision.

In answer, Maxie made an instinctive and instantaneous shift across the seat towards the passenger door. But, before she could try to jump back out of the car, a powerful hand whipped out to close over hers and hold her fast. The limousine quickened speed.

Black eyes clashed with hers. 'Are you suicidal?' Angelos bit out crushingly.

Maxie shakily pulled free of his grasp.

The heavy silence clawed at her nerves. Such a simple question, such a lethally simple, clever question, yet it had flummoxed her. If she had truly wanted to avoid him, why *had* she let something as trivial as wet clothes push her back into his company?

Angelos extended a lean brown hand again, with the aspect of an adult taking reluctant pity on a sulky child. 'Come here,' he urged.

Without looking at him again, Maxie curled into the far corner of the back seat instead. His larger-than-life image was already engraved inside her head. She didn't know what was happening to her, why she was reacting so violently to him. Her own increasing turmoil and the suspicion that she was adrift in dangerously unfamiliar territory frankly frightened her. Angelos Petronides was bad news in every way for a woman like her. Avoiding him like the plague was the only common sense response. And she should've been freezing him out, not screaming at him.

With a languorous sigh, Angelos shrugged fluidly out of his suit jacket. Without warning he caught her hand and pulled her to him. Taken by surprise, Maxie went crazy, struggling wildly to untangle herself from those powerful fingers. 'Let go! What are you trying to——?'

'Stop it!' Angelos thundered down at her, and he released her again in an exaggerated movement, spreading both arms wide as if to demonstrate that he carried no offensive weapon. 'I don't like hysterical women.'

'I'm not...I'm not like that.' Maxie quivered in shock and stark embarrassment as he draped his grey jacket round her slim, taut shoulders. The silk lining was still warm from his body heat. The faint scent of him clung to the garment and her nostrils flared. Clean, husky male, laced with the merest tang of some citrus-based lotion. She lowered her damp head and breathed that aroma in deep. The very physicality of that spontaneous act shook her.

'You're as high-strung as some of my racehorses,' Angelos contradicted. 'Every time I come close you leap about a foot in the air—'

'I didn't yesterday,' she muttered with sudden lancing bitterness.

'You didn't get the chance...I crept up on you.' With a tormentingly sexy sound of indolent amusement, Angelos reached out his hands and closed them over the sleeves of the jacket she now wore, tugging on them like fabric chains of captivity to bring her to him.

'No!' Maxie gasped, wide-eyed, her hands flying up, only to find that the only place she could plant her palms was against his broad, muscular chest.

'If you like, you can bail out after the first kiss—no questions asked, no strings attached,' Angelos promised thickly.

Even touching him through his shirt felt so incredibly intimate that guilty quivers ran through her tautening length. He was so hot. Her fingers spread and then shifted over the tactile silk barrier, learning of the rough whorls of hair below the fabric and enthralled. She was used to being around male models with shiny shaven chests. She shivered deliciously, appallingly tempted to rip open the shirt and explore.

Heavily lidded black eyes lambent with sensual indulgence intercepted hers. 'You look like a guilty child with her hand caught in the biscuit tin,' he confided with a lazy smile.

At the power of that smile, the breath tripped in Maxie's throat, her pupils dilating. His proximity mesmerised her. She could see tiny gold lights in his eyes, appreciate the incredible silky length and luxuriance of those black lashes and the faint blue shadow on his strong jawline. The potency of her own fascination filled her with alarm. 'You're all wrong for me,' she said in breathless panic, like a woman trying to run through a swamp and inexplicably finding herself standing still and sinking fast.

'Prove it,' Angelos invited in that velvet-soft drawl that fingered down her spine like a caress. A confident hand pushed into her drying hair and curved to the nape of her neck. 'Prove that anything that feels this good could possibly be wrong for either of us.'

He was so stunningly gorgeous, she couldn't think straight. Her heartbeat seemed to be racing in her tight throat. The insidious rise of her own excitement was like a drowning, overwhelming wave that drove all before it. He dropped his eyes to the pouting distended buds clearly delineated by the clinging bodice of her dress and her face burned red.

Slowly Angelos tilted her back, his arms banding round her spine to support her, and, bending his dark, arrogant head, he pressed the mouth she craved on hers to the thrusting sensitivity of an aching nipple instead. Her whole body jumped, throat arching, head falling back, teeth clenching on an incoherent whimper of shock.

Angelos lifted her up again, black eyes blazing with primal male satisfaction. 'It hurts to want this much. I don't think you were familiar with the feeling...but *now* you are.'

Trembling, Maxie stared at him, sapphire eyes dark with shaken arousal. Cold fear snaked through her. He was playing with her just as he might have played with a toy. Using his carnal expertise he was taunting her, winding her up, demonstrating his sexual mastery.

'Don't touch me!' Her hand whipped up and caught him across one hard cheekbone, and then she froze in dismay at what she had done.

With striking speed Angelos closed his fingers round that offending hand, and slowly he smiled again. 'Frustration *should* make you angry.'

Beneath her strained and bemused gaze, he bent his glossy dark head and pressed his lips hotly to the centre of her stinging palm. It was electrifying. It was as if every tiny bit of her body was suddenly programmed to overreact. And then, while she was still struggling to comprehend the incredible strength of his power over her, he caught her to him with indolent assurance and simply, finally, kissed her.

Only there was nothing simple about that long-awaited kiss. It blew Maxie away with excitement. It was like no kiss she had ever received. That hard, sensual mouth connected with hers and instantly she needed to be closer to him than his own skin. Pulses pounding at an insane rate, she clutched at him with frantic hands, reacting to the violent need climbing inside her, craving more with every passing second.

And then it was over. Angelos studied her with burnished eyes of appreciation, all virile male strength and supremacy as he absorbed the passion-glazed blankness of her hectically flushed and beautiful face.

'Come on,' he urged her thickly.

She hadn't even realised the limousine had stopped. Now he was closing his jacket round her again with immense care, practically lifting her back out into the rain and the sharp fresh air which she drank in great thirsty gulps. She felt wildly disorientated. For timeless minutes the world beyond the limousine just hadn't existed for her. In confusion, she curved herself into the support of the powerful arm welded to her narrow back and bowed her head.

Without warning, Angelos tensed and vented a crushing oath, suddenly thrusting her behind him. Maxie looked up just in time to see a photographer running away from them. Simultaneously two powerfully built men sprinted from the car behind the limo and grabbed him before he could make it across to the other side of the street.

Angelos untensed again, straightening big shoulders. 'My security men will expose his film. That photo of us will never see the light of day.'

In a daze, Maxie watched that promise carried out. As a demonstration of ruthlessness it took her breath away. She had often wished that she could avoid the intrusive cameras of the paparazzi, but she had never seen in action the kind of brute power which Angelos exercised to protect his privacy.

And it was *his* privacy that he had been concerned about, she sensed. Certainly not hers. Why was it that she suspected that Angelos would go to great lengths to avoid being captured in newsprint by her side? Why was it that she now had the strongest feeling that Angelos was determined not to be seen in public with her?

Shivering with reaction at that lowering suspicion, she emerged from her tangled thoughts to find herself standing in a stark stainless steel lift. 'Where are we?' she muttered then, with a frown of bewilderment.

The doors sped soundlessly back on a vast expanse of marble flooring.

'My apartment…where else?'

Maxie flinched in dismay, her brain cranking back into sudden activity. If that paparazzo had escaped, he would've had a highly embarrassing and profitable picture of her entering Angelos Petronides's apartment wrapped intimately in his jacket. No prizes for guessing what people would've assumed. She just could not believe how stupid she had been.

'I thought you were taking me back to Liz's,' she admitted rather unsteadily.

Angelos angled up a mocking brow. 'I never said I was…and, after our encounter in the car, I confess that I prefer to make love in my own bed.'

Maxie could feel her teeth starting to chatter, her legs shaking. Like a whore, that was how she would've looked in that photo, and that was exactly how he was treating her.

'Maxie…' Angelos purred, reading her retreat and switching channel to high-powered sensual persuasion as he strolled with animal grace towards her, strong, hard-boned face amused. 'You think I'm likely to respect you more if you suggest that we should wait another week, another month? I have no time for outdated attitudes like that—'

'Obviously not.' Agreement fell like dropped stones from Maxie's tremulously compressed lips.

'And I cannot credit that you should feel any differently. We will still be together six months from now,' Angelos forecast reflectively. 'Possibly even longer. I burn for you in a way I haven't burned for a woman in a very long time.'

'Try a cold shower.' Ice-cool as her own shrinking flesh, Maxie stood there, chin tilting as high as she could hold it even though she felt as if she was falling apart behind her façade. She shrugged back her shoulders so that his jacket slid off and fell in a rejected heap on the floor. 'I'm not some bimbo you can bed before you even date me—'

'The original idea was only to offer you lunch…' A dark rise of blood accentuated the tautening slant of his bold, hard cheekbones as he made that admission.

'But why waste time feeding me?' Maxie completed for him, her distaste unconcealed. 'In my time I have met some fast movers, but you have to qualify as supersonic. A kiss in the limo and that was consent to the whole menu?'

Angelos flung his arrogant dark head back, black eyes thudding like steel arrows into a target. 'The desire between us was honest and mutual and very strong. Do you expect me to apologise for a hunger you answered with a passion as powerful as my own?'

Maxie flinched. 'No...I don't think you make a habit of apologising.'

'I'm very straight...what you see is what you get. You put out conflicting signals and then back off. You have the problem,' Angelos informed her in cool condemnation. 'Don't put it on me. When I became an adult, I put childish games behind me.'

Although every strained muscle in her taut length ached, Maxie remained as outwardly poised as a queen surveying a less than satisfactory subject. But violent loathing powered her now. It took its strength from her shame that she had allowed him to touch her at all.

'I won't say it's been nice getting to know you over the past twenty-four hours, Angelos...it's been lousy,' Maxie stated, and turned in the direction of the lift.

'Goddamn you...don't you dare walk away from me!' Angelos slashed across the distance that separated them. 'Who are you, Maxie Kendall, to speak to *me* like that?'

'No more...I don't want to hear it,' Maxie muttered shakily.

'This time you will listen to me,' Angelos raked at her in wrathful forewarning. In one powerful stride he imposed his intimidating size between her and the lift. His lean, strong face hard as steel, bold black eyes hurled a ferocious challenge. 'Do you think I don't know you moved in with Leland between one day and the next? You hardly knew him. You came out of nowhere into his life. Do you think I didn't notice that you weren't remotely attracted to him?'

Quite unprepared for that angle of attack, Maxie stammered, 'I...I—'

'In fact, Leland bored you to death and you couldn't hide it. You could hardly bear him to touch you but you stuck it for three years all the same. Does that strike you as the behaviour of a sensitive woman with principles? You sold yourself for a wardrobe of designer clothes—'

'No, I didn't!' Maxie gasped strickenly.

'At no stage did you wake up and say to yourself, "I could do better than this. I'm worth more than this. This isn't the way I should be living!"' Angelos roared at her in a rage of shockingly raw derision. 'So don't tell me I got the wrong impression. I trust the evidence of my own eyes and senses. You felt nothing for him. But you put yourself on the market and he was still able to buy!'

Nausea stirring in her stomach, Maxie was retreating deeper into the penthouse apartment, her hands coming up in a fluttering movement in front of her as if she could somehow ward him off. 'No...no,' she mumbled sickly.

'And I was the bloody fool who, even knowing all that, *still* wanted you!' Angelos slung, spreading his arms in an extravagant gesture of outrage at her, at himself. 'I didn't want to buy you...or maybe I wanted the cosy pretence that it didn't have to be like that between us...that because you lusted after me too I could gloss over the knowledge that my immense wealth might have anything to do with your presence in my life!'

Maxie was like a statue, terrified to risk a step in case she cracked and broke into shattered pieces. He had forced her into cruel confrontation with the image he had of her. Like an explosion of glass, countless shards pierced her cringing flesh as every painful word drew blood.

'I'll never forgive you for this,' she whispered, more to herself than to him. 'But Leland was never my lover. We had an agreement. It was a charade we played—'

Angelos spat something guttural in Greek. 'Don't talk to me like I'm stupid!'

Maxie looked through him then, and despised herself for even attempting self-defence. It suggested a weakness inside her, a need for this arrogant Greek's good opinion that her savaged pride could not allow. 'You stay away from me from now on—'

'You made your choices in life long before you met me. What is it that you want now?' Angelos demanded contemptuously.

A semi-hysterical laugh erupted from Maxie and she choked it off, twisting her head away defensively before he could see the burning tears in her eyes. 'Just the usual things.' Then she whipped her golden head back, shimmering eyes as unwittingly bright as stars. 'And some day, when all this is behind me, I'll have them. I wouldn't have you as a gift, Angelos. I wouldn't make love with you unless you tied me to the bed and held me down and forced me...is that clear enough? What you want you will *never* have!'

Angelos stared at her as if he couldn't take his eyes off her and hated her for it.

Maxie stared back with a stab of malicious satisfaction new to her experience. 'Bad news, eh? I'll be the one who got away,' she breathed tautly, frighteningly aware of the thunderous charge of violence in the atmosphere but unable to silence her own tongue and her helpless need to taunt him. 'But then why should that bother you? It's not like you have a shred of *real* emotion in you—'

'What do you want from me?' Angelos ripped back at her with suppressed savagery. 'I will not and could not love a woman like you!'

'Oh, that honesty...hits me right where it hurts,' Maxie trilled, a knife-like pain scything through her. She was shaking like a leaf without even being aware of it. 'But for all that you still want me, don't you? Do you know something, Angelos? I *like* knowing that.'

A muscle jerked at the corner of his wide, sensual mouth, his strong jawline clenching. Those stunning black eyes burned with rage and seething pride.

'Thanks, you've just done wonders for my low self-esteem,' Maxie informed him with a jagged catch in her voice.

'What a bitch you can be…I never saw that in you before.' His accent was so thick she could have sliced it up, but that contemptuous intonation would still have flamed over her like acid, hurting wherever it touched. 'So, quote me a price for one night in your bed. What do you think you would be worth?'

The derisive suggestion coiled like a whip around her and scarred her worse than a beating. Her backbone went rigid. Hatred fired her embittered gaze. 'You couldn't even make the bidding,' Maxie asserted, looking him up and down as if he had crawled out from under a stone. 'I'd want a whole lot more than a wardrobe of designer clothes. You see, I learn from my mistakes, Angelos. The next man I live with will be my husband…'

Shock turned Angelos satisfying pale. 'If you think for one *insane* second that I—'

'Of course you wouldn't,' Maxie slotted in, each word clipped and tight with self-control. 'But you must see now why I'm not available for lunch, in bed or out of it. A woman can't be too careful. Being associated with a randy Greek billionaire could be very harmful to my new image.'

'I will work this entire dialogue out of your wretched hide every day you are with me!' Angelos snarled at her with primal force, all cool abandoned.

'You are just so slow on the uptake. I am not ever going to be *with* you, Angelos,' Maxie pointed out, and with that last word she strolled past him, holding herself taut and proud to the last, and walked into the lift.

Outside in the street again, she discovered that she was trembling so violently it was an effort to put one leg in front of the other. For once disregarding her straitened circumstances, she chose to hail a cab. Her mind was working like a runaway express train, disconnected images bombarding her…

How *could* two people who scarcely knew each other spend so long tearing each other apart? How could she have been that bitchy? How could she have actually enjoyed striking back at him and watching him react with impotent black fury? And yet now she felt sick at the memory, and astonishingly empty, like someone who had learned to thrive on electric tension and pain...and who now could not see a future worth living without them.

Angelos Petronides had devastated her but he wouldn't bother her again now, she told herself in an effort at consolation. Even the toughest male wouldn't put himself in line for more of the same. And Angelos least of all. He had expected her to fall into his bed with the eagerness of an avaricious bimbo, scarcely able to believe her good fortune. Instead she had hit that boundless ego of his, watched him shudder in sheer shock from the experience...and yet inside herself she felt the most awful bewildering sense of loss.

Reluctant to dwell on reactions that struck her as peculiar, Maxie chose instead to look back on their brief acquaintance with self-loathing. She squirmed over her own foolishness. Like an adolescent fighting a first powerful crush, she had overreacted every step of the way.

She had fancied him like mad but, blind and naive as a headstrong teenager, she hadn't even admitted that to herself until it was too late to save face. 'I have not been unaware of your interest in me.' She shuddered with shame. Had she surrendered to that physical attraction, it would've been a one-way ticket to disaster. She knew she couldn't afford to make any more wrong choices. She hadn't needed *him* to tell her that. Dear heaven, as if becoming his mistress would've been any kind of improvement on the humiliating charade Leland had forced her to live for so long!

Angelos hadn't believed her about Leland, of course he hadn't—hadn't even paused to catch his breath and listen. And in pushing the issue she would've made an ass of herself, for nothing short of medical proof of her virginity, if there was such a thing, would've convinced him otherwise. In any case the level of her experience wouldn't count with a male like Angelos Petronides. He viewed her the same way people viewed a takeaway snack. As something quick and cheap to devour, not savour. Her stomach lurched sickly. Even had she been tempted, which she hadn't been, had he thought for one moment that she would've believed she was likely to hold his interest as long as six months?

'A man will tell a girl who looks like you *anything* to get her into the bedroom,' her father had once warned her grimly. 'The one who is prepared to wait, the one who is more interested in how you feel, is the one who *cares*.'

That blunt advice had embarrassed her at a time when she was already struggling to cope with the downside of the spectacular looks she had been born with. Girlfriends threatened by the male attention she attracted had dumped her. Grown men had leered at her and tried to touch her and date her. Even teenage boys who, alone with her, had been totally intimidated by her, had told crude lies about her sexual availability behind her back. Eight years on, Maxie was still waiting without much hope to meet a man who wasn't determined to put the cart before the proverbial horse.

An hour after she got back to Liz's house, the phone rang. It was Catriona Ferguson, who ran the Star modelling agency which had first signed Maxie up at eighteen.

'I've got no good news for you, Maxie,' she shared in her usual brisk manner. 'The PR people over at LFT Haircare have decided against using you for another series of ads.'

'We were expecting that,' Maxie reminded the older woman with a rueful sigh of acceptance.

'I'm afraid there's nothing else in the pipeline for you. Hardly surprising, really,' Catriona told her. 'You're too strongly associated with one brand name. I did warn you about that risk and, to be blunt, your recent coverage in the tabloids has done you no favours.'

It had been a month since Maxie had moved out of Leland's townhouse. She hadn't worked since then and now it looked as if she was going to have to find some other means of keeping herself. Her bank account was almost empty. She couldn't afford to sit waiting for work that might never come, nor could she blame Catriona for her lack of sympathy. Time and time again the older woman had urged Maxie to branch out into fashion modelling, but Leland's frantic social life and the demands he had made on her time had made that impossible.

Hours later, Maxie hunched over both bars of the electric fire in Liz's lounge as she tried to keep warm while she brooded. Angelos was gone. That was good, she told herself, that was one major problem solved. She scratched an itchy place on her arm and then gazed down in surprise at the little rash of spots there.

What had she eaten that had disagreed with her? she wondered, but she couldn't recall eating anything more than half a sandwich since breakfast time. She just couldn't work up an appetite. She fell asleep on the settee and at some timeless stage of the night wakened to feel her way down to the guest-room and undress on the spot before sinking wearily into bed.

When she woke up late the next morning, she wasn't feeling too good. As she cleaned her teeth she caught a glimpse of her face in the tiny mirror Liz had on the wall for visitors and she froze. There was another little rash of spots on her forehead. It looked remarkably like… chickenpox. And she itched, didn't she? But only children got that, didn't they? And then she remembered one of Liz's neighbours calling in a couple of weeks back with a child in tow who had borne similiar spots.

'She's not infectious any more,' the woman had said carelessly.

Lower lip wobbling, Maxie surveyed the possible proof of that misapprehension. A dry cough racked her chest, leaving her gasping for breath. Whatever she had, she was feeling foul. Getting herself a glass of water, she went back to bed. The phone went. She had to get out of bed again to answer it.

'What?' she demanded hoarsely after another bout of coughing in the cold hall.

'Angelos here, what's wrong with you?'

'I have...I have a cold,' she lied. 'What do you want?'

'I want to see you—'

'No way!' Maxie plonked down the phone at speed.

The phone rang again. She disconnected it from its wall-point. A couple of hours later the doorbell went. Maxie ignored it. Getting out of bed yet again felt like too much trouble.

She dozed for the rest of the day, finally waking up shivering with cold and conscious of an odd noise in the dim room. Slowly it dawned on her that the rasping wheeze was the sound of her own lungs straining to function. Her brain felt befogged, but she thought that possibly she might need a doctor. So she lay thinking about that while the doorbell rang and rang and finally fell silent.

Fear got a healthy grip on her when she stumbled dizzily out of bed and her legs just folded beneath her. She hit the polished wooden floor with a crash. Tears welled up in her sore eyes. The room was too dark for her to get her bearings. She started to crawl, trying to recall where the phone was. She heard a distant smash. It sounded like glass breaking, and then voices. Had she left the television on? Trying to summon up more strength, she rested her perspiring brow down on the boards beneath her.

And then the floor lit up...or so it seemed.

CHAPTER FOUR

A DISTURBINGLY familiar male voice bit out something raw in a foreign language and a pair of male feet appeared in Maxie's limited view. Strong hands turned her over and began to lift her.

'You're all...*spotty*...' Angelos glowered down at her with unblinking black eyes, full of disbelief.

'Go away...' she mumbled.

'It just looks a little...strange,' Angelos commented tautly, and after a lengthy pause, while Maxie squeezed shut her eyes against the painful intrusion of that overhead light *and* him, he added almost accusingly, 'I thought only children got chickenpox.'

'Leave me alone...' Maxie succumbed weakly to another coughing fit.

Instead, he lifted her back onto the bed and rolled the bulky duvet unceremoniously round her prone body.

'What are you doing?' she gasped, struggling to concentrate, finding it impossible.

'I was on my way down to my country house for the weekend. Now it looks like I'll be staying in town and you'll be coming home with me,' Angelos delivered, with no visible enthusiasm on his strong, hard face as he bent down to sweep her up into his powerful arms.

Maxie couldn't think straight, but the concept of having nothing whatsoever to do with Angelos Petronides was now so deeply engrained, his appearance had set all her alarm bells shrieking. 'No...I have to stay here to look after the house—'

'I wish you could...but you can't.'

55

'I promised Liz…she's away and she might be burgled again…put me down.'

'I can't leave you alone here like this.' Angelo stared down at her moodily, as if he was wishing she would make his day with a sudden miraculous recovery but secretly knew he didn't have much hope.

Maxie struggled to conceal her spotty face against his shoulder, mortified and weak, and too ill to fight but not too ill to hate. 'I don't want to go anywhere with you.' Gulping, she sniffed.

'I don't see any caring queue outside that door ready to take my place…and what have you got to snivel about?' Angelos demanded with stark impatience as he strode down the hall. Then he stopped dead, meshing long fingers into her hair to tug her face round and gaze accusingly down into her bemused eyes. 'I smashed my way in only because I was aware that you were ill. Decency demanded that ΐ check that you were all right.'

'I do not snivel,' Maxie told him chokily.

'But the only reason I came here tonight was to return your ''something on account'' and to assure you that it would be a cold day in hell before I ever darkened your door again—'

'So what's keeping you?'

But Angelos was still talking like a male with an ever-mounting sense of injustice. 'And there you are, lying on the floor in a pathetic shivering heap with more spots than a Dalmatian! What's fair about that? But I'm not snivelling, am I?'

Maxie opened one eye and saw one of his security men watching in apparent fascination. 'I do not snivel…' she protested afresh.

Angelos strode out into the night air. He ducked down into the waiting limousine and propped Maxie up in the farthest corner of the seat like a giant papoose that had absolutely nothing to do with him.

Only then did Maxie register that the limousine was already occupied by a gorgeous redhead, wearing diamonds and a spectacular green satin evening dress which would've been at home on the set of a movie about the Deep South of nineteenth-century America. The other woman gazed back at Maxie, equally nonplussed.

'Have you had chickenpox, Natalie?' Angelos enquired almost chattily.

Natalie Cibaud. She was an actress, a well-known French actress, who had recently won rave reviews for her role in a Hollywood movie. It had not taken Angelos long to find other more entertaining company, Maxie reflected dully while a heated conversation in fast and furious French took place. Maxie didn't speak French, but the other woman sounded choked with temper while Angelos merely got colder and colder. Maxie curled up in an awkward heap, conscious she was the subject under dispute and wishing in despair that she could perform a vanishing act.

'Take me home!' she cried once, without lifting her sore head.

'Stay out of this…what's it got to do with you?' Angelos shot back at her with positive savagery. 'No woman owns me…no woman ever has and no woman ever will!'

But Angelos was fighting a losing battle. Natalie appeared to have other ideas. Denied an appropriately humble response, her voice developed a sulky, shrill edge. Angelos became freezingly unresponsive. Strained silence finally fell. A little while later, the limousine came to a halt. The passenger door opened. Natalie swept out with her rustling skirts, saying something acid in her own language. The door slammed again.

'I suppose you thoroughly enjoyed all that,' Angelos breathed in a tone of icy restraint as the limousine moved off again.

Opening her aching eyes a crack, Maxie skimmed a dulled glance at the space Natalie had occupied and recently vacated. She closed her eyes again. 'I don't understand French…'

Angelos grated something raw half under his breath and got on the phone. He had been ditched twice in as many days. And, wretched as she was, Maxie was tickled pink by that idea. Angelos, who got chased up hill and down dale by ninety-nine out of a hundred foolish women, had in the space of forty-eight hours met two members of the outstanding and more intelligent one per cent minority. And it was good for him—really, really good for him, she decided. Then she dozed, only to groggily resurface every time she coughed. Within a very short time after that, however, she didn't know where she was any more and felt too ill to care.

'Feeling a bit better, Miss Kendall?'

Maxie peered up at the thin female face above hers. The face was familiar, and yet unfamiliar too. The woman wore a neat white overall and she was taking Maxie's pulse. Seemingly she was a nurse.

'What happened to me?' Maxie mumbled, only vaguely recalling snatches of endless tossing and turning, the pain in her chest, the difficulty in breathing.

'You developed pneumonia. It's a rare but potentially serious complication,' the blonde nurse explained. 'You've been out of it for almost five days—'

'Five…days?' Maxie's shaken scrutiny wandered over the incredibly spacious bedroom, with its stark contemporary furniture and coldly elegant decor. She was in Angelos's apartment. She knew it in her bones. Nowhere was there a single piece of clutter or feminine warmth and homeliness. His idea of housing heaven, she reflected absently, would probably be the wide open spaces of an under-furnished aircraft hangar.

'You're very lucky Mr Petronides found you in time,' her companion continued earnestly, dragging Maxie back

from her abstracted thoughts. 'By recognising the serious-
ness of your condition and ensuring that you got immediate
medical attention, Mr Petronides probably saved your
life—'

'No...I don't want to owe him *anything*...never mind
my life!' Maxie gasped in unconcealed horror.

The slim blonde studied her in disbelief. 'You've been
treated by one of the top consultants in the UK...Mr
Petronides has provided you with the very best of round-
the-clock private nursing care, and you say—?'

'While Miss Kendall is ill, she can say whatever she
likes,' Angelos's dark drawl slotted in grimly from the far
side of the room. 'You can take a break, Nurse. I'll stay
with your patient.'

The woman had jerked in dismay at Angelos's silent entrance and intervention. Face pink, she moved away from
the bed. 'Yes, Mr Petronides.'

In a sudden burst of energy, Maxie yanked the sheet up
over her head.

'And the patient is remarkably lively all of a sudden,'
Angelos remarked as soon as the door closed on the nurse's
exit. 'And ungrateful as hell. Now, why am I not surprised?'

'Go away,' Maxie mumbled, suddenly intensely conscious of lank sweaty hair and spots which had probably
multiplied.

'I'm in my own apartment,' Angelos told her drily. 'And
I am not going away. Do you seriously think that I haven't
been looking in on you to see how you were progressing
over the past few days?'

'I don't care...I'm properly conscious now. If I was so
ill, why didn't you just take me to hospital?' Maxie demanded from beneath the sheet.

'The top consultant is a personal friend. Since you responded well to antibiotics, he saw no good reason to
move you.'

'Nobody consulted me,' Maxie complained, and shifted to scratch an itchy place on her hip.

Without warning, the sheet was wrenched back.

'No scratching,' Angelos gritted down at her with raking impatience. 'You'll have scars all over you if you do that. If I catch you at that again, I might well be tempted to tie your hands to the bed!'

Aghast at both the unveiling and the mortifying tone of that insultingly familiar threat, Maxie gazed up at him with outraged blue eyes bright as jewels. 'You pig,' she breathed shakily, registering that he was getting a kick out of her embarrassment. 'You had no right to bring me here—'

'You're in no fit state to tell me what to do,' Angelos reminded her with brutal candour. 'And even I draw the line at arguing with an invalid. If it's of any comfort to your wounded vanity, I've discovered that once I got used to the effect the spotty look could be surprisingly appealing.'

'Shut up!' Maxie slung at him, and fell back against the pillows, completely winded by the effort it had taken to answer back.

While she struggled to even out her breathing, she studied him with bitter blue eyes. Angelos looked soul-destroyingly spectacular. He wore a beige designer suit with a tie the shade of rich caramel and a toning silk shirt. The lighter colours threw his exotic darkness into prominence. He exuded sophistication and exquisite cool, and at a moment when Maxie felt more grotty than she had ever felt in her life, she loathed him for it! Rolling over, she presented him with her back.

Maddeningly, Angelos strolled round the bed to treat her to an amused appraisal. 'I'm flying over to Athens for the next ten days. I suspect you'll recover far more happily in my absence.'

'I won't be here when you get back...oh, no, Liz's house

has been left empty!' Maxie moaned in sudden guilty dismay.

'I had a professional housesitter brought in.'

Maxie couldn't even feel grateful. Her heart sank even further. He had settled Leland's loan. He had paid for expensive private medical care within his own home. And now he had shelled out for a housesitter as well. If it took her the rest of her life, she would still be paying off what she now had to owe him in total!

'Thanks,' she muttered ungraciously, for her friend's sake.

'Don't mention it,' Angelos said with considerable irony. 'And you *will* be here when I return. If you're not, I'll come looking for you in a very bad mood—'

'Don't talk like you own me!' she warned him in feverish, frantic denial. 'You were with that actress only a few days ago...you were never going to darken my door again—'

'You darkened mine. Oh...yes, before I forget...' Angelos withdrew something small and gold from his pocket and tossed it carelessly on the bed beside her.

Stunned, Maxie focused on the bracelet which she had pawned.

' *"Ice Queen in pawnshop penury"* ran the headline in the gossip column,' Angelos recounted with a sardonic elevation of one ebony brow as he watched Maxie turn brick-red with chagrin. 'The proprietor must've tipped off the press. I found the ticket in your bag and had the bracelet retrieved.'

Wide-eyed and stricken, Maxie just gaped at him.

Angelos dealt her a scorching smile of reassurance. 'You won't have to endure intrusive publicity like that while you are with me. I will protect you. You will never have to enter a pawnshop again. Nor will you ever have to shake your tresses over a misty green Alpine meadow full of wildflowers…unless you want to do it for my benefit, of course.'

Maxie simply closed her eyes on him. She didn't have the energy to fight. He was like a tank in the heat and fury of battle. Nothing short of a direct hit by a very big gun would stop his remorseless progress.

'Silence feels good,' Angelos remarked with silken satisfaction.

'I hate you,' Maxie mumbled, with a good deal of very real feeling.

'You hate *wanting* me,' Angelos contradicted with measured emphasis. 'It's poetic justice and don't expect sympathy. When I had to think of you lying like a block of ice beneath Leland, I did not enjoy wanting you either!'

Maxie buried her burning face in the pillow with a hoarse little moan of self-pity. He left her nothing to hide behind. And any minute now she expected to be hauled out of concealment. Angelos preferred eye-to-eye contact at all times.

'Get some sleep and eat plenty,' Angelos instructed from somewhere alarmingly close at hand, making her stiffen in apprehension. 'You should be well on the road to recovery by the time I get back from Greece.'

Maxie's teeth bit into the pillow. Her blood boiled. For an instant she would have sacrificed the rest of her life for the ability to punch him in the mouth just once. She thought he had gone, and lifted her head. But Angelos, who never, ever, it seemed, did anything she expected, was still studying her from the door, stunning dark features grave. 'By the way, I also expect you to be extremely discreet about this relationship—'

'We don't have a relationship!' Maxie bawled at him. 'And I wouldn't admit to having been here in your apartment if the paparazzi put thumbscrews on me!'

Angelos absorbed that last promise with unhidden satisfaction. And then, with a casual inclination of his dark, arrogant head, he was gone, and she slumped, weak and shaken as a mouse who had been unexpectedly released from certain death by a cat.

Maxie finished packing her cases. While she had been ill, Angelos had had all her clothes brought over from Liz's. The discovery had infuriated her. A few necessities would have been sensible, but *everything* she possessed? Had he really thought she would be willing to stay on after she recovered?

For the first thirty-six hours after his departure she had fretted and fumed, struggling to push herself too far too fast in her eagerness to vacate his unwelcome hospitality.

The suave consultant had made a final visit to advise her to take things slowly, and the shift of nursing staff had departed, but Maxie had had to face that she was still in no fit state to look after herself. So she *had* been sensible. She had taken advantage of the opportunity to convalesce and recharge her batteries while she was waited on hand and foot by the Greek domestic staff...but now she was leaving before Angelos returned. In any case, Liz was coming home at lunchtime.

Two of Angelos's security men were hovering in the vast echoing entrance hall. Taut with anxiety, they watched her stagger towards them with her suitcases. Neither offered an ounce of assistance.

'Mr Petronides is not expecting—' the bigger, older one finally began stiffly.

'If you know what's good for you, you'll stay out of this!' Maxie thumped the lift button with a clenched fist of warning.

'Mr Petronides doesn't want you to leave, Miss Kendall. He's going to be annoyed.'

Maxie opened dark blue eyes very, very wide. *'So?'*

'We'll be forced to follow you, Miss Kendall—'

'Oh, I wouldn't do that, boys,' Maxie murmured gently. 'I would hate to call in the police because I was being harassed by stalkers. It would be sure to get into the papers too, and I doubt that your boss would enjoy *that* kind of publicity!'

In the act of stepping forward as the lift doors folded back, both men froze into frustrated stillness. Maxie dragged her luggage into the lift.

'A word of advice,' the older one breathed heavily. 'He makes a relentless enemy.'

Maxie tossed her head in a dismissive movement. Then the doors shut and she sagged. No wonder Angelos threw his weight around so continually. Everybody was terrified of him. Unlimited wealth and power had made him what he was. His ruthless reputation chilled, his lethal influence threatened. The world had taught him that he could have whatever he wanted. Only not her...never ever *her*, she swore vehemently. Her mind was her own. Her body was her own. She was inviolate. Angelos couldn't touch her, she reminded herself bracingly.

The housesitter vacated Liz's house after contacting her employer for instructions. Alone then, and tired out by the early start to the day, Maxie felt very low. Making herself a cup of coffee, she checked through the small pile of post in the lounge. One of the envelopes was addressed to her; it had been redirected.

The letter appeared to be from an estate agent. Initially mystified, Maxie struggled across the barrier of her dyslexia to make sense of the communication. The agent wrote that he had been unable to reach her father at his last known address but that she had been listed by Russ as a contact point. He required instructions concerning a rental property which was now vacant. Memories began to stir in Maxie's mind.

Her father's comfortably off parents had died when she was still a child. A black sheep within his own family even then, Russ had inherited only a tiny cottage on the outskirts of a Cambridgeshire village. He had been even less pleased to discover that the cottage came with an elderly sitting tenant, who had not the slightest intention of moving out to enable him to sell up.

Abandoning the letter without having got further than the third line, Maxie telephoned the agent. 'I can't tell you where my father is at present,' she admitted ruefully. 'I haven't heard from him in some time.'

'The old lady has moved in with relatives. If your father wants to attract another tenant, he'll have to spend a lot on repairs and modernisation. However,' the agent continued with greater enthusiasm, 'I believe the property would sell very well as a site for building development.'

And of course that would be what Russ would want, Maxie reflected. He would sell and a few months down the road the proceeds would be gone again, wasted on the racecourse or the dog track. Her troubled face stiffening with resolve, Maxie slowly breathed in and found herself asking if it would be in order for her to come and pick up the keys.

She came off the phone again, so shaken by the ideas mushrooming one after another inside her head that she could scarcely think straight. But she *did* need a home, and she had always loved the countryside. If she had the courage, she could make a complete fresh start. Why not? What did she have left in London? The dying remnants of a career which had done her infinitely more harm than good? She could find a job locally. Shop work, bar work; she wasn't fussy. As a teenager Maxie had done both, and she had no false pride.

By the time Liz came home, Maxie was bubbling with excitement. In some astonishment, Liz listened to the enthusiastic plans that the younger woman had already formulated.

'If the cottage is in a bad way, it could cost a fortune to put it right, Maxie,' she pointed out anxiously. 'I don't want to be a wet blanket, but by the sound of things—'

'Liz…I never did want to be a model and I'm not getting any work right now,' Maxie reminded her ruefully. 'This could be my chance to make a new life and, whatever it takes, I want to give it a try. I'll tell the agency where I am so that if anything does come up they can contact me, but I certainly can't afford to sit around here doing nothing. At least if I start earning again, I can start paying back Angelos.'

If Maxie could've avoided telling Liz about the house-sitter and her own illness, she would've done so. But Liz had a right to know that a stranger had been looking after her home. However, far from being troubled by that revelation, Liz was much more concerned to learn that Maxie had been ill. She was also mortifyingly keen to glean every detail of the role which Angelos Petronides had played.

'I swear that man is madly in love with you!' Liz shook her head in wonderment.

Maxie vented a distinctly unamused laugh, her eyes incredulous. 'Angelos wouldn't know love if it leapt up and bit him to the bone! But he will go to any lengths to get what he wants. I suspect he thinks that the more indebted he makes me, the easier he'll wear down my resistance—'

'Maxie…if he'd left you lying here alone in this house, you might be dead. Don't you even feel the slightest bit grateful?' Liz prompted uncomfortably. 'He could've just called an ambulance—'

'Thereby missing out on the chance to get me into his power when I was helpless?' Maxie breathed cynically. 'No way. I know how he operates. I *know* how he thinks.'

'Then you must have much more in common with him than you're prepared to admit,' Liz commented.

Maxie arrived at the cottage two days later. With dire mutters, the cabbie nursed his car up the potholed lane. In the sunshine, the cottage looked shabby, but it had a lovely setting. There was a stream ten feet from the front door and a thick belt of mature trees that provided shelter.

She had some money in her bank account again too. She had liquidated a good half of her wardrobe. Ruthlessly piling up all the expensive designer clothes which Leland had insisted on buying her, Maxie had sold them to a couple of those wonderful shops which recycle used quality garments.

Half an hour later, having explored her new home, Maxie's enthusiasm was undimmed. So what if the accommodation was basic and the entire place crying out for paint and a seriously good scrub? As for the repairs the agent had mentioned, Maxie was much inclined to think he had been exaggerating.

She was utterly charmed by the inglenook fireplace in the little front room and determined not to take fright at the minuscule scullery and the spooky bathroom with its ancient cracked china. Although the furnishings were worn and basic, there were a couple of quite passable Edwardian pieces. The new bed she had bought would be delivered later in the day.

She was about a mile from the nearest town. As soon as she had the bed made up, she would call in at the hotel she had noticed on the main street to see if there was any work going. In the middle of the tourist season, she would be very much surprised if there wasn't an opening somewhere...

Five days later, Maxie was three days into an evening job that was proving infinitely more stressful than she had anticipated. The pace of a waitress in a big, busy bar was frantic.

And why, oh, why hadn't she asked whether the hotel bar served meals *before* she accepted the job? She could carry drinks orders quite easily in her head, but she had been driven into trying to employ a frantic shorthand of numbers when it came to trying to cope at speed with the demands of a large menu and all the innumerable combinations possible. She just couldn't write fast enough.

Maxie saw Angelos the minute he walked into the bar. The double doors thrust back noisily. He made an entrance. People twisted their heads to glance and then paused to stare. Command and authority written in every taut line of his tall, powerful frame, Angelos stood out like a giant among pygmies.

Charcoal-grey suit, white silk shirt, smooth gold tie. He looked filthy rich, imposing and utterly out of place. And Maxie's heart started to go bang-bang-bang beneath her uniform. He had the most incredible traffic-stopping presence. Suddenly the crowded room with its low ceiling and atmospheric lighting felt suffocatingly hot and airless.

For a split second Angelos remained poised, black eyes raking across the bar to close in on Maxie. She had the mesmerised, panicked look of a rabbit caught in car headlights. His incredulous stare of savage impatience zapped her even at a distance of thirty feet.

Sucking in oxygen in a great gulp, Maxie struggled to finish writing down the order she was taking on her notepad. Gathering up the menus again, she headed for the kitchens at a fast trot. But it wasn't fast enough. Angelos somehow got in the way.

'Take a break,' he instructed in a blistering undertone.

'How the heck did you find out where I was?'

'Catriona Ferguson at the Star modelling agency was eager to please.' Angelos watched Maxie's eyes flare with angry comprehension. 'Most people are rather reluctant to say no to me.'

In an abrupt move, Maxie sidestepped him and hurried into the kitchen. When she re-emerged, Angelos was sitting at one of *her* tables. She ignored him, but never had she been more outrageously aware of being watched. Her body felt uncoordinated and clumsy. Her hands perspired and developed a shake. She spilt a drink and had to fetch another while the woman complained scathingly about the single tiny spot that had splashed her handbag.

Finally the young bar manager, Dennis, approached her. 'That big dark bloke at table six…haven't you noticed him?' he enquired apologetically, studying her beautiful face with the same poleaxed expression he had been wearing ever since he'd hired her. With an abstracted frown, he looked across at Angelos, who was tapping long brown fingers with rampant impatience on the tabletop. 'It's odd. There's something incredibly familiar about the bloke but I can't think where I've seen him before.'

Maxie forced herself over to table six. 'Yes?' she prompted tautly, and focused exclusively on that expensive gold tie while all the time inwardly picturing the derision in those penetrating black eyes.

'That uniform is so short you look like a bloody French maid in a bedroom farce!' Angelos informed her grittily. 'Every time you bend over, every guy in here is craning his neck to get a better view! And that practice appears to include the management.'

Maxie's face burned, outrage flashing in her blue eyes. The bar had a Victorian theme, and the uniform was a striped overall with a silly little frilly apron on top. It did look rather odd on a woman of her height and unusually long length of leg, but she had already let down the hemline as far as it would go. 'Do you or do you not want a drink?' she demanded thinly.

'I'd like the table cleared and cleaned first,' Angelos announced with a glance of speaking distaste at the cluttered surface. 'Then you can bring me a brandy and sit down.'

'Don't be ridiculous…I'm working.' Maxie piled up the dishes with a noisy clatter, and in accidentally slopping coffee over the table forced him to lunge back at speed from the spreading flood.

'You're working for me, and if I say you can sit down,

I expect you to do as you're told,' Angelos delivered in his deep, dark, domineering drawl.

Engaged in mopping up, Maxie stilled. 'I beg your pardon? You said...I was working for *you*?' she queried.

'This hotel belongs to my chain,' Angelos ground out. 'And I am anything but impressed by what I see here.'

Maxie turned cold with shock. Angelos *owned* this hotel? She backed away with the dishes. As she was hailed from the kitchen, she watched with a sinking stomach as Angelos signalled Dennis. When she reappeared with a loaded tray, Dennis was seated like a pale, perspiring graven image in front of Angelos.

She hurried to deliver the meals she had collected but there was a general outcry of loud and exasperated complaint.

'I didn't order this...' the first customer objected. 'I asked for salad, not French fries—'

'And I wanted garlic potatoes—'

'This steak is *rare*, not well-done—'

The whole order was hopelessly mixed up. A tall, dark shadow fell menacingly over the table. In one easy movement, Angelos lifted Maxie's pad from her pocket, presumably to check out the protests. 'What *is* this?' he demanded, frowning down at the pages as he flipped. 'Egyptian hieroglyphics...some secret code? Nobody could read this back!'

Maxie was paralysed to the spot; her face was bone-white. Her tummy lurched with nausea and her legs began to shake. 'I got confused, I'm sorry. I—'

Angelos angled a smooth smile at the irate diners and ignored her. 'Don't worry, it will be sorted out as quickly as possible. Your meals are on the house. Move, Maxie,' he added in a whiplike warning aside.

Dennis, she noticed sickly, was over at the bar using the internal phone. He looked like a man living a nightmare. And when she came out of the kitchen again, an older man, whom she recognised as the manager of the entire hotel, was with Angelos, and he had the desperate air of a man walking a tightrope above a terrifying drop. Suddenly Maxie felt like the albatross that had brought tragedy to an entire ship's crew. Angelos, it seemed, was taking out his black temper on his staff. Her own temper rose accordingly.

How the heck could she have guessed that he owned this hotel? She recalled the innumerable marble plaques in the huge foyer of the Petronides building in London. Those plaques had listed the components of Angelos's vast and diverse business empire. Petronides Steel, Petronides Property, and ditto Shipping, Haulage, Communications, Construction, Media Services, Investments, Insurance. No doubt she had forgotten a good half-dozen. PAI—Petronides Amalgamated Industries—had been somewhat easier to recall.

'Maxie...I mean, Miss Kendall,' Dennis said awkwardly, stealing an uneasy glance at her and making her wonder what Angelos had said or done to make him behave like that. But not for very long. 'Mr Petronides says you can take the rest of the night off.'

Maxie stiffened. 'Sorry, I'm working.'

Dennis looked aghast. 'But—'

'I was engaged to work tonight and I need the money.' Maxie tilted her chin in challenge.

She banged a brandy down in front of Angelos. 'You're nothing but a big, egocentric bully!' she slung at him with stinging scorn.

A lean hand closed round her elbow before she could stalk away again. Colour burnished her cheeks as Angelos forced her back to his side with the kind of male strength that could not be fought without making a scene. Black eyes as dark as the legendary underworld of Hades slashed threat into hers. 'If I gave you a spade, you would happily dig your own grave. Go and get your coat—'

'No...this is my job and I'm not walking out on it.'

'Let me assist you to make that decision. You're sacked…' Angelos slotted in with ruthless bite.

With her free hand, Maxie swept up the brandy and up-ended it over his lap. In an instant she was free. With an unbelieving growl of anger, Angelos vaulted upright.

'If you can't stand the heat, stay out of the kitchen!' Maxie flung fiercely, and stalked off, shoulders back, classic nose in the air.

CHAPTER FIVE

DENNIS was waiting for Maxie outside the staff-room when she emerged in her jeans and T-shirt. Pale and still bug-eyed with shock, he gaped at her. 'You must be out of your mind to treat Angelos Petronides like that!'

'Envy me...I don't work for him any more.' Maxie flung her golden head high. 'May I have my pay now, please?'

'Y-your pay?' the young bar manager stammered.

'Is my reaction to being forcibly held to the spot by the owner of this hotel chain sufficient excuse to withhold it?' Maxie enquired very drily.

The silence thundered.

'I'll get your money...I don't really think I want to raise that angle with Mr Petronides right now,' Dennis confided weakly.

Ten minutes later Maxie walked out of the hotel, gri-macing when she realised that it was *still* pouring with rain. It had been lashing down all day and she had got soaked walking into town in spite of her umbrella. Every passing car had splashed her. A long, low-slung sports car pulled into the kerb beside her and the window buzzed down.

'Get in,' Angelos told her in a positive snarl.

'Go take a hike! You can push around your staff but you can't push *me* around!'

'Push around? Surely you noticed how sloppily that bar was being run?' Angelos growled in disbelief. Thrusting open the car door, he climbed out to glower down at her in angry reproof. 'Insufficient and surly staff, customers kept waiting, the kitchens in chaos, the tables dirty and even the carpet in need of replacement! If the management don't

73

get their act together fast, I'll replace them. They're not doing their jobs.'

Taken aback by his genuine vehemence, Maxie nonetheless suppressed the just awareness that she herself had been less than impressed by what she had seen. He had changed too, she noticed furiously. He must have had a change of clothes with him, because now he was wearing a spectacular suit of palest grey that had the exquisite fit of a kid glove on his lean powerful frame.

Powered by sizzling adrenaline alone, Maxie studied that lean, strong face. 'I hate you for following me down here—'

'You were waiting for me to show up…'

Her facial muscles froze. The minute Angelos said it, she knew it was true. She had *known* he would track her down and find her.

'I'm walking home. I'm not getting into your car,' she informed him while she absently noted that, yet again, he was getting wet for her. Black hair curling, bronzed cheekbones shimmering damply in the street lights.

'I have not got all night to waste, waiting for you to walk home,' Angelos asserted wrathfully.

'So you know where I'm living,' Maxie gathered in growing rage, and then she thought, What am I doing here standing talking to him? 'Well, don't you dare come there because I won't open the door!'

'You could be attacked walking down a dark country road,' Angelos ground out, shooting her a flaming look of antipathy. 'Is it worth the risk?'

Angling her umbrella to a martial angle, Maxie spun on her heel and proceeded to walk. She hadn't gone ten yards before her flowing hair and long easy stride attracted the attention of a bunch of hard-faced youths lounging in a shop doorway. Their shouted obscenities made her stiffen and quicken her pace.

From behind her, she heard Angelos grate something savage.

A hand came down without warning on Maxie's tense shoulder and she uttered a startled yelp. As she attempted to yank herself free, everything happened very fast. Angelos waded in and slung a punch at the offender. With a menacing roar, the boy's mates rushed to the rescue. Angelos disappeared into the fray and Maxie screamed and screamed at the top of her voice in absolute panic.

'Get off him!' she shrieked, laying about the squirming clutch of heaving bodies with vicious jabs of her umbrella and her feet as well.

Simultaneously a noisy crowd came out of the pub across the street and just as suddenly the scrum broke and scattered. Maxie knelt down on the wet pavement beside Angelos's prone body and pushed his curling wet black hair off his brow, noting the pallor of his dark skin. 'You stupid fool...you stupid, stupid fool,' she moaned shakily.

Angelos lifted his head and shook it in a rather jerky movement. Slowly he began to pick himself up. Blood was running down his temples. 'There were five of them,' he grated, with clenched and bruised fists.

'Get in your car and shut up in case they come back,' Maxie muttered, tugging suggestively at his arm. 'Other people don't want to get involved these days. You could've been hammered to a pulp—'

'*Them and who else?*' Angelos flared explosively, all male ego and fireworks.

'The police station is just down the street—'

'I'm not going to the police over the head of those little punks!' Angelos snarled, staggering slightly and spreading his long powerful legs to steady himself. 'I got in a punch or two of my own—'

'Not as many as they did.' Maxie hauled at his sleeve and by dint of sustained pressure nudged him round to the passenger side of his opulent sports car.

'What are you doing?'

'You're not fit to drive—'

'Since when?' he interrupted in disbelief.

Maxie yanked open the door. 'Please, Angelos…you're bleeding, you're probably concussed. Just for once in your wretched life, do as someone else asks.'

He stood there and thought about that stunning concept for a whole twenty seconds. There was a definite struggle taking place and then, with a muffled curse, he gradually and stiffly lowered himself down into the passenger seat.

'Can you drive a Ferrari?' he enquired.

'Of course,' Maxie responded between clenched teeth of determination, no better than him at backing down.

The Ferrari lurched and jerked up the road.

'Lights,' Angelos muttered weakly. 'I think you should have the lights on…or maybe I should just close my eyes—'

'Shut up…I'm trying to concentrate!'

Having mastered the lights and located the right gear, Maxie continued, 'It was typical of you to go leaping in, fists flying. Where are your security guards, for goodness' sake?'

'How *dare* you?' Angelos splintered, leaning forward with an outrage somewhat tempered by the groan he emitted as the seat belt forced him to rest back again. 'I can look after myself—'

'Against five of them?' Maxie's strained mouth compressed, her stomach still curdling at what she had witnessed. Damn him, damn him. She felt so horribly guilty and shaken. 'I'm taking you to Casualty—'

'I don't need a doctor…I'm OK,' Angelos bit out in exasperation.

'If you drop dead from a skull fracture or something,' she said grimly, 'I don't want to feel responsible!'

'I have cuts and bruises, nothing more. I have no need

of a hospital. All I want to do is lie down for a while and then I'll call for a car.'

He sounded more like himself. Domineering and organised. Maxie mulled over that unspoken demand for a place to lie down while she crept along the road in the direction of the cottage at the slowest speed a Ferrari had probably ever been driven at. Then the heavy rain was bouncing off the windscreen and visibility was poor. 'All right…I'll take you home with me—but just for an hour,' she warned tautly.

'You are so gracious.'

Maxie reddened, conscience-stricken when she recalled the amount of trouble he had taken to ensure that she was properly looked after when she was ill. But then Angelos had not been personally inconvenienced; he had paid others to take on the caring role. In fact, as she drove up the lane to the cottage, she knew she could not imagine Angelos allowing himself to be inconvenienced.

Her attention distracted, she was wholly unprepared to find herself driving through rippling water as she began to turn in at the front of the cottage. In alarm, she braked sharply, and without warning the powerful car went into a skid. 'Oh, God!' she gasped in horror as the front wheels went over the edge of the stream bank. The Ferrari tipped into the stream nose-first with a jarring thud and came to rest at an extreme angle.

'God wasn't listening, but at least we're still alive,' Angelos groaned as he reached over and switched off the engine.

'I suppose you're about to kick up a whole macho fuss now, and yap about women drivers,' Maxie hissed, unclamping her locked fingers from the steering wheel.

'I wouldn't dare. Knowing my luck in your radius, I'd step out of the car and drown.'

'The stream is only a couple of feet deep!'

'I feel so comforted knowing that.' With a powerful

thrust of his arm, Angelos forced the passenger door open and staggered out onto the muddy bank. Then he reached in to haul her out with stunning strength.

'I'm sorry... I got a fright when I saw that water.'

'It was only a large puddle. What do you do when you see the sea?'

'I thought the stream had flooded and broken its banks, and I wanted to be sure we didn't go over the edge in the dark...that's *why* I jumped on the brakes!' Fumbling for her key, not wishing to dwell on quite how unsuccessful her evasive tactics had been, Maxie unlocked the battered front door and switched on the light.

Angelos lowered his wildly tousled dark head to peer, unimpressed, into the bare lounge with its two seater hard-backed settee. Without the fire lit or a decorative face-lift, it didn't look very welcoming, she had to admit.

'All right, upstairs is a bit more comfortable. You can lie down on my bed.'

'I can hardly believe your generosity. Where's the phone?'

Maxie frowned. 'I don't have one.'

Tangled wet black lashes swept up on stunned eyes. 'That's a joke?'

'Surely you have a mobile phone?'

'I must've dropped it in the street during the fight.' With a mutter of frustrated Greek, Angelos started up the narrow staircase.

He was a little unsteady on his feet, and Maxie noted that fact anxiously. 'I think you need a doctor, Angelos.'

'Rubbish...just want to lie down—'

'Duck your head!' she warned a split second too late as he collided headfirst with the lintel above the bedroom door.

'Oh, no,' Maxie groaned in concert with him, and shot out both arms to support him as he reeled rather danger-ously on the tiny landing. Hurriedly she guided him into the bedroom before he could do any further damage to himself.

'There's puddles on the floor,' Angelos remarked, blinking rapidly.

'Don't be silly,' Maxie told him, just as a big drop of water from somewhere above splashed down on her nose.

Aghast, she tipped back her head to gaze up at the vaulted wooden roof above, which she had thought was so much more attractive and unusual than a ceiling. Droplets of water were suspended in several places and there *were* puddles on the floorboards. The roof was leaking.

'I'm in the little hovel in the woods,' Angelos framed.

Maxie said a most unladylike word and darted over to the bed to check that it wasn't wet. Mercifully it appeared to be occupying the only dry corner in the room, but she wrenched back the bedding to double-check. Angelos dropped down on the edge of the divan and tugged off his jacket. It fell in a puddle. She snatched up the garment and clutched it as she met dazed black eyes. 'I shouldn't have listened you. I should've taken you to Casualty.'

'I have a very sore head and I am slightly disorientated. That is *all*.' Angelos coined the assurance with arrogant emphasis. 'Stop treating me like a child.'

'How many fingers do you see?' In her anxiety, Maxie stuck out her thumb instead of the forefinger she had intended.

'I see one thumb,' he said very drily. 'Was that a trick question?'

Flushing a deep pink, Maxie bridled as he yanked off his tie. 'Do you have to undress?'

'I am not lying down in wet clothes,' Angelos informed her loftily.

'I'll leave you, then…well, I need to get some bowls for the drips anyway,' Maxie mumbled awkwardly on her passage out through the door.

Just the thought of Angelos unclothed shot a shocking

current of snaking heat right through her trembling body. It was only nervous tension, Maxie told herself urgently as she went downstairs, the result of delayed shock after that horrendous outbreak of masculine violence in the street. *She* had been really scared, but Angelos was too bone-deep macho and stupid to have been scared. However, she should have forced him to go to the local hospital…but how did you force a male as spectacularly stubborn as Angelos to do something he didn't want to do, and surely there couldn't be anything really serious wrong with him when he could still be so sarcastic?

In the scullery, she picked up a bucket and a mop, and then abandoned them to pour some disinfectant into a bowl of water instead. She needed to see close up how bad that cut was. Had he been unconscious for several seconds after the youths had run off? His eyes had been closed, those ridiculously long lashes down like black silk fans and almost hitting his cheekbones. Dear heaven, what was the matter with her? Her mind didn't feel like her own any more.

Angelos was under her rosebud-sprigged sheets when she hesitantly entered the bedroom again. His eyes seemed closed. She moistened her lower lip with a nervous flick of her tongue. She took in the blatant virility of his big brown shoulders, the rough black curls of hair sprinkling what she could see of his powerful pectoral muscles and that vibrant golden skintone that seemed to cover all of him, and which looked so noticeable against her pale bedding…

'You're supposed to stay awake if you have concussion,' she scolded sharply in response to those unnecessarily intimate observations. Stepping close to the bed, she jabbed at a big brown shoulder and swiftly withdrew her hand from the heat of him again as if she had been scalded, her fair skin burning.

Those amazing black eyes snapped open on her.

'You're bleeding all over my pillow,' Maxie censured, her throat constricting as she ran completely out of breath.

'I'll buy you a new one.'

'No, you buy nothing for me...and you lie still,' she instructed unevenly. 'I need to see that cut.'

With an embarrassingly unsteady hand and a pad of kitchen towelling, Maxie cleaned away the blood. As she exposed the small seeping wound, a beautifully shaped brown hand lifted and closed round the delicate bones of her wrist. 'You're shaking like a leaf.'

'You might've been knifed or something. I still feel sick thinking about it. But I could've dealt with that kid on my own—'

'I think not...his mates were already moving in to have some fun. Nor would it have cost them much effort to drag you round the corner down that alleyway—'

'Well, I'm not about to thank you. If you had stayed away from me, it wouldn't have happened,' Maxie stated tightly. 'I'd have stayed in the hotel until closing time and got a lift home with the barman. He lives a couple of miles on down the road.'

With that final censorious declaration, Maxie pulled herself free and took the bowl downstairs again. She would have to go back up and mop the floor but it was true, she *was* shaking like a leaf and her legs felt like jelly. Unfortunately it wasn't all the result of shock. Seeing Angelos in her bed, wondering like a nervous adolescent how much, if anything, he was wearing, hadn't helped.

Five minutes later she went back up, with a motley collection of containers to catch the drips and the mop and bucket. In silence, she did what had to be done, but she was horribly mortified by the necessity, not to mention furious with herself for dismissing the agent's assessment of the cottage's condition on the phone. This was the first time it had rained since she had moved in and clearly either a new roof or substantial repairs would be required to make the cottage waterproof before winter set in. It was doubtful that she could afford even repairs.

As each receptacle was finally correctly positioned to catch the drips from overhead, a cacophany of differing noises started up. Split, splat, splash, plop…

'How are you feeling?' Maxie asked thinly above that intrusive backdrop of constant drips.

'Fantastically rich and spoilt. Indoors, water belongs in the bathroom or the swimming pool,' Angelos opined with sardonic cool. 'I can't credit that you would prefer to risk drowning under a roof that leaks like a sieve sooner than come to me.'

'Credit it. Nothing you could do or say would convince me otherwise. I don't want to live with any man—'

'I wasn't actually asking you to live with me,' Angelos delivered in gentle contradiction, his sensual mouth quirking. 'I like my own space. I would buy you your own place and visit—'

An angry flush chased Maxie's strained pallor. 'I'm not for sale—'

'Except for a wedding ring?' Angelos vented a roughened laugh of cynical amusement. 'Oh, yes, I got the message. Very naive, but daring. I may be obsessed with a need to possess that exquisite body that trembles with sexual hunger whenever I am close,' he murmured silkily, reaching up with a confident hand to close his fingers over hers and draw her down beside him before she even registered what he was doing, 'but, while I will fulfil any other desire or ambition with pleasure, that one is out of reach, *pethi mou*. Concentrate on the possible, not the wildly improbable.'

'If you didn't already have a head injury, I'd swing for you!' Maxie slung fiercely. 'Let go of me!'

In the controlled and easy gesture of a very strong male, Angelos released her with a wry smile. 'At the end of the day, Leland did quite a number on your confidence, didn't he? Oh, yes, I know that *he* dispatched *you* from the hospital and screeched for Jennifer. Suddenly you found yourself back on the street, alone and without funds. So I quite understand why you should decide that a husband would be a safer bet than a lover next time around. However, I am *not* Leland…'

Maxie stared down into those stunning dark golden eyes. Fear and fascination fought for supremacy inside her. She could feel the raw magnetism of him reaching out to entrap her and she knew her own weakness more and more with every passing second in his company. She hated him but she wanted him too, with a bone-deep yearning for physical contact that tormented her this close to him. She was appalled by the strength of his sexual sway over her, shattered that she could be so treacherously vulnerable with a male of his ilk.

'Come here…stop holding back,' Angelos urged softly. 'Neither of us can win a battle like this. Do we not both suffer? I faithfully promise that I will never, ever take advantage of you as Leland did—'

'What are you trying to do right now?' Maxie condemned strickenly.

'Trying to persuade you that trusting me would be in your best interests. And I'm not laying a finger on you,' Angelos added, as if he expected acclaim for that remarkable restraint.

And the terrible irony, she registered then, was that she *wanted* him to touch her. Her bright eyes pools of sapphire-blue dismay and hunger, she stared down at him. Reaching up to loosen the band confining her hair to the nape of her neck, Angelos trailed it gently free to wind long brown fingers into the tumbling strands and slowly tug her down to him.

'But that's not what you want either, is it?' he said perceptively.

'No…' Her skin burning beneath the caress of the blunt

forefinger that skated along her tremulous and full lower lip, she shivered violently. 'But I won't give in. This attraction means nothing to me,' she swore raggedly. 'It won't influence my brain—'

'What a heady challenge...' Black eyes flaring with golden heat held her sensually bemused gaze.

'I'm not a challenge, I'm a woman...' Maxie fumbled in desperation to make her feelings clear but she didn't have the words or, it seemed, the self-discipline to pull back from his embrace.

'A hell of a woman, to fight me like this,' Angelos confirmed, with a thickened appreciation that made her heart pound like mad in her eardrums and a tide of disorientating dizziness enclose her. 'A woman worth fighting for. If you could just rise above this current inconvenient desire to turn over a new leaf—'

'But—'

'No buts.' Angelos leant up to brush his lips in subtle glancing punishment over her parted ones, scanning her with fierce sexual hunger and conviction. 'You *need* me.'

'No...' she whispered feverishly.

'*Yes...*' Dipping his tongue in a snaking explorative flick into her open mouth, Angelos jolted her with such an overpowering stab of excitement, she almost collapsed down on top of him.

Pressing his advantage with a ruthless sense of timing, Angelos tumbled her the rest of the way and gathered her into his arms. She gasped again, 'No.'

The palm curving over a pouting, swollen breast stilled. Her nipple was a hard, straining bud that ached and begged for his attention, and she let her swimming head drop down on the pillow while she fought desperately for control. She focused on him. The brilliant eyes, the strong nose, the ruthless mouth. And that appalling tide of painful craving simply mushroomed instead of fading.

'No?' Angelos queried lazily.

She inched forward like a moth to a candle flame, seeking the heat and virility she could not resist, all thought suspended. He recognised surrender when he saw it, and with a wolfish smile of reward he closed his mouth hungrily over hers and she burned up like a shooting star streaking through the heavens at impossible speed, embracing destruction as if she had been born to seek it.

He curved back from her when her every sense was thrumming unbearably, her whole body shaking on a peak of frantic anticipation, and eased one hand beneath the T-shirt to curve it to her bare breasts. She whimpered and jerked, the most terrifying surge of hunger taking over as his expert fingers tugged on her tender nipples and then his caressing mouth went there instead. For long, timeless minutes, Maxie was a shuddering wreck of writhing, gasping response, clutching at him, clutching at his hair, her denim-clad hips rising off the bed in helpless invitation.

Abruptly Angelos tensed and jerked up his dark head, frowning. 'What's that?' he demanded.

'W-what's what?' she stammered blankly.

'Someone's thumping on the front door.'

By then already engaged in gaping down at her own shamelessly bared breasts, the damp evidence of his carnal ministrations making the distended pink buds look even more wanton, Maxie gulped. With a low moan of distress she threw herself off the bed onto quaking legs.

'You swine,' she accused shakily, hauling down her T-shirt, crossing trembling arms and then rushing for the stairs.

She flung open the front door. Her nearest neighbour, Patrick Devenson, who had called in to introduce himself the day before, stared in at her. 'Are you aware that you have a Ferrari upended in your stream?'

Dumbly, still trembling from the narrowness of her escape from Angelos and his seductive wiles, Maxie nodded like a wooden marionette.

The husky blond veterinary surgeon frowned down at her. 'I was driving home and I saw this strange shape from the road, and, knowing you're on your own here, I thought I'd better check it out. Are you OK?'

'The driver's upstairs, lying down,' Maxie managed to say.

'Want me to take a look?'

'No need,' she hastened to assert breathlessly.

'Do you want me to ring a doctor?'

Maxie focused on the mobile in its holder at his waist. 'I'd be terribly grateful if you'd let me use that to make a call.'

'No problem…' Patrick said easily, and passed the phone over. 'Mind if I step in out of the rain?'

'Sorry, not at all.'

Maxie walked upstairs rigid-backed, crossed the room and plonked the phone down on the bed beside Angelos. 'Call for transport out of here or I'll throw you out in the rain!'

His stunningly handsome features froze into impassivity, but not before she saw the wild burn of outrage flare in the depths of his brilliant eyes. He stabbed the buttons, loosed a flood of bitten-out Greek instructions and then, cutting the connection, sprang instantly out of bed. Maddeningly, he swayed slightly.

But Maxie was less affected by that than by her first intimidating look at a naked and very aroused male. Colouring hotly, she dragged her shaken scrutiny from him and fled downstairs again.

'Thanks,' she told Patrick.

'Had a drink or two, had he? Wicked putting a machine like that in for a swim,' Patrick remarked with typical male superiority as he moved very slowly back to the door. 'Your boyfriend?'

'No, he's not.'

'Dinner with me then, tomorrow night?'

Words of automatic refusal brimmed on Maxie's lips, and then she hesitated. 'Why not?' she responded after that brief pause for thought. She was well aware that Angelos had to be hearing every word of the conversation.

'Wonderful!' Patrick breathed with unconcealed pleasure. 'Eight suit you?'

'Lovely.'

She watched him swing cheerfully back into his four-wheel drive and thought about how open and uncomplicated he was in comparison to Angelos, who was so devious and manipulative he would contrive to zigzag down a perfectly straight line. And she hated Angelos, she really did.

Hot tears stung her eyes then, and she blinked them back furiously. She hated him for showing her all over again how weak and foolish she could be. She hated that cool, clever brain he pitted against her, that brilliantly persuasive tongue that could make the unacceptable sound tempting, and that awesome and terrifying sexual heat he unleashed on her whenever she was vulnerable.

Barely five minutes later, Angelos strode fully dressed into the front room where she was waiting. He radiated black fury, stormy eyes glittering, sensual mouth compressed, rock-hard jawline at an aggressive angle. His hostile vibrations lanced through the already tense atmosphere, threatening to set it on fire.

'You bitch...' Angelos breathed, so hoarsely it sounded as if he could hardly get the words out. 'One minute you're in bed with me and the next you're making a date with another man within my hearing!'

'I wasn't in bed with you, not the way you're implying.' Her slender hands knotted into taut fists of determination by her side, Maxie stood her ground, cringing with angry self-loathing only inside herself.

'You don't *want* any other man!' Angelos launched at her with derisive and shocking candour. 'You want *me*!'

Maxie was bone-white, her knees wobbling. In a rage, Angelos was pure intimidation; there was nothing he would not say. 'I won't be your mistress. I made that clear that from the start,' she countered in a ragged rush. 'And even if I had slept with you just now, I would still have asked you to leave. I will not be cajoled, manipulated or seduced into a relationship that I would find degrading—'

'Only an innocent can be seduced.' His accent harshened with incredulity over that particular choice of word. '*Degrading?*' Outrage clenched his vibrant dark features hard. 'Fool that I am, I would have treated you like a precious jewel!'

Locked up tight somewhere, to be enjoyed only in the strictest privacy, Maxie translated, deeply unimpressed.

'I know you don't believe me, but I was never Leland's mistress—'

'Did you call yourself his lover instead?' Angelos derided.

Maxie swallowed convulsively. 'No, I—'

Grim black eyes clashed with hers in near physical assault. '*Theos*…how blind I have been! All along you've been scheming to extract a better offer from me. One step forward, two steps back. You run and I chase. You tease and I pursue,' he enumerated in harsh condemnation. 'And now you're trying to turn the screw by playing me off against another man—'

'No!' Maxie gasped, unnerved by the twisted light he saw her in.

Angelos growled, 'If you think for one second that you can force me to offer a wedding ring for the right to enjoy that beautiful body, you are certifiably insane!'

His look of unconcealed contempt sent scorching anger tearing through Maxie. 'Really…? Well, isn't that just a shame, when it's the only offer I would ever settle for,' she stated, ready to use any weapon to hold him at bay.

Evidently somewhat stunned to have his worst suspicions

so baldly confirmed, Angelos jerked as if he had run into a brick wall. He snatched in a shuddering breath, his nostrils flaring. 'If I ever marry, my wife will be a lady with breeding, background and a decent reputation.'

Maxie flinched, stomach turning over sickly. She had given him a knife and he had plunged it in without compunction. But ferocious pride as great as his own, and hot, violent loathing enabled her to treat him to a scornful appraisal. 'But you'll still have a mistress, won't you?'

'Naturally I would choose a wife with my brain, not my libido,' Angelos returned drily, but he had ducked the question and a dark, angry rise of blood had scoured his blunt cheekbones.

Maxie gave an exaggerated little shiver of revulsion. The atmosphere was explosive. She could feel his struggle to maintain control over that volatile temperament so much at war with that essentially cool intellect of his. It was etched in every restive, powerfully physical movement he made with his expressive hands and she rejoiced at the awareness, ramming down the stark bitterness and sense of pained inadequacy he had filled her with. 'You belong in the Natural History Museum alongside the dinosaur bones.'

'When I walk through that door I will never come back...how will you like that?'

'Would you like to start walking now?'

'What I would *like* is to take you on that bed upstairs and teach you just once exactly what you're missing!'

Wildly unprepared for that roughened admission, Maxie collided with golden eyes ablaze with frustration. It was like being dragged into a fire and burned by her own hunger. She shivered convulsively. 'Dream on,' she advised fiercely, but her voice shook in self-betrayal.

The noise of a car drawing up outside broke the taut silence.

Angelos inclined his arrogant dark head in a gesture of grim dismissal that made her squirm, and then he walked.

CHAPTER SIX

MAXIE drifted like a sleepwalker through the following five days. The Ferrari was retrieved by a tow-truck and two men who laughed like drains throughout the operation. She contacted a builder to have the roof inspected and the news was as bad as she had feared. The cottage needed to be reroofed, and the quote was way beyond her slender resources.

She dined out with Patrick Devenson. No woman had ever tried harder to be attracted to a man. He was good-looking and easy company. Desperate to feel a spark, she let him kiss her at the end of the evening, but it wasn't like falling on an electric fence, it was like putting on a pair of slippers. Seriously depressed, Maxie made an excuse when he asked when he could see her again.

She didn't sleep, *couldn't* sleep. She dreamt of fighting with Angelos. She dreamt of making wild, passionate love for the first time in her life. And, most grotesque of all, she dreamt of drifting down a church aisle towards a scowling, struggling Greek in handcuffs. She felt like an alien inside her own head and body.

She sat down and painstakingly made a list of every flaw that Angelos possessed. It covered two pages. In a rage with herself, she wept over that list. She loathed him. Yet that utterly mindless craving for his enlivening, domineering Neanderthal man presence persisted, killing her appetite and depriving her of all peace of mind.

How could she miss him, how could she possibly? How *could* simple sexual attraction be so devastating a leveller? she asked herself in furious despair and shame. And, since she could only be suffering from the fallout of having repressed her own physical needs for so long, why on earth hadn't she fancied Patrick?

At lunchtime on the fifth day, she heard a car coming up the lane and went to the window. A silver Porsche pulled up. When Catriona Ferguson emerged, Maxie was startled. She had never in her life qualified for a personal visit from the owner of the Star modelling agency and couldn't begin to imagine what could've brought the spiky, city-loving redhead all the way from town.

On the doorstep, Catriona dealt her a wide, appreciative smile. 'I've got to hand it to you, Maxie…you have to be the Comeback Queen of the Century.'

'You've got some work for me?' Maxie ushered her visitor into the front room.

'Since the rumour mill got busy, you're really *hot*,' Catriona announced with satisfaction. 'The day after tomorrow, there's a Di Venci fashion show being staged in London…a big splashy charity do, and your chance to finally make your debut on the couture circuit.'

'The rumour mill?' Maxie was stunned by what the older woman was telling her. One minute she was yesterday's news and the next she was being offered the biggest break of her career to date? That didn't make sense.

Having sat down to open a tiny electronic notepad, Catriona flashed her an amused glance. 'The gossip columns are rumbling like mad…don't you read your own publicity?'

Maxie stiffened. 'I don't buy newspapers.'

'I'm very discreet. Your private life is your own.' However, Catriona still searched Maxie's face with avid curiosity. 'But what a coup for a lady down on her luck, scandalously maligned and dropped into social obscurity… Only one of the richest men in the world—'

Maxie jerked. 'I don't know what you're talking about.'

Catriona raised pencilled brows. 'I'm only talking about the guy who has just single-handedly relaunched your career without knowing it! The paparazzo who had his film exposed howled all over the tabloids about who he had seen you with—'

'You're talking about Angelos…'

'And when I received a cautious visit from a tight-mouthed gentleman I know to be close to the Greek tycoon himself, I was just totally *amazed*, not to mention impressed to death,' Catriona trilled, her excitement unconcealed. 'So I handed over your address. They say Angelos Petronides never forgets a favour…or, for that matter, a slight.'

Maxie had turned very pale. 'I…'

'So why are you up here vegetating next door to a field of sheep?' Catriona angled a questioning glance at her. 'Treat 'em mean, keep 'em keen? Popular report has it that this very week he dumped Natalie Cibaud for you. Whatever you're doing would appear to be working well. And he's an awesome catch, twenty-two-carat gorgeous, and as for that delicious *scary* reputation of his—'

'There's nothing between Angelos and me,' Maxie cut in with flat finality, but her head buzzed with the information that Angelos had evidently still been seeing the glamorous French film actress.

The silence that fell was sharp.

'If it's already over, keep it to yourself.' Catriona's disappointment was blatant. 'The sudden clamour for your services relates very much to *him*. The story that you've captured his interest is enough to raise you to celebrity status right now. So keep the people guessing for as long as you can…'

When Maxie recalled how appalled she had been at the threat of being captured in newsprint with Angelos and being subjected to more lurid publicity, she very nearly choked at that cynical advice. And when she considered how outraged Angelos must be at the existence of such rumours, when he had demanded her discretion, she sucked in a sustaining breath.

Catriona checked her watch. 'Look, why don't I give you a lift back to town? I suggest you stay with that friend in the suburbs again. The paparazzi are scouring the pavements for you. You don't want to be found yet. You need to make the biggest possible impact when you appear on that catwalk.'

It took guts, but Maxie nodded agreement. The old story, she thought bitterly. She needed the money. Not just for the roof but also to pay off Angelos as well. Yet the prospect of all those flashing cameras and the vitriolic pens of the gossip columnists made her sensitive stomach churn. Money might not buy happiness, but the lack of it could destroy all freedom of choice. And Maxie acknowledged then that the precious freedom to choose her own way of life was what she now craved most.

Scanning Maxie's strained face, Catriona sighed. 'Whatever *has* happened to the Ice Queen image?'

As she packed upstairs, Maxie knew the answer to that. Angelos had happened. He had chipped her out from behind the safety of her cool, unemotional façade by making her feel things she had never felt before...painful things, hurtful things. She wanted the ice back far more desperately than Catriona did.

Maxie came off the catwalk to a rousing bout of thunderous applause. Immediately she abandoned the strutting insolent carriage which was playing merry hell with her backbone. Finished, *at last*. The relief was so huge, she trembled. Never in her life had she felt so exposed.

Before she could reach the changing room, Manny Di Venci, a big bruiser of a man with a shaven head and sharp eyes, came backstage to intercept her. 'You were brilliant! Standing room only out there, but now it's time to beat a fast retreat. No, you don't need to get changed,' the designer laughed, urging her at a fast pace down a dimly lit corridor that disorientated her even more after the glaring spotlights of the show. 'You're the best PR my collection has ever had, and a special lunch-date demands a touch of Di Venci class.'

Presumably Catriona had set up lunch with some VIP she had to impress.

Thrust through a rear entrance onto a pavement drenched in sunlight, Maxie was dazzled again. Squinting at the open door of the waiting vehicle, she climbed in. The car had pulled back into the traffic before she registered that she was in a huge, opulent limo with shaded windows, but she relaxed when she saw the huge squashy bag of her posses-sions sitting on the floor. She checked the bag; her clothes were in it too. Somebody had been very efficient.

Off the catwalk, she was uncomfortable in the daring peacock-blue cocktail suit. She wore only skin below the fitted jacket with its plunging neckline, and the skirt was horrendously tight and short. She would have preferred not to meet a potential client in so revealing an outfit, but she might as well make the best of being sought after while it lasted because it wouldn't last long. The minute Angelos appeared in public with another woman, she would be as 'hot' as a cold potato. But oh, how infuriating it must be for Angelos to have played an accidental part in pushing her back into the limelight!

When the door of the limo swung open, Maxie stepped out into a cold, empty basement car park. She froze in astonishment, attacked by sudden mute terror, and then across the vast echoing space she recognised one of Angelos's security men, and was insensibly relieved for all of ten seconds. But the nightmare image of kidnapping which had briefly gripped her was immediately replaced by a sensation of almost suffocating panic.

'Where am I?' she demanded of the older man standing by a lift with the doors wide in readiness.

'Mr Petronides is waiting for you on the top floor, Miss Kendall.'

'I didn't realise that limo was *his*. I thought I was meeting up with my agent and a client for lunch…this is o-outrageous!' Hearing the positively pathetic shake of rampant nerves in her own voice, Maxie bit her lip and stalked into the lift. She was furious with herself. She had been the one to make assumptions. She should have spoken to the chauffeur before she got into the car.

Like a protective wall in front of her, the security man stayed by the doors, standing back again only after they had opened. Her face taut with temper, Maxie walked out into a big octagonal hall with a cool tiled floor. It was not Angelos's apartment and she frowned, wondering where on earth she was. Behind her the lift whirred downward again and she stiffened, feeling ludicrously cut off from escape.

Ahead of her, a door stood wide. She walked into a spacious, luxurious reception room. Strong sunlight was pouring through the windows. The far end of the room seemed to merge into a lush green bank of plants. Patio doors gave way into what appeared to be a conservatory. Was that where Angelos was waiting for her?

Her heart hammered wildly against her ribs. Utterly despising her own undeniable mix of apprehension and excitement, Maxie threw back her slim shoulders and stalked out into…*fresh air*. Too late did she appreciate that she was actually out on a roof garden. As she caught a dizzy glimpse of the horrific drop through a gap in the decorative stone screening to her right, her head reeled. Freezing to the spot, she uttered a sick moan of fear.

'Oh, hell…you're afraid of heights,' a lazy drawl murmured.

A pair of hands closed with firm reassurance round her whip-taut shoulders and eased her back from the parapet and the view that had made her stomach lurch to her soles. 'I didn't think of that. Though I suppose I could keep you standing out here and persuade you to agree to just about anything. Sometimes it's *such* a challenge to be an honourable man.'

Shielding her from the source of her mindless terror with his big powerful frame, Angelos propelled her back indoors at speed. Appalled by the attack of panic which had thrown her off balance, Maxie broke free of him then, on legs shaking like cotton wool pins, and bit out accusingly, 'What would *you* know about honour?'

'The Greek male can be extremely sensitive on that subject. Think before you speak,' Angelos murmured in chilling warning.

Maxie stared at him in surprise. Angelos stared levelly back at her, black eyes terrifyingly cold.

And it tore her apart just at that moment to learn that she couldn't *bear* him to look at her like that. As if she was just anybody, as if she was nobody, as if he didn't care whether she lived or died.

'You get more nervy every time I see you,' Angelos remarked with cruel candour. 'Paler, thinner too. I thought you were pretty tough, but you're not so tough under sustained pressure. Your stress level is beginning to show.'

Colour sprang into Maxie's cheeks, highlighting the feverish look in her gaze. 'You're such a bastard sometimes,' she breathed unevenly.

'And within itself, that's strange. I've never been like this with a woman before. There are times when I aim to hurt you and I shock myself,' Angelos confided, without any perceptible remorse.

Yet he still looked so unbelievably good to her, and that terrified her. She couldn't drag her attention from that lean, strong face, no matter how hard she tried. She couldn't forget what that silky black hair had felt like beneath her fingertips. She couldn't stop herself noticing that he was wearing what had inexplicably become the colour she liked best on him. Silver-grey, the suit a spectacular fit for that magnificent physique. And how had she forgotten the way that vibrant aura of raw energy compelled and fascinated her? Cast into deeper shock by the raging torrent of her own frantic thoughts, Maxie felt an intense sense of her own vulnerability engulf her in an alarming wave.

'Relax…I've got a decent proposal to put on the table before lunch,' Angelos purred, strolling soundlessly forwards to curve a confident arm round her rigid spine and guide her across the hall into a dining-room. 'Trust me…I think you'll feel like you've won the National Lottery.'

'Why won't you just leave me alone?' Maxie whispered, taking in the table exquisitely set for two, the waiting trolley that indicated they were not to be disturbed.

'Because you don't want me to. Even the way you just looked at me…' Angelos vented a soft husky laugh of very masculine appreciation. 'You really *can't* look at me like that and expect me to throw in the towel.'

'How did I look?'

'Probably much the same way that I look at you,' he conceded, uncorking a bottle of champagne with a loud pop and allowing the golden liquid to foam expertly down into two fluted glasses. 'With hunger and hostility and resentment. I am about to wipe out the last two for ever.'

Angelos slotted the moisture-beaded glass between her taut fingers. Absorbing her incomprehension, he dealt her a slashing smile. 'The rumour that Angelos Petronides cannot compromise is a complete falsehood. I excell at seeing both points of view and a period of reflection soon clarified the entire problem. The solution is very simple.'

Maxie frowned uneasily. 'I don't know what you're driving at…'

'What *is* marriage? Solely a legal agreement.' Angelos shrugged with careless elegance but she was chilled by that definition. 'Once I recognised that basic truth, I saw with clarity. I'll make a deal with you now that suits us both. *You* sign a prenuptial contract and I *will* marry you…'

'S-say that again,' Maxie stammered, convinced she was hallucinating.

Angelos rested satisfied eyes on her stunned expression. 'The one drawback will be that you won't get the public kudos of being my wife. We will live apart much of the time. When I'm in London and I want you here, you will stay in this apartment. I own this entire building. You can have it all to yourself, complete with a full complement of staff and security. The only place we will share the same roof will be on my island in Greece. How am I doing?'

Maxie's hand was shaking so badly, champagne was slopping onto the thick, ankle-deep carpet. Was he actually asking her to marry him? Had she got that right or imagined it? And, if she was correct and hadn't misunderstood, why was he talking about them living apart? And what had that bit been concerning 'public kudos'? Her brain was in a hopelessly confused state of freefall.

Angelos took her glass away and set it aside with his own. He pressed her gently down onto the sofa behind her and crouched down at her level to scan her bewildered face.

'If a marriage licence is what it takes to make you feel secure and bring you to my bed, it would be petty to deny you,' Angelos informed her smoothly. 'But, since our relationship will obviously not last for ever, it will be a private arrangement between you and I alone.'

Maxie stopped breathing and simply closed her eyes. He had hurt her before but never as badly as this. Was her reputation really *that* bad? In his eyes, it evidently was, she registered sickly. He didn't want to be seen with her. He didn't want to be linked with her. He would go through the motions of marrying her only so long as it was a 'private arrangement'. And a temporary one.

Cool, strong hands snapped round her straining fingers as she began to move them in an effort to jump upright. 'No…think about it, don't fly off the handle,' Angelos warned steadily. 'It's a fair, realistic, what-you-see-is-what-you-get offer—'

'A mockery!' Maxie contradicted fiercely.

And that had to be the most awful moment imaginable to realise that she was very probably in love with Angelos. It was without doubt her lowest hour. Devastated to suspect just how and why he had come to possess this power to tear her to emotional shreds, Maxie was shorn of her usual fire.

'Be reasonable. How do I bring Leland's former mistress into my family and demand that they accept her as my wife?' Angelos enquired with the disorientating cool of someone saying the most reasonable, rational things and expecting a fair and understanding hearing. 'Some things one just does not do. How can I expect my family to respect me if I do something I would kill any one of them for doing? The family look to me to set an example.'

Maxie still hadn't opened her eyes, but she knew at that instant how a woman went off the rails and killed. There was so much pain inside her and so much rage—at her, at him—she didn't honestly know how she *could* contain it. Mistress within a marriage that nobody would ever know about because she was too scandalous and shameful a woman to deserve or indeed expect acceptance within the lofty Petronides clan…that was what he was offering.

'I feel sick…' Maxie muttered raggedly.

'No, you do not feel sick,' Angelos informed her with resolute emphasis.

'I…feel…sick!'

'The cloakroom is across the hall.' Angelos withdrew his strong hands from hers in a stark demonstration of disapproval. Only when he did so did she realise how tightly she had been holding onto him for support. The inconsistency of such behaviour in the midst of so devastating a dialogue appalled her. 'I didn't expect you to be so difficult about this. I can appreciate that you're a little disappointed with the boundaries I'm setting, but when all is said and done, it is *still* a marriage proposal!'

'Is it?' Maxie queried involuntarily, and then, not trusting herself to say anything more, she finally, mercifully made it into the sanctuary of the cloakroom.

She locked the door and lurched in front of a giant mirror that reflected a frightening stranger with the shocked staring eyes of tragedy, pallid cheeks and a horribly wobbly mouth. You do *not* love that swine—do you hear me? she mouthed with menace at the alien weak creature in the reflection. The only thing you're in love with is his *body*! She knew as much about love as a fourteen-year-old with a crush! And she could not imagine where that insane impulsive idea that she might love such a unreconstructed pig could've come from…it could only have been a reaction to overwhelming shock.

She wanted to scream and cry and break things and she knew she couldn't, so she hugged herself tight instead and paced the floor. As there was a great deal of floor available, in spite of the fact it was only a cloakroom, that was not a problem.

He's prepared to give you a whole blasted building to yourself. But then he does like his own space. He's prepared to do virtually anything to get you into bed except own up to you in public. Love and hate. Two sides of the same coin. A cliché but the brief, terrifying spasm of that anguished love feeling had now been wholly obliterated by loathing and a desire to hit back and hurt that was ferocious.

A *marriage* proposal? A bitter laugh erupted from Maxie. Angelos was still planning to use her, still viewing her as a live toy to be acquired at any cost for his bedroom. And evidently her reluctance had sent what he was prepared to pay for that pleasure right through the roof! Grimacing, she could not help thinking about the two men before Angelos who had most influenced her life. Her father and

Leland. For once she thought about her father without sentimentality…

Russ had gambled away her earnings and finally abandoned her, leaving her to work off *his* debts. Leland had stolen three years of her life and destroyed her reputation. How often had she sworn since never to allow any man to use her for his own ends again?

Like a bolt from the blue an infinitely more ego-boosting scenario flashed into Maxie's mind. She froze as the heady concept of turning the tables occurred to her. What if *she* were to do the using this time around?

Didn't she require a husband to inherit a share of her godmother's estate? When she had heard that news, she had taken disappointment on the chin. She had not foreseen the remotest possibility of a husband on the horizon, and the concept of looking for one with the sole object of collecting that inheritance had made her cringe

Only no longer did Maxie feel so nice in her notions. Angelos had done that to her. He was a corrupting influence and no mistake. He had distressed her, humiliated her, harassed her, not to mention committed the ultimate sin of taking the holy bond of matrimony and twisting it into a sad, dirty joke.

Angelos saw her as an ambitious, money-grabbing bimbo without morals. No doubt he despised what he saw. He probably even despised his own obsessive hunger to possess her. The marriage, if it could be called such, wouldn't last five minutes beyond the onset of his boredom.

But what if she were to take the opportunity to turn apparent humiliation into triumph? She *could* break free of everything that had ruined her life in recent years. That debt to Angelos, a career and a life she hated, Angelos himself. If she had the courage of her convictions, she could have it *all*. Yes, she really could. She could marry him and walk out on him six months later. She pictured herself breezily throwing Angelos a cheque and telling him no, she didn't

need his money, she now had her own. She looked back in
the mirror and saw a killer bimbo with a brain and not a
hint of tears in her eyes any more.

Maxie was surprised to find Angelos waiting in the hall
when she emerged.

'Are you OK?' he enquired, as if he really cared.

Her lip wanted to curl but she controlled it. The rat. An
extraordinarily handsome rat, but a rat all the same.

'I was working out my conditions of acceptance.' Maxie
flashed him a bright smile of challenge.

Angelos tensed.

'I'll need to be sure I *will* feel like a Lottery winner at
the end of this private arrangement,' she told him for good
measure.

Angelos frowned darkly. 'My lawyer will deal with such
things. Do you have to be so crude?'

Crude? My goodness, hadn't he got sensitive all of a
sudden? He didn't want to be forced to dwell on the actual
cost of acquiring her. And even if she didn't go for the
whole package, and indeed considered herself insulted beyond belief, it *was* quite a hefty cost on his terms, Maxie
conceded grudgingly. A marriage licence as the ultimate
assurance of financial security—the lifestyle of a very
wealthy woman and no doubt a very generous final settlement at the end of the day.

Mulling over those points, Maxie decided that he certainly couldn't accuse her of coming cheap, but she was
entranced to realise that Angelos had no desire to be reminded of that unlovely fact. Just like everybody else, it
seemed, Angelos Petronides preferred to believe that he
was wanted for himself. She stored up that unexpected
Achilles' heel for future reference.

Maxie widened her beautiful eyes at his words. 'I
thought you admired the upfront approach?'

'I brought you here to celebrate a sane and sensible
agreement, not to stage another argument.'

With that declaration, heated black eyes watched her flick her spectacular mane of golden hair over her slim shoulders and stayed to linger on her exquisite face. As his intent appraisal slowly arrowed down over the deep shadowy vee of her neckline, Maxie stiffened. At an almost pained pace of ever-deepening lust, his appreciative gaze wandered on down to take in the full effect of her slim hips and incredibly long legs. 'No, definitely not to have another argument,' Angelos repeated rather hoarsely.

'If your idea of celebration encompasses what I think it might, I'm afraid no can do.' Maxie swept up her glass of champagne with an apologetic smile pasted on her lips and drank deep before continuing at a fast rate of knots, 'I'll share your bed on our wedding night, but not one single second, minute, hour or day before. I suggest that we have lunch—'

'Lunch?' Angelos repeated flatly.

'We might as well do lunch because we are not about to do anything else,' Maxie informed him dulcetly.

'*Theos*...come here,' Angelos groaned. He hauled her resisting frozen length into his arms. 'Why are you always so set on punishing me?' He gave her a frustrated little shake, black eyes blazing over her mutinous expression. 'Why do you always feel the need to top everything I do and turn every encounter into a fight? That is not a womanly trait. Why cannot you just one time give me the response I expect?'

'I suppose I do it because I don't like you,' Maxie admitted, with the kind of impulsive sincerity that was indisputably convincing.

In an abrupt movement, Angelos's powerful arms dropped from her again. He actually looked shocked. 'What do you mean you don't *like* me?' he grated incredulously. 'What sort of a thing is that to say to man who has just asked you to marry him?'

'I wrote two whole pages on the subject last week...all

the things I don't like...but why should you let that bother you? You're not interested in what goes on inside my head...all you require is an available body!'

'You're overwrought, so I won't make an issue of that judgement.' Angelos frowned down into her beautiful face with the suggestion of grim self-restraint. 'Let's have lunch.'

As she sat down at the table Maxie murmured sweetly, 'One more little question. Are you planning to generously share yourself between Natalie Cibaud and me?'

Angelos glared at her for a startled second. 'Are you out of your mind?'

'That's not an answer—'

Angelos flung aside his napkin, black eyes glittering hard and bright as diamonds. 'Of course I do not intend to conduct a liaison with another woman while I am with you,' he intoned in a charged undertone.

Relaxing infinitesimally, Maxie said flatly, 'So when will the big event be taking place?'

'The wedding? As soon as possible. It will be very private.'

'I think it is so sweet that you had not a single doubt that I would say yes.' Maxie stabbed an orange segment with vicious force.

'If you want me to take you to bed to close that waspish mouth, you're going the right way.'

Looking up, Maxie clashed with gleaming black eyes full of warning. She swallowed convulsively and coloured, annoyed that she was unable to control her own fierce need to attack him.

'You told me yourself that the one offer you would settle for is marriage. I have delivered...stop using me as target practice.'

Maxie tried to eat then, but she couldn't. All appetite had ebbed, so she tried to make conversation, but it seemed rather too late for that. Angelos now exuded brooding dissatisfaction. She saw that she had already sinned. He had expected to pour a couple of glasses of champagne down her throat and sweep her triumphantly off to bed. She felt numb, for once wonderfully untouched by Angelos's incredibly powerful sexual presence.

'Are you aware that all those rumours about you and I have actually relaunched my career?' she murmured stiffly.

'Today was your swansong. I don't want you prancing down a catwalk half-naked and I don't want you working either,' Angelos framed succinctly.

'Oh,' Maxie almost whispered, because it took so much effort not to scream.

'Be sensible…naturally I want you to be available when I'm free.'

'Like a harem slave—'

'Maxie…' Angelos growled.

'Look, I've got a ripping headache,' Maxie confessed abruptly and, pushing her plate away, stood up. 'I want to go home.'

'This will be your home in London soon,' he reminded her drily.

'I don't like weird pictures and cold tiled floors and dirty great empty rooms with ugly geometric furniture…I don't want to live in a building with about ten empty floors below me!' Maxie flung, her voice rising shrilly.

'You're just overexcited—'

'Like one of your racehorses?'

With a ground-out curse, Angelos slung his napkin on the table and, thrusting his chair back, sprang to his full commanding height. As he reached for her she tried to evade him, but he simply bent and swept her up into his powerful arms and held her tight. 'Maxie…why are you suddenly behaving like a sulky child?'

'How *dare*—?'

In answer, Angelos plunged his mouth passionately hard down on hers and smashed his primal passage through every barrier. Her numbness vanished. He kissed her breathless until she was weak and trembling with tormented need in his arms. Then he looked down at her, and he stared for a very long while.

The silence unnerved her, but she was too shaken by the discovery that even a few kisses could reduce her to wanton compliance to speak.

His bronzed face utterly hard and impassive, he finally murmured flatly, 'I'll call the car for you and I'll be in touch. I don't feel like lunch now either.'

Maxie registered his distance. The sense of rejection she felt appalled her. And she thought then, If I go through with this private arrangement, if I try to play him at his own game, I will surely tear myself apart…

No—no, she wouldn't, she told herself urgently, battening down the hatches before insidious doubt could weaken her determination. One way or another she would survive with her pride intact. Wanting Angelos was solely a physical failing. Ultimately she would overcome that hunger and look forward to the life she would have *after* him.

CHAPTER SEVEN

'SO, EVEN though it was a rather unconventional proposal, Angelos *did* have marriage in mind,' Liz finally sighed with satisfaction.

'Only when he saw it was his only hope.'

'I hear a lot of men are like that. Angelos is only thirty-three, but he's bound to be rather spoilt when it comes to his…well, when many other women would be willing to sleep with him without commitment,' Liz extended with warming cheeks. 'I expect you've been something of a learning experience for him, and if *you* were more sensible, he could learn a lot more.'

'Meaning?'

'This marriage will be what you make of it.'

'Haven't you been listening to what I've been saying?' Maxie muttered in confusion. 'It isn't going to *be* a proper marriage, Liz.'

'Right now you are very angry with Angelos. I refuse to credit that you could really go through with walking out on your marriage in six months' time,' Liz told her with a reproving shake of her head.

'I will, Liz…believe me, I *will*—'

'This time I'm definitely not listening,' Liz asserted wryly. 'And as for Angelos's apparent fantasy that he can marry you and live with you on an occasional basis without people finding out that he's involved with you…he's almost as off the wall on this as you are, Maxie!'

'No, he knows exactly what he's doing. He just doesn't expect me to be in his life for very long.'

Liz compressed her lips. 'I have only one real question

to ask you. Why can't you just sit down and tell Angelos the whole truth about Leland?'

Taken aback, Maxie protested, 'He didn't want to listen when I did try—'

'You could've made him listen. You are no shrinking violet.'

'Do you seriously think that Angelos is likely to believe that Leland took advantage of me in every way but the *one* in which, of course, everyone thinks he did, even though he didn't?' Maxie was shaken into surprised defensiveness by Liz's attitude.

'Well, your silence on the subject has defined your whole relationship with Angelos. Indeed, I have a very strong suspicion that you don't really *want* him to know the real story.'

'And why on earth would I feel like that?'

'I think that *you* think you're a much more exciting proposition as a bad girl,' Liz admitted reluctantly, and Maxie turned scarlet. 'You get all dolled up in your fancy clothes and you flounce about getting a bitter thrill out of people thinking you're a real hard, grasping little witch—'

Maxie was aghast. 'Liz, *that's*—'

'Let me finish,' the older woman insisted ruefully. 'I believe that that's the way you've learnt to cope with those who have hurt you, not to mention all the mud you've had slung at you. You hide away inside that fancy shell and sometimes you get completely carried away with pretending to be what you're not…so ask yourself—is it any wonder that Angelos doesn't know you the way he should? He's never seen the real you.'

The *real* me, Maxie reflected, cringing where she sat. He would be bored stiff by the real Maxie Kendall, who, horror of horrors, couldn't even read or write properly. And was it really likely that a male as sexually experienced as Angelos would be equally obsessed with possessing a woman who turned out to be just one big pathetic bluff? A woman who had never yet shared a bed with any man? A virgin?

Unaware of the younger woman's hot-cheeked distraction, Liz was made anxious by the lingering silence. 'You're the closest thing to a daughter I'll ever have,' she sighed. 'I just want you to be happy…and I'm afraid that if you keep up this front with Angelos, you'll only end up getting very badly hurt.'

Her eyes prickling, Maxie gave her friend a hug. She blamed herself for being too frank and worrying Liz. From here on in, she decided shamefacedly, she would keep her thoughts and her plans to herself.

Angelos phoned her at six that evening. He talked with the cool detachment of someone handing out instructions to an employee. She knew herself unforgiven. His London lawyer would visit her with the prenuptial contract. The ceremony would take place the following week in the north of England.

'*Next week?*' Maxie exclaimed helplessly.

'I'm organising a special licence.'

'Why do we have to go north?'

'We couldn't marry in London without attracting attention.'

Maxie bit her lower lip painfully. So, Liz innocently assumed that such secrecy couldn't be achieved? She didn't know Angelos. Employing his wealth in tandem with his naturally devious mind, Angelos clearly intended to take every possible precaution.

'Do we travel up together in heavy disguise?'

'We'll travel separately. I'll meet you up there.'

'Oh…' Even facetious comments were squashed by such attention to detail.

'I'm afraid that I won't be seeing you beforehand—'

'Why *not*?' Maxie heard herself demand in disbelief, and then was furious with herself for making such an uncool response.

'Naturally I intend to take some time off. But in order to free that space in a very tight schedule, I'll be flying to Japan later this evening and moving on to Indonesia for the rest of the week.'

'You'll be seriously jet lagged by the time you get back.'

'I'll survive. I suggest you disengage yourself from your contract with the modelling agency—'

'I was on the brink of signing a new one,' Maxie admitted.

'Excellent. Then you can simply tell them that you have changed your mind.'

Maxie was still recovering from Catriona Ferguson's angry incredulity at their brief and unpleasant interview when she was subjected to the visit from Angelos's lawyer.

At her request the older man read out the document she was expected to sign. If Maxie had been as avaricious as Angelos apparently believed, she would've been ecstatic. In return for her discretion she was offered a vast monthly allowance on top of an all-expenses-paid lifestyle, and when the marriage ended she was to receive a quite breathtaking settlement.

By the time he had finished speaking, Maxie's nails were digging into her palms like pincers and she was extremely pale. She signed, but the only thing that gave her the strength to do so was the bitter certainty that in six months' time she would tear up her copy of that agreement and throw the pieces scornfully back at Angelos's feet. Only then would he appreciate that she could neither be bought nor paid off.

The church sat on the edge of a sleepy Yorkshire hamlet. Mid-morning on a weekday, the village had little traffic and even fewer people. Maxie checked her watch for the tenth time. Angelos was *now* eleven minutes late.

Having run out of casual conversation, the elderly rector

and his wife were now uneasily anchored in the far corner of the church porch while Maxie hovered by the door like a pantomime bride, on the watch in terror that the groom had changed his mind. And it *was* possible, wasn't it? The arrangements had been so detached they now seemed almost surreal.

A car had picked her up at a very early hour to ferry her north. And Angelos had phoned only twice over the past week. He would have been better not phoning at all. Her spontaneity vanished the instant she recognised her own instinctive physical response to that rich, dark drawl. It had not made for easy dialogue.

Today, I am getting married. This is my wedding day, she told herself afresh in a daze of disbelief, and of course he would turn up, but he would get a tongue-lashing when he did. Angelos... Hatred was so incredibly enervating, Maxie conceded grimly. He kept her awake at night and he haunted her dreams. That infuriated and threatened her.

In defiance of the suspicion that she was taking part in some illegal covert operation, she was wearing her scarlet dress. A scarlet dress for a scarlet woman. No doubt that would strike Angelos as an extremely appropriate choice.

Hearing the sound of an approaching car, Maxie tensed. A gleaming Mercedes closely followed by a second car pulled up. Angelos emerged from the Mercedes. Sheathed in a wonderfully well-cut navy suit, pale blue tie and white silk shirt, he looked stupendous. As his London lawyer appeared from the second car, Angelos paused to wait for him. As if he had all the time in the world, Maxie noted incredulously. Her ready temper sizzled. How *dared* Angelos keep her waiting and then refuse to hurry himself?

Stepping into full view, her attention all for Angelos as he mounted the shallow steps to the door, Maxie snapped, 'And what sort of a time do you call this? Where the heck have you been?'

As his lawyer froze into shattered stillness, Angelos's

black eyes lit on Maxie like burnished blazing gold. And then a funny thing happened. A sudden scorching smile of raw amusement wiped the disturbing detachment from his savagely handsome features. 'We had to wait thirty minutes for a landing slot at the airport. Short of a parachute jump, there wasn't much I could do about that.'

Suddenly self-conscious, her cheeks flaming, Maxie shrugged. 'OK.'

'Thanks for wearing my favourite outfit. You look spectacular,' Angelos murmured huskily in her ear, before he moved smoothly forward to offer his apologies to the rector for his late arrival.

Minutes later, they were walking down the aisle. As the ceremony began Maxie looked tautly around herself and then down at her empty hands. Not even a flower to hold. And her dress—so inappropriate, so strident against the timeworn simplicity of the church and its quiet atmosphere of loving piety. But then what did love have to do with her agreement with Angelos?

Suddenly she felt the most terrible fraud. Like any other woman, she had had wedding day dreams. Not one of them had included marrying a man who didn't love her. Not one of them had included the absence of her father and of even a single friend or well-wisher. Her eyes prickled with tears. Finding herself all choked up, Maxie blinked rapidly, mortified by her own emotionalism. A ring was slid onto her wedding finger. And then it was over. When Angelos tried to kiss her, she twisted her golden head away and presented him with a cool, damp cheek.

'What's the matter with you?' Angelos demanded as he strode down the steps, one big hand stubbornly enclosing hers in spite of her evasive attempts to ease free of him. 'Why the tears?'

'I feel horribly guilty…we just took vows we didn't mean.'

Maxie climbed into the Mercedes. After a brief exchange

with his lawyer, Angelos swung into the driver's seat and slammed the door. Starting the engine, he drove off. The silence between them screeched louder with every passing minute.

'Tell me, is there the slightest hope of any bridal joy on the horizon?' Angelos finally enquired in a charged and sardonic undertone.

'I don't feel like a bride,' Maxie responded flatly. 'I thought you'd be pleased about that.'

Angelos brought the Mercedes to a sudden halt on the quiet country road. As he snapped free his seat belt Maxie turned to look at him, wondering why he had stopped. With a lack of cool that took her completely by surprise, Angelos pulled her into his powerful arms and sealed his mouth to hers in a hot, hard, punishing kiss. Maxie struck his broad muscular back with balled fists of outrage, but all that pent-up passion he unleashed surged through her like a lightning bolt of retribution.

Her head swam; her heartbeat thundered insanely fast. Her fists uncoiled, her fingers flexed and then rose to knot round the back of his strong neck. She clung. He prised her lips apart and with a ragged groan of need let his tongue delve deep. Excited beyond belief at that intensely sexual assault, Maxie reacted with a whimpering, startled moan of pleasure, and then as abruptly as he had reached for her Angelos released her again, his hard profile taut.

'We haven't got time for this. I don't want to have to hang around at the airport.'

Maxie's swollen mouth tingled. She lowered her head, but as Angelos shifted restlessly on the seat and switched the engine back on she could not help but notice that he was sexually aroused. Her face burning from that intimate awareness, she swiftly averted her attention again. He seemed to get that way very easily, she thought nervously. And only then did Maxie admit to herself that her own lack of sexual experience had now become a source of some anxiety to her.

For a cool, sophisticated male, Angelos had seemed alarmingly close to the edge of his control. If he could react like that to one kiss, what would he be like tonight?

That Greek temperament of his was fiery. Virile, over-whelming masculinity powered his smouldering passion to possess, which she had already frustrated more than once. And, since he believed that she had had other lovers, maybe he wouldn't bother too much with preliminaries. Maybe he would just expect her to be as hot and impatient as he was for satisfaction...

For goodness' sake, Angelos wasn't a clumsy teenager, she told herself in exasperation. As experienced as he un-doubtedly was in the bedroom, he was sure to be a skilled and considerate lover. And he would never guess that she was inexperienced. She had once read on a problem page that most men couldn't even tell whether a woman was a virgin or not.

Honestly, she was being ridiculous! Embarrassed for her-self, Maxie stared stonily out at the passing scenery and forced her mind blank. She smothered a yawn. As the fe-rocious tension drained gradually out of her muscles, tired-ness began to creep in to take its place.

Angelos helped her out of the car at the airport. He frowned down at her pale, stiff face. 'Are you OK?'

'I'm just a bit tired.'

They were flying straight to Greece and they were able to board his private jet immediately. He tucked her into a comfortable seat and, after takeoff, a meal was served. Maxie had about two mouthfuls and a glass of wine. In the middle of the conversation Angelos was endeavouring to open, she noticed that she still had the wedding ring on her finger.

He *is* my husband, Maxie suddenly registered in shock. And then, just as suddenly, she erased that thought. She didn't want to think of him as her husband because she was all too well aware that he did not think of her as his wife. A private arrangement, a temporary one, not a normal marriage, she reminded herself. Her troubled eyes hardened. Sliding the slender band from her finger, she studied it with a slightly curled lip before leaning forward to set it down on the table between them.

'You'd better take that back,' she told him carelessly.

Angelos stared at her as if she had slapped him. A faint arc of colour scored his high cheekbones. His fulminating gaze raked over her. 'You are a ravishingly beautiful woman…but sometimes you drive me clean up the wall!' he admitted grittily. 'Why should you remove that ring now, when we are alone?'

'Because I don't feel comfortable with it.' To evade that hard, assessing scrutiny, Maxie rested her head back and closed her eyes. He was acting as if she had mortally insulted him. But she had no intention of sporting a ring that she would eventually have to take off. On that awareness, she fell asleep.

Angelos shook her awake just after the jet had landed at Athens.

'You've been tremendous company,' he drawled flatly.

Maxie flushed. 'I'm sorry, I was just so tired I crashed.'

'Surprisingly enough, I did get that message.'

They transferred from the jet onto a helicopter for the final leg of their journey to the island. As the unwieldy craft rose into the air and then banked into a turn, providing Maxie with a frighteningly skewed panoramic view of the city far below, her stomach twisted sickly. She focused on the back of the pilot's seat, determined not to betray her fear to Angelos. A long, timeless period of mute suffering followed.

'We're almost there. I want you to see the island as we come in over the bay,' Angelos imparted. His warm breath fanned her cheekbone as the helicopter gave an alarming lurch downward and she flinched. 'Go on...*look.*' Angelos strove to encourage her while she shut her eyes tight and her lips moved as she prayed.

'I totally forgot you were afraid of heights,' he murmured ruefully as he lifted her down onto solid ground again and steadied her with both hands. 'I always come to Chymos in the helicopter. You'll have to get used to it some time.'

All Maxie could think about was how soon she would have to undergo that ordeal again.

'What you need is more of the same,' Angelos announced in a tone of immoveable conviction. 'I have a pilot's licence. I'll take you up in the helicopter every day for longer and longer periods and you'll soon get over your phobia.'

Welded to the spot by such a threat, Maxie gave him an aghast look. 'Is it your mission in life to torture me?'

Angelos dealt her a smouldering appraisal, his hard, sensual mouth curving in consideration while his black eyes glittered over her with what could only be described as all-male anticipation. 'Only with pleasure, in my bed, *pethi mou.*'

CHAPTER EIGHT

WARM colour fingered into Maxie's pale cheeks.

Thirty yards from them a long, low white villa sprawled in isolated splendour across the promontory. It overlooked a pale sandy beach, and the rugged cliffs and dark blue sea supplied a majestic backdrop for Angelos's island home.

'I was born on Chymos. As a child I spent all my vacations here. Although I was an only child, I was never lonely because I had so many cousins. Both my parents came from large families. Since my father died, this island has become my retreat from the rest of the world.' Dropping an indolent and assured arm round her stationary figure, Angelos guided her towards the villa. 'You're honoured. I have never brought a woman here before, *pethi mou.*'

As they entered the charming hall she saw into the spacious lounge opposite. In one glance she took in the walls covered with pictures, the photographs scattered around, the shelves of books and the comfortable sofas and rugs. It was full of all the character of a family home. 'It's not like your apartment at all!' Maxie surprise was unconcealed.

'One of my cousins designed my London apartment. I did tell her what I wanted but it didn't quite turn out the way I had imagined it would.' Angelos closed his arms round her from behind. 'We're alone here. I gave the staff some time off.'

Maxie tensed. He pressed his wickedly expert mouth to the smooth skin just below her ear. Every treacherous pulse jumped in response. Maxie quivered, knees wobbling. With an earthy chuckle of amusement, Angelos scooped her off

117

her feet as if she weighed no more than a doll and strode out of the hall down a long tiled corridor.

It was the end of the line of restraint and Maxie knew it. She parted her dry lips nervously. 'Angelos?' she muttered urgently. 'I know you think I've slept with—'

'I do *not* want to hear about the other men who have preceded me,' Angelos interrupted with ruthless precision, glowering down at her in reproof. 'Why do women rush to make intimate revelations and then lie like mad about the number of lovers they've had? Why can't you just keep quiet?'

Not unnaturally silenced by that unexpected attack, Maxie chewed her lower lip uncertainly as he settled her down on the thick carpet in a beautifully furnished bedroom. Her entire attention immediately lodged on the bed.

Seemingly unable to tolerate an instant of physical separation, Angelos encircled her with his arms again and loosed a husky sigh of slumberous pleasure above her head. Curving her quiescent length into glancing contact with his hard, muscular physique, Angelos tugged down the zip on her dress. As cooler air hit her taut shoulder-blades, followed by the sensual heat of Angelos's exploring mouth, Maxie braced herself and surged back into speech.

'Actually,' she confided in an uneven rush, 'all I wanted to say is that I'm really not that experienced!'

'*Theos...*' Angelos ground out, abruptly dropping his arms from her and jerking away to stride across the room. Peeling off his jacket and pitching it aside under her bemused gaze, he sent her a look as dark and threatening as black ice under spinning wheels.

'Sorry, what—?' Maxie began.

'Why are you *doing* this to me?' Angelos demanded rawly as he wrenched at his tie with an exasperated hand. 'Why tell me these foolish lies? Do you think I need to hear them? Do you honestly believe that I could credit such a plea from you for one second?'

Marooned in the centre of the carpet, her dress lurching awkwardly off one bare and extremely taut shoulder, Maxie let her gaze fall from his in a mixture of fierce embarrassment and resentment. If that was his response to the mere admission that she was not a bedroom sophisticate likely to wow him with the unexpected, or possibly even with moves he *did* expect, she could only cringe from the possibility of what an announcement of complete inexperience would arouse. And she did not want to go to bed with an angry man.

'No doubt next you will be offending me beyond belief by referring to the man who kept you for three years...don't *do* it,' Angelos told her in emphatic warning. 'I do not wish to hear one more word about your past. I accept you as you are. I have no choice but to do otherwise.'

Maxie tried to shrug her dress back up her arm

'And why are you standing there like a child put in the corner? Are you trying to make me feel bad?'

Hot colour burnished her cheeks. 'You're in a very volatile mood—'

'Put it down to frustration...you've done nothing but freeze me out since I married you this morning,' Angelos drawled with raw impatience.

'And you have done nothing but think about sex.'

Having made that counter-accusation, Maxie collided with scorching black eyes of outrage and tilted her chin. Like a child in a corner, was she? How *dare* he? Her bright eyes blazed. The silence thundered. She shrugged her slim shoulders forward and extended her slender arms.

Angelos tensed, eyes narrowing. The scarlet dress shimmied down to Maxie's feet, unveiling her lithe, perfect figure clad in a pair of minuscule white panties and a no more substantial gossamer-fine bra. Angelos looked as if he had stopped breathing. Stepping out of the dress, she slung him a catwalk model's look of immense boredom and, strolling

over to the bed, kicked off her shoes and folded herself
down on it.

'What are you waiting for? A white flag of surrender?'
Maxie enquired drily, pride vindicated by the effect she had
achieved.

'Something rather less choreographed, a little warmer and
more enthusiastic,' Angelos purred with sudden dangerous
cool, strolling over to the side of the bed to stare down at
her with slumberous eyes of alarming shrewdness. 'I'm de-
veloping a strong suspicion that to date your bedroom forays have been one big yawn, because you really *don't*
understand how I feel, do you?'

Face pink, and uneasy now, Maxie levered herself up on
one elbow. 'What are you trying to imply?'

'You're about to find out.' Disorientatingly, his bold
black eyes flamed with amusement as he began unbuttoning
his shirt.

'Is that a threat?' Maxie said breathlessly.

'Is that fear or hope I hear?' With a soft, unbearably sexy
laugh, Angelos dispensed with his shirt and gazed down
mockingly into very wide blue eyes. 'Your face...the expression is priceless!'

Maxie veiled her scrutiny, her fair complexion redden-
ing.

Angelos strolled across the room, indolent now that he
had her exactly where he wanted her, fully in control. 'As
for me thinking about sex all the time...don't you know
men? I've been celibate for many weeks. I've wanted you
for an incredibly long time. I'm not used to waiting and
fighting every step of the way for what I want. When you
have everything, what you cannot have naturally assumes
huge importance—'

'And when you finally get it, I suppose it means next to
nothing?' Maxie slotted in tightly.

Angelos elevated a slanting ebony brow. 'Lighten up,'
he advised, not even pretending not to comprehend her

meaning. 'Only time will decide that. I live in the present and so should you, *pethi mou.*'

He undressed with fluid ease. She watched him. Ever since that night at the cottage, his powerful image had been stamped into her brain like a Technicolor movie still. But she was still hopelessly enthralled, shaken by the extent to which she responded to his intensely physical allure. Yet she had never seen beauty in the male body until he came along. But from his wide brown shoulders, slim hips and long, powerful hair-roughened thighs, Angelos made her mouth run dry, her pulses race and her palms perspire.

'You've been so quiet since that ceremony…and now you recline like a very beautiful stone statue on my bed.' Angelos skimmed off his black briefs in one long, lazy movement. 'If it wasn't so ridiculous, I would think you were scared of me.'

Maxie managed to laugh but her throat was already constricting with nerves. He was so relaxed about his nudity, quite unconcerned that he was hugely aroused. And while common sense was telling her that of course God had fashioned men and women to fit, Maxie just could not begin to imagine *how* at that moment.

Angelos came down on the wide bed beside her. He scanned the sudden defensive upward tilt of her perfect profile, trailed a slow and appreciative hand through the lush tumble of golden strands of hair cascading off the pillows. He threw himself back and closed his hands round her slender forearms to bring her gently down to him. 'And now my reward for waiting,' he breathed with indolent satisfaction. 'Nothing can disturb or part us here.'

Maxie gazed down into smouldering golden eyes full of expectancy. 'Angelos…'

He reached up to run the tip of his tongue erotically along the tremulous line of her generous mouth. 'You feel like ice. I'll melt you,' he promised huskily, deft fingers already engaged in releasing the catch on her bra.

Maxie trembled, feeling her whole body filled with delicious tension. She closed her eyes. He kissed her, and every time he kissed her it got just that little bit more tormenting, and she would open her lips wider, needing more pressure, more passion, begging for it as the floodtide of unstoppable hunger began to build and race through her veins.

He rolled her over and closed a hand over the pouting swell of one pale breast. Her taut body jumped as he smiled brilliantly down into her shaken eyes. 'And yet you are so red-hot, responsive when I touch you. Every time that gives me a high,' Angelos confessed thickly. 'I love seeing you out of control.'

Threatened by that admission, Maxie shifted uneasily. 'I don't like that—'

'You'll have to learn to like it.' Angelos bent his dark, arrogant head over a pink straining nipple and laved that achingly tender tip with his tongue, engulfing her in sensation that she now struggled instinctively to resist.

'No...' she gasped.

'Don't fight what I can make you feel...' he urged hoarsely, employing expert fingers on her sensitive flesh, making her squirm in breathless, whimpering excitement.

Her body wasn't her own any more, but by then she didn't want it to be. With every atom of her being she craved those caresses. Wild sensation was addictive. She was hooked between one second and the next, her mind wiped clean of all thought. The hot wire of his seduction pulled tight as heat flared between her shifting thighs. She moaned his name low in her throat.

He took her mouth with a hot, sexual dominance then. He sealed her to the abrasively masculine angles of his hard, hungry body. She panted for breath when he released her swollen lips, sensually bemused eyes focusing on the brooding intensity of that darkly handsome face now curiously stilled above hers.

'Angelos…?' she mumbled, her fingers rising without her volition to trace the unremittingly harsh compression of his mouth.

He jerked back his head, so that she couldn't touch him. In pained bewilderment Maxie lowered her hand again and stared up at him.

'You used to watch me all the time,' he breathed grimly. 'But the instant I turned in your direction, you looked away…except that once, seven months ago. Then I knew you were mine, as much *mine* as if I had a brand on you!'

Stricken by that assurance slung at her out of the blue, Maxie twisted her head away, feeling naked, exposed. Even then Angelos had been able to see inside her, see below the surface which had dazzled other men. And, worst of all, he had immediately recognised the hunger she had refused to recognise within herself.

'So I waited for you to make your move,' Angelos admitted in a tone of growing condemnation. 'I waited and I waited for you to dump him. But you still stayed *with* him! I began to wonder if you had a single living brain cell inside that gorgeous head!'

He was talking about Leland. Shocked rigid by what he was telling her, Maxie muttered, 'But I…I didn't—'

Angelos vented a harsh, cynical laugh. 'Oh, I know why you stayed with him *now*! You owed him too much money to walk out. Did you think I hadn't worked that out yet? But that's when you reduced yourself to the level of a marketable commodity, and when I think about that it makes me want to smash things! Because, having learnt that wonderful lesson with him, you then sold yourself to me for an even higher price.'

'How *can* you—?'

'What else is this marriage but the price I had to pay for you?'

'You…swine,' Maxie whispered brokenly, white as

death as the contempt he had concealed from her sank into
her sensitive flesh like poison.

'And I'll get you out of my system soon if it kills me,'
Angelos swore with ragged force as he gazed broodingly
down at her.

'Start by letting me out of this bed,' she demanded unevenly.

'No way…I paid with a wedding ring and millions of
pounds for this pleasure.'

'No!'

'But you're no good at saying no to me,' Angelos murmured with roughened menace against her tremulous lips.
'Sexually you are one very weak reed where I'm concerned.
It's my one and only consolation while I'm making a
bloody fool of myself over a woman like you!'

'How dare you?' Maxie gulped.

But Angelos skimmed an assured hand down the taut
length of one quivering thigh and kissed her with fierce,
angry hunger. And it was like instantaneous combustion.
She went up in flames. He didn't hold her down. He didn't
pin her to the mattress. He kissed her into submission, tormented her with every erotic trick in his extensive reper-
toire and the most overpowering physical passion. He swept
away her defences with terrifying ease.

Stroking apart her slender thighs, Angelos traced the
swollen, moist sensitivity at the very heart of her with
knowing fingers. With a strangled moan, Maxie clutched at
him in desperation. He controlled her with the hunger she
could not deny and made her ache for him. That ache for
satisfaction tortured her. He groaned something in Greek,
pushing her tumbled hair back off her brow with an unsteady hand, circling her mouth caressingly with his one
more time.

As Angelos shifted over her she couldn't get him there
fast enough. Her own urgency was as screamingly intense
as his. And then she felt him, hot and hard and gloriously

male, seeking entrance, and she shivered convulsively, on a high of such anticipation and excitement she was mindless.

So when he thrust hungrily into her willing body she was quite unprepared for the jagged pain of that forceful intrusion. Pain ripped apart the fog of sensual sensation and made her jerk and cry out in shock as she instinctively strove to push him away from her. But Angelos had already stilled to frown down at her with stunned, disbelieving black eyes. 'Maxie—?'

'What are you looking at me like that for?' Maxie whispered in stricken embarrassment, utterly appalled and outraged that her own body could have betrayed her to such an extent.

With a sudden shift of his hips, Angelos withdrew from her again. But he kept on staring down at her in the most mortifying way, his bewilderment blatant. A damp sheen accentuated the tautness of the bronzed skin stretched over his hard cheekbones and the pallor spreading beneath. '*Cristo*…a virgin…' he breathed, not quite levelly.

Maxie lay there, feeling horribly rejected and inadequate and wishing she could vanish.

'And I really hurt you,' Angelos groaned even more raggedly, abruptly levering his weight from her, black eyes holding hers with the same transfixed incredulity with which he might have regarded the sudden descent of an alien spaceship in his bedroom, 'Are you in a lot of pain?'

In one driven movement Maxie rolled off the bed and fled in the direction of the bathroom. Dear heaven, he had been so repulsed he had just abandoned their lovemaking.

'Maxie?' Angelos murmured grimly. 'I think *this* is something we definitely need to talk about—'

Maxie slammed the bathroom door so loudly it rocked on its hinges and then she depressed the lock double-quick. Bang went the image of the cool sophisticate! And without that glossy image she felt naked and exposed. The last thing she could've faced right then was awkward questions. And as she turned on the bath taps she recalled his swinging verbal attack on her before they made love and she burst into gulping tears.

Angelos banged on the door. 'Maxie? Come out of there!'

'Go to hell!' she shouted, cramming her hand to her wobbling mouth before a sob could escape and betray her.

'Are you all right?'

'I'm having a bath, Angelos…not drowning myself! Although with that technique of yours, I understand your concern!'

But no sooner had Maxie hurled those nasty words than she was thoroughly ashamed of herself. He hadn't meant to hurt her, he hadn't known, and lashing out in retaliation because she felt horribly humiliated was unjust and mean. Silence fell. Slowly, miserably, Maxie climbed into the bath.

Only then did it occur to her that it was foolish to be distressed by what Angelos had said in temper earlier. After all, he had now discovered that she could not possibly have been Leland's mistress. So that had to make a difference to the light in which he saw her, *surely*? Only what she had been given with one hand had seemingly been taken with the other. Angelos had been repulsed by her inexperience.

Devastated by that awareness, Maxie thought back seven months to that single exchanged glance with Angelos across that long table in the Petronides boardroom, that charged clash of mutual awareness which seemed to have changed her entire life. Angelos had actually been waiting for her to ditch Leland on his behalf and he had been furious when she hadn't.

Furthermore, Angelos could not now bring himself to speak Leland Coulter's name out loud. In fact he had said she would offend him beyond belief with any reference to Leland before they'd even got into bed. Yet Angelos had been in no way that sensitive to that former relationship when he'd first come to announce his intentions at Liz's house... Men were strange, Maxie decided limply, and none more strange than Angelos.

It took her a long time to emerge from the bathroom, but when she did, wrapped in an over-large short silk robe she had found, the bedroom was empty. It was something of an anticlimax. Maxie got back into bed, not remotely sleepy and very tense, while she waited and waited for Angelos to reappear. A postmortem to end all postmortems now threatened. Having emerged from shock, Angelos would take refuge in anger, she forecast glumly. He would demand to know why she hadn't told him the truth about Leland. He would utterly dismiss any claim that he would never have believed her.

She lay back, steeling herself for recriminations as only Angelos could hurl them. Like deadly weapons which struck a bull's-eye every time. He never missed. And she hadn't been fair to him; she knew now that she hadn't been fair. Liz had been right. She *had* reaped a twisted kind of relish out of pretending to be something she wasn't while she goaded Angelos on and taunted him. And so why had she reacted to him in a way she had never reacted to any other man? Maxie discovered that she was miserable enough without forcing herself to answer that question.

The door opened. She braced herself. Angelos stood poised in the doorway. Barefoot, black hair tousled, strong jawline already darkening with stubble, he looked distinctly unfamiliar in a pair of black tight-fitting jeans, with a black shirt hanging loose and unbuttoned on his bare brown hair-roughened chest.

'I now know *everything*...' he announced in the most peculiar slurred drawl. 'But I am too bloody drunk to fly!'

Maxie sat up. Eyes huge, she watched Angelos collide with the door and glower at it as if it had no business being there in his path. He was drunk all right. And he just looked so helpless to Maxie at that moment that she abandoned her stony, defensive aspect. Concern for him took over instead.

Leaping out of bed and crossing the room, she put her hand on his arm. 'Come and lie down,' she urged.

'Not on that bed.' As he swayed Angelos surveyed the divan with an extraordinary force of antagonism. 'Right at this moment I want to burn it.'

Assuming that her vindictive comment on his technique had struck home with greater force and efficacy than she could ever have imagined, Maxie paled with guilt but continued to try and ease him in the same direction. Was that why he had gone off to hit the bottle? Some intrinsically male sense of sexual failure because he had inadvertently hurt her? Maxie endeavoured to drag him across the carpet. He was obstinate as ever.

'Lie down!' she finally launched at him in full-throttle frustration.

And Angelos *did* lie down. Maxie couldn't believe it but he sprawled down on the bed as if she had a gun trained on him. And he looked so utterly miserable. It was true, she decided in fascination, women were definitely the stronger sex. Here was the evidence. Disaster had befallen Angelos when he had least expected it in a field he prided himself on excelling in and he couldn't handle it.

Crawling onto the bed beside him, Maxie gazed down at him until her eyes misted over. She was shattered to discover that all she wanted to do was cocoon him in lashings of TLC.

'You were really great until the last moment,' she told him in tender consolation. 'I didn't mean what I said. You mustn't blame yourself—'

'I blame Leland,' Angelos gritted.

In complete confusion, Maxie frowned. 'You blame... you blame *Leland*?' she stressed, all at seas as to his meaning.

Angelos growled something in Greek that broke from him with the aggressive force of a hurricane warning.

'English, Angelos…'

'He's a slime-bag!'

Focusing on her properly for the first time, Angelos dug a hand into the pocket of his jeans and withdrew a great wodge of crumpled fax paper.

Maxie took it from him and spread the paper out. It was so long it kept on spreading, across his chest and finally right off the edge of the bed. She squinted down and recognised her own signature right at the very foot. In such dim light, it left her little the wiser as to its content, and in his presence she didn't want to be seen peering to comprehend all that tiny type.

'Leland took advantage of your stupidity—'

'Excuse me?' Maxie cut in, wide-eyed.

'Only a financially very naive person would've signed that loan contract,' Angelos extended, after a long pause during which he had visibly struggled to come up with that more diplomatic term. 'And a moneylender from a back-street would've offered more generous terms than that evil old bastard!'

Clarity shone at last for Maxie. Angelos had somehow obtained a copy of the loan agreement she had signed three years earlier. That was what was on the fax paper. 'Where did you get this from?'

'I got it,' Angelos responded flatly.

'Why did you say I was stupid…? Because I'm *not*!'

'You'd still have been paying that loan off ten years from now.' He got technical then, muttering grimly about criminal rates of interest and penalty clauses. She couldn't bring herself to tell him that she had become trapped in such an agreement because she had been too proud to ask someone else to read the small print out and explain the conditions.

'You were only nineteen,' Angelos grated finally. 'You

signed that the day before you moved in with Leland. He blackmailed you—'

'No...I agreed. There was never any question of us sharing a bedroom or anything like that. All he ever asked for was the right to show me off. I was just an ego-trip for him but I didn't know what I was getting into until it was too late to back out,' Maxie muttered tightly, squashing the fax paper into a big crunched-up ball again and throwing it away.

'And Leland was getting his own back on an unfaithful wife,' Angelos completed grimly.

Unsurprised that he should have known about Jennifer Coulter's affair, Maxie breathed in deep and decided to match his frankness. 'My father is a compulsive gambler, Angelos. He got into trouble with some very tough men and he couldn't pay up what he owed them. It was nothing to do with Leland but I went to him for advice, and that's when he told me he'd loan me the money if I moved in with him.'

'Lamb to the slaughter,' Angelos groaned, as if he was in agony. 'Compulsive gambler?' he queried in sudden bemusement.

'Dad would sell this bed out from under you if he got the chance.'

'Where have you kept this charming character concealed?'

'I don't know where he is right now. We haven't been close...well, not since I took on that loan to settle his debts. Naturally Dad feels bad about that.'

'The debt was *his*?' Angelos bit out wrathfully as that fact finally sunk in. 'Your precious father stood back and watched you move in with Leland just so that he could have his gambling debts paid?'

'It was life or death, Angelos...it *really* was,' Maxie protested. 'He'd already been badly beaten up and he was terrified they would kill him the next time around. Leland

gave me that money when nobody else would have. It saved
Dad's life.'

'Dad doesn't sound like he was worth saving—'

'Don't you dare say that about my father!' Maxie censured chokily. 'He brought me up all on his own!'

'Taught you how to go to the pawnshop? Flogged anything he could get his hands on? Your childhood must've
been a real blissfest, I *don't* think!'

'He did his best. That's all anyone can do,' Maxie whispered tautly. 'Not everyone is born with your advantages
in life. You're rich and selfish. Dad's poor and selfish, but,
unfortunately for him, he has too much imagination.'

'So have I…oh, *so* have I. I imagined you,' Angelos
confided, his deep dark drawl slurring with intense bitterness. 'The only quality I imagined right was that you *do*
need me. But all the rest was my fantasy. Tonight…
deservedly…it exploded right in my face.'

Maxie slumped as if he had beaten the stuffing out of
her. She wanted to tell him that she *didn't* need him but
her throat was so clogged up with tears she couldn't trust
herself to speak. A fantasy? He had *imagined* her? That
was even worse than being a one-dimensional trophy, she
realised in horror. At the end of the day, when fantasy met
reality and went bang, there was just nothing left, was
there?

'I don't want to sober up,' Angelos admitted morosely.
'The more I find out about you, the worse I feel. I don't
like regret or guilt. Some people love to immolate themselves in their mistakes. I don't. How could I have been so
bloody stupid?'

'Sex,' Maxie supplied, even more morosely.

Angelos shuddered. It was a very informative reaction.

'Was it that bad?' she couldn't help asking.

'Worse,' Angelos stressed feelingly. 'I felt like a rapist.'

'Silly…just bad luck…life kicking you in the teeth…you

get used to it after a while…least, I do,' Maxie mumbled, on the brink of tears again.

'You should be furious with me—'

'No point…you're drunk. I like you better drunk than I like you sober,' she confided helplessly. 'You're more human.'

'*Christos*…when you go for the deathblow, you don't miss, do you?' Unhealthily pale beneath his bronzed skin, Angelos let his tousled head fall heavily back on the pillows. His lashes swept down on his shadowed black eyes. 'So now I know where I stand with you…basement footing—possibly even right down level with the earth's core,' he muttered incomprehensibly.

'Go to sleep,' Maxie urged.

'When one is that far down, one can only go up,' Angelos asserted with dogged resolution.

Well, at least he wasn't talking about flying again. With a helicopter parked thirty yards away that had been a genuine cause for concern. She ought to hate him. She knew she ought to hate him for breaking her heart with such agonising honesty. But the trouble was, she loved him in spite of that two-page list of flaws. She didn't know why she loved him. She just did. And she was in really deep too. He had just rejected her in every possible way and all she wanted to do was cover him up and hug him to death. Flaked out, silenced and vulnerable, Angelos had huge appeal for Maxie.

Why had she spent so long telling herself that she hated this guy? She had been cleverer than she knew, she conceded. Loving him hurt like hell. She felt as if she had lost an entire layer of skin and every inch of her was now tender and wounded. There she had been, naively imagining that he might have been upset because his sexual performance had not resulted in her impressed-to-death ecstasy. And all the time he had been ahead of her, whole streets ahead of her…

The minute he had found out that *he* was her first lover, he had fairly leapt into seeking out what her relationship with Leland had been based on, since it had self-evidently not been based on sex. Naturally he had immediately thought of that loan and probed deeper. And now he knew the whole sorry story and her name had been cleared. But much good it seemed to have done her…

Liz had said Maxie enjoyed pretending to be what she had called a 'bad girl'. Maxie suppressed a humourless laugh. Poor Liz had never allowed for the painful possibility that Angelos, who had exceedingly poor taste in women, was more excited by bad girls than he was by virgins.

CHAPTER NINE

MAXIE wakened the next morning in the warm cocoon of Angelos's arms. It felt like heaven.

Some time during the night he had taken off his shirt. She opened her lips languorously against a bare brown shoulder and let the tip of her tongue gently run over smooth skin. He tasted wonderful. She breathed in the achingly familiar scent of him with heady pleasure. Hot husky male with a slight flavour of soap. She blushed for herself, but the deep, even rise and fall of his broad chest below her encircling arm soothed her sudden tension. He was still out for the count.

And she would probably never lie like this with Angelos again. He was only here now because he had fallen asleep. She had plummeted from the heights of obsessive desirability like a stone. She had lost him but then she had never really had him. He had craved the fantasy, the Ice Queen, not the ordinary woman, and when in so many ways she had played up to that fantasy of his, how could she really blame him for not wanting her any more?

Easing back her arm, she let her palm rest down on that hair-roughened expanse of chest which drew her attention like a magnet. Her fingertips trailed gently through black springy curls, delicately traced a flat male nipple, slid downward over the rippling muscular smoothness of his abdomen, discovering a fascinating little furrow of silky hair that ran…and then she tensed in panic as she recognised the alteration in his breathing pattern. She was waking him up!

And just at that moment Maxie didn't feel strong enough to face Angelos waking up, sober and restored to intimidating normality. Angelos would bounce back from last night's shock and humility like a rubber ball aiming for the moon. Lying absolutely still, she waited until his breathing had evened out again and then, sidling out from under his arm, she slid off the bed.

Gathering up her discarded garments, she crept out into the corridor. Through the open doorway of the bedroom opposite she could see her single suitcase sitting at the foot of the bed. And that sight just underlined Maxie's opinion of her exact marital status. She had *no* status whatsoever. Her possessions belonged in a guest-room because she was supposed to be a casual visitor, not a wife.

Pulling out a white shift dress, fresh lingerie and strappy sandals, Maxie got dressed at speed. It was only seven but the heat was already building. The house was silent. Finding her way into a vast, gleaming kitchen, she helped herself to a glass of pure orange juice and swiped a couple of apples from a lush display of fruit. Determined not to face Angelos until she had sorted herself out, she left the house. Traversing the beautiful gardens, she wandered along the rough path above the beach.

Then she let her thoughts loose, and she winced and she squirmed and she hurt. Their wedding night had been a disaster. And how much of that final confessional dialogue would Angelos recall when he woke up? Would he remember the stupid, soppy way she had hung over him? Would he recognise the pain she had not been able to conceal for what it was? The mere idea that Angelos might guess that she was in love with him was like the threat of death by a thousand cuts for Maxie.

Last night, for the very first time, Angelos hadn't treated her as an equal. Maxie shrank from that lowering awareness. Funny how she hadn't really noticed or even appreciated that Angelos had *always* met her on a level playing field until he suddenly changed tack. Now everything was different. She had been stripped of her tough cookie glossy image and exposed as a pathetic fraud. A virgin rather than a sultry, seductive object of must-have desire. A blackmail victim rather than a calculating gold-digger and the former mistress of an older man.

And who would ever have guessed that Angelos Petronides had a conscience? But, amazingly, he *did*. Angelos had been appalled by what he'd discovered. Even worse, he had pitied her for her less than perfect childhood and her gullible acceptance of that hateful loan agreement. *Pitied*. That acknowledgement was coals of fire on Maxie's head.

Angelos now regretted their strange marriage but he felt guilty. Maxie didn't want his guilt or his pity, and suddenly she saw how she could eradicate both. It would be so simple. All she had to do was tell Angelos about the conditions of Nancy Leeward's last will and testament. When Angelos realised that she had had an ulterior motive in marrying him, he would soon stop feeling sorry for her…at least she would retain her pride that way.

As Maxie rounded a big outcrop of rock, she saw two little boys trying to help a fisherman spread a net on the beach below. As she watched, unseen, their earnest but clumsy efforts brought a warm, generous smile to her lovely face.

'You have never once shown me that ravishing smile.' Maxie was startled into a gasp by the intervention of that soft, rich, dark drawl, and her golden head spun.

Angelos stood several feet away. Clad in elegant chinos and a white polo shirt, he stole the very breath from Maxie's lungs. Her heart crashed violently against her breastbone. He looked drop-dead gorgeous. But her wide eyes instantly veiled. She knew how clever he was. She was terrified he would somehow divine her feelings for him.

'But then possibly I have done nothing to inspire such a reward,' Angelos completed tautly.

He stared at her, black eyes glittering and fiercely intent. In the brilliant sunlight, with her hair shimmering like a veil of gold and the simple white dress a perfect foil for her lithe figure, she was dazzling. Moving forward slowly, as if he was attuned to her pronounced tension, he closed a lean hand over one of hers and began to walk her back along the foreshore.

'From today, from this moment, *everything* will be different between us,' Angelos swore with emphasis.

'Will it be?' Briefly, involuntarily, Maxie stole a glance at him, nervous as a cat on hot bricks.

'You should have told me the truth about Leland the very first day—'

'You wouldn't have believed me...'

His long brown fingers tightened hard on hers. He looked out to sea, strong profile rigid. He released his breath in a sudden driven hiss. 'You're right. I wouldn't have. Nothing short of the physical proof you gave me last night would've convinced me that you weren't the woman I thought you were.'

'At least you're honest,' Maxie muttered tautly.

Apparently enthralled by the view of the single caique anchored out in the bay, Angelos continued to stare out over the bright blue water. 'Considering that there were so many things that didn't add up about you, I can't say that I can pride myself on my unprejudiced outlook...or my judgement. You asked me to stay away from you and I wouldn't. You even left London...'

He was talking as if someone had a knife bared at his throat. Voice low, abrupt, rough, every word clenched with tension and reluctance.

'I have never treated a woman as badly as I have treated you...and in the manner of our marriage I really did surpass myself, *pethi mou*.'

He sounded like a stranger to Maxie. Angelos having a guilt trip. She trailed her fingers free of his, cruel pain

slashing at her. It was over. She didn't need to hear these
things when she had already lived them, and most of all
she did not want *him* feeling sorry for *her*. In fact that
humiliation stung like acid on her skin.

'Look, I have something to tell you,' Maxie cut in stiffly.

'Let me speak…do you think this is *easy* for me?'
Angelos slung at her in a gritty undertone of accusation.
'Baring my feelings like this?'

'You don't have any feelings for me,' Maxie retorted
flatly, her heart sinking inside her, her stomach lurching.

'You seem very sure of that—'

'Get real, Angelos. There are rocks on this beach with
more tender emotions than you've got!' Having made that
cynical assurance, Maxie walked on doggedly. 'And why
should you feel bad for trying to use me when I was planning to use you too? It's not like I'm madly in love with
you or anything like that!' She paused to stress that point
and vented a shrill laugh for good measure. 'I only married
you because it *suited* me to marry you. I needed a husband
for six months…'

Against the soft, rushing backdrop of the tide, the silence
behind her spread and spread until it seemed to echo in her
straining ears.

'What the hell are you talking about?' Angelos finally
shattered the seething tension with that harsh demand.

Maxie spun round, facial muscles tight with self-control.
'My godmother's will. She was a wealthy woman but I
can't inherit my share of her estate without a marriage licence. All I wanted was access to my own money, not
yours.'

Angelos stood there as if he had been cast in granite,
black eyes fixed to her with stunning intensity. 'This is a
joke…right?'

Maxie shook her golden head in urgent negative. She
was so tense she couldn't get breath enough to speak.
Angelos was rigid with incredulity and in the stark, drench-

ing sunlight reflecting off the water he seemed extraordinarily pale.

'You do realise that if what you have just told me is true, I am going to want to kill you?' Angelos confided, snatching in a jagged breath of restraint.

'I don't see why,' Maxie returned with determined casualness. 'This marriage wasn't any more real to you than it was to me. It was the only way you could get me into bed.' His hard dark features clenched as if she had struck him but she forced herself onward to the finish. 'And you didn't expect us to last five minutes beyond the onset of your own boredom. So that's why I decided I might as well be frank.'

Turning on her heel, trembling from the effect of that confrontation, Maxie walked blindly off the path and up through the gardens of the house. He wasn't going to be feeling all sorry and superior now, was he? The biter bit, she thought without any satisfaction as she crossed the hall. Now they would split up and she would never see him again…and she would spend the rest of her life being poor and wanting a man she couldn't have and shouldn't even want.

'Maxie…?'

She turned, not having realised in her preoccupation that Angelos was so close behind her. The world tilted as he swept her off her startled feet up into his powerful arms. A look of aggressive resolution in his blazing golden eyes, Angelos murmured grittily, 'It should've occurred to you that I might not be bored yet, *pethi mou*!'

'But—'

The kiss that silenced her lasted all the way down to the bedroom. It was like plunging a finger into an electric socket. Excitement and shock waved through her. He brought her down on the bed. Surfacing, Maxie stammered in complete bewilderment, 'B-but you don't want me any more…you imagined me—'

Engaged in ripping off his clothes over her, Angelos

glowered down at her. 'I didn't *imagine* that clever little brain or that stinging tongue of yours, did I?'

'What are you *doing*?' she gasped.

'What I should have done when I woke up this morning to find you exploring me like a shy little kid...I didn't want to embarrass you.' Angelos focused on her, his sheer incredulity at that decision etched in every line of his savagely attractive features. 'How could I possibly have dreamt that you *could* be embarrassed? Beneath that angelic, perfect face you're as tough as Teflon!'

Maxie was flattered to be called that tough. She didn't mind being told she was clever, or that she had a sharp tongue either. This was respect she was getting. It might not be couched in terms most women would've recognised but she knew Angelos well enough to see that she had risen considerably in his estimation since the previous night. Indeed, it crossed her mind that Angelos responded beautifully to a challenge, and that acknowledgement shone a blinding white light of clarity through her thoughts. She sat there transfixed.

'Why are you so quiet?' Angelos enquired suspiciously. 'I don't trust you quiet.'

Maxie cast him an unwittingly languorous smile over one shoulder. 'I presume we're not heading for a divorce right at this moment...?'

'*Theos*, woman...we only got married yesterday!'

The heat of his hungry gaze sent wild colour flying into her cheeks. He still wanted her. He still seemed to want her every bit as much as he had ever wanted her, she registered in renewed shock. And then he brought his mouth to hers again and her own hunger betrayed her. Her hands flew up to smooth through his hair, curve over his hard jawline. The need to touch, to hold was so powerful it made her eyes sting and filled her with instinctive fear.

'I won't hurt you this time...I promise,' Angelos groaned against her reddened mouth while he eased her out

of her dress virtually without her noticing. He cupped her
cheekbones to stare down into her sensually bemused eyes,
his own gaze a tigerish, slumberous gold. 'To be the first
with you...that was an unexpected gift. And telling me
crazy stories in an effort to level some imaginary score is
pointless. You ache for me too...do you think I don't see
that in you with every look, every touch?'

Crazy stories? The will, her godmother's will. Obviously, after a moment of reflection, he hadn't believed
her after all. But Maxie couldn't keep that awareness in
mind. She did part her lips, meaning to contradict him, but
he kissed her again and she clutched at him in the blindness
of a passion she could not deny.

'Why should you still fight me?' Angelos purred as he
freed her breasts from the restraint of her bra and paused
to run wondering dark eyes over her. He brushed appreciative fingers over the engorged tip of one pale breast and
then lingered there in a caress that stole the very breath
from her quiveringly responsive body. 'Why should you
even *want* to fight me?'

There was something Maxie remembered that she needed
to tell him, but looking up into those stunning golden eyes
she could barely recall what her own name was, never mind
open a serious conversation. Angelos angled a blinding
megawatt smile of approval down at her and it was as if
she had been programmed from birth to seek that endorse-
ment. She reached up and found his lips again, a connection
she now instinctively craved more than she had ever craved
anything in her life before.

His tongue played with hers as he lay half over her. He
smoothed a hand down over her slim hips and eased off
the scrap of lace that still shielded her from him. With
skilled fingers he skimmed through the golden curls at the
apex of her slender thighs and sought the hot, moist centre
of her. A whimper of formless sound was torn from Maxie

then. Suddenly she was burning all over and she couldn't stay still.

And, as straying shards of sunlight played over the bed, Angelos utilised every ounce of his expertise to fire her to the heights of anguished desire. When she couldn't bear it any more, he slid over her. He watched her with hungry intimacy as he entered her, the fierce restraint he exercised over his own urgency etched in every taut line of his dark, damp features.

The pleasure came to her then, in wave after drugging wave. In the grip of it, she was utterly lost. 'Angelos...' she cried out.

And he stilled, and Maxie gasped in stricken protest, and with an earthy sound of amusement he went on. She didn't want him ever to stop. The slow, tormenting climb to fevered excitement had raised her to such a pitch, she ached for more with every thrust of his possession. And when finally sensation took her in a wild storm of rocketing pleasure, she uttered a startled moan of delight. As the last tiny quiver of glorious fulfilment evaporated she looked up at him with new eyes.

'Wow,' she breathed.

Struggling to catch his breath, Angelos dealt her a very male smile of satisfaction. 'That was the wedding night we should have had.'

Maxie was still pretty much lost in wonder. Wow, she thought again, luxuriating in the strong arms still wrapped around her, the closeness, the feeling of tenderness eating her up alive and threatening to make her eyes overflow. Oh, yes, wouldn't tears really impress him? Blinking rapidly, she swallowed hard on the surge of powerful emotion she was struggling to control.

'I think it's time I made some sort of announcement about this marriage of ours,' Angelos drawled lazily.

Maxie's lashes shot up, eyes stunned at all that went unsaid in that almost careless declaration. Evidently

Angelos no longer saw the slightest need to keep their true relationship a secret from the rest of the world.

'Don't you think?' he prompted softly, and then with a slumberous sigh he released her from his weight and rolled off the bed in one powerfully energetic movement. 'Shower and then breakfast…I don't think I've ever been so hungry in my life!'

Only then did Maxie recall what he had said about 'crazy stories' before they'd made love. Her face tensed, her stomach twisting. 'Angelos…?'

He turned his tousled dark head and he smiled at her again.

Her fingers knotted nervously into a section of sheet. 'What I mentioned earlier…what I said about my godmother's will…that *wasn't* a story, it was the truth.'

Angelos stilled, his smile evaporating like Scotch mist, black eyes suddenly level and alert.

Maxie explained again about the will. She went into great detail on the subject of her godmother's lifelong belief in the importance of marriage, the older woman's angry disapproval when Maxie had moved in with Leland. But Maxie didn't look at Angelos again after that first ten seconds when she had anxiously registered the grim tautening of his dark features.

'You see, at the time…after the way you proposed…I mean, I was angry, and I didn't see why I shouldn't make use of the fact that you were actually offering me exactly what I required to meet that condition of inheritance…' Maxie's voice petered out to a weak, uncertain halt because what had once seemed so clear now seemed so confused inside her own head. And the decision which once had seemed so simple and so clever mysteriously took on another aspect altogether when she attempted to explain it out loud to Angelos.

The silence simmered like a boiling cauldron.

Slowly, hesitantly, Maxie lifted her head and focused on Angelos.

Strong face hard with derision, black eyes scorching slivers of burning gold, he stared back at her. 'You are one devious, calculating little vixen,' he breathed with raw anger. 'When I asked you to marry me, I was honest. Anything *less* than complete honesty would've been beneath me because, unlike you, I have certain principles, certain standards!'

Maxie had turned paper-pale. 'Angelos, I—'

'Shut up…I don't want to hear any more!' he blazed back at her with sizzling contempt. 'I'm thinking of the generous financial settlement you were promised should our marriage end. You had neither need nor any other excuse to plot and plan to collect on some trusting old lady's will as well!'

A great rush of hot tears hit the back of Maxie's aching eyes. Blinking rapidly, she looked away. He was looking at her as if she had just crawled out from under a stone and sudden intense shame engulfed her.

'How could you be so disgustingly greedy?' Angelos launched in fierce condemnation. 'And how could you try to use me when I never once tried to use you?'

'It wasn't like that. You've got it all wrong,' Maxie fumbled in desperation, deeply regretting her own foolish mode of confession on the beach when saving face had been uppermost in her mind. 'It was a spur-of-the-moment idea…I was hurt and furious and I—'

'When a man gives you a wedding ring, he is honouring you, *not* using you!' Angelos gritted between clenched teeth.

Maxie started to bristle then. 'Well, I wouldn't know about that…I only had the supreme honour of wearing that ring for about five minutes—'

'You gave it back—'

Maxie lifted shimmering blue eyes and tilted her chin.

'You *took* it!' she reminded him wrathfully. 'And I don't want it back either…and I don't want you making any announcement to anybody about our marriage…because I wouldn't want anybody to know I was *stupid* enough to marry you!'

'That cuts both ways,' Angelos asserted with chilling bite, temper leashed back as he squared his big shoulders. 'And I'll be sure to ditch you before the six months is up!'

He strode into the bathroom.

Maxie flung herself back against the pillows, rolled over and pummelled them with sheer rage and frustration. Then she went suddenly still, and a great rolling breaker of sobs threatened because just for a little while she had felt close to Angelos and then, like a fairy-tale illusion, that closeness had vanished again…driven away by her own foolish, reckless tongue.

Yes, sooner or later she would naturally have had to tell Angelos about Nancy Leeward's will. But on the beach she had blown it, once and for all. After all, who was it who had told him that she had planned to use him? And the whole thing had struck him as so far-fetched that within minutes of being told he had decided it wasn't true. Indeed he had assumed that she was childishly trying to 'level the score.' Maxie shivered, belatedly appalled by the realisation that Angelos could understand her to that degree…

That was exactly what she had been doing. Believing that their relationship was over, she had been set on saving face and so she had told him about the will in the most offensive possible terms. Now that she had convinced him that she was telling him the truth, she was reaping the reward she had invited…anger, contempt, distaste.

And how could she say now, I wanted to marry you anyway and I needed a good excuse to allow myself to do that and still feel that I was control? There was no way that she could tell Angelos that she loved him. There was no way she could see herself *ever* telling Angelos that she loved him…

When he came out of the bathroom, a towel knotted round his lean brown hips, Maxie studied him miserably. 'Angelos, I was going to tear up that prenuptial contract—'

'You should be writing scripts for Disney!' Angelos countered with cutting disbelief, and strode towards the dressing-room.

'You said…you said you couldn't pride yourself on your judgement where I was concerned,' Maxie persisted tightly, wondering if what she was doing qualified as crawling, terrified that it might be.

'I'm back on track now, believe me.' Angelos sent her an icy look of brooding darkness. 'I'm also off to London for a couple of days. I have some business to take care of.'

Business? What business? They had only arrived yesterday. Maxie wasn't stupid. She got the message. He just didn't want to be with her any more.

'Are you always this unforgiving in personal relationships?' Maxie breathed a little chokily when he had disappeared from view, but she knew he could still hear her.

'I love that breathy little catch in your voice but it's wasted on me. You wouldn't cry if I roasted you over a bonfire!'

'You're right,' Maxie said steadily, hastily wiping the tears dripping down her cheeks with the corner of the sheet.

Angelos reappeared, sheathed in a stupendous silver-grey suit. Lean, dark face impassive, he looked as remote as the Himalayas and even colder.

Maxie made one final desperate attempt to penetrate that armour of judgemental ice. 'I really don't and never did want your money, Angelos,' she whispered with all the sincerity she could muster.

Angelos sent her a hard, gleaming scrutiny, his expressive mouth curling. 'You may not be my conception of a wife but you will make the perfect mistress. In that role you can be every bit as mercenary as you like. You spend my money; I enjoy your perfect body. Randy Greek billionaires understand that sort of realistic exchange best of all. And at least this way we both know where we stand.'

Maxie gazed back at him in total shock. Every scrap of colour drained from her cheeks. But in that moment the battle lines were drawn…if Angelos wanted a mistress rather than a wife, a mistress, Maxie decided fierily, was what he was jolly well going to get!

'Angelos doesn't *know* where you are? You mean he's not aware that you're back in London yet?' Liz breathed in astonishment when the fact penetrated.

Maxie took a deep breath. 'I came straight here from the airport. I'm planning to surprise him,' she said, with more truth than the older woman could ever have guessed.

'Oh…you, of course.' Liz relaxed again and smiled. 'What a shame business concerns had to interrupt your honeymoon! It must've been something terribly important. When was it you said Angelos left the island?'

'Just a few days ago…' Maxie did not confide that she had left on the ferry exactly twenty-four hours later—the very morning, in fact, when her credit cards had been delivered. Credit cards tellingly made out in her maiden name. The die had been cast there and then. Angelos's goose had been cooked to a cinder.

And, faced with that obvious invitation to spend, spend, spend, as any sensible mistress would at the slightest excuse, Maxie had instantly risen to the challenge. She had flown to Rome and then to Paris. She had had a whale of a time. She had repaired the deficiencies of her wardrobe with the most beautiful designer garments she could find. And if she had seen a pair of shoes or a handbag she liked, she had bought them in every possible colour…

Indeed, she could now have papered entire walls with credit card slips. If Angelos had been following that impressive paper trail of gross extravagance and shameless avarice across Rome and Paris, he would probably still think she was abroad, but he wouldn't know where because she had deliberately used cash to pay for flights and hotel bills.

'Are you happy?' Liz pressed anxiously.

'Incredibly...' Well, about as happy as she could be when it had been six days, fourteen hours and thirty-seven minutes since she had last laid eyes on Angelos, Maxie reflected ruefully. But to vegetate alone, abandoned and neglected on Chymos, would've been even worse.

'Do you think Angelos might come to love you?'

Maxie thought about that. She had set her sights on him loving her but she wasn't sure it was a very realistic goal. Had Angelos ever been in love? It was very possible that she might settle for just being *needed*. Right now, all she could accurately forecast was that Angelos would be in a seething rage because she had left the island without telling him and hadn't made the slightest effort to get in touch.

But then that was what a mistress would do when the man in her life departed without mention of when he would return. A mistress was necessarily a self-sufficient creature. And if Angelos hadn't yet got around to putting in place the arrangements by which he intended to see her and spend time with her, then that was his oversight, not hers. No mistress would tell her billionaire lover when *she* would be available...that was *his* department.

Maxie had tea with Liz and then she called a cab. With the mountain of luggage she had acquired, it was quite a squeeze. She directed the driver to the basement car park of the building Angelos had informed her was to be exclusively hers. She was a little apprehensive about how she was to gain entry. After all, Angelos didn't even know she was back in London yet, and possibly the place would be locked up and deserted.

But on that point she discovered that she had misjudged him. There was a security man in the lift.

'Miss Kendall…?'

'That's me. Would you see to my luggage, please?' Maxie stepped into the lift to be wafted upwards and wondered why the man was gaping at her.

When the doors slid back, she thought she had stopped on the wrong floor. The stark modern decor had been swept away as if it had never been. In growing amazement, Maxie explored the spacious apartment. The whole place had been transformed with antique furniture, wonderful rugs and a traditional and warm colour scheme. King Kong on stilts couldn't have seen over the barriers ringing the roof garden and, just in case she still wasn't about to bring herself to step out into the fresh air, a good third of the space now rejoiced in being a conservatory.

The apartment was gorgeous. No expense had been spared, nothing that might add to her comfort had been overlooked, but, far from being impressed by Angelos's consideration of her likes and dislikes, and even her terror of heights, Maxie was almost reduced to grovelling tears of despair. Angelos had had all this done just so that they could live *apart*. Looked at from that angle, the lengths he had gone to in his efforts to make her content with her solitary lot seemed like a deadly insult and the most crushing of rejections.

Maxie unpacked. That took up what remained of the evening and her wardrobe soon overflowed into the guest-room next door. She took out the two-page list of Angelos's flaws that had become her talisman. Whenever she got angry with him, whenever she missed him, she took it out and reminded herself that while she might not be perfect, he was not perfect either. It was a surprisingly comforting exercise which somehow made her feel closer to him.

How long would it take him to work out where she was? She lay in her sunken bath under bubbles, miserable as sin.

She wanted to phone him but she wouldn't let herself. The perfect mistress did not phone her lover. That would be indiscreet. She put on a diaphanous azure-blue silk nightdress slit to the thigh and curled up on the huge brass bed in the master suite.

The arrival of the lift was too quiet and too far away for her to hear. But she heard the hard footsteps ringing down the corridor. Maxie tensed, anticipation filling her. The bedroom door thrust wide, framing Angelos.

In a black dinner jacket that fitted his broad shoulders like a glove, and narrow black trousers that accentuated the long, long length of his legs, he was breathtakingly handsome. Her heart went thud...and then *thud* again. His bow tie was missing; the top couple of studs on his white dress shirt were undone to reveal a sliver of vibrant brown skin.

Poised in the doorway, big hands clenched into fists and breathing rapidly as if he had come from somewhere in a heck of a hurry, he ran outraged golden eyes over her relaxed pose on the brass bed as she reclined back against the heaped-up luxurious pillows as if she hadn't a single care in the world.

'You're here on my first night back...what a lovely surprise!' Maxie carolled.

CHAPTER TEN

MOMENTARILY disconcerted by that chirpy greeting, Angelos stilled. His lush black lashes came down and swept up again as if he wasn't quite sure what he was seeing, never mind what he was hearing.

Having learned some very good lessons from him, Maxie took the opportunity to sit forward, shake back her wonderful mane of golden hair and stretch so that not one inch of the remarkably sexy nightdress hugging her lithe curves could possibly escape his notice.

'What do you think?' she asked gaily. 'I bought it in—'

His entire attention was locked on her, darker colour highlighting his taut high cheekbones and the wrathful glitter of incredulity in his brilliant eyes. 'Where the hell have you been for the past week?' he launched at her with thunderous aggression as he strode forward. 'Do you realise that I flew back to Chymos before I realised you'd left the island?'

'Oh, *no*,' Maxie groaned. 'I would've felt awful if I'd known that!'

'Why the blazes didn't you phone me to tell me what you were thinking of doing?' Angelos demanded with raw incredulity. 'You can shop any time you like but you don't need to do it in time that you could be with me!'

'Why didn't you phone me to tell me that you were coming back?' Maxie's eyes were as bright as sapphires. 'You see, I couldn't phone you. None of the villa staff spoke a word of English and I don't have your phone number—'

Angelos froze. 'What do you mean you don't have my number?'

'Well, you're not in the directory and I'm sure your office staff are very careful not to hand out privileged information like that to just anybody—'

'*Theos*...you're not just anybody!' Angelos blazed, in such a rage he could hardly get the words out. 'I expect to know where you are every minute of the day! And the best I could do was follow your credit card withdrawals as they leapfrogged across Europe!'

What Maxie was hearing now was bliss. She had been missed. 'I think it really would be sensible for you to give me a contact number,' she said gently. 'I'm sorry, but I honestly never realised how possessive you could be—'

'*Possessive?*' Angelos snatched in a shuddering breath of visible restraint, scorching golden eyes hot as lava. 'I am *not* possessive. I just wanted to know where you were.'

'Every minute of the day,' Maxie reminded him helplessly. 'Well, how was I to know that when you didn't tell me?'

Angelos drove raking fingers through his luxuriant black hair. 'You do not *ever* take off anywhere again without telling me where you're going...is that clear?' he growled, withdrawing a gold pen from the inside pocket of his well-cut jacket and striding over to the bedside table.

To her dismay he proceeded to use the blank back page of her list of his flaws to write on. She had left it lying face-down on the table. 'What are you doing?'

'I am listing every number by which I can be reached. Never again will you use the excuse that you couldn't contact me! My portable phone, my confidential line, the apartment, the car phones, and when I'm abroad...'

And he wrote and he wrote and he wrote while Maxie watched in fascination. He had more access numbers than a telecommunications company. It was as if he was drawing up a network for constant communication. Mercifully it had not occurred to him, however, to take a closer look at what he was writing on.

'I got the news that you had reappeared while I was

entertaining a group of Japanese industrialists,' Angelos supplied grittily. 'I had to sit through the whole blasted evening before I could get here!'

'If only I'd known,' Maxie sighed, struggling to keep her tide of happiness in check. Angelos was no longer cold and remote. He had been challenged by the shocking discovery that she did not sit like an inanimate object stowed on a shelf when he was absent. He had been frustrated by not knowing where she was or exactly when or where she might choose to show up again. As a result, Angelos had had far more to think about than the argument on which they had parted on Chymos.

Angelos was still writing. He stopped to sling her a penetrating look of suspicion. 'You were in Rome...you were in Paris...who were you with?' he demanded darkly.

'I was on my own,' Maxie responded with an injured look of dignity.

Angelos's intent gaze lingered. A little of his tension evaporated. Dense lashes screened his eyes. 'I was pretty angry with you...'

She knew that meant he had been thumping walls and raising Cain. From the instant he'd found her absent without leave from the island, he had been a volcano smouldering, just longing for the confrontational moment of release when he could erupt.

'I'd offer you a drink but I'm afraid all the cupboards are bare,' Maxie remarked.

'Naturally...I wasn't expecting you to move in here.'

Maxie frowned. 'How can you say that when this entire apartment has obviously been remodelled for my occupation?'

Setting down his pen, Angelos straightened and settled gleaming dark eyes on her. 'Look, that was *before* we got married...you might not have noticed, but things have changed since then.'

Maxie looked blank. 'Have they?'

Angelos's beautiful mouth compressed hard. 'I've been thinking. You might as well come home with me. I'll stick a notice about our marriage in the paper—'

'No…I like things the way they are.' Saying that was the hardest thing Maxie had ever done, but pride would not allow her to accept the role of wife when it was so grudgingly offered. 'I love this apartment and, like you, I really do appreciate my own space. And there is no point in firing up a media storm about our marriage when it's going to be over in a few months.'

Angelos studied her intently, like a scientist peeling layers off an alien object to penetrate its mysteries. And then, without the slightest warning, his brilliant eyes narrowed and the merest hint of a smile lessened the tension still etched round his mouth. 'OK…fine, no problem. You're being very sensible about this.'

Inside herself, Maxie collapsed like a pricked balloon. He sounded relieved by her decision. He saw no point in them attempting to live as a normal married couple. Evidently he still saw no prospect of them having any kind of a future together. But Maxie wanted him *begging* her to share the same roof. Clearly she had a long way to go if she was to have any hope of achieving that objective.

'But I would appreciate an explanation for your sudden departure from Chymos,' Angelos completed.

Maxie tautened. 'I didn't know when you were coming back. You were furious. It seemed a good idea to let the dust settle.'

'Do you know *why* I came back to London?' Strong face taut, Angelos drew himself up to his full commanding height, the two-page list still clasped in one hand and attracting her covert and anxious attention.

'I haven't a clue.'

'I had to sort out Leland.'

Quite unprepared for that announcement, Maxie gasped. *'Leland?'*

With an absent glance at the loose pages in his hand, Angelos proceeded to fold them and slot them carelessly into the pocket of his jacket. Utterly appalled by that development, and already very much taken back by his reference to Leland Coulter, Maxie watched in sick horror as her defamatory list disappeared from view.

'Leland had to be dealt with. Surely you didn't think I planned to let him get away with what he did to you?' Angelos drawled in a fulminating tone of disbelief. 'He stole a whole chunk of your life and, not content with that, he ripped you off with that loan—'

'Angelos…L-Leland is a sick man—'

'Since he had the bypass op he is well on the road to full recovery,' Angelos contradicted grimly. 'But he's thoroughly ashamed of himself now, and so he should be.'

'You actually confronted him?' Maxie was still reeling in shock.

'*And* in Jennifer's presence. Now that she knows the real story of your dealings with her husband, she's ecstatic. Leland had no plans to confess the truth and his punctured vanity will be his punishment. He trapped you into a demeaning, distressing charade just to hit back at Jennifer!' Angelos concluded harshly.

'I never dreamt you would feel so strongly about it,' Maxie admitted tautly.

'You're mine now,' Angelos countered with indolent cool. 'I look after everything that belongs to me to the very best of my ability.'

'I don't belong to you…I'm just passing through…' Hot, offended colour had betrayingly flushed Maxie's cheeks. She wanted to hit him but, surveying him, she just gritted her teeth because she *knew* that the instant she got that close she would just melt into his arms and draw that dark, arrogant head down to hers. Almost seven days of sensory and emotional deprivation were making her feel incredibly weak.

Poised at the foot of the bed, lean brown hands flexing round the polished brass top rail, Angelos rested slumbrous yet disturbingly intent dark eyes on her beautiful face. 'Leland and Jennifer *do*, however, lead one to reflect on the peculiarity of the games adults play with each other,' he commented levelly. 'What a mistake it can be to under-estimate your opponent…'

A slight chill ran down Maxie's backbone. Games? No, surely he couldn't have recognised what she was trying to do, she told herself urgently, for, apart from anything else, she did not consider herself to be playing a game. 'I don't follow…'

'Leland neglected his wife. Jennifer had a silly affair. She wouldn't say sorry. He was too bitter to forgive her. So they spent three years frantically squabbling over the terms of their divorce, enjoying a sort of twisted together-ness and never actually making it into court. Neither one of them allowed for the other's intransigence or stamina.'

'Crazy,' Maxie whispered very low.

'Isn't it just?' Angelos agreed, flicking a glance down at the thin gold watch on his wrist. He released a soft sigh of regret. 'I'd love to stay. However, I did promise to show my face at my cousin Demetrios's twenty-first celebration at a nightclub…and it's getting late.'

Maxie sat there as immobile as a stone dropped in a deep pond and plunged into sudden dreadful suffocating dark-ness. 'You're…*leaving*?' she breathed, not quite levelly.

'I lead a fairly hectic social life, *pethi mou*. Business, family commitments,' Angelos enumerated lazily. 'But the pressure of time and distance should ensure that the snatched moments we share will be all the more exciting—'

'Snatched moments?' Maxie echoed in a strained and slightly shrill undertone as she slid off the bed in an abrupt movement. 'You think I am planning to sit here and wait for "snatched moments" of your precious time?'

'Maxie…you're beginning to sound just a little like a

wife,' Angelos pointed out with a pained aspect. 'The one thing a mistress must never ever do is nag.'

'Nag?' Maxie gasped, ready to grab him by the lapels of his exquisitely tailored dinner jacket and shake him until he rattled like a box of cutlery in a grinding machine.

'Or sulk, or shout or look discontented...' Angelos warmed to his theme with a glimmering smile of satisfaction. 'This is where I expect to come to relax and shrug off the tensions of the day... I'll dine here with you tomorrow night—'

Maxie was seething and ready to cut off her nose to spite her face. 'I'm going out.'

'Maxie...' Angelos shook his imperious dark head in reproof. 'Naturally I expect your entire day to revolve round being available when I want you to be.'

'For snatched moments?' Maxie asserted in outrage. 'What am I supposed to do with myself the rest of the time?'

'Shop,' Angelos delivered with the comforting air of a male dropping news she must be dying to hear. 'Any woman who can spend for an entire week without flagging once is a serious shopaholic.'

Maxie flushed to the roots of her hair, assailed by extreme mortification. She had spent an absolute fortune.

'And if it's a phobia, you should now be very happy,' Angelos continued bracingly. 'With me bankrolling you, you won't ever need to take the cure.'

Maxie was mute. Her every objective, her script, everything she had dreamt up with which to challenge him over the past week now lay in discarded tatters round her feet. As yet she couldn't quite work out how that had happened. Angelos had started out angry, fully meeting her expectations, but he was now in a wonderfully good mood...even though he was about to walk out on her.

During that weak moment of inattention, Angelos reached out to tug her into his arms with maddeningly confident hands. Maxie was rigid, and then she just drooped, drained of fight. He curved her even closer, crushing her up against him with a groan of unconcealed pleasure and sending every nerve in her body haywire with wanton longing.

'If it wasn't for this wretched party, I'd stay...' Angelos pushed against her with knowing eroticism, shamelessly acquainting her with the intensity of his arousal. Maxie's heartbeat went from a race into an all-out sprint. Heat surged between her thighs, leaving her weak with lust.

'I could throw you down on the bed and sate this overpowering ache for fulfilment—'

Maxie said, 'Yes...'

'But it would be wicked and unforgivable to make a snack out of what ought to be a five-course banquet.' Even as he talked Angelos was tracing a passage down her extended throat with his mouth in hot, hungry little forays. He slid a long, powerful thigh between hers to press against the most sensitive spot in her entire shivering body. 'I really do have to go...'

'Kiss me,' Maxie begged.

'Absolutely not...I'd go up in flames,' Angelos groaned with incredulous force, tearing himself back from her with shimmering golden eyes full of frustration.

Maxie clutched the bed to stay upright. Angelos backed away one slow step at a time, like a recovering alcoholic struggling to resist the temptation of a drink. '*Christos*...you're so beautiful, and so totally perfect for me,' he murmured with hoarse satisfaction.

Maxie blinked. All she could focus on was the fact that he was leaving. Everything that mattered to her in the whole world was walking out, and it felt as if it was for ever. The shock of separation from him was so painful it swallowed her alive. And a kind of terror swept over her then, because for the first time she tasted the full extent of her own agonising vulnerability.

She watched him until the last possible moment. She listened to him striding fast down the corridor. She even strained to hear the lift but she couldn't. And then she collapsed in a heap on the soft thick carpet and burst into floods of tears. Dear heaven, what an idiot she had been to set out to provide Angelos with a challenge! All of a sudden she could not credit that she had been so insane as to refuse the chance of making something of their marriage.

He had said that he hadn't expected her to move into this apartment. He had said that she might not have noticed but things had changed. He hadn't even mentioned that wretched argument over that equally wretched will of her godmother's. 'You might as well come home with me,' he had drawled. Her stupid, stupid pride had baulked; he had sounded for all the world like a disgruntled male grudgingly facing up to an inevitable evil. But no matter how half-hearted that offer had seemed, shouldn't she have accepted it?

She would've had something to build on then. Her rightful place as his wife. Instead, she had turned it down, gambled her every hope of happiness on the slender hope that Angelos would learn to love her and want her to be more than a mistress in his life. But, judging by his behaviour in the aftermath of that refusal, she appeared to have offered Angelos exactly what *he* wanted.

No, she had *not* made a mistake in rejecting that offer, she conceded heavily. How long would it have been before he resented the restraints of such a marriage? He had only married her for sex. She shuddered. There had to be a lot more than that on offer before she would risk figuring in the tabloids as the ultimate discarded bimbo yet again.

Angelos certainly wouldn't have been offering a wife snatched moments of his time...nor would he have been taking off for a nightclub on his own. Maxie sobbed her heart out and then, after splashing her swollen face with loads of cold water, she surveyed her weak reflection in the mirror with loathing and climbed into her lonely bed.

Tonight she had got some things wrong, but ultimately she had still made the right decision. She had played right into his hands but it was early days yet, she reminded herself bracingly. Stamina—she needed buckets of stamina to keep up with Angelos. It was so strange, she reflected numbly, every time she rejoiced in the belief that she had got Angelos off balance, he retaliated by doing the exact same thing to *her*...

The instant Maxie was engulfed by the hard heat of a hair-roughened male body, she came awake with a start. Pulling away with a muffled moan of fright, she sat up in a daze. Dawn light was filtering through the curtains.

'I didn't mean to wake you up...' Angelos murmured.

Utterly unconvinced by that plea of innocence, Maxie struggled to focus on him in the dim light. Against the pale bedlinen, he was all intriguing darkness and shadow. Her heart was still palpitating at such a rate, she pressed a hand to her breast and suppressed the lowering suspicion that Angelos might have more stamina than she had. 'What are you d-doing here?' she stammered helplessly.

'It was a long drive home...what do you *think* I'm doing here?' Angelos demanded with sudden disturbing amusement. He rolled over to her side of the bed at the speed of light to haul her back into his arms and seal her into all-pervasive contact with every charged line of his big, powerful frame.

'Oh...' Maxie said breathlessly.

'I know anticipation is supposed to be the cutting edge of erotic pleasure but I am not really into self-denial, *agape mou*,' Angelos confided huskily, his warm breath fanning her cheekbone. 'It's been a hell of a week...seven very rough days of wondering if you had left me and found another man.'

As it had genuinely not occurred to her that Angelos might interpret her departure from Chymos in that melodramatic light, Maxie was shaken. 'But—'

'The thought of you out there...*loose*,' Angelos framed with a hoarse edge to his dark, deep drawl.

'What do you mean by..."loose"?'

'The world is full of men like me. If I saw a ravishing beauty like you walking down a street alone, I'd make a move on her like a shot!'

Maxie was not best pleased by that assurance. 'If I ever have the slightest reason to think you're two-timing me, I'll be out of here so fast—'

'How can a husband two-time his wife?'

'He has an affair...*or* a mistress.'

'Well, you've got the market cornered there, haven't you?' Angelos breathed with galling amusement, running his hands down to the curvaceous swell of her hips to cup them and urge her even closer.

Maxie quivered, her body responding with a wanton life all of its own, but she struggled desperately to keep on talking because potential infidelity was an extremely important subject, to be tackled and dealt with on the spot. 'Wh-who was it said that when the mistress becomes the wife, a vacancy is created?'

'Some guy who hadn't had the good fortune to discover you,' Angelos growled with blatant satisfaction. 'You are not like other women.'

Maxie blossomed at what sounded like a true compliment. 'Did you have a good time at the club?'

'What do *you* think?' Angelos nipped at the tender lobe of her ear in sensual punishment and curved her suggestively into contact with the straining evidence of his arousal. 'I've been like this all night, hot and hungry and *aching*—''

Maxie kissed him to shut him up; he was embarrassing her. He seized on that invitation with a fervour that fully bore out his frustration. She came up for air again, awash with helpless tenderness. He was irredeemably oversexed but she just adored him. Something to build on. Obviously being a sex object was the something to build on. How the mighty had fallen, she conceded, and then Angelos kissed her again and all rational thought was suspended...

Maxie crept out of bed and tiptoed across the carpet to the chair where she could see Angelos's clothing draped. She would get the list back before he found it. The very last thing their relationship needed now was the short, sharp shocking result of Angelos seeing that awful list of all that she had once thought was wrong with him. That list had been a *real* hatchet job. After all, when she had written it, she'd been trying to wean herself off him.

Maxie couldn't believe her eyes when she discovered that the jacket she was searching *wasn't* his dinner jacket! Before he had returned to her at dawn, Angelos had evidently gone back to his own apartment to change. She could've screamed... *Stamina*, she reminded herself, but her nerves were already shot to hell.

'Maxie...what are you doing?'

Maxie jerked and dropped his jacket as if she had been burnt. 'Nothing!'

'What time is it?' he queried softly.

'Eight...'

'Come back to bed, *agape mou*.'

Maxie was so relieved he hadn't noticed what she was doing, she responded with alacrity.

An hour and a half later she sat across the dining-room table while breakfast was served by Angelos's manservant, Nikos. He had imported his own staff to remedy the empty cupboards in the kitchen. His efficiency in sweeping away such problems just took her breath away. Now he lounged back, skimming through a pile of newspapers and onto his third cup of black coffee.

He was a fantastic lover, she thought dreamily. He could be so gentle and then so…so wild. And he ought to be exhausted after only a couple of hours of sleep, but instead Angelos emanated a sizzling aura of pent-up energy this morning. I'm never, ever going to get over him, she thought in sudden panic. I *need* my list back to deprogramme myself from this dependency.

Without warning, Angelos bit out something raw and incredulous in Greek and sprang upright, sending half his coffee flying. Volatile, volcanic, like a grizzly bear, Maxie reminded herself studiously. He strode across the dining-room, swept up the phone, punched out some numbers and raked down the line, 'That piece on Maxie Kendall on the gossip page…who authorised that? You print a retraction tomorrow. And after that she's the invisible woman…you tell that malicious poison-pen artist to find another target. She's supposed to be writing up society stuff, not trawling the gutter for sleaze!'

About thirty seconds later, Angelos replaced the receiver. Maxie was suffering from dropped-jaw syndrome. Only Nikos, evidently inured to the liveliness of life with Angelos, was functioning normally. Having mopped up the split coffee, he had brought a fresh cup, and he now removed himself from the room again with admirable cool.

Angelos slapped the offending newspaper down in front of Maxie. 'This is what happens when you stroll round Paris without protection,' he informed her grimly. 'You didn't even realise you'd been caught on camera, did you?'

'No,' she confided, and swallowed hard, still in shock from that startling knee-jerk demonstration of male protectiveness. She cast a brief glance at the photo. 'But do you really think that newspaper is likely to pay the slightest heed to your objections?'

'I *own* that newspaper,' Angelos breathed flatly, his lean face sardonic. 'And just look at what that stupid columnist has written!'

Maxie obediently bent her head. She put a finger on the lines of italic type to the right of the photo. The tiny words blurred and shifted hopelessly because she couldn't even begin to concentrate with Angelos standing over her as he was.

The silence thundered.

Then a lean brown forefinger came down to shift hers to the section of type *below* the photograph. 'It's that bit, actually,' Angelos informed her, half under his breath.

Maxie turned white, her stomach reacting with a violent lurch. 'I never read this kind of stuff…and you've caught me out. I'm horribly long-sighted…'

The silence went on and on and on. She couldn't bring herself to look up to see whether or not he had been fooled by that desperate lie.

In an abrupt movement, Angelos removed the newspaper. 'You shouldn't be looking at that sort of sleazy trash anyway. It's beneath your notice!'

The sick tension, the shattering fear of discovery drained out of Maxie, but it left her limp, perspiration beading her short upper lip. How *could* she tell him? How could she admit a handicap like dyslexia to someone like Angelos? Like many, he might not even believe that the condition really existed; he might think that it was just a fancy name coined to make the not very bright feel better about their academic deficiencies. Over the years Maxie had met a lot of attitudes like that, and had learnt that any attempt to explain the problems she had often resulted in contempt or even greater discomfiture.

'Maxie…' Angelos cleared his throat with rare hesitancy. 'I don't think there's anything wrong with your eyesight, and I don't think it's a good idea at this stage in our relationship to pretend that there is.'

As that strikingly candid admission sank in, appalled humiliation engulfed Maxie. This was her worst nightmare. Angelos had uncovered her secret. She could have borne anybody but him seeing through the lying excuses that came so readily to her lips when her reading or writing skills were challenged. She sat there just staring into space, blocking him out.

'Maxie...I don't like upsetting you but I'm not about to drop the subject.' Angelos bent and hauled the chair around by the arms, with her still sitting in it. 'You are very intelligent so there has to be a good reason why you can't read ten lines in a newspaper with the same ease that I can. And, you see, I remember your notebook when you were waitressing...like a type of shorthand instead of words.'

Maxie parted compressed lips like an automaton. 'I'm dyslexic...OK?'

'OK...do you want some more coffee?' Angelos enquired without skipping a beat as he straightened.

'No, I've had enough...I thought you'd want to drag it all out of me,' she said then accusingly.

'Not right now, if it's upsetting you to this degree,' Angelos returned evenly.

'I'm *not* upset!' Maxie flew upright and stalked across the room in direct contradiction of the statement. 'I just don't like people prying and poking about in what is my business and nobody else's!'

Angelos regarded her in level enquiry. 'Dyslexia is more widespread than perhaps you realise. Demetrios, whose twenty first I attended last night, is also dyslexic, but he's now in his second year at Oxford. His two younger brothers also have problems. Didn't you get extra tuition at school to help you to cope?'

Relaxing infinitesimally, Maxie folded her arms and shook her head dully. 'I went to about a dozen different schools in all—'

'A dozen?' Angelos interrupted in astonishment.

'Dad and I never stayed in one place for long. He always ended up owing someone money. If it wasn't the landlord it was the local bookie, or some bloke he had laid a bet with and lost…so we would do a flit to pastures new.'

'And then the whole cycle would start again?' Angelos questioned tautly.

'Yes…' Maxie pursued her lips, her throat aching as she evaded his shrewd appraisal. 'I was ten before a teacher decided that there might be an explanation other than stupidity for my difficulties and I was assessed. I was supposed to get extra classes, but before it could be arranged Dad and I moved on again.' She tilted her chin, denying her own agonising self-consciousness on the subject. 'In the next school, after I'd been tested, they just stuck me in the lowest form alongside the rest of the no-hopers.'

Angelos actually winced. 'When did you leave school?'

'As fast as my legs could carry me at sixteen!' Maxie admitted with sudden explosive bitterness. 'As my godmother once said to me, "Maxie, you can't expect to be pretty *and* clever."''

'I don't think I like the sound of her very much.'

'She was trying to be kind but she thought I was as thick as a brick because I was such a slow reader, and my writing was awful and my spelling absolutely stinks!' Feeling the tears coming on, Maxie shot across the room like a scalded cat and fled back to the bedroom.

Angelos came down on the bed beside her.

'And don't you dare try to pretend that you don't see me differently now!' Maxie sobbed furiously.

'You're right. You are incredibly brave to cope with something like that all on your own and still be such a firecracker,' Angelos breathed grittily. 'And if I'd known this when I had Leland in my sights, I'd have torn him limb from limb…because you couldn't *read* that bloody loan contract, could you?'

'Bits of it…I can get by…but it takes me longer to read things. I didn't want to show myself up, so I just signed.'

'Demetrios was fortunate. His problems were recognised

when he was still a child. He got all the help he needed
but you were left to suffer in frustration…you shouldn't
be—you *mustn't* be ashamed of the condition.'

Tugging her back against him, Angelos smoothed her
hair off her damp brow as if he was comforting a distressed
and sensitive child, and she jerked away from him. He persisted. Out of pride, she tried to shrug him off again, but
it was a very half-hearted gesture and recognised as such.
Somehow, when Angelos closed his powerful arms round
her, she discovered, nothing could possibly feel that bad.

'What did that piece in the gossip column say anyway?'
Maxie wiped her eyes on her sleeve.

'That the rumours about you and I were complete non-
sense. But that it looked like you had attracted another
wealthy "friend"—the implication being that he was another married man.'

'The columnist got that bit right.' An involuntary laugh
escaped Maxie.

Angelos's grip tightened. 'It didn't amuse me.'

Maxie then dug up the courage to ask something that had
been puzzling her all night. 'Why aren't you still furious
about me deciding to marry you because of my godmother's will?'

'In your position, I might have reacted the same way. I
fight fire with fire too,' Angelos admitted reflectively. 'I
don't surrender, I get even. But, you see, there comes a
time when that can become a dangerously destructive
habit…'

'I'll stop trying to top everything you do,' Maxie promised tautly.

'I'll stop trying to set you up for a fall,' Angelos swore,
and then he surveyed her with sudden decision. 'And we'll
fly back the island to enjoy some privacy.'

'You really are a fabulous cook,' Angelos commented appreciatively as Maxie closed the empty picnic hamper.

Maxie tried to look modest and failed. In the most unexpected ways, Angelos was a complete pushover. With all those servants around, and the ability to eat every meal at five-star locations if he chose, no woman had ever, it seemed, made the effort to cook for him, and he was wildly and unduly impressed by the domestic touch. If she cracked an egg, he made her feel like Mother Earth.

'You could make some lucky guy a really wonderful wife,' Angelos drawled indolently.

Maxie leant over him and mock-punched him in the ribs. Bronzed even deeper by the sun, narrow hips and long powerful thighs sheathed in a pair of low-slung cut-off jeans, Angelos was all lean, dark, rampantly virile male. She stared down at him, entrapped, heart thumping, breathing constricted. He threaded a lean hand into her tumbling hair to imprison her in that vulnerable position.

Disturbingly serious black eyes focused on her. 'Tell me, have you *ever* trusted a member of my sex?'

'No,' Maxie admitted uneasily.

'I feel as if I'm on trial. We're married. You won't wear my ring. You still don't want anyone to know you're my wife—'

'You made the offer to announce our marriage out of guilt.'

'I'm not that big a fool. I think you're paying me back for refusing to do it the right way from the start,' Angelos countered steadily. 'I hurt you and I'm sorry, but we have to move on from there.'

Maxie's gaze was strained, wary. 'I'm not ready for that yet.'

'Thanks for that vote of faith.' Releasing her with startling abruptness, Angelos sprang upright and strode up the beach.

Fighting a sensation of panic, and the urge to chase after him, Maxie hugged her knees tightly and stared out at the sun-drenched blue of the sea. The first row since they had left London. It totally terrified her. She could not overcome the fear that she was just a fascinating interlude for Angelos, that she did not have what it would take to hold him. She could not face the prospect of being his wife in public and then being dumped a few months down the line when he lost interest...

And yet, to be fair, so far Angelos had not shown the slightest sign of becoming bored with her. In fact, with every passing day Angelos made her feel better about herself, so much more than a beautiful face and body—something no man had ever achieved or even *tried* to achieve.

Yesterday he had had to fly to Athens for the day on business. Three gorgeous bouquets of the white lilies she loved had been flown in during his absence. And every one of them had carried a personal message, carefully block-printed by his own hand. 'Missing you.' 'Missing you more.' 'Missing you even more,' Maxie recalled headily. So impractical, so over-the-top. Not bad for a guy she had believed didn't have a romantic, imaginative, thoughtful, sensitive or tender bone in his entire beautiful body.

But for the past ten days Angelos had been proving just how wrong she had been to attribute such flaws to him. The list? Well, as yet, since that dinner jacket was still in London, she hadn't had a chance to get hold of it, and the list might well have been dumped by Nikos or trashed at the dry-cleaners or some such thing by now. She knew Angelos *couldn't* have found it before they left London. He couldn't possibly have kept his mouth shut on the subject if he had.

He had presented her with a laptop computer with a wonderful spellcheck mechanism on it so that she could write things with ease. He read newspapers with her. He was so patient with her efforts and, as her confidence had risen from absolute rock-bottom inadequacy, she had improved amazingly. How had she ever imagined he was selfish and inconsiderate? And how had she ever thought she could bask in such generosity and not be expected to give something back? And she knew what he wanted back. Total, unconditional surrender. That was what trust was. She was being such a terrible, selfish coward...

Maxie found him in the airy lounge. Hovering in the doorway, she studied him, her heart jumping worse than it did when he took her up in the helicopter most mornings. 'I trust you,' she said tautly, a betraying shimmer brightening her eyes.

Angelos dealt her a pained, unimpressed look, and then he groaned with suppressed savagery. Striding across the room, he pulled her into his arms in one powerful motion. '*Christos*...don't look at me like that, *agape mou*!' he urged ruefully. 'Forget that whole conversation. I'm just not very good at patience...not a lot of practice and too big an ego.'

'I like you the way you are.'

'The lies women tell in certain moods,' Angelos sighed with an ironic look.

'It's *not* a lie, Angelos—'

'Possibly it won't be...some time in the future.' And with that last word he sealed his sensual mouth to hers with a kind of hungry desperation.

The ground beneath Maxie's feet rocked. In that one way Angelos controlled her. He understood that. He used it. She accepted it; the passion he unleashed inside her was more than she could withstand. But, most importantly of all, it was the one time she could show him affection without the fear that she might be revealing how much she loved him. And if anything, after the past ten days, she loved him ten times more.

She was enslaved, utterly, hopelessly enslaved. So the minute Angelos touched her she let all that pent-up emotion loose on him. She clutched, she clung, she heaved ecstatic sighs and she hugged him tight. And he responded with a flattering amount of enthusiasm every time.

Probing her mouth with hot, sexual intimacy, Angelos unclipped her bikini bra. As her breasts spilt full and firm into his palms, he uttered a hungry sound of pleasure. He let his thumbs glance over her urgently sensitive pink nipples. Maxie moaned, her spine arching as he used his mouth to torment those straining buds. She was so excited she couldn't breathe. Reaching down, he unclipped the bikini briefs clasped at her slim hips and pulled them free, leaving her naked.

'I love exciting you,' Angelos confided hoarsely, and he kissed her again, slowly, sensually this time. A long, powerful thigh nudged hers apart. A surge of unbearable heat left her boneless as he bent her back over his supporting arm, splaying his hand across the clenched muscles of her stomach. His skilled fingers skated through the cluster of damp golden curls and into the hot, melting warmth beneath. She whimpered and squirmed under his mouth, and at the exact moment when her legs began to buckle he picked her up with easy strength and carried her down to the bedroom.

He stood over her, unzipping the cut-offs, peeling them off. And then he came down to her. 'Angelos...' she pleaded, aroused beyond bearing.

Answering the powerful need he had awakened, he took her hard and fast, as always disturbingly attuned to the level of her need. And then there was nothing, nothing but him and the wild sensation that controlled her as surely as he did. She cried out as he drove her to a peak of exquisite pleasure and then slumped, absolutely, totally drained.

'Have you ever been in love?' Angelos asked lazily then.

Unprepared for serious conversation, Maxie blinked and met brilliant assessing eyes. 'Yes.'

'What happened?'

Maxie lowered her lashes protectively. 'He didn't love me back...er, what about you?'

'Once...'

Maxie opened her eyes wide. *'And?'*

Angelos focused on her swollen mouth, ebony lashes screening his gaze. 'I fell victim to a feminist with high expectations of the man in her life. She thought I was great in bed but that was kind of it.'

'Tart!' Maxie condemned without hesitation, absolutely outraged to discover he had loved somebody else and, worst of all, somebody wholly undeserving of the honour. There was just so much more to Angelos than his ability to drive her crazy with desire, she thought furiously. He was highly entertaining company and such a wretched tease sometimes...

Dark eyes met hers with disturbing clarity. 'She wasn't and isn't a tart...is that jealousy, I hear?'

'I'm not the jealous type,' Maxie lied, and, snaking free of him with the Ice Queen look she hadn't given him in weeks, she slid off the bed. 'I feel like a shower.'

On the flight back to London, Maxie contemplated the wedding ring now embellishing her finger. It was new, a broad platinum band. It was also accompanied by a gorgeous knuckleduster of sapphires and diamonds.

'An engagement ring?' she had asked him incredulously.

'A *gift*,' Angelos had insisted. But he had produced both at spectacular speed.

Indeed, her finger was now so crowded, a glance at a hundred yards would give the news that she was married to even the most disinterested onlooker. But why couldn't Angelos mention the prospect of having children...or something, *anything* that would make her feel like a really permanent fixture in his life? she wondered ruefully. Maybe he didn't want children. Or maybe he just couldn't contemplate the idea of having children with her. Certainly he hadn't taken a single risk in that department.

They parted at the airport. Angelos headed for the Petronides building and Maxie travelled back to *his* apartment, her new home. Barely stopping to catch her breath, she found the main bedroom, went into the dressing-room and searched through wardrobe after wardrobe of fabulous suits in search of that dinner jacket with her list in the pocket. She found half a dozen dinner jackets, but not one of them contained what she sought. Obviously that list had been dumped. She relaxed.

Angelos called her at lunchtime. 'Something's come up. I may be very late tonight,' he informed her.

Maxie's face fell a mile but her response was upbeat. 'Don't worry, I'll amuse myself—'

'*How?*' Angelos interrupted instantaneously.

'I'll have an early night.' Maxie worked hard to keep the amusement out of her voice.

'I have this recurring image of you hitting the town on your own.'

'Because you know you got away with going to that nightclub by yourself, but you won't ever again,' Maxie murmured with complete sincerity.

Maxie couldn't believe how much she missed him that night. She thought she would turn over at some stage and find him there in the bed beside her, and it was something of a shock to wake up at eight and discover she was still alone.

By the time she sat down to breakfast, however, the table was rejoicing in a huge bunch of white lilies. 'Missing you too much,' the card complained. Maxie heaved a happy sigh, consoled by the sight. Her portable phone buzzed.

'Thank you for the flowers,' she said, since nobody else but Angelos had her number. 'Where are you?'

'The office. I was out of town last night. It was too late to drive back and I didn't want to wake you up by phoning in the early hours.'

'The next time, phone,' Maxie urged.

'What are you wearing, *agape mou*?' Angelos enquired huskily.

Maxie gave a little shiver and crammed the phone even closer to her ear. The sound of that honeyed drawl just knocked her out. 'Shocking pink…suit…four-inch stilettos,' she whispered hoarsely. 'I can't wait to take them all off.'

'How am I supposed to concentrate when you say things like that?' Angelos demanded in a driven undertone.

'I want you to miss me.'

'I'm missing you…OK?'

'OK…when can I expect a snatched moment?'

'Don't go out anywhere. I'll pick you up at eleven. I've got a surprise for you.'

Maxie flicked through the topmost newspaper and went as usual to the gossip column. She saw the picture of Angelos instantly. Her attention lodged lovingly on how wonderfully photogenic he was, and then her gaze slowly slewed sideways to take in the woman who occupied the photo with him, the woman whose hand he was intimately clasping across a table.

Aghast, she just stared for a full count of ten seconds. Her stomach twisted, her brow dampened. She felt sick. Natalie Cibaud, the movie actress…

CHAPTER ELEVEN

Fresh from reports of an on-off affair with the model Maxie Kendall, Greek tycoon Angelos Petronides, our all-time favourite heartbreaker, seen dining last night with the ravishing actress Natalie Cibaud. Is it off with Maxie and on with Natalie again? Or is this triangle set to run and run?

Last night? Dear heaven, Angelos had been with another woman? With Natalie Cibaud? Maxie just couldn't believe it. She kept on laboriously re-reading the column and staring an anguished hole into the photo. Then her stomach got the better of her. She lost her breakfast in the cloakroom.

Sick and dizzy, she reeled back to the table to study the card she had received with her flowers. 'Missing you *too* much.' There was a certain appalling candour in that admission, wasn't there? Evidently Angelos couldn't be trusted out of her sight for five minutes. And, trusting woman that she was, Angelos had been out of her sight for almost *twenty-four* hours...

Maxie asked Nikos to have the car brought around. She swept up her portable phone. No, she wasn't going to warn Angelos. Nor was she about to sit and wait for him to arrive with whatever surprise his guilty conscience had dreamt up. She would confront him in the Petronides building. Her phone buzzed in the lift. She ignored it.

The phone went again in the limousine. Angelos trying to call her. She switched the phone off with trembling fingers. Offered the car phone some minutes later, she uttered a stringent negative. Getting a little nervous, was he? By now, Angelos would've been tipped off about that piece in the gossip column. He knew he had been caught out. He had been unfaithful to her. He *must* have been. He had been out all night. *All night.* Maxie shivered, gooseflesh pricking her clammy skin. She was in sick shock. Why…*why*? was all she could think.

Until now she hadn't appreciated just how entirely hers Angelos had begun to seem. She had trusted him one hundred per cent. And now she couldn't comprehend how her trust had become so unassailable. He had never mentioned love, never promised to be faithful. On the very brink of making a public announcement of their marriage, Angelos had betrayed her. Why? Was this one of those male sexual ego things women found so incomprehensible? Or was an adulterous fling his revealing reaction to the prospect of fully committing himself to her?

Magnificent in her rage, Maxie stalked into the Petronides building. Every head in the vicinity seemed to turn. They did a double-take at the bodyguards in her wake. Maxie stepped into the executive lift.

Angelos had to be gnashing his teeth. Famous for his discretion in his private life, and his success in keeping his personal affairs out of the gossip columns, he would've assumed he was safe from discovery. Or had he deliberately sought to be found out? Was she becoming paranoid? The simplest explanations were usually the most likely, she reflected wretchedly. Had Angelos just met up with Natalie Cibaud again and suddenly realised that *she* was the woman he really wanted?

The receptionist on the top floor stared and rose slowly to her feet.

Maxie strode on past, the stillness of her pale features dominated by eyes as brilliant as sapphires. Agog faces appeared at doorways. Without breaking her stride, Maxie reached the foot of the corridor and, thrusting wide the door of Angelos's office, she swept in and sent the door slamming shut behind her again.

Angelos was standing in the centre of the room, lean, hard-boned face whip-taut, black eyes shimmering.

A pain as sharp as a knife cut through Maxie. She could read nothing but angry frustration in those startlingly handsome features. That neither shame nor regret could be seen savaged her. 'Before I walk out of your life for ever, I have a few things to say to you—'

Angelos moved forward and spread silencing hands. 'Maxie—'

'Don't you dare interrupt me when I'm shouting at you!' Maxie launched. 'And don't say my name like that. The only way you could get around me at this moment is with a rope! When I saw that photo of you with Natalie Cibaud, I couldn't believe my eyes—'

'Good,' Angelos slotted in fiercely. 'Because you shouldn't have believed what you were seeing. That photo was issued by Natalie's agent *three* months ago! That dinner date took place *three* months ago!'

'I don't believe you,' Maxie breathed jerkily, studying him with stunned intensity.

'Then call my lawyer. I've already been in touch with him. I intend to sue that newspaper.'

Maxie's lashes fluttered. Her legs trembled. She slumped back against the door. Widening blue eyes dazed, she framed raggedly, 'Are you saying that…you *weren't* with Natalie last night?'

'Maxie, I haven't laid eyes on Natalie since the night you took ill. We did not part the best of friends.'

The tremble in Maxie's lower limbs was inexorably spreading right through her entire body. 'But I thought you saw her after that—'

'You thought wrong. I have neither seen nor spoken to her since that night, and as far as I'm aware she's not even in the UK right now. Maxie…you should know I haven't the smallest desire for any other woman while you are in my life,' Angelos swore, anxiously searching her shaken face and then lapsing into roughened Greek as he reached for her and held her so tight and close she couldn't breathe.

'You s-said if you saw a beautiful woman walk down the street—'

'No, I said, "a ravishing beauty like *you*",' Angelos contradicted with strong emphasis. 'And there *is* no other woman like you. When I realised you must've seen that picture, it was like having my own heart ripped out! I can't bear for you to be hurt—not by me, not by anyone, *agape mou*.'

Strongly reassured by that unexpectedly emotional speech, Maxie gazed wordlessly up at him. Angelos breathed in deep and drew back from her. Black eyes meeting her bemused scrutiny, he murmured tautly, 'I have so much I want to say to you…but there is someone waiting to see you and it would be cruel to keep him waiting any longer. Your father is already very nervous of his reception.'

'My…my father?' Maxie whispered shakily. 'He's *here*?'

'I put private detectives on his trail and they contacted me as soon as they found him. I went to see him yesterday. I had planned to bring him back to the apartment to surprise you.' Angelos guided her over to one of the comfortable armchairs and settled her down carefully, seeming to recognise that she was in need of that assistance. 'I'll send him in…'

Stiff with strain, Maxie breathed unevenly, 'Just tell me one thing before you go…has Dad asked you for money?'

'No. No, he hasn't. He's cleaned up his act, Maxie. He's holding down a job and trying to make a decent life for himself.' Angelos shrugged. 'But he would be the first one to admit that he still has to fight the temptation to go back to his old habits.'

Her troubled eyes misted with tears. As Russ Kendall stepped uncertainly through the door through which Angelos had just departed, Maxie slid upright. Her father looked older, his hair greyer, and he had put on weight. He also looked very uncertain of himself.

'I wasn't sure about coming here after what I did,' her father admitted uncomfortably. 'It's very hard for me to face you now. I let you down the whole time I was bringing you up but I let you down worst of all three years ago, when I left you to pay the price for my stupidity.'

Maxie's stiffness gave way. Closing the distance between them, she gave the older man a comforting hug. 'You loved me. I *always* knew that. It made up for a lot,' she told him frankly. 'You did the best you could.'

'I hit rock-bottom when I saw you having to dance to the tune of that old coot, Leland Coulter.' Russ Kendall shook his head with bitter regret. 'There was no way I could avoid facing up to how low I'd sunk and how much I'd dragged you down. I leeched off you, off everyone. All I lived for was the next game, the next bet—'

Maxie drew him up short there. 'Angelos says you've got a job. Tell me about that,' she encouraged.

For the past year he had been working as a salesman for a northern confectionery firm. It was now eighteen months since he had last laid a bet. He still attended weekly meetings with other former gamblers.

Maxie told him that the cottage no longer had a sitting tenant. Her father frowned in surprise, and then slowly he smiled. Rather apprehensively, he then admitted that he had met someone he was hoping to marry. He would sell the cottage and put the proceeds towards buying a house. Myrtle, he explained, had some savings of her own, and it was a matter of pride that he should not bring less to the relationship.

Now he was middle-aged, she registered, her father finally wanted the ordinary things that other people wanted.

Security, self-respect, to be loved, appreciated. And wasn't that exactly what *she* had always wanted for herself? Her father had needed her forgiveness and she had needed to shed her bitter memories. As they talked, her gratitude to Angelos for engineering such a reconciliation steadily increased. Russ had built a new life and she wished him well with her whole heart.

'You've got yourself a good bloke in Angelos,' her father commented with a nod as he took his leave. 'I shouldn't like to cross him, though.'

Maxie was mopping her eyes when Angelos reappeared. She didn't look at him. 'This has been a heck of morning…but I'm really grateful that you found Dad for me. It's like a whole big load of worry has dropped off my shoulders. Tell me, would you have brought us together again if he'd still been down on the skids?'

From the corner of her eye, she saw Angelos still. 'Not immediately,' he confessed honestly. 'I would have tried to get him some help first. But he wouldn't have come if he hadn't sorted himself out. He wouldn't have had the courage to face you.'

Angelos curved a supportive hand round her spine and walked her towards the door. 'We have a helicopter to catch.'

'Where on earth are we going?'

'Surprise…'

'I thought Dad was my surprise.'

'Only part of it.' He urged her up a flight of stairs and they emerged onto the roof, where a helicopter waited. Maxie grimaced and gave him a look of reproach which he pretended not to notice.

He held her hand throughout the flight. Maxie was forced to admit that it wasn't so bad. She was even persuaded to look out of the windows once or twice. But she still closed her eyes and prayed when they started coming in to land.

Angelos restored her to solid ground again with careful hands. 'You're doing really great,' he told her admiringly.

Only then did Maxie open her eyes. She gaped. A hundred yards away stood a very large and imposing nineteenth-century country house surrounded by a gleaming sea of luxury cars. Three other helicopters were parked nearby. 'Where are we? What's going on?'

'I did once mention having a house in the country but you were ill at the time,' Angelos conceded with a wolfish smile. 'Welcome to the wedding reception you never had, Mrs Petronides…'

'I beg your pardon?' Maxie prompted unevenly.

'All my relatives and all my friends are waiting to meet you,' Angelos revealed. 'And the advantage of inviting them for lunch is that they all have to go home before dinner. Two weeks ago, the only reason I agreed to hold fire on announcing our marriage was that I hadn't the *slightest* desire to share you with other people. I wanted you all to myself for a while—'

'*All* your relatives…*all* your friends?'

'Maxie…this little celebration has been in the pipeline for two weeks. The invitations went out while we were in Greece.' He hesitated and cast her a rueful glance. 'I did ask your father to join us but he preferred not to.'

Maxie nodded without surprise and wondered absently why they were dawdling so much on their passage towards the house. 'Was Dad the something that came up yesterday?'

'I went up to Manchester to see him. That took up quite a few hours and then I came back here for the night. I wanted to check everything was ready for us.' Angelos stilled her steps altogether, casting an odd, frustrated glance of expectancy up at the sky.

'What's wrong…?'

The whine of an aircraft approaching brought a smile back to Angelos's impatient dark features. As a low-flying plane approached over the trees, he banded both arms round Maxie and turned her round. 'Look up,' he urged.

Maxie's eyes widened. In the wake of the strange trail of pink smoke left by the plane, words appeared to be forming.

'That's an I,' Angelos informed her helpfully. 'And that's an L and an O and a V—'

'Even I can read letters that big!' Maxie snapped.

The words 'I love you' stood there in the sky, picked out in bright pink. Maxie's jaw dropped.

Somewhat pained by this lack of response, Angelos breathed, 'I wanted you to know that I am proud of my feelings for you...and it was the only way I could think of doing it.'

Never in Maxie's wildest dreams would it have occurred to her that Angelos would do something so public and so deeply uncool. 'You love me?' she whispered weakly.

'You ought to know that by now!' Angelos launched in frustration. 'I've been tying myself in knots for weeks trying to *show* you how much I care!'

Maxie surveyed him with eyes brimming with happiness, but was conscious of a very slight sense of female incomprehension. 'Angelos...couldn't you just *say* the words?'

'You weren't ready to hear them. You had a very low opinion of me...and, let me tell you, few men would've emerged from reading that written character assassination of yours with much in the way of hope!' Angelos asserted with a feeling shudder.

Maxie was aghast. 'You *found* my list—?'

'How could you write all those things about me?'

'There was no name on it, so if you recognised the traits...' Maxie fell silent and studied him with dismayed and sympathetic eyes. 'Oh, Angelos...you kept quiet all this time, and that must've killed you—'

'I used that list as a blueprint for persuading you that I wasn't the man you imagined I was.'

'And you improved so much,' Maxie completed rather tactlessly.

With a helpless groan, Angelos hauled her close and kissed her with devouring passion. Maxie's impressionable heart went crazy. She submitted to being crushed with alacrity and hugged him tight, finally resting her golden head down on his broad shoulder as she struggled to catch her breath again. 'Oh, dear, *I* was the tart who thought you were great in bed and that was all…you were playing games with me when you said that, Angelos!' she condemned.

'That is really rich…coming from a wife who announced she preferred to be a mistress—'

'Only after being told she would be perfect in that role—'

'Perfect wife, perfect mistress, perfect…you are the love of my life,' Angelos confessed rather raggedly. 'Why the hell did I arrange the reception for today?'

Maxie squinted across the sea of big cars at the house. A lot of faces were looking out of the windows. But she didn't squirm. She threw her head high. Angelos *loved* her. The one and only love of his life? She felt ten feet tall. She would never, ever, no matter how long she lived, tell him how utterly naff that pink trail in the sky had been—particularly not when he was so pleased with himself for having come up with the idea.

'I love you too,' she confided as they threaded a passage through the parked cars on their way to the impressive front doors that already stood wide for their entrance. 'I really don't think I ought to tell you, but it wasn't the new improved you that did the trick entirely. I got sort of irrationally attached to you even before I wrote the list.'

'How can you tell me you love me with all these people hovering?' Angelos slung in a gritty hiss of reproach, but he smiled and their eyes met and that devastating smile of his grew even more brilliant.

'I want you to meet my wife,' Angelos announced a few minutes later, with so much pride and pleasure that Maxie felt her eyes prickle.

A whole host of people lined up to greet them. They were mobbed. At one stage it was something of a surprise to find herself looking down on Leland Coulter's balding little head, and then meeting his faded, discomfited blue eyes. 'I'm sorry,' he breathed tightly.

'I made him sorry,' his wife, Jennifer, said very loudly, and Leland flinched and seemed to shrink into himself. 'Everyone knows the whole story now. There's no fool like an old fool.'

The older woman shook hands with brisk efficiency and passed on.

Somewhat paralysed by that encounter, Maxie whispered to Angelos, 'I feel so sorry for him now.'

'Don't you dare…if it hadn't been for Leland, we'd have been together three years sooner!' Angelos responded without pity.

'I couldn't have coped with you at nineteen.'

'I never knew anyone learn to cope with me faster,' Angelos countered, guiding her through the crush to a quiet corner.

Maxie focused on her friend, Liz, in delighted surprise. Petting Bounce, she sat down beside her. 'How did you get here?' she demanded.

'Angelos phoned me last night. We travelled down in a limousine this morning. Bounce was most impressed. Now, didn't I tell you that man loved you? Oh, dear, is he listening?' Liz said with comic dismay.

'Your senses are so much more acute than Maxie's,' Angelos told Liz cheerfully. 'To convince her, I had to hire a plane to spell out "I love you" in the sky.'

'How did that feel?' Liz asked Maxie eagerly.

'It felt…it *felt* absolutely fantastic,' Maxie swore. 'It was so imaginative, so unexpected, so—'

'Naff?' Angelos slotted in tautly.

'No, it was the moment I realised that I loved you most.' And truthfully it had been, when he had unerringly betrayed to her just how hard he found it to put his pride on the line and say those three little words before she said them.

Lunch was a vast buffet served in the ballroom by uniformed waiters. Maxie sipped champagne and drifted about on an ecstatic cloud with Angelos's arm curved possessively round her. She met his aunts and his uncles and his cousins and his second cousins and his third cousins, and all the names just went right over her head.

And then, when the band struck up the music, rising to the role expected of the bridal couple, they circled the floor and the dancing began. Given an excuse to remain constantly within Angelos's hold, Maxie was initially content. Curving herself round him like a vine, she breathed in the hot, familiar scent of his body and inevitably turned weak with longing. 'Any sign of anyone leaving yet?' she kept on asking hopefully.

At last a trickle of departures led to a generalised flood. They saw Liz back out to the limo. Then Maxie and Angelos mounted the stairs hand in hand at a stately pace. 'When did you realise you were in love with me?' she pressed.

'When you had the chickenpox and I still couldn't wait to take you home.'

'But you weren't prepared to admit it—'

'Torture wouldn't have made me confess I was that vulnerable. This is our bedroom.' Angelos cast wide a door with a flourish.

'"Our" has a warm sound,' Maxie savoured. 'I still can't believe you love me...'

'You wouldn't have had to wait so long to find out if you had kept quiet on the beach the morning after I got drunk.' In exasperation Angelos framed her surprised face with loving hands. 'I was ready to tell you. Since I was painfully aware that I had got everything wrong, and I was feeling unusually humble, I was planning to go for the sympathy vote…and what did *you* do?'

'I told you about my godmother's will… I think I'll give my share to Nancy's favourite children's charity.' She stared dizzily into dark eyes blazing with love and gave him a glorious smile. 'I had to tell you about the will some time, but I was just trying to save face. I didn't want you to realise how much I loved you—'

'You're a total dreamer.'

'I'm the love of your life,' Maxie reminded him rather smugly as she flicked loose his tie and slid his jacket down off his broad shoulders with the intent air of one unwrapping a wonderful parcel. 'And you're the love of mine.'

Angelos brought her down on the four-poster bed with a husky laugh of amusement. 'Let me remind you of what you said in your list. Chauvinistic, bad-tempered, selfish, unromantic, insensitive, domineering—'

'A woman always reserves the right to change her mind,' Maxie inserted before he could get really warmed up.

Black eyes were burnished to pure gold as he met her dancing eyes. 'You may be gorgeous…but I think it was your mind I fell in love with…all those snappy replies and sneaky moves, *agape mou.*'

'To think I once thought you were cold.' Maxie ran a tender loving hand over his hair-roughened chest. 'How many children are we going to have?' she asked.

Angelos gave her a startled smile of appreciation that turned her heart over and inside out. 'You want my baby?'

Maxie nodded. The prospect just made her melt.

'You really are tremendous,' Angelos breathed hoarsely.

And then he took her readily parted lips with urgent, speaking hunger and the passion took over, gloriously reaffirming their love for each other.

* * *

Ten months later, they had their first child. Maxie gave birth to a baby girl with blue eyes as bright and bossy as her own. Angelos took one look at his daughter and he just adored her too.

THE PRICE OF A BRIDE

MICHELLE REID

CHAPTER ONE

JANUARY had arrived with an absolute vengeance. Standing in the window behind her father's desk, Mia watched the way the wind was hurling the rain against the glass in fiercely gusting squalls—while behind her a different kind of storm was raging, one where two very powerful men pitched angry insults at each other.

Not that she was taking much notice of what they were actually fighting about. She knew it all already, so her presence here was really quite incidental.

Merely a silent prop to use as leverage.

'Look, that's the deal, Doumas!' she heard her father state with a brittle grasp on what was left of his patience. 'I'm not into haggling so either take what's on offer or damn well leave it!'

'But what you are proposing is positively barbaric!' the other man hit back furiously. 'I am a businessman, not a trader in white slavery! If you have difficulty finding a husband for your daughter try a marriage agency,' he scathingly suggested, 'for I am not for sale!'

No? Way beyond the point of being insulted by remarks like that one, Mia's startlingly feminine mouth twitched in a cross between bitter appreciation for the clever answer Alexander Doumas had tossed back at her father and a grimace of scorn. Did he truly believe he would be standing here at all if Jack Frazier thought he couldn't be bought?

Jack Frazier dealt only in absolute certainties. He was a rough, tough, self-made man who, having spent most of his life clawing his way up from nothing to become the corporate giant he was today, had learned very early on that

5

attention to fine detail before he went in for the kill was the key to success.

He left nothing whatsoever to chance.

Alexander Doumas, on the other hand, was the complete antithesis of Jack. He was smooth, sleek and beautifully polished by a top-drawer Greek pedigree which could be traced back so far into history it made the average mind boggle, only, while the Frazier fortunes had been rising like some brand new star in the galaxy during the last thirty odd years, the Doumas fortunes had been steadily sinking—until this man had come on the scene.

To be fair, Alexander Doumas had not only stopped the rot in his great family's financial affairs but had spent the last ten years of his life repairing that rot, and so successfully that he had almost completely reversed the deterioration—except for one final goal.

And he was having the rank misfortune of coming up against Jack Frazier in his efforts to achieve that one goal.

Poor devil, Mia thought with a grim kind of sympathy, because, ruthless and unswerving though he was in his own way, Alexander Doumas didn't stand a chance of getting what he wanted from her father, without paying the price Jack Frazier was demanding for it.

'Is that your final answer?' Jack Frazier grimly challenged, as if to confirm his daughter's prediction. 'If so, then you can get out for I have nothing left to say to you.'

'But I am willing to pay double the market price here!'

'The door, Mr Doumas, is over there…'

Mia's spine began to tingle, the fine muscles lining its long, slender length tensing as she waited to discover what Alexander Doumas was going to do next.

He had a straight choice, the way she saw it. He could walk out of here with his arrogant head held high and his monumental pride still firmly intact, but put aside for ever the one special dream that had brought him to this point in the first place, or he could relinquish his pride, let his own principles sink to Jack Frazier's appalling level and pay the price being asked for that dream.

'There has to be some other way we can resolve this,' he muttered.

No there isn't, Mia countered silently. For the simple reason that her father did not *need* another way. The Greek had called Jack Frazier barbaric, but barbarism only half covered what her father really was. As she, of all people, should know.

Jack Frazier didn't even bother to answer. He just sat there behind his desk and waited for the other man to give in to him or leave as suggested.

'Damn you to hell for bringing me down to this,' Alexander Doumas grated roughly. It was the driven sound of a grudging surrender.

The next sound Mia heard was the creak of old leather as her father came to his feet. It was a familiar sound, one she had grown to recognise with dread when she was younger, and even now, at the reasonably mature age of twenty-five, she was still able to experience the same stomach-clutching response as she had in childhood.

Jack Frazier was a brute and a bully. He always had been and always would be. Man or woman. Friend or foe. Adult or child. His need to dominate made no exceptions.

'Then I'll leave you to discuss the finer details with my daughter,' he concluded. 'Get in touch with my lawyer tomorrow. He will iron out any questions you may have, then get a contract drawn up.'

With that, and sounding insultingly perfunctory now that he had the answer he wanted from the other man, Jack Frazier, cold, cruel, ruthless man that he was, walked out of the room and left them to it.

And with the closing of the study door came quite a different silence. Bitter was the only word Mia could come up with to describe it—a silence so bitter it was attacking the back of her neck like acid.

I should have left my hair down, she mused in the same dry, mockingly fatalistic way she had dealt with all of this.

It was the only way, really. She couldn't fight it so she mocked it. It was either that or weep, and she'd done enough weeping during her twenty-five years to know very well that tears did nothing but make you feel worse.

'Drink?'

The sound of glass chinking against fine crystal had her turning to face the room for the first time since the interview had begun. Alexander Doumas was helping himself to some of her father's best whisky.

'No, thank you,' she said, and stayed where she was, with her arms lightly folded beneath the gentle thrust of her breasts, while she watched him toss back a rather large measure.

Poor devil, she thought again. Men of his ilk just weren't used to surrendering anything to anyone—never mind to a nasty piece of work like her father.

Alexander Doumas had arrived here this afternoon, looking supremely confident in his ability to strike a fair agreement with Jack Frazier. Now he was having to deal with the very unpalatable fact that he had been well and truly scuppered—caught hook, line and sinker by a man who always knew exactly what bait to use to catch his prey. And even the fine flavour of her father's best malt whisky wasn't masking the nasty taste that capture had placed in his mouth.

He glanced at her, his deep-set, dark brown Mediterranean eyes flicking her a whiplashing look of contempt from beneath the glowering dip of his frowning black eyebrows. 'You had a lot to say for yourself,' he commented in a clipped voice.

Mia gave an empty little shrug. 'Better men than me have taken him on and failed,' she countered.

She was referring to him, of course, and the way he grimaced into his glass acknowledged the point.

'So you are quite happy to agree to all of this, I must presume.'

Happy? Mia picked up the word and tasted it for a few moments, before deciding ruefully, that—yes—she was, she supposed, *happy* to do whatever it would take to fulfil her side of this filthy bargain.

'Let me explain something to you,' she offered in a tone gauged to soothe not aggravate. 'My father never puts any plan into action unless he is absolutely sure that all participants are going to agree to whatever it is he wants from them. It's the way he works. The way he has *always* worked,' she tagged on pointedly. 'So, if you are hoping to find your redemption through me, I'm sorry to disappoint you.'

'In other words—' His burning gaze was back on her again '—you are willing to sleep with anyone if Daddy commands it.'

'Yes.' Despite the deliberate insult, her coolly composed face showed absolutely nothing—no hint of offence, no distaste, not even anger.

His did, though, showing all of those things plus a few others all meant to label her nothing better than a trollop.

Maybe she was nothing better than a trollop, allowing her father to do this to her, Mia conceded. Certainly, past history had marked her as a trollop.

'Did you do the choosing yourself?' he asked suddenly. 'Is that what this is really all about?'

Taken by surprise by the suggestion, her eyes widened. Then she laughed—a surprisingly pleasant sound amidst all the bitterness and tension. 'Oh, no,' she said. 'You said yourself that my father is a barbarian. It would go totally against his character to allow me to choose anything for myself. But how conceited of you to suggest it…' she added softly.

'It had to be asked,' he said, stiffening slightly at the gentle censure.

'Did it?' Mia was not so sure about that. 'It seems to me that you're seeing yourself as the only victim here, Mr Doumas,' she said more soberly. 'And at this juncture it may well help if I remind you that there tend to be different kinds of victims in most disasters.'

'And you are a victim of your own father's tyranny—is that what you are trying to tell me?'

His scepticism was clear. Her green eyes darkened. If Alexander Doumas came to know her better he would take careful note of that. She was Jack Frazier's daughter after all.

'I am not *trying* to tell you anything,' Mia coolly countered. 'I don't have to justify myself to you, you see.'

After all, she thought, why should she defend herself when his own reasons for agreeing to this were not that defensible?

Not that he was seeing it like that, she wryly acknowledged. Alexander Doumas was looking for a scapegoat on which to blame his own shortcomings.

'No,' he murmured cynically. 'You merely have to go to bed with me.'

And she, Mia noted, was going to be his scapegoat.

'Of course, I do understand that my lot is the much easier one,' she conceded, with that same dangerously deceptive mildness. 'Being a woman, all I need to do is lie down, close my eyes and mentally switch off, whereas you have to bring yourself to…er…perform. But God help us both,' she added drily, 'if you find me so repulsive that you can't manage it because we will really have a problem then.'

She had managed to actually shock him, Mia was gratified to note—had managed to make him look *at* her and *see* her, instead of just concentrating on showing her his contempt.

With a wry smile of satisfaction she deserted her post by the window at last to come around her father's desk and walk across the room towards the two high wing-backed leather armchairs that flanked the polished mahogany fireplace.

A log fire was burning in the grate, the leaping flames trying their best to add some warmth to a room that did not know the meaning of the word—not in Jack Frazier's house, anyway.

But the flames did manage to highlight the rich, burnished copper of Mia's hair as she walked towards them. Although she didn't look at Alexander Doumas as she moved, she felt his narrowed gaze following her.

Eyeing up the merchandise, she thought, cynically mocking that scrutiny.

Well, let him, she thought defiantly as she felt his gaze sweep over the smooth lines of her face, which she had been told was beautiful although she did not see any beauty in it herself.

But, then, she didn't like herself very much and they did say that beauty was in the eyes of the beholder.

Therefore, it followed that neither would this man be seeing any beauty in her right now, she supposed, as he was so actively despising her at this moment.

Oh, she was no hound-dog. Mia wasn't so eaten up with self-hate that she couldn't see that her hair, face, body and legs combined to present a reasonably attractive picture.

Whatever this man was feeling about her right now, she knew that he had looked at her before today and had wanted her so his expression of distaste simply failed to impress her.

Reaching the two chairs, she turned, felt his gaze dip over the slender curves of her figure—so carefully muted by the simple coffee-coloured pure wool dress she was wearing—and chose the chair which would place him directly in her sight so she could watch those eyes draw down the long length of her silk-stockinged legs as she sat and smoothly crossed one knee over the other.

Alexander Doumas was no hound-dog himself, Mia had

to acknowledge. In fact, she supposed he was what most fanciful females would have seen as ideal husband material—tall, tanned and undeniably handsome, with the kind of tightly contoured Greek-god body on which top designers liked to hang their very exclusive clothes.

Indeed, that iron grey silk suit looked very definitely top designer wear. He wore his straight black hair short at the back and neat at the front, and the rich smoothness of his olive-toned skin covered superb bone structure that perhaps said more about his high-born lineage than anything else about him.

He had a good mouth, too—even if it was being spoiled by anger and disgust at the moment—and his long, rather thin nose balanced well with the rest of his cleanly chiselled features.

But it was his eyes that made him special—deep-set, dark brown, lushly fringed, deceptively languid eyes that, even when they were showing disdain, could still stir the senses.

Her senses, she noted as she watched those eyes settle on the point where her slender legs disappeared under the hem of her dress and felt a warm, tingling sensation skitter along her inner thighs in response.

'Well,' she prompted, unable to resist the dig, 'do you have a problem there?'

He stiffened, the finely corded muscles along his strong jawbone clenching when he realised he had been caught staring. 'No,' he admitted on a rasping mutter.

At least he's being honest about it, Mia reflected ruefully. And so he should be, having spent the last month trying to get her into his bed!

'Then your only problem,' she went on coolly, 'is having to decide whether you want your lost island of Atlanta— or whatever it is called,' she mocked flippantly, 'badly enough to relinquish your single status to get it.'

'But it isn't just my single status I'm being tapped for, is it?' he threw back sourly.

'No,' she agreed, with another wry smile of appreciation at his wit, even in the face of all this horror. 'And you are going to have to…er…produce pretty potently, too, if you want this arrangement kept short-term.'

That had his gaze narrowing sharply on her studiedly impassive green eyes. He didn't like the tone of voice she had used but she didn't care that he didn't like it. She didn't *like* Alexander Doumas.

However, she would go to bed with him, if that was what it would take to get what she needed to gain from this dastardly deal.

'And what is the incentive that makes *you* agree to all of this?'

Mia didn't answer, wondering bleakly what his reaction would be if she told him the truth.

He was still standing by her father's drinks cabinet, his body tense and his expression tight with anger and contempt—for her, for himself, or even for both of them, she wasn't sure. And it really didn't matter because there was a whole lot more at stake here than his personal contempt—or even her own self-contempt, come to that.

Her father wanted a grandson to replace the son who had foolishly got himself killed in a car accident several months ago. Alexander Doumas had been chosen to father that grandson—Mia to be the vessel in which the poor child would be seeded.

This man's reasons for agreeing to any of this were based on his own personal ambitions. He wanted to get back the family island that lay somewhere off the Greek mainland, which his father had been forced to sell during the downfall of the family fortunes. Jack Frazier was the only person who could return it to him since he now owned the deeds to the island.

Mia, on the other hand, stood to gain far more than what amounted to a pile of ancient Greek rock. What was more, she was quite prepared to do anything to complete her side of the bargain she had made with her father.

'Like you, I get back something that once belonged to me,' she murmured eventually.

'Am I to be told what?'

Her eyes clouded over, her mind shooting off to some dark, dark place inside her that made her look so bleak and saddened it actually threatened to breach his bristling contempt.

Then her lashes flickered, bringing her eyes back into focus, and the bleak look was gone. 'No,' she replied, and rose to her feet. 'That, I'm afraid, is none of your business.'

'It is if we are going to be man and wife,' he claimed.

'And are we?' Mia raised her sleek brows in counterchallenge. 'Going to be man and wife?'

'Why me?' he asked suddenly. 'Why, if you did not make the selection yourself, did your father set me up for this?'

'Are you serious?' she gasped, her green eyes widening in scathing incredulity. 'Last week you virtually undressed me with your eyes right in front of him! The week before that you invited me to spend the weekend in Paris with you in front of a room full of people—including my father! And there wasn't a person present who misunderstood what your intentions were, Mr Doumas,' she informed him. 'You certainly were not offering to show the city sights to me!'

From the moment they'd met, he'd not even attempted to hide the attraction he felt for her!

'You set yourself up for it!' she told him. 'I tried to head you off, freeze you out as best as I could do in front of my father. I even told you outright at one point that you were playing with fire, coming anywhere near me! Did you take any notice?' Her green eyes flashed. 'Did you hell!' she snapped, ignoring the way his expression was growing darker the more she threw at him. 'You just smiled an amused little smile that told me you had the damned conceit to think I was playing hard to get with you—and kept on coming on to me!

'And I'll tell you something else,' she continued, while he stood there, stiff-backed and riveted to the spot by what she was tossing at him. 'Until you started pursuing me, you weren't even up for consideration for this deal! But as soon as my father saw the way you looked at me you went right to the top of his carefully collected short-list of men fit to father his precious grandson! So, if you need to blame someone for this predicament you now find yourself in, blame yourself,' she suggested. 'You looked at me, you wanted me, you were offered me—on my father's terms.'

'In other words, your father is really your pimp,' he hit back.

Oh, very good, Mia grimly acknowledged. She'd cut into him, and he had cut right back.

'If you prefer to think of your future wife as a whore, then fine,' she parried. 'Though what that makes you doesn't really bear thinking about.'

He jerked as if she'd stabbed him—and so he damn well should! He might not like what he was being dealt here, but it didn't mean he could ride roughshod over her feelings!

'As it happens,' she tagged on, simply to twist the knife, 'you also had to pass several other tests before you qualified. You were younger than the other candidates on my father's list, as well as being more physically attractive—which was an important factor when my father was creating his grandson and heir,' she explained. 'But, most important of all, your family has a reputation for conceiving male children.' There hadn't been a female born to the Doumas line this century.

'And, of course, you were hungrier than the rest, not only for me,' she emphasized, 'but for your precious island.' And, therefore, so much easier to capture than the rest, was the bit she kept to herself.

But he took it as said. She saw that confirmed as his mouth took on a wryly understanding twist.

'And what happens to this—grandson and heir once he arrives in this world?' he asked next. 'Does your father come and snatch him from your breast an hour after his birth and expect me to forget I ever sired him?'

'Good heavens, no.' To his annoyance, she laughed again. 'My father has a real abhorrence of children in any shape or form.' Despite the laugh, her own bitter experience showed gratingly through. 'He simply desires a male heir to leave all his millions to. A legitimate male heir,' she added succinctly. 'I am afraid I can't go out and just get one from anywhere, if that's what you were going to suggest next...'

It had been a half-question, which his shrug completely dismissed. 'I'm not a complete fool,' he drawled. 'I would not suggest anything of the kind to you when it would mean my losing what I aim to gain from this.'

'And the child would lose a whole lot more, when you think about it,' Mia pointed out, referring to the size of Jack Frazier's well-known fortune. 'But I get full custody,' she announced with a lift of her chin that said she expected some kind of argument about it. 'That is not up for negotiation, Mr Doumas. It is my own condition before I will agree to any of this, and will be written into that contract my father mentioned to you.'

'Are you saying that I will have no control at all over this child?' he questioned sharply.

'Not at all,' Mia said. 'You will have all the rights any man would expect over his own son—so long as we stay married. But once the marriage is over I get full custody.'

'Why?'

Now there was a good question, Mia mused whimsically.

'I mean,' he qualified when she didn't answer him immediately, 'since you are making it damned obvious to me that you are no more enthusiastic about all of this than I am, why should you demand full custody of a child you don't really want in the first place?'

'I will *love* it,' she declared, 'no matter what his beginnings. I will *love* this child, Mr Doumas, not resent him, not look at him and despise him for who and what he means to me.'

'And you think I will?'

'I know you will,' she said with an absolute certainty. 'Men like you don't like to be constantly faced with their past failures.' She'd had experience of men of his calibre, after all—plenty of it. 'And agreeing to this deal most definitely represents a failure to you. So I get full custody,' she repeated firmly. 'Once the marriage is dissolved you will receive all the visitation rights legally allowed to you— if you still want them by then, of course,' she added, although her tone did not hold any optimism.

His eyes began to flash—the only warning she got that she had ignited something potentially dangerous inside him before he was suddenly standing right in front of her.

Her spine became erect, her eyelashes flickering warily as he pushed his angry face close to hers. 'You stand here with your chin held high and your beautiful eyes filled with a cold contempt for me, and dare to believe that you know exactly what kind of man I am—when you do not know me at all!' he rasped. 'For my son...' His hands came up to grip her shoulders. '*My son*,' he repeated passionately, 'will be *my* heir also!'

And it was a shock. Oh, not just the power of that possessiveness for something which was, after all, only a means to an end to him, but the effect his touch was having on her. It seemed to strike directly at the very heart of her, contracting muscles so violently that it actually squeezed the air from her tightened chest on a short, shaken gasp.

'*My son* will remain under *my* wing, no matter who—or what—his mother is!' he vowed. 'And if that means

trapping us both into a lifelong loveless marriage, then so
be it!'

'Are we?' Despite his anger, his biting grip, the bitter
hatred he was making no effort to hide, Mia's beautiful,
defiant eyes held his. 'Are we going to marry?'

His teeth showed, gleaming white and sharp and disturbingly predatorial between the angry stretch of his lips, his
eyes like hard black pebbles that displayed a grinding distaste for both herself and the answer he was about to give
her.

'Yes,' he hissed with unmasked loathing. 'We will
marry. We will do everything expected of us to meet your
father's filthy terms! But don't,' he warned, 'let yourself
think for a moment that it is going to be a pleasure!'

'Then get your hands off me.' Coldly, she swiped his
hands away. 'And don't touch me again until it is absolutely necessary for us to touch!'

With that she turned and walked back to the window
where she stood, glaring outside at the lashing rain, while
she tried to get a hold on what was straining to erupt inside
her.

It didn't work. She could no more stop the words from
flowing than she could stop the rain outside from falling.
'You seem to think you have the divine right to stand there
and be superior to me. But you do not,' she muttered. 'You
have your price, just like the rest of us! Which makes you
no better than my father—no better than myself!'

'And what exactly is your price?' he challenged grimly.
'Give me one good reason why you are agreeing to all of
this and I might at least try to respect you for it!'

It was an appeal. An appeal that caught at her heart because, even through his anger, Mia could hear his genuine
desire for her to give him just cause for her own part in
this.

Her green eyes flashed then filmed over, as for a moment—for a tiny breathless space in time—the sheer

wretched truth to that question danced on the very edge of her tongue.

But she managed to smother the feeling, bite that awful truth down and keep it back, then spun to face him with her eyes made opaque by tears that had turned to ice.

'Money, of course,' she replied. 'What other price could there be?'

'Money...' he repeated, as though she had just confirmed every avaricious suspicion he'd held about her.

'On the day I present my father with a grandson I receive five million pounds as payment,' she went on. 'No better reason to agree to this—no worse than a man who can sell himself for a piece of land and a pile of ancient stone.'

He wasn't slow—he got her meaning. She was drawing a neat parallel between the two of them—or three people if she counted her father's willingness to give away a Greek island to get what he wanted out of this rotten deal.

'So make this a marriage for life if it suits you,' she defied him. 'I don't care. I will be wealthy in my own right and therefore independent of you no matter how long the marriage lasts! But we will soon know how strong your resolve is,' she added derisively, 'once the marriage is real and your sense of entrapment begins to eat away at you!'

'Entrapment?' he picked up on the word and shot it scornfully back at her. 'You naïvely believe I will feel trapped by this marriage? That I am prepared to change a single facet of my life to accommodate you or the vows we will make to each other?'

It was his turn to discharge a disdainful laugh, and Mia's turn to stiffen as his meaning began to sink in. 'I will change nothing!' he vowed. 'Not my way of life or my freedom to enjoy it wherever the mood takes me!'

His eyes were ablaze, anger and contempt for her lancing into her defiant face.

'I have a mistress in Athens with whom I am very happy,' he announced, using words like ice picks that he thrust into her. 'She will remain my mistress no matter what I have to do to fulfil my side of this filthy bargain! I will not be discreet.' he warned. 'I will not make any concessions to your pride while you live with me as my so-called wife! I will hate and despise you—and bed you with alacrity at regular intervals until this child of the devil is conceived, after which I will never touch you again!

'But,' he added harshly, 'if you truly believe I will also let you walk away with that child then you are living in a dream world because I will not!'

'Then the deal is off,' Mia instantly retaliated, using her father's tactics to make her own point.

After all, he hadn't given in to the big one—namely, agreeing to marry her and produce Jack Frazier's grandchild in what amounted to cold blood—without being desperate! And she would have her way in this if only because she had to glimpse some light at the end of this long dark tunnel or she knew she would not survive.

'Try telling your father that,' he derided, his eyes narrowing as her cheeks went white. 'You are afraid of him. I saw that from the first moment I set eyes on you.'

'And you want what only he can give you *more* than you want a child!' Mia countered. 'So I am telling *you* that you agree to my having full custody or the deal is off! This may also be a good moment for me to remind you of the shortlist of other names waiting to be called upon at a moment's notice,' she added, playing what she saw as her trump card.

To her immense satisfaction, his handsome face fell into harsh lines of raw frustration. 'You are as cold-blooded about this as your damned father!' he spat at her in disgust.

Mia said nothing, her chin up and eyes cool, her defiance in the face of his disdain so palpable it could almost be tasted in the air between them. Air that seemed to sing with enmity, picking at her flesh and tightening her throat as she watched him turn and stride angrily for the door.

'I will speak to my lawyers,' he said in a clipped voice

as he reached it, 'and let you know tomorrow what I decide.'

'F-fine,' Mia said, not quite managing to hide the sudden tremor of anxiety in her voice.

He heard it, and read it for exactly what it was. 'Your father is going to be bloody furious with you for not clinching this here and now, isn't he?' he taunted.

She merely shrugged one finely sculptured shoulder. 'My father knew my requirements before you arrived here. Why else do you think he left us alone like this when he actually had you so nicely caught in the bag?'

Take that, you nasty swine, she thought, her eyes gleaming with her own contempt.

One set of long, brown, lean fingers was gripping the brass doorhandle in preparation to open the door, but that final taunt had them sliding away again, and on a quiver of real alarm, which made her spine warily straighten, Mia watched him turn and begin to walk slowly towards her. Her heart began to hammer, her tongue cleaving to the dry roof of her mouth as he came to a halt mere inches away.

He was tall—taller than herself by several daunting inches. It meant she had to tilt her chin to maintain that most necessary eye-to-eye contact bitter adversaries always used as a weapon on each other.

His eyes were black, hard and narrowed, the finger he used to stroke a feather-light caress down the arched column of her throat an electric provocation that had her teeth gritting behind the firm set of her lips as she fought to stop herself from flinching away from him.

'You know...' he murmured, super-light, super-soft, 'you are in real danger of provoking me one step too far. I wonder why that is?'

'I d-don't know what you're talking about,' she said tremulously, feeling that trailing finger make its electrifying journey back up her throat again.

'No?' he said quizzically.

Then he showed her exactly what he meant as that taunting finger suddenly became a hand that cupped her jaw then tilted her head as his mouth came down to capture hers.

It was not a passionate kiss or even a punishing one. He simply crushed her slightly parted lips against his own, tasted her, using his tongue to lick a lazy passage along the vulnerable curve of her mouth, then straightened, his eyes still like dark glass as they gazed into her own rather startled ones.

'W-why did you do that?' she gasped.

'Why do you think?' he replied mockingly. 'I wanted to know if I would taste the acid that drips constantly from your lips. It wasn't there,' he softly confided. 'In fact, you tasted so sweet I think I will have to taste you again...'

And he did, that warning all she had before he was crushing her lips again, only this time his exploring tongue was sliding sinuously along the edge of her own, and as she released a protesting gasp his free hand snaked round her waist and pulled her against the long lean length of his body—a body she could feel already tightening with an arousal that actually shocked her.

But what shocked her more was the way her own senses went absolutely haywire, slinging out all kinds of demands that had her simmering from head to toe. The static-packed build-up of sensual excitement set her quivering all over and it was an effort not to give in.

What was the matter with her? she wondered deliriously. She didn't even like this man!

Yet she was on fire already, and she had to admit he was good. He seduced her mouth with an expertise that had her groaning, the splay of his hands across her body holding her trapped so he could move against her in a blatant demonstration of what the friction between their two bodies was doing to him.

To her horror, her own inner thighs began to pulse in hungry answer, her mouth quivered, her breathing quickened and her hands came up to cling to his shoulders as, on another helpless groan, her defences finally collapsed, and she was kissing him back with a passion that held her totally captivated.

It was raw and it was hot and it was so utterly basic that his deep-throated laugh of triumph against her clinging mouth had to be the worst humiliation she had ever experienced.

'Now this is a surprise,' he murmured silkily as he drew away. 'I knew our sparring was arousing me, but I did not realise it was having the same effect upon you. That adds a little spice to my final decision, does it not?'

Mia took a shaky step backwards, her trembling fingers falling from his shoulders and her cheeks blooming with shock and a dreadful consternation.

'Lie back and mentally switch off?' He mocked her earlier remark 'I think you will be doing a whole lot more than that, Mia Frazier.'

'I never said I was frigid,' she shot back stiffly.

'But your father must think you are or why else does he believe he has to pay to get a man to bed you?'

'Not just any man, but the man of his own choice!' Her chin was up again and, despite the quivers still shaking her body, her eyes still managed to spit out defiance. 'Please remember that while you make your decision—you are not my personal choice. I am simply willing to do anything for that five millions pounds.'

Which was about as good as a slap in the face for him. He stepped right away from her, his expression so utterly disgusted that she almost—almost—wished the words unsaid.

'I will call you with my decision tomorrow,' he said abruptly as he moved back to the door.

'It's my father you will be dealing with, not me.'

'You,' he repeated. 'I will deal personally with *you*. Your father will be dealt with through my lawyers.'

CHAPTER TWO

MIA was staring out of the study window again when her father entered the room. She had just watched Alexander Doumas take off down the driveway with enough angry force to forge a vacuum through the storm still raging outside. There were tears in her eyes, though she didn't know why—unless those tears had something to do with the awful person she had been forced to play here today who bore no resemblance to the real Mia Frazier.

'Well, how did it go?'

'He has until tomorrow to agree to my terms or the deal is off,' she replied, without bothering to turn.

In the small silence that followed she sensed her father's frown of irritation. 'Don't spoil this for me, Mia,' he warned her very grimly, 'or you will be spoiling it for yourself.'

'I was taught by an expert.' Mia's smile was bleak. 'He will come around to my way of thinking simply because he has no choice.'

'Neither do you.'

'He doesn't know that, though.'

'Ah.' Jack Frazier lowered himself into the chair behind his desk with a sigh of satisfaction. 'You didn't tell him.'

'You warned me not to.'

'So, what does he think I am holding up as your incentive to agree to all of this?'

'I get five million pounds from you on the day I produce your grandson,' she informed him.

'Five million?' he grimaced. 'A nice round figure.'

'I thought so, too,' Mia agreed. 'It makes me a really expensive whore, don't you think?'

'You've always been a whore, darling,' Jack Frazier murmured insultingly. 'Expensive or cheap, a whore is still a whore. Tell Mrs Leyton I'm ready for some coffee now that the Greek has gone.'

Just like that. His low opinion of her stated, he was now calmly changing the subject.

Moving over to the desk, Mia lifted the internal phone which would connect her to the kitchen and held tightly locked inside herself the few choice replies that rattled around her brain regarding this man whom she was so ashamed to have to call her father.

Which was why neither Jack Frazier nor Alexander Doumas would ever have any control over her son. They could lay legal claims as mere blood relatives—she didn't mind that. They could even leave him every penny they possessed when they both decided to make this world a better place by leaving it.

But they would not have any control over who and what her son grew into. She already had in her possession her father's written agreement to that. And when tomorrow came she would be getting the same written agreement from Mr Doumas.

And how could she feel so sure about that? Because she had his measure. She had watched her father carefully mark it when he got the arrogant Greek to agree to any of this in the first place. If Alexander Doumas was prepared to wed and bed a woman just to get his hands on his old family pile then he would give away his first-born child also.

'If he surprises us both and doesn't give in to your terms,' her father posed quietly, 'what will you do then?'

'Wait until you come up with someone who will agree.'

His eyes began to gleam. 'The next on the list is Marcus Sidcup,' he reminded her silkily. 'Can you honestly bring yourself to let him touch you, Mia?'

Marcus Sidcup was a grotesque little man several years

older than her father who turned her stomach every time she set eyes on him. 'I'm a whore,' she replied. 'Whores can't be too picky. I'll close my eyes and think nice thoughts, like what to wear at your funeral.'

He laughed. Her opinion of him had never mattered simply because she didn't matter to him, the main reason being that she reminded him too much of his dead wife's many infidelities. Her brother Tony's conception had been just as suspect as her own, but because he had been male her father had been willing to accept him as his own. Mia being female, though, her paternity was an entirely different matter.

'If all goes well with Mr Doumas tomorrow,' she tossed in as a mere aside, 'I intend to go and visit Suzanna at school. She will need to know why I won't be around much for the next year or so.'

'You will tell her only what she needs to be told.' her father commanded sharply.

'I'm not a complete fool,' Mia replied. 'I have no wish to raise her hopes, but neither do I want her to think that I've deserted her.'

'She will be making no trips to visit you in Greece, either,' Jack Frazier warned her, 'so don't go all soft and try to placate her with promises that I might agree to it because I will not.'

Mia never for one moment thought that he would. Her eyes bleak and her heart aching for that small scrap of a seven-year-old who had seen even less of this man's love than she herself had, she walked out of the room before she was tempted to say something really nasty.

She couldn't afford to be nasty. She couldn't afford to get her father's back up, not when she was this close to achieving her own precious dream.

And she couldn't afford to lose Alexander Doumas either, she admitted heavily to herself, because no matter how much she despised him for being what he was he was her best option in this deal she had made with her father.

Pray to God he was as hungry as her father claimed he was, was the final thought she allowed herself to have that day on the subject.

The call came early the next morning just as Mia was emerging from her usual twenty laps of their indoor swimming pool. Mrs Leyton came to inform her that a Mr Doumas was waiting to speak to her on the phone. Wringing the water out of her hair as she walked across the white tiles, she went to the pool phone extension and picked up the receiver.

'Yes?' she said coolly.

'Yes,' he threw right back with a grim economy of words that showed every bit of his angry distaste. 'Be here at my offices at noon,' he commanded. 'My lawyers will have something ready for you to sign by then.'

Click. The phone went dead. Mia stood and grimaced at the inert piece of plastic, then ruefully replaced it on its wall rest.

At noon exactly she presented herself in the foyer of the very luxurious Doumas Corporation. Dressed in a severely tailored black pin-striped wool suit and plain white blouse, she looked the epitome of cool business elegance with her long, silky, copper hair neatly contained, as usual, in a knot high on her head and her make-up as understated as everything always was about her.

But, then, Mia Frazier did not need to make dress statements to look absolutely stunning. She was tall and incredibly slender, with legs so long that even a conservative knee-length skirt couldn't diminish their sensational impact.

Her skin was wonderful, so clear and smooth and white that it made the ocean greenness of her eyes stand out in startling contrast and the natural redness of her small heart-shaped mouth look lush and inviting and unwittingly sensual.

Add to all of that the kind of feminine curves that promised perfection beneath the severe clothing, and men stopped and stared when she walked into a room—as if they could recognise by instinct that beneath the cloak of cool reserve hid an excitingly sensual woman.

Alexander Doumas had been one man who had looked and instinctively seen her like that. One evening, a month ago, he had been standing with a group of people at a charity function when Mia had walked into the room on her father's arm.

He had been aware of who she was, of course, and who her father was, and how important Jack Frazier was to his reasons for being in London at all. But, still, he had taken one look at Jack's beautiful daughter and had made the most colossal tactical error of his life, by deciding he would like to mix business with a bit of pleasure.

It had been his downfall, which was how Mia liked to remember that moment. He had seen, he had desired and had done nothing whatsoever to hide that desire from either herself or her watching father. Maybe he had even seen his own actions as a way to ingratiate himself with Jack Frazier. Flatter the daughter to impress the father—that kind of thing—she had never really been sure.

Whatever, he had signed his own death warrant that very same evening when he had detached himself from his friends so he could come and introduce himself to Jack Frazier. His words might have been directed at her father but his eyes had all but consumed Mia.

In her own defence, Mia had tried to head him off before he had sunk himself too deeply into her father's clutches. She'd remained cool, aloof, indifferent to every soft-voiced compliment he had paid her—had tried to freeze him out when he wouldn't be frozen out.

For her own reasons. Alexander Doumas was one of the most attractive men she had ever laid eyes on, but for what she already knew her father was planning for her the Greek was just too much of everything. Too young, too dynamic, too sensually charismatic. Too obviously used to handling power, and just too confident in his own ability to win—both in the boardroom and the bedroom.

She needed a weaker man, a man with less of an aura of strength about him—a man with whom she could carry out her father's wishes and then walk away, spiritually unscathed, once the dastardly deal was done.

She certainly did not need a man who could make her heart race just by settling his lazily admiring dark eyes on her, or one whose lightest touch on her arm could make her flesh come alive with all kinds of unwanted sexual murmurings. A man whose voice made her toes curl and whose smile rendered her breathless. In other words, a man with all the right weapons to hurt her. She had been hurt enough in her life by men of Alexander Doumas's calibre.

She'd tried very hard to freeze him out during the last few weeks when her father made sure they were thrown together at every opportunity, but the stupid, stubborn man refused to be pushed away.

Now he was paying the consequences—or was about to pay them, Mia amended as she paused just inside the foyer.

The Doumas name had once been connected exclusively with oil and shipping, but since Alexander Doumas had taken over the company had diversified into the far more lucrative business of holidays and leisure. Now the name was synonymous with all that was the best and most luxurious in accommodation across the world. Their hotel chain and fleet of holiday cruise liners were renowned for their taste and splendour.

And all in ten years, Mia mused appreciatively as she set herself moving across the marble floor towards the reception desk. Before that the Doumas family had been facing bankruptcy and, from what her father had told her, had only just managed to stave it off by selling virtually everything they possessed.

Alexander Doumas had managed to hang on to one

cruise liner and a small hotel in Athens, which no one had actually known the family owned until he had begun to delve into their assets.

But that one cruise liner and hotel had been all that had been needed for the man to begin the rebuilding of an empire. Now he had by far outstripped what the family had once had, and the only goal left in his corporate life was regaining the family island.

Quite how her father had come by the island Mia had no idea. It was his way, though, to pick the bones clean of those in dire straits. He bought at rock-bottom prices from the absolutely desperate then moved in his team of business experts, who would pull the ailing company back into good health before he sold it on for the kind of profit that made one's hair curl.

Some things he didn't bother to sell on—like the house they lived in now, which he'd acquired for a snip from a man who'd lost everything in the last stockmarket crash. Jack Frazier had simply moved into it himself as it was in one of the most prestigious areas of London. The yacht and the plane had been acquired the same way, and of course the tiny Greek island that he'd held onto because—whatever else her father was that she hated and despised—he was astute.

He would have watched Alexander Doumas begin to rebuild the family fortunes. He would have known that the proud Greek would one day want his island back, and he had simply waited until the price was right for him to offer it back.

'I am here to see Mr Doumas,' Mia informed the young woman behind the reception desk. 'My name is Mia Frazier.'

'Oh, yes, Miss Frazier.' The girl didn't even need to glance down at the large appointment book she had open in front of her. 'You'll need to take the lift to the top floor, where someone will meet you.'

With a murmured word of thanks, Mia moved off as gracefully as always, and so well controlled that no one would have known how badly her insides were shaking or that her throat was tight with a mixture of dread and horror at what she was allowing herself to walk into. Yet, abhor herself as she undoubtedly did, her footsteps did not falter nor did her resolve. The stakes were too high and the rewards at the end of it too great to allow any room for doubt.

She walked into a waiting lift and pressed the button for the top floor without a pause. She kept her chin firm and her teeth set behind steady lips as she took that journey upwards, her clear green eyes fixing themselves on the framed water-colour adorning the back wall of the lift.

It was a painting of the most beautiful villa, set on the side of a hill and surrounded by trees. The walls were white, the roof terra-cotta and the garden a series of flower strewn terraces sweeping down to a tiny bay where a primitively constructed old wooden jetty protruded into deeper, darker waters and a simple fishing boat stood tied alongside it.

What really caught her interest was the tiny horseshoe-shaped clearing in a cluster of trees to the left of the house. It seemed to be a graveyard. She could just make out the shapes of simple crosses amongst a blaze of colourful flowers.

A strange detail to put in such a pretty picture, she mused frowningly. *Vision* it was simply titled. Whose vision? she wondered. That of the man she was here to see or the artist who had painted it?

'Miss Frazier?'

The slightly accented cool male voice brought her swinging round to discover in surprise that not only had the lift come to a stop without her realising it, but the doors had opened and she was now being spoken to by a tall, dark, olive-skinned stranger. A stranger who was eyeing her so coldly that she had to assume he knew exactly why she was here today.

'Yes,' she confirmed, with a tilt of her chin that defied his right to judge her.

Something flashed in his eyes—surprise at her clear challenge? Or maybe it was more basic than that, she suggested to herself as she watched his dark eyes dip in a very male assessment of her whole body, as if he had some kind of right to check her out like a prime piece of saleable merchandise!

Which is exactly what you are, Mia reminded herself with her usual brutal honesty.

'And you are?' she countered in her crispest, coldest upper-class English, bringing those roving eyes flicking back up to clash with the clear green challenge reflected in her own.

His ears darkened. It was such a boyish response to being caught, blatantly staring, that she almost found it in her to laugh. Only… It suddenly hit her that there was something very familiar about this young man's features.

'I am Leonadis Doumas,' he informed her. 'My brother is this way, if you would follow me…'

Ah, the brother. She smiled a rueful smile. No wonder he looked familiar. The same eyes, the same physique—though without the same dynamic impact as his brother. Perhaps he was more handsome in a purely aesthetic way but, by the way his colour remained heightened as she followed him towards a pair of closed doors, she judged he lacked his brother's cool sophistication.

Leonadis Doumas paused, then knocked lightly on one of the closed doors, before pushing it open, and Mia used that moment to take a deep breath to prepare herself for what was to come next.

It didn't help much, and a fresh attack of nerves almost had her turning to run in the opposite direction before this thing was taken right out of her hands.

But, as she had told Alexander Doumas only yesterday, her father did not deal in uncertainties. He knew she would go ahead with this, just as he had known that Alexander Doumas would go ahead with it, no matter how much it made him despise himself.

Leonadis Doumas was murmuring something in Greek. Mia heard the now-familiar deep tones of his brother in reply before the younger man stepped aside to let her pass him.

She did so reluctantly, half expecting to find herself walking into a room full of grey-suited lawyers. Instead, she found herself facing the only other person present in the room. Alexander was sitting at his desk, with the light from the window catching the raven blackness of his neatly styled hair.

Behind her the door closed. She glanced back to find that Leonadis had gone. Mia's stomach muscles clenched into a tight knot of tension as she turned back to face the man with whom—soon—she was going to have to lie and share the deepest intimacy.

'Very businesslike,' he drawled. 'I believe it's called power dressing. But I feel I should warn you that it's lost on me.'

Startled by the unexpected choice of his first attack, Mia glanced down at her severely tailored suit, with its modest-length skirt and prim white blouse, and only then realised that he had completely misinterpreted why she was dressed like this.

Not that it mattered, she decided as her chin came back up and she levelled her cool green eyes on him. She had dressed like this because she was going on to Suzanna's very strict boarding school directly from here, where strait-laced conservatism was insisted upon from family and pupils alike.

'When you marry me,' he went on, 'I will expect something more...womanly. I find females in masculine attire a real turn-off.'

'*If* I marry you,' Mia corrected, and made herself walk forward until only the width of his desk was separating them. 'Your brother looks like you,' she observed as a mere aside.

For some reason, the remark seemed to annoy him. 'Wondering if your father tapped the wrong brother?' he asked. 'Leon is nine years younger than me, which places him just about in your own age group, I suppose. But he is also very much off-limits, as far as you are concerned,' he added with a snap that made his words into a threat.

'I have no inclination to so much as touch him,' she countered, smiling slightly because she knew then that big brother must have noticed and correctly interpreted the reason his younger brother was looking so warm about the ears. 'Though, you never know,' she couldn't resist adding, 'it may be worth my while to look into whether he would be a better bet than you before I commit myself.'

Again there was the hint of anger. 'Leon is already very much married to a wonderful creature he adores,' he said abruptly. 'Which makes him of absolutely no use to you.'

'Ah, married.' She sighed. 'Shame. Then it looks as if you will have to do.'

With that little ego-deflater, she lowered herself into a chair and waited for his next move.

To her surprise, his mouth twitched, appreciation for her riposte suddenly glinting in his eyes. He was no one's fool. He knew without vanity that he was a better, more attractive, more sensually appealing man than his younger, less dynamic brother.

'A contract my lawyers have drawn up this morning,' he announced, reaching out with a long fingered hand for a document of several pages which he slid across the desk towards her. 'I suggest you read that thoroughly before you sign it.'

'I have every intention of doing so,' she said, picking up the contract. She proceeded to ignore him while she immersed herself in its detail.

It was a comprehensive document, which set out point by point the guidelines by which this so-called marriage of theirs would proceed. In a way, Mia supposed the first part read more like a prenuptial agreement than a business contract, with its declarations on how small an allowance he would be giving her on a monthly basis and what little she could expect from him if the marriage came to an end—which was a pittance, though she wasn't surprised by that.

The man believed she would be a wealthy woman in her own right once all this was over. It suited her to continue to let him go on thinking that way so she didn't care that he was offering her nothing.

It was only on the third page that things began to get nasty. She would live where he wanted her to live, it stipulated. She would sleep where he wanted her to sleep. If she went out at all she would never do so without one of his designated people as a companion.

She would be available at all times for sex on his demand...

Mia felt his eyes on her, following, she was sure, line by line as she read. Her cheeks wanted to redden, but she refused to allow them to, her lips drawing in on themselves because it seemed so distasteful to add such a clause when, after all, they were only marrying because of the sex, which was necessary to make babies.

She would conduct herself at all times in a way which made her actions as his wife above reproach, she grimly read on. She would not remark on his own personal life outside their marriage, and she accepted totally that he intended to maintain a mistress...

The fact that several slick lawyers were privy to all of this, as well as the person who had typed it, made her want to cringe in horror.

In anticipation of her falling pregnant, she would not step off Greek soil without his permission during her pregnancy. The child must be born in Greece and registered as Greek. In the event of the marriage irretrievably breaking down, yes, she would get full custody of their child, she was relieved to read.

Then came his own proviso to that concession, and it made her heart sink. It had to be *his* decision that the marriage must end. If Mia walked out on the marriage of her own volition then she did so knowing she would be forfeiting full custody...

'I can't agree to that,' she protested.

'You are not being given a choice,' he replied, leaning back in his chair yet reading with her word for word of the contract. 'I did warn you that I would not relinquish control of my own son and heir. I have the right to safeguard myself against that contingency, just as you have the right to safeguard yourself against my walking out on you. So it is covered both ways by that particular clause.

'If I decide I cannot bear having you as my wife any longer, then I get rid of you, knowing I will be relinquishing all rights to our child. If you decide the same thing then you, too, will relinquish all rights over him. I think that is fair, don't you?'

Did she? She had a horrible feeling she was being scuppered here, though the logic of his argument gave her no clue as to where. And, in the end, did it matter? she then asked herself. She had no intention of marrying any man ever again after this. If Alexander Doumas wanted to tie himself to this wife for life, let him.

'Is there anything else you want to add to this?' he asked, once she'd read the contract to the end without further comment.

Mia shook her head. Whatever she felt she needed to safeguard for herself would be done privately with her own lawyer in the form of a last will and testament.

Getting to her feet, she picked up her handbag. 'I'll let my father look at this then get back to you,' she informed him coolly.

'No.'

In the act of turning towards the door Mia paused, her neat head twisting to let her eyes clash with his for the first time since this interview had begun. Her heart stopped beating for a moment and her porcelain-like skin chilled at the uncompromising grimness she saw in those dark eyes.

'This is between you and me,' he insisted. 'Whatever is agreed between your father and myself—or even your father and yourself—will be kept completely separate from this contract. But you decide now and sign now or—to use your own words—the deal is off.'

'I would have to be a complete fool if I didn't get this checked out by someone professional before I put my signature to it,' she protested.

'You want a professional here? Give me the name of your lawyer and I will have him here in half an hour,' he said. 'But I think it only fair to warn you first that I refuse to alter one single word on that contract, no matter what advice he offers you. So...' A shrug threw the ball back into her court.

Well, Mia, what are you going to do? she asked herself as she stood, gazing at this man with his intractable expression that so reminded her of her father.

She shivered. He was contemptuous of who she was and what she was, indifferent to what she felt or even *if* she felt. He was ready, she was sure, to make her pay in every way he could, for bringing him down to this.

Oh, yes, she thought grimly. Just like her father. Every bit the same kind of man. Which made her wonder suddenly if that was why Jack Frazier had chosen Alexander Doumas in the first place. Was it because he saw in this man a more than adequate successor to himself as her tormentor?

'Are you at last beginning to wonder if five million pounds is worth the kind of purgatory you are about to embark upon if you marry me?' this particular tormentor prodded silkily.

'No,' she said, dropping both the contract and her handbag back onto the desk. 'I was merely trying to decide whether it was worthwhile calling your bluff,' she explained, 'but, since I have another pressing engagement, I've decided not to bother haggling with you. So...' Her chin came up, her green eyes as cool and as indifferent as they had ever been. 'Where do I sign?'

It took the whole of the long drive into Bedfordshire to pull her utterly ragged senses back into some semblance of calm because from the moment she'd agreed to sign his rotten contract the meeting had sunk to an all-time low in the humiliation stakes.

He hadn't liked her consigning him to second place behind whatever engagement she had, she knew that. It had been exactly why she had said it, hadn't it?

But what had come afterwards had made her wish she'd kept her reckless mouth shut. Punishment was the word that came to mind. He'd punished her by introducing her to the two lawyers he'd called in to witness their signatures as 'the woman who is this desperate to bear my child' as he'd tossed the contract towards them to sign.

It had been cruel and unnecessary but he hadn't cared. The way his hard eyes had mocked the hot colour that swept up her cheeks had shown he'd even enjoyed seeing her so discomfited.

Then had come the final humiliation once the lawyers had been dismissed again.

The kiss.

Her whole body quivered in appalled reaction, her lips still throbbing in memory of the ruthless way he had devoured them. He'd done it so cavalierly, coming around his desk in what she'd foolishly believed had been an intention to escort her politely to the door. What he'd actually done had been to reach out and pull her into his arms then capture her mouth with the same grim precision he had achieved the day before.

Only this time he had taken that kiss a whole lot further, Staking his claim, she realised now. Staking his claim on a piece of property he had just bought, by deepening the kiss with all the casual expertise of a man who knew exactly how to make a woman's senses catch fire at his will.

And she had caught fire—that was the truly humiliating part of it. She had just stood there in his arms and had gone up like a Roman candle! She'd quivered and groaned and clung to his mouth, as though her very survival had depended on it.

Where had her pride been? Her self-control? Her determination to remain aloof from him, no matter what he did to her?

What he did to you? her mind screamed jeeringly back at her. What about what you did to him?

'No…' The word escaped as a wretched groan from anguished lips, and she had to slow the car down because her vision was suddenly misted. Misted by terrible visions of her fingers clutching at him—at his nape, and his hair—holding him to her when she should have been pushing him away!

He'd muttered something—she could still hear that driven groan echoing inside her shell-shocked head. Could still feel the burning pressure of his body against hers, of buttons parting, of flesh preening to the pleasure of his touch and the sudden flare of a powerful male arousal, the crush of his arms as he'd pressed her even closer.

It had been awful. They'd devoured each other like hungry animals, so fevered by desire that when he'd suddenly let go of her she'd staggered backwards with flushed skin and dazed eyes, her pulsing mouth parted and gasping for

air as she'd stood there, staring blankly at him as he'd
swung away from her.

'Cover yourself,' he'd rasped.

A shudder of self-revulsion shot through her, making her
foot slip on the accelerator when she saw in her mind's eye
what he must have seen as he'd stood there, glowering at
her, with the desk once more between them.

Her jacket, her blouse—even her fine lacy bra—gaping
wide to reveal the fullness of her breasts in tight, tingling
distension!

'I can't believe you did that,' she whispered, turning her
back to him while useless fingers fumbled in their attempts
to put her clothing back in order.

'Why not?' he countered flatly. 'It is what you signed
up for.'

Humiliation almost suffocated her. 'I hate you,' she
choked.

'But I don't think you're going to find the sex a problem,
do you?'

Recognising her own taunt from yesterday being flung
right back at her, she shuddered again.

'Not surprising, really,' he continued remorselessly,
'when rumour has it that you were a bit of a raver in your
teens…'

Her teens? She went very still. The fact that he knew
about her wild teenage rebellion was enough to keep her
ready tongue locked inside her kiss-numbed mouth.

'Well, let's get one more thing straight before you leave
this room,' he continued very grimly. 'You will behave like
a lady while you belong to me. There will be no wild parties, no rave-ups. No sleeping around when the mood happens to take you.'

'I'm not like that.' She was constrained to defend herself.

'Now? Who knows?' he said derisively. 'While you are
married to me? No chance. I want to know that the child
you will eventually carry is my child,' he vowed, 'or you

will be wishing you'd never heard the name Doumas! Now, pull yourself together before you walk out of this room,' he concluded dismissively. 'We will marry in three days' time.'

'Three days?' she gasped, spinning round to stare at him. 'But—'

It was as far as she got. 'Three days,' he repeated. 'I see no reason to delay—especially when I know what a receptive little thing you're going to be in my bed,' he added silkily at her white-faced shock. 'The sooner we get this show on the road the sooner I get you pregnant, and you get your five million pounds and I get back what should be mine.'

He meant his island, of course. The stupid bit of Greek rock he was prepared to sell his soul for—or, at the very least, his DNA. The man had no concept of which was really more important. She could have told him, but she didn't.

In fact, she wanted him to go right on believing that his island was worth more to him than his DNA. That way she could finally beat him, which was really all that mattered to her.

The only thing she could do now was think ahead. A long way ahead to a time when—God willing—the awful man would grow tired of her and eventually let her go.

Suzanna was heart achingly pleased to see her. But the seven-year-old broke down and wept her heart out when Mia told her gently that she was going away for a while.

Pulling her onto her lap, she let the little girl weep herself dry. Heaven knew, there were too few moments when she could give her emotions free rein like this.

'It will only be for a year or two,' she murmured soothingly, 'and I will come and see you as often as I can.'

'But not like you do now,' the child protested, 'because Greece is a long, long way away! And it's going to mean that I will have to spend the school holidays alone with Daddy!'

The alarm that prospect caused the poor child cut deeply into Mia's heart. 'Mrs Leyton will be there for you,' Mia reminded her. 'You like her, don't you?'

'But I can't bear not having you there, too, Mia!' she sobbed. 'He h-hates me! You know he does because he hates you too!'

Mia sighed and hugged the child closer because she knew she couldn't even lie and deny the charge. Jack Frazier did hate them both. He had poured what bit of love he had ever had in him into their brother, Tony. With Tony gone, their father had just got more and more resentful of their very existence.

'Look,' she murmured suddenly out of sheer guilt and desperation, even though her father's warning was ringing shrilly in her ears, 'I promise to call you once a week so we can talk on the telephone.'

'You promise?' the child whispered.

'I promise,' Mia vowed.

She hugged the thin little body tightly to her because it wasn't fair—not to herself, not to Suzanna. May God forgive me, she prayed silently, for deserting her like this.

'I love you, my darling,' she whispered thickly. 'You are and always will be the most important thing in my life.'

She got back to the house after dark, feeling limp and empty.

'Your father's flown off to Geneva,' Mrs Leyton informed her. 'He said to tell you not to expect him back before you leave here. Why are you leaving here?'

The poor old lady looked so shocked that it took the very last dregs of Mia's strength to drag up another set of explanations. 'I'm going to be living in Greece for a year or two,' she said.

'With that Greek fellow that was here the other day?'

'Yes.' Her tired mouth tightened. 'We are—getting married,'

'And your father agrees?' Mrs Layton sounded stunned.

'He—arranged it,' Mia said, with a smile that wasn't a smile but more a grimace of irony. Then she added anxiously, 'You'll keep an eye on Suzanna for me, won't you, while I'm away?'

'You should be staying here to do that yourself,' the housekeeper said sternly.

'I can't, Cissy.' At last the tears threatened to fall. 'Not for the next year or so, anyway. Please don't quiz me about it—just promise me you'll watch her and keep my father away from her as much as you can!'

'Don't I always?' the housekeeper snapped, but her old eyes were shrewd. Mia had a suspicion that she knew exactly what was going on. 'That Greek chap has been on the telephone, asking for you, umpteen times today. He didn't sound very pleased that you weren't here to take his calls.'

'Well, that's his hard luck.' Mia dismissed Alexander Doumas and all he represented. 'I'm tired. I'm going to bed.'

'And if he rings again?'

'Tell him to leave a message then go to hell,' she said, walking away up the stairs and into her room where she stripped herself with the intention of having a shower. But it couldn't even wait that long and the next moment she had thrown herself down on her bed and was sobbing brokenly into her pillow, just as Suzanna had sobbed in her arms this afternoon.

CHAPTER THREE

'WHERE the hell have you been for the last three days?'

Mia's insides jumped, her eyes jerking sideways to skitter briefly over the dark-suited figure seated next to her in the car.

Alexander looked grim-faced and tense. She didn't blame him. She felt very much the same way herself, hence her jumping insides, because he had actually spoken to her directly for the first time since that dreadful marriage ceremony had taken place.

'I had things to do,' she replied, her nervous fingers twisting the unfamiliar gold ring that now adorned her finger.

'And I had things I needed to check with you,' he bit back.

'Mrs Leyton answered all your questions,' Mia parried coolly. Hadn't it occurred to him that she was the one who was having to uproot her whole life for this? He'd given her three days to do it in—three damn days!

But that hadn't been the real reason she had refused to accept any of his phone calls. She'd needed these last few days to get a hold on herself, to come to terms with what had erupted between them in his office.

It hadn't worked. She was still horrified by it all, frightened by it all.

'Well, fob me off like that again, and you won't like the consequences,' he muttered.

I already don't like them, she thought heavily, but just shrugged a slender shoulder and kept her gaze fixed firmly on the slowly changing scenery beyond the limousine window.

And it was strange, really, she mused, but here she sat, married to this man. He had kissed her twice, ruthlessly violated her sexual privacy once, had insulted her and shown her his contempt and disgust in so many ways during their two short interviews that it really did not bear thinking about. Yet during all of that, including the brief civil ceremony which had taken place this morning with no family present on either side, not even his own brother, Leon—which had acted as a clear message in itself to Mia—their eyes had barely ever clashed.

Oh, they'd looked at each other, she conceded drily. But it had been a careful dance as to when he looked or she looked, but they had not allowed themselves to look at the same time.

Why? she asked herself. Because neither of them were really prepared to accept that they were actually doing this It went so against the grain of civilised society that even the Greek in him must be appalled at the depths to which he had allowed himself to sink in the name of desire.

Not sexual desire but the desire for property.

'Why the smile?'

Ah, she thought, his turn to look at me. 'I was wondering if my father was enjoying a glass of champagne somewhere in Geneva,' she lied. 'Celebrating his success in getting us both this far.'

'He isn't in Geneva,' he said, watching impassively as her slender spine straightened. 'He has been staying with his mistress in Knightsbridge since I signed his bloody contract. I presume he wanted to keep out of your way in case you started asking awkward questions about what he actually got me to sign in the end.'

Her chin turned slowly, supported by a neck that was suddenly very tense, her wary eyes flickering over his face without really focusing before she lowered them again. There was something—something snake-like in the way he had imparted all that which made her feel slightly sick inside.

'The two of you can't possibly have agreed anything else to do with me without my say-so,' she declared rather shakily.

'True. We didn't.' He relieved her mind with his confirmation. 'But we did discuss the fact that you have a younger sister…'

Oh, no. She closed her eyes, her heart sinking to her stomach. Her father would not have told this man about Suzanna, surely?

'He wanted me to know what a bad influence you are on the child,' that hateful voice continued, while Mia's mind had shot off in another direction entirely. 'Therefore, while you are with me you are to have no contact with—Suzanna, isn't it? Apparently, you are very jealous of her and can, if allowed to, make her young life a misery…'

So that was how her father was playing it. Her eyes bleak and bitter behind her lowered lids, Mia pressed her lips together and said nothing. No contact with Suzanna would keep her striving to make the grandson her father wanted so badly. No contact with Suzanna was meant as a warning—do your job or forget all about her.

'Is that why he married you off to the highest bidder?' her new husband continued remorselessly. 'To get you right out of your sister's life?'

'You didn't bid for me—you were *bought!*' She hit back at him. 'For the specific purpose of producing my father's precious grandson! So, if the reputation for making sons in your family lets you down,' she finished shakily, 'make sure you don't blame me for the mistake!'

He should have been angry. Heavens, she'd said it all to make him angry! But all he did was huff a lazy laugh of pure male confidence.

'My mother had three sons and my grandmother five. I don't think I need worry on that score. And,' he added as he shifted his lean bulk to glance out of the car window, 'that was not the point I was trying to make. I was simply letting you know that I now know why your father was willing to pay you five million pounds to get you out of his life.'

'Plus a Greek island,' Mia added. 'Please don't forget the island—how much is that worth in cold, hard cash?'

His face hardened at the reminder, the link she was making between them so clear that even he, for all his arrogance, could not deny it was there.

'We have arrived,' he said, bringing an end to the conversation.

Sure enough, the car pulled to a stop and Mia looked out to find they had come to one of the private airfields just outside London. A gleaming white Gulfstream jet sat glinting in the weak winter sunlight, the Doumas logo painted in gold on its side.

Ten minutes after that Mia found herself ensconced in luxurious cream leather—alone.

Her new husband, she discovered, was apparently going to fly them wherever they were going. He disappeared into the cockpit the moment they boarded and she did not set eyes on him again until they landed—in Greece she had to assume because no one had bothered to inform her.

He came striding into the main cabin minus his jacket and silk tie. He looked different somehow, less formal, but all the more intimidating for it.

Male—that was the word that suddenly came to mind. He looked more aggressively male than he had done before. Once again she lowered her eyes before he could glimpse what she was thinking, and bent to pick up her jacket which she, too, had discarded during the flight.

So she didn't see the way his eyes narrowed on the firm thrust of her breasts, outlined by the close fit of her clinging white top. She didn't see those eyes dip lower, over her flat stomach to her slender thighs and then down over pale stockinged legs, before they made the same journey back up her face again.

'Where are we?' she asked, using the cover of fastening her jacket buttons.

'The island of Skiathos,' he told her. 'I have a villa here. It will, of course, be sold when I get back the family island,' he added stiffly.

The family island… Mia shuddered, swallowing on the thick dry lump that formed in her throat at the grim reminder of what this was all about for him.

Then he went on, in a completely different tone of voice, 'That green colour suits you,' he murmured huskily. 'It does something spectacular to your eyes.'

She was so disconcerted by the unexpected compliment that she just stared blankly at the mint green suit with its little fitted jacket and short straight skirt. She hadn't bought it for its colour, but out of respect for the icy winter weather back in London. The suit was made from pure cashmere with matching dyed fake fur collar and cuffs to the jacket.

'Thank you,' she replied, having to fight the rather pathetic urge to blush because he had said something nice to her.

A small silence fell, she wasn't sure why. The two of them stood there, seemingly imprisoned by it, she with her head lowered and he—well, she didn't know what he was doing because she didn't dare look. But the sudden tension between them was almost palpable. Then someone was opening the outer door of the plane and, thankfully, the strange tension was broken.

He left the aircraft first, obviously expecting her to follow. She did so reluctantly, to find another car was waiting for them at the bottom of the short flight of steps—a silver Mercedes.

The sun was shining and the air was much warmer than it had been back in England, but not so hot that she didn't appreciate the warm suit she was wearing.

Alexander was striding round to the driver's side of the car while their luggage was being stowed in the boot. Taking a deep breath, Mia stepped up to the passenger door and then, on a strange kind of compulsion, she paused to glance across the shimmering silver bonnet towards him.

And there it was—the first time that their eyes truly met. Her heart stopped, the breath squeezing painfully in her stilled lungs. He looked grim, those dark eyes frowning back at her with a resentment that utterly belied his earlier compliment.

He hated and despised her for bringing him down to this level. And, what was worse, she didn't even blame him. She hated and despised herself! So why should it hurt?

Yet it did. Of course it hurt. She had feelings, like anyone else! It was her eyes that dropped first, hiding the sudden sharp stab of pain she was experiencing—hiding the deep, dragging sense of self loathing with which she was having to live.

Heart-weary, she made herself get into the car. He didn't join her immediately. In fact, he remained standing out there for such a long, long time that Mia began to wonder if he had finally come to his senses and changed his mind about all of this. Eventually he appeared, folding his long body into the seat beside her.

He didn't look at her again, and she didn't look at him. The car began to move, and the atmosphere inside it was so thick you could almost suffocate in it. 'It isn't too late to stop this if you want to,' she heard herself whisper, hoping... Hoping for what? she asked herself.

'No,' he replied.

Relief washed through her because that, she realised bleakly, was what she'd been hoping he'd say. No matter how much she hated this she still wanted it—needed it. Needed him.

Her new surroundings were lush and green, with bright splashes of colour from a flush of very early blooming flowers. Give it another few months and the green would be baked brown by the heat of the sun, she mused sadly. The flowers would be mostly gone. It was Mother Nature's way of maintaining a balance—hours of unrelenting sunshine but at the expense of floral colour.

Was she destined to wilt along with the flowers as the months went by? she wondered. She had the feeling that that was exactly what she would do, living a life in an emotion-starved desert with this man.

So, what's new? She mocked her own maudlin fancy. You've been living just like that with your own father. Swapping one heartless despot for another isn't going to be that much of a hardship, is it?

They were travelling along a high, winding road with the sea to the left of them. They passed through tiny hamlets of whitewashed buildings, which would probably be alive with tourists in high season but were at present almost deserted. There was hardly anyone about, in fact. It was a point she dared to remark upon to the man beside her.

'Most people here spend their winters on the mainland,' he explained. 'There is work for them there out of season, and the weather here can be as cold as England sometimes. But in another couple of months the place will come alive again.'

'Is it a big island?' she asked curiously.

He shook his dark head. 'We have driven almost its full length already,' he said. 'The house is situated in the next bay.'

Five minutes later they were driving through the gates of what appeared to be a vast private property hidden from the road by a high wall flanked by tall shrubs and trees. The house itself nestled lower down so the only view she got of it was its red slate rooftop.

It was impossible to tell just how big it was, but as they dropped lower she counted six separate windows on the upper floor and four on the lower, split by a wide white arched double door in the centre of a veranda.

By the time they came to a halt at the veranda steps she had counted at least four men who could only have been security guards by the way they made themselves evident as the car pulled in each one of them in turn, giving an acknowledging flick of his hand before he slunk out of sight again.

'Well, this is it,' Alexander announced, leaning back in his seat as the car engine died into silence. 'Your new home for the duration.'

Mia made no comment—what could she say? Oh, how lovely? How enchanting? I'm sure I will be happy here? She knew for a fact he had no interest in making her happy.

Anyway, she was too busy stifling the fresh set of butterflies that were attacking her system, apprehension for what was in store for her next being their stimulus.

She opened her door and made herself climb out into the late afternoon sunshine. Once again Alexander took his time to do the same, remaining seated inside the car as though it gave him a chance to relax his cold features and let them show what he was really feeling.

Anger, mostly, she guessed, a bitter sense of resentment at her presence in his life, which was going to be her close companion for what he had called the duration.

The white entrance doors began to open. Mia stood, watching, as they swung wide and a short stocky woman stepped out, dressed in uniform grey.

Her expression was utterly impassive as she studied Mia for a few short seconds, then turned her attention away as Alexander Doumas uncoiled himself from the car. Then a smile of such incredible warmth lit the woman's rugged features that it made the comparison between welcome and no welcome with a hard, cruel alacrity.

She said something in Greek, and he replied in the same language as he strode up the steps towards her. They did not embrace, which killed Mia's suspicion that this woman might be his mother. Then they were both turning to gaze in her direction, and all warmth left both of them. Mia's chin came up accordingly, pride insisting she outface the enemy to her last breath.

'Come.' That was all he said, as if he were talking to a pet dog.

Come. Sucking back the wretched desire to tell him to go to hell, she walked around the car and up the steps with her clear green gaze fixed defiantly somewhere between the two of them.

'This is Elena,' she was informed. 'She is my house-keeper here. Anything you require you refer to her. Elena will show you to your room,' he added coolly. 'And get Guido to bring up your luggage. I have some calls to make.'

And he was gone. Without a second look in Mia's direction, he strode into the house and disappeared.

'This way, madam...' Surprising Mia with her nearly accent-free English, the housekeeper turned and led the way into the house.

It was warmer inside, with sunlight seeping in through silk-draped windows onto apricot walls and lovingly polished wooden floors and doors. The furniture was old, un-doubtedly antique, but solid, with a well used, well lived with look to it. Not what she would have expected of him somehow.

A highly polished wooden staircase climbed up the wall to the left of her, then swept right around the upper landing.

Elena led the way up and across the polished floor to a door directly opposite the stairs. She threw it open then stood back to allow Mia to move past her.

Her feet were suddenly sinking into a deep-piled oatmeal carpet, and her eyes drifted around soft lemon walls and white woodwork. Oatmeal curtains were caught back from the windows with thick lemon ropes.

'Your bathroom is to your right,' Elena informed her

coolly. 'The master's bedroom is through the door to your left.'

Separate bedrooms, then, Mia was relieved to note. 'Thank you,' she murmured, and forced herself to step further into the room.

Elena did not join her, instead remaining in the open doorway. 'My daughter, Sofia, will come and unpack for you. If you need anything tell her and she will tell me.'

In other words, don't speak to me yourself unless it is absolutely necessary, Mia ruefully assumed from that cold tone.

'Guido, my husband, will bring your luggage shortly,' the housekeeper continued. 'Dinner here is served at nine. Will you require some refreshment before then?'

And doesn't it just stick in your throat to offer it? Mia thought with a sudden blinding white smile that made the other woman's face drop at the sheer unexpectedness of it.

'Yes,' she said lightly. 'I require a large pot of coffee, milk—not cream—to go with it and a plate of sandwiches—salad, I think. Thank you, Elena. Now you may go.'

The woman's face turned beetroot red as she stepped back over the threshold, then pulled the door shut with a barely controlled click. Almost immediately Mia wilted, the stress of maintaining this level of indifference towards everyone taking the strength out of her legs so that she almost sank shakily into the nearest chair.

Right in the very midst of that telling little weakness she sucked in a deep breath, straightening her shoulders and grimly defying it. She had many long months of this to put up with, and if she started turning into a quivering wreck at each new obstacle she wouldn't stay the course.

With that now aching chin held high again, she turned to view the room in general. It was large and light and airy, with two full-length windows standing open to a light breeze beyond. Appropriate furniture stood around the room—a couple of oatmeal upholstered bedside chairs and a small matching sofa scattered with pale lemon cushions. A large dark wood wardrobe stood against the wall opposite the windows, a dressing-table against another, and a tall chest of drawers. Her eyes kept moving, picking out occasional tables and table lamps sitting on lace doilies to protect the polished wood—all very old-fashioned and reminiscent of a different era when tender loving care was poured into furniture like this in the form of beeswax, which she could smell in the air.

And then, of course, there was the bed.

Gritting her teeth, Mia made herself turn and face her major fear. The bed was huge, standing in pride of place between the two open windows, its heavily carved head- and footboards suggesting that the bed was antique. The sheets were white and folded back neatly over a pale lemon bedspread, the headboard piled with snowy white pillows.

Her heart stopped beating, her stomach muscles contracting with dread as she stood there staring at it. She made herself imprint the image of two heads on those snowy white pillows—one dark and contemptuous but grimly determined, the other red-gold and frightened but resolutely defiant.

She shuddered suddenly, realising that contempt and defiance were not going to make good bed partners. Contempt and mute submission would be a far less volatile mixture, she told herself in an attempt at wry mockery.

It didn't work. In fact, there wasn't even the merest hint of the usual mockery that she relied on so much to keep her going.

Oh, hell, she thought heavily, and moved around the bed to go and went to open one of the windows, her lungs pulling in short tugs of clean fresh air in an effort to dispel the ever-present sense of dread—a dread that was drawing nearer with every passing hour.

There was a pretty view outside, she noted in a deliberate

snub to those other grim thoughts. Carefully attended gardens rolled down towards a shallow rock face, but she couldn't see a beach or any obvious way down the cliff to the sea below.

But there was a glass-walled swimming pool glinting off to the left of her, which cheered her up a bit because at least the temperature was mild enough to allow her to take her usual exercise while she was stuck here. Further out, she could see the misted bulk of several other islands not very far away. It made her wish she'd had the foresight to ask where he was bringing her so she could have bought herself a map and acquainted herself with what she was seeing out there.

Then another thought hit her, making a connection that she should have made ages ago. For this was Skiathos, and Skiathos belonged to the Sporades group of islands. The island her father owned was also in the Sporades group. She could actually be looking at her new husband's dream, without actually knowing it.

Suddenly she felt surrounded by reminders of what she was here for. The island. The bed. The isolation in which she was supposed to fulfil her part of the bargain.

Her blood ran cold and she shivered, any pleasure she had experienced because of the beauty of her new surroundings spoiled for ever. She turned away from the window, from the islands, from the bed, and walked straight into the bathroom.

She needed a shower, she decided grimly—needed to soak the tension out of her body with warmth. She had to keep herself together because this was the beginning, not the end, of it.

Guido had arrived with her luggage while she was still in the bathroom and Sofia was there when Mia eventually came back to the bedroom, wrapped in a white terry bathrobe she had found hanging on the bathroom door and with her hair hidden beneath a turban-wrapped towel.

Sofia's glance was very guarded. 'I bring food,' she said in badly broken English, 'and have unpacked for you.'

'Thank you.' No smile was offered so none was returned.

The girl left and Mia moved over to the tray set on a low table beside the sofa. The coffee was too strong and the crusty bread sandwiching the salad too thickly cut for her to have any hope of swallowing it past that lump that was still constricting her throat. Luckily, someone had had the foresight to place a pitcher of iced water on the tray with the coffee so she contented her thirst with that and picked the salad off the bread.

By the time she had finished she felt suddenly and utterly bone-weary. Despite her long shower, the strain of it all was still dragging at her muscles and she could now feel the dull throb of a tension headache coming on.

With a heavy sigh, she at last did what her brain and her body had been pleading with her to do since she'd arrived here. She got up and walked over to that dreaded bed, threw herself face downwards across it and simply switched off.

For the next few blissful hours Mia was aware of nothing, not the day slowly closing in around her or the towel turban slowly uncoiling itself from her head then sliding lazily to the carpet—trailing her hair along with it so the long silken strands spilled over the edge of the bed like a wall of fire lit by the glowing sunset.

When she did eventually come awake she did so abruptly, not sure what had woken her but certain that something had. Her eyes flicked open, her senses coming to full alert and setting her flesh tingling.

She continued to lie there for a few more seconds, listening intently to the silence surrounding her, then something brushed against her cheek and on a strangled gasp she rolled over—and found herself wedged up against a hard male body that was reclining beside her. Alexander's dark head was casually propped up on the heel of one hand.

'I wondered how long your hair was,' he remarked idly. 'Now I know…'

It was then she realised that he was gently fondling a silky skein of her hair. Her scalp was tingling, as well as her cheek, as if he'd teasingly brushed the lock of hair across it.

It must have been his touch that had woken her. 'W-what are you doing here?' she demanded unsteadily.

Stupid question, his mocking eyes said, and he grinned, all white teeth and predatorial amusement.

With a flash of annoyance, meant to disguise the real shaft of alarm that went streaking through her, Mia made to roll away from him again but he stopped her, his arm snaking around her waist to keep her clamped against him.

She met with rock-solid immovable muscle and soft white terry towelling. Her breath caught her eyes dropping to stare at the gap in his bath-robe where tight black curls of rough chest hair lay clustered against warm golden skin.

Her heart stuttered. Her mouth went dry. Something clicked into motion deep inside her—the slowly turning gears of sexual awakening, she realized with dread.

'You sleep like an innocent, do you know that?' he informed her very softly. 'I've been lying here for ages, just watching you, and you barcly movcd, barcly breathed, and your lovely mouth looked so vulnerable it was a strain not to kiss it.'

He did now, though, bending his dark head just enough to brush his lips against her own. Her own head jerked backwards in rejection. 'L-let go of me,' she stammered. 'I n-need—'

'Sex on demand,' he reminded her, speaking right over her protest. 'You agreed to it. Here I am to collect it.'

Oh, God. Her eyes closed, her lips folding in on themselves in an effort to moisten what had gone way beyond being moistened. 'Please,' she whispered with the first hint of weakness she had let herself show him. 'I'm not used to…'

'Performing on demand?' he suggested when her voice trailed off into silence. 'That's not the way I heard it…'

Silence. Mia went perfectly still, a slither of horror sliding down her spine. 'I don't know what you mean,' she said.

'No?' he murmured. 'Then, please, correct me if I am wrong,' he drawled. 'You did have your first full-blown affair at the tender age of sixteen, did you not? With a struggling rock star, I believe. He died several years later of a cocktail of drink and drugs. But not before your wild whoring ways forced your father to place you in a closed institution while they dried you out, made you a half-fit human being then disgorged you back on society in the hope that you had learned your lesson. Did you learn your lesson?'

Mia felt sick, but said nothing. Her father, she was thinking desolately, just couldn't let her do anything with a modicum of dignity. He had to soil it—soil everything—for her.

'Certainly,' that cruel voice went on when she offered no defence, 'you've kept a very low profile for the last seven years. Do you still indulge in drugs?'

She shook her head. Her eyes were closed, and her face so white it looked brittle. It would be no use telling him that she had never—ever—abused her body with illegal drugs because she knew he wouldn't believe her.

'I don't want any child of mine born a drug addict because his mother had no control over herself. What about sex?' he pushed on remorselessly. 'Should I have had you tested before we reached this point? Is there any chance I am likely to put my health at risk if I indulge myself with you?'

Her heart heaved, her aching lungs along with it. 'I have not had a sexual relationship with a man in years,' she told him with as much pride as she could muster.

'You expect me to believe that?'

'It's the truth,' she retorted, her green eyes despising him so much that they actually sought glacial contact with his. 'Believe it or not. I don't care. I don't care if you get a whole army of doctors in here to make sure I am clean enough for you to use. But just do it quickly, will you, so we can get the whole sordid conception over with?'

With that, she managed to break free from him and rolled sideways across the bed. His hand shot out and caught her.

'Oh, no, you don't,' he breathed, and began to pull her to him.

He came to lean right over her, his face tight with anger, his eyes alive with it and his body tense with it. 'Is it true?' he demanded rawly. 'Is everything I've just said the truth?'

The truth? she repeated to herself with skin-blistering mockery. He would like the truth even less than he was liking her father's lies!

'I sold myself for five million pounds,' she spat. 'Does that answer your question?'

It had been a reckless thing to say—foolish, when it was so obvious that he was angry. His dark eyes flashed contemptuously. 'Then start paying your damned dues,' he muttered, and his mouth crushed hers.

It was an insult, an invasion. It promised nothing but punishment for believing she could answer him like that. Yet what actually happened to her then was perhaps more of a punishment than the fierceness of his kiss.

Because she pushed and punched out at him—and then went up like an exploding volcano, her mouth drawing greedily on his like someone with a raging thirst. It was awful—she could feel herself shattering into a million fiery particles but couldn't do a single thing to stop it from happening.

'My God,' he gasped, dragging his mouth free so he could stare down at her. He was shocked. She didn't blame him—she was feeling utterly shattered by it herself!

'You are now contaminated!' she snarled at him in sheer seething reaction.

He just laughed, but it was a rather shocked sound with nothing amused about it. Then he caught her mouth again, sending her spinning back to where she'd gone off to with no apparent effort. It was different now. There was no anger feeding the flames, just a white-hot passion that sang through her blood and sizzled across her skin.

His hands were all over her, his long fingers knotting in her hair, trailing the arching length of her throat, urgently searching for and finding the thrusting tightness of her breast. Then, frustratingly, his hands moving on downwards, finding the knot holding her robe together and impatiently freeing it.

Cool fresh air touched her burning skin and she cried out when it actually hurt. His mouth had left hers and she hadn't even noticed, his body sliding sideways so he could completely unwrap her.

Her eyes were closed, her body trembling with an overload of sensation. He knelt there beside her and watched it all happen while he rid himself of his own robe, his dark face taut and muscles bunched, his own sensual urgency no less controlled than hers was.

When he came back to her, her arms wrapped round him, her fingers clawing into his hair. Their mouths fused hungrily again, and she felt the stinging pleasure of his hair-roughened chest grazing the sensitised tips of her breasts. She felt the power of his arousal pressing against her thighs and instinctively opened them so she could accept him into the cradle of her slender hips.

He groaned something, she didn't know what. She didn't even care. But her eyes snapped open in protest when he denied her his mouth again.

He was glaring hotly down at her. 'Wild,' he muttered. 'I knew you would be wild. No one with this glorious colour of hair and the amount of self-control you exhibit could be anything but wild once you let go.'

'I haven't let go!' she denied, wishing it was the truth! 'I hate you!' she added helplessly

'I hate you too.' He laughed. 'Interesting, isn't it? How two people who can hate each other this much can also feel this naked kind of passion.'

'The passion is all yours,' she said, tight-lipped, then gasped when he suddenly lifted himself away from her to kneel between her parted thighs.

Eyes like black lasers skimmed over her body from firm proud, thrusting breasts to the cluster of tight golden curls protecting her sex.

'Oh…' she choked in appalled embarrassment. No man had ever looked on her quite like this!

But what was a worse humiliation was the way her oonoos were responding to the way he was looking at her— throbbing and pulsing with an excitement that threatened to completely engulf her.

'I can see you are dying for me to touch you.'

'Please,' she groaned in pained mortification. 'Don't do this to me!'

'You will be wishing me inside you before this hour is through,' he promised darkly.

Then he touched her, sliding a long and silkenly practised finger along the hot moist crevice he had exposed with such a bold disregard to her modesty, and claimed possession by delving deep inside.

It shook her, shook her right through to the very centre of everything she had ever imagined to do with this kind of intimacy. At sixteen she had been too young and too inexperienced to know that she was supposed to have been enjoying this as much as the man who had eventually taken her virginity.

But this—this wild hot surge of stinging pleasure which was taking her over was completely new territory to her. And the fact that it was caused by a man she so utterly despised was enough to send her reeling into shock—the kind of shock that held her helpless as he arched his body over her, capturing her mouth with a hunger that devoured while his fingers began to work a magic on her flesh she had never experienced in her life before.

Oh, help me, she thought on a wave of helpless despair. She couldn't believe this was happening to her, couldn't believe she could lose control like this!

He knew it too, and played with her, like a cat with a mesmerised mouse. An arm slid beneath her shoulders, his body shifting sideways so he was no longer completely covering her, then the real torture began, with slow, light, lazy caresses that told him everything he needed to know about the woman he was exploring.

He touched her face, her nose, her lips, and ran those same fingers down her neck and between the throbbing upthrust of her breasts. He followed the flat line of her ribcage to her tightly muscled stomach, traced the line of her hips, then delved once again into the very core of her, but only fleetingly—too fleetingly—before he was exploring her silken thighs, watching with a dark intensity, which really frightened her, each quiver and jolt of her flesh as he learned what gave her pleasure and what did not.

'Why do you always hide your hair?' he murmured huskily into the dark chasm of sensation that her whirling mind had become. 'I find it very exciting that the same colour nestles here between your thighs. I adore it that your skin is so pale against my own skin, that your breasts are so very sensitive to my slightest touch even though you fight me. And even the fact that you fight me excites me. It makes me wonder what I will feel when you decide to torment me in return...'

'No.' Out of her head with sensation as she was, she heard the silky invitation in his voice and breathlessly refused the offer. 'I won't touch you. You don't need me to.'

The obvious fact that his manhood lay in such daunting erection against her thigh confirmed that fact.

'I will drive you wild,' he warned her, seeming even to enjoy this battle. As if any battle with her was an excitement for him. 'I will make you beg…'

Mia kept her hands clenched in tight fists by her sides as a stubborn answer.

She heard his soft laugh at her stubbornness, then he took one pointed stinging nipple into his mouth and sucked hard at the same time as he slid a finger deep inside her.

Wild, he'd called her. Well, she went wild. It flared up with no constraint. Her hands snaked up and caught at his hair, her fingernails raking into his scalp as she cried out in a wretchedly raw response to what he was doing to her.

He muttered something—it sounded shaken. Then he was repeating the sequence of events so that she reacted in the same way. It was so utterly, mind-blowingly pleasurable that she didn't even feel ashamed of herself, just elated— so exquisitely elated because she had truly believed that she did not have it in her to respond to any man as violently as this.

'You will beg me or caress me,' he warned.

Her eyes flicked open, green fire lasering into burning black. 'I never beg,' she informed him with amazing coolness.

'No?'

With a sudden bright glow in his eyes he slid down the full length of her, landing on his knees beside the bed. 'Beg?' he offered silkily.

'Go to hell, Mr Doumas,' she bit out, using that formal title as an insult.

What he did was bury his mouth between her thighs.

Mia begged. She clutched at him in exquisite agony, and pleaded with him to stop. She wrapped her long legs around him and tried to pull him up and over her. She dug long anxious fingers into his sweat-slicked shoulders. She gasped and writhed and panted and hated him with a vengeance as he held her fast with hands at her hips and drove her to the very edge of sanity.

'Oh—please,' she sobbed, 'please stop now!'

'Say my name,' he muttered against her flesh, his tongue making a snake-like flick at her with the cruel intention of ripping the breath from her body. 'Beg me again and use my name.'

'Alexander,' she whispered helplessly.

'Alex,' he corrected. 'My lovers call me Alex.'

'Alex!' she groaned. 'Alex, please, please…' she murmured deliriously.

'Please—what?' he demanded.

'Please come inside me!' she cried out in aching agony.

It was so humiliating because he laughed as he slid his long, lean, hot body along the full length of her, then entered her with no more warning than that.

'Like this?' he taunted. 'Is this what the five-million-pound wife requires?'

But it was too late for Mia. The cruelty and the insult went sailing right past her because she had shot straight into an orgasm that went on and on and on, and made him go very still in stunned reaction.

He could feel her—actually feel her beating all around him on wave after wave of pulsing ecstasy. It shook him, shook to the very roots his conviction that he'd often experienced what was best in a sexual climax. This woman was experiencing what had to be the best, and not one part of her missed out on the raging feast. Not her fingers where they flexed and clutched at his body, not her breasts as they heaved and arched and quivered, not her mouth as it gasped and groaned and panted.

He caught her mouth. He needed to capture it, needed to join in that wild experience, and at last he began to move inside her, feeling that incredible orgasm go on and on and on while driving him towards his own mind-blowing finish.

When it came he lost touch with himself, with her, with everything. His mind shut down. He felt it happen—felt the flow of blood leave his brain as it surged down to that point of such unbelievable pleasure that it was almost agony to feel it eventually fade away.

Mia thought she might have died a little afterwards. Certainly something deep inside her had been lost for ever. She didn't know what, couldn't begin to try and work out what. But as he lay there, heavy on her, his big body still attacked by the pulsing aftershocks of what they had just created between them, she knew that something vital had gone from her—had been passed, maybe, from her to him, she didn't know.

But it was most definitely gone.

When he eventually moved, sliding sideways onto the mattress to bury his face in the pillow, Mia turned and curled up away from him. She was shocked, shocked by the uninhibited wildness of what had just taken place. Shocked by the power of his passion and her own ability to let go of every ounce of self-control.

And now came the aftermath, she thought bleakly as they continued to lie there, together but separate, intimate but strangers.

Silent, appalled strangers who had been caught in the tangled web of their own sexuality, only to find after it all that they were still very separate entities.

He moved first, sending her muscles into wary tension as he moved to the edge of the bed and sat up with his feet on the floor. She heard him utter a heavy sigh, sensed him raking angry fingers through hair that had been disarrayed by her own restless fingers. She felt the mattress dip as he bent and she knew he was picking up his discarded robe. She felt him begin to cover himself as he pushed himself to his feet.

Tears burned in her eyes as she lay there, facing away from him with her arms and hands clutched protectively across her curved and naked body. She sensed his eyes raking over her, sensed him considering what to say, and waited with baited breath and a hammering heart for the clever insult to hit her eardrums.

But in the end he said nothing, and maybe that was just about the biggest insult he could have paid her as he walked out of her bedroom in total silence.

CHAPTER FOUR

IT TOOK every ounce of determination Mia could muster to step out of that bedroom at precisely nine o'clock that evening, but she had to pause at the top of those highly polished stairs as a bout of cowardly tremors made a sudden last-minute attack.

She was still suffering from shock, she knew. Her body was in shock at the unrestrained way it had behaved this afternoon. Her mind was in shock because it just could not believe it had allowed her to go so out of control with Alex, a man she supposedly felt nothing for. But, more to the point, she was finding it more difficult to come to terms with the knowledge that she had allowed all of it to happen with a man who felt so little for her.

Where had her pride been? Her self-respect?

She didn't know, could not understand what had possessed her during that wild, hot frenzy that had taken place in the bedroom. But she certainly knew where her pride was at this moment. It was floundering around at her feet, along with her lost self-respect.

And the urge to simply turn right around and lock herself in that bedroom rather than have to face *him* again tonight was so powerful at the moment that she almost gave in to it.

Then the sound of a door opening downstairs caught her attention, and she suddenly discovered that her pride was not completely demolished because, with a bracing of her slender shoulders and a defiant lifting of her chin, she found herself walking down the stairs, instead of dashing for cover behind a locked door, because she knew she would rather die than let him see how utterly degraded she felt.

A sound to her left as she reached the hallway set her feet moving in that direction. A door was standing slightly ajar, with golden light shining gently through the gap.

She took a deep breath, ran trembling fingers down her equally trembling thighs then stepped forward, silently pushing the door open just enough to allow her to enter whatever room was on the other side of it.

She saw Alex immediately. Her heart turned over, her throat locking on a fresh lump of tension. He was dressed very formally in a black silk dinner suit, white dress shirt and black bow tie—though what he was wearing barely registered with her at that moment because she was so busy coming to terms with the way she was seeing him now.

Naked.

She shuddered, horrified at herself—appalled by the sudden flare of sexual awareness that went sizzling through her as her eyes looked at him and saw firm golden flesh, covering a beautifully structured framework, instead of the reality of conventional black fabric.

She saw wide satin-smooth shoulders and rock-solid biceps, a hair-roughened chest that was so powerfully muscled it made her own breasts sting in memory of what it had felt like to be crushed against it. She saw a long lean torso with a tight waist, flat hips and strong thighs, supporting a pelvis that housed the full-blooded and dynamic essence of the man.

An essence that made her inner thighs clench, made her go hot all over, made her lungs completely shut down as a whole gamut of sensation went racing right through her. She looked at his mouth and felt it crushing her own mouth, looked at his hands and felt them caressing her skin.

She looked at the man in his entirety and saw a tall dark stranger—now an intimate stranger. But one who had suddenly become so physically real to her that she now realised just how successfully she had been blanking him out before as a flesh and blood person.

Was he aware she had done that? she wondered as she stood there, staring at him in nerve-tightening tension. Did he know that to get herself this far in this dastardly deal they had struck she'd had to pretend he was nothing more than a shadow?

Standing there by a drinks cabinet, seemingly lost in thought as he frowned into what looked like a crystal tumbler lightly splashed with whisky, the only thing she could be sure about concerning him now was that at this moment, while he believed himself alone, he was doing nothing to hide his own sense of loathing at what had erupted between them.

And why not? she asked herself. He despised her as much as she despised him so it followed automatically that he felt the same revulsion for what they'd done to each other.

Shame trickled through her, followed by a wave of pained helplessness. Because this was only the beginning, not the end.

The beginning.

She must have moved, though she hadn't been aware of doing it, because something made his dark head turn. Then he became still, his brooding stare fixing on hers, knowledge making his dark brown irises glint and then burn, which sent a wild flush of hot embarrassment sweeping through her because their new intimacy, she realised, was catching him out, too.

Then the flame changed to contempt, a hard, biting, cruel contempt, before he hooded the expression with long black lashes. Hooded it so he could let his gaze run over her carefully controlled hair and the dramatically plain deep turquoise silk shift dress she was wearing, which skimmed her slender figure without clinging anywhere—deliberately chosen for that reason.

Yet he missed nothing—like herself, she suspected, seeing not the fully dressed woman standing here but the naked one, the wild one, the woman who had surprised him with the power of her own passions. He was seeing her spread out, fully exposed to him and ready.

She felt sick suddenly. Stomach-churningly, head-swimmingly sick.

'Take your hair out of that unflattering knot,' he said in an oddly flattened tone. 'And don't wear it up in my company again.'

It was a shock. The very last thing she had expected him to say, in fact. Her hair? An impulsive hand went to touch the simple knot held in place by a tortoiseshell clasp. Her cheeks warmed and her eyes dropped away from him because she didn't know why he was suddenly attacking her and why he had used that strange tone to do it.

'No,' she said, grimly pulling herself together, the coolly indifferent Mia sliding back into place. 'It's more comfortable for me to wear it like this. It annoys me when it's loose.'

'Then suffer,' he said unsympathetically. 'I hate liars. And that prim hairstyle makes such a damned liar of you. At least when your hair is down...' he took a tense gulp at the drink in his glass '...people are forewarned about what you really are.'

'And what am I?' she asked, the green eyes glinting with challenge—while every fine muscle in her body was held tensely, waiting for him to say the word her father had been throwing at her for so many years now that she couldn't remember when he had not seen her as a whore.

This man would be no different. This man and her father had so much in common it would shock and appal Alexander Doumas to know just how much.

Or maybe he did know, she corrected herself when he didn't say it but took another deep slug from his glass instead.

'Do it,' he commanded as he lowered the glass again. 'Or I will make you do it.'

'Dinner,' a carefully neutral voice announced behind Mia.

She turned abruptly and caught Elena's frosty expression. She knew the other woman had overheard most of their telling little conversation, and looked right through the housekeeper as she strode proudly past her.

But the hand landing on her shoulder brought her to a sudden standstill. How Alex had managed to move across the room so quickly Mia didn't know, but it was certainly his hand, burning its already familiar brand as he detained her.

'Leave us.' He grimly dismissed the housekeeper.

She turned and left as he propelled Mia back into the room then closed the door. A half-moment later and the tortoiseshell clasp that was holding up her hair was springing free, and the silken coil of hair was unfurling over his fingers in a heavy fall of fire that rippled its way to the base of her spine.

The tortoiseshell clasp was discarded and she heard it land with a clunk on a nearby table. Then he turned her round to face him.

'Don't fight me,' he warned her very grimly, 'because you won't like the consequences.'

To prove his point, the hand still lost in her hair tightened, tugging her head backwards until she had no choice but to look at him. His eyes were still hooded, but she could see the anger simmering beneath those heavy eyelids as he began to rearrange her hair to his own satisfaction.

It hurt her inside. For some reason Mia could not work out at all the way he was asserting his control over her like this hurt—when it shouldn't. It was only what she had expected from him from the very beginning after all.

'You don't like who you are, do you?' he murmured suddenly.

'No,' she replied. It was blunt and it was honest.

'It is why you hide your true nature behind prim clothes and stark hairstyles. You are ashamed of what you are.'

'Yes,' she confirmed, again with the same cool bluntness.

'But you could not keep the passion hidden in that bed upstairs, could you? It broke free and virtually consumed you.'

'You weren't so controlled yourself,' she hit back.

'I didn't quite reach the point where I completely stopped breathing,' he countered grimly.

Her cheeks went pale, her lowered eyes squeezing together on a fresh bout of self-revulsion.

'Was it like that with the rock star?' he questioned. 'Did you fall apart as spectacularly for him as you did for me?'

She didn't answer that one—refused to answer. Whatever had gone on in her life *before* this man was none of his business, and she was damned if she was going to feed his ego by telling him she had *never* lost control of herself like that before—ever.

His hand came to her chin, closed around it then tightened, demanding an answer, but her eyes showed him nothing except cold, green defiance. Her mouth, so red and full and still clearly swollen from his kisses, remaining resolutely shut.

'Well, I tell you this much, *yineka mou,*' he murmured very softly. 'You have set your own boundaries with what took place up there. You will not move from this estate without my say-so. You will not be left alone—either in this house of out of it—with another man. You are now, in effect, my personal prisoner.'

'Points you had written into my contract,' she reminded him. 'Did you see me arguing with you about them then?'

'Ah, but I have a… worrying suspicion that you were not so aware of your own passions when you agreed to that contract. Now you do know, and I am going to take no chances with you falling apart like that for any other man— understand me?'

'Yes.' Once more she refused to give him the satisfaction of arguing the point with him because, whatever lessons he thought he had learned about her in that blasted bedroom, she, too, had learned her own lessons about him. This man thrived on argument. His sexual drive fed off it, but he would not be fed by her again.

He knew exactly what she was doing, of course. He was not an idiot. He could read silent messages just as well as she could. But to her surprise, he laughed, a warm, dark, sexily amused sound that curled up her toes inside her shoes as his mouth came down to cover her own.

Their bodies fused, that quickly and that easily, from mouth to breast to hips. They came together as though someone or something had simply thrown a switch to let the whole wretched current of electric pleasure wrap itself around them.

His tongue blended with hers, and her hands jerked up to clutch at his warm, tightly muscled neck where her fingers spread along his jawbone, his cheeks and the smooth line of his chin. She felt his body respond by tensing, felt his hands drag their way downwards until they were clasping her low on the hips, drawing her even closer to the pulsing throb where his manhood was thickening, tightening.

Her own body melted—melted on the inside, melted on the outside, a hot, honeyed meltdown that poured into her bloodstream, filling her breasts and that aching junction between her thighs so she moved wantonly against him. She couldn't stop herself, couldn't put a halt to what was beginning to happen all over again.

She groaned—at least she thought it was her but it might have been him—and her thighs flexed and parted, searching out an even deeper intimacy against the grinding thrust of him. It was terrible. She didn't know herself, couldn't seem to control what was suddenly raging through her system.

When he dragged his mouth free she whimpered and

went in blind search of reconnection while his hands bit like twin vices into the flesh around her hips to keep her pressed tightly against him, though he denied her his mouth. Denied it ruthlessly. So much so that her eyes flickered open, glazed by need and a confusion that went so deep that it took several long agonising seconds for her to realise what he was doing.

Watching her.

Watching her with a bite in his eyes that told her exactly what he thought of her lack of control.

Whore, that expression said. Whore.

She almost fainted on the wave of self-loathing that went sweeping through her.

He despised her for responding like this—as much as he despised her for being here at all.

'Save it,' he said insolently, 'until later. I have a mistress to console before I can come back here and console you.'

It was cruel but, then, he had meant to be. Anger was driving him—anger at himself for wanting her like this, anger at her for making him want her and anger at the whole situation which he could only relieve by venting it on her.

With that final humiliation biting deep into her senses, he let go and stepped back from her. Two seconds after that he was pulling open the door and striding from the room. Not just from the room but from the villa. Standing there, trembling, aching and shamed, she listened to the front door slam in his wake, heard a car start up and drive away with a powerful roar.

And through it all she barely breathed, barely blinked, barely functioned on any level.

Why? Because it had finally sunk in just how much he hated her. It didn't matter that he had already told her so as far back as in her father's study—the point was that she hadn't really taken the full thrust of his words on board.

Words like, 'I will hate and despise you and bed you

with alacrity,' were suddenly taking on their full true meaning. As did his most recent statement, 'I have a mistress to console before I can come back here and console you...'

She would come second. Second to that lucky lady who probably came fairly far down his list of priorities, which made second a very low status indeed.

She was here for one purpose and one purpose only—to conceive his child so he could claim his prize.

'Your dinner, madam...' Sofia appeared from nowhere, her eyes lowered, her expression carefully guarded. 'The dining room is this way,' she prompted quietly.

It took another few moments to pull herself together but Mia managed it, following Sofia into the long narrow grandeur of a formal dining room where only one place setting waited.

He had always meant to leave her alone like this, she realised on a fresh wave of agony.

Then, thankfully, right out of the centre of that very same agony emerged the other Mia—the pragmatic, invulnerable, very mocking Mia. The one who could smile wryly at herself for actually being hurt by Alex's treatment of her.

The one who could sit quite comfortably at a table and eat alone because eating alone was far more preferable to eating with cruel swines like Alexander Doumas—a man like her father.

When the long silent meal was over she left alone, walking out of the dining room with her chin held high as she trod those polished stairs back to the relative sanctuary of her own room where she calmly prepared for bed—and felt the protective casing she had built around herself threaten to crack only once.

That was when she glanced at the bed she had so carefully tidied, before leaving the room earlier. Someone had stripped it, changed the sheets and put on a clean lemon top cover, one which gave not a single hint of what had taken place on that bed earlier—no tell-tale creases, nothing. An act which told tales in itself.

They knew.

She shuddered. The whole damned staff must know what had been going on in this bed earlier.

Did that mean they also knew why it had been going on? By their cold unwelcoming attitude she had to assume that they knew *exactly* why she was here and, worse, that their employer was accepting the situation only under the severest duress.

That brought her swiftly on to the next soul-crushing point—did they therefore know just where he had gone tonight?

The mistress.

The other woman.

Did they know that he had climbed out of her bed only to climb into another bed with his mistress?

Humiliation poured into her blood, searing a path to a temper few knew she possessed. With a flash from her glinting green eyes, she reached down and grabbed hold of that lemon cover, yanking it clear away from the bed and tossing it in a heap on the ground at her feet.

From now on, she vowed, every time she walked into this room she would mess up this rotten bed! If they wanted to bear witness to their employer's bed duty, let them! Let them change this damned bed fifteen times a day and wonder at his incredible stamina!

Keeping two women busy at the same time—the rotten, crass bastard!

Not that she cared! she told herself tightly as she crawled between those pristine white sheets. She couldn't give a damn what the man got up to so long as he was practising safe sex with the other woman. Other than that, she had no interest whatsoever in his sex life!

That was the exact point at which she made her brain switch off because she had a horrible feeling that she might begin to care if she let herself dwell on the subject too much.

Thankfully, sleep came to her rescue with a single lowering of her eyelids. Wearing a nightdress of cream satin and curled on her side with her long hair flowing across the white pillow, she didn't know another thing for hours. Hours and hours of blessed oblivion from the bleak prospect of what her life was going to be like from now on.

A hand grasped her shoulder. 'Wake up,' a deeply masculine voice insisted.

Just as she had managed to push it all away with the single blink of an eye, it was suddenly all back again. 'W-what?' she mumbled in sleepy confusion. 'What do you think you're doing!' she gasped as he rolled her onto her back and pinned her there with his weight. 'No—!'

'Not a word I recognise,' he informed her with a grim kind of sardonicism.

Her lashes flicked upwards, her eyes finding themselves trapped by glinting dark irises that confirmed exactly what his words and actions were stating.

'What's the matter?' she taunted. 'Wasn't she very consolable tonight?'

He frowned, his eyes narrowing for the few moments it took him to grasp her meaning. Then his teeth were suddenly gleaming in the darkness, cruel and incisive like the next few words he lashed her with. 'She was fine,' he muttered, 'but now I want you.'

'You're disgusting,' she said, and tried to wriggle free, but he wasn't about to let her.

'Nevertheless, when I want I take and you deliver,' he said harshly. 'Don't ever say no to me again.'

Then he did take, passionately and ruthlessly, his hungry mouth covering hers, his tongue probing with a dark, knowing intimacy that appalled her even as her own desires leapt like the traitors they were to greet him eagerly.

He still smelled of whisky. His lips were warm with it,

his tongue tasted of it, transferring the evocative taste to her own tongue and filling her lungs with its heady fumes. His hands were trembling slightly as though his urgency was so great he was having difficulty controlling it. His long fingers ran over the smooth slide of satin, skimming her breasts, her ribcage, her abdomen and eliciting sharp little stinging responses that made her gasp, her spine arch, her muscles tighten and her hands move upwards to clutch at his shoulders with the intention of pushing him away.

Only her hands never pushed. They made contact with his hard, warm, naked flesh and clung to him, a wretched groan escaping her smothered mouth as his fingers slid upwards to find her breasts again. In seconds her nipples were erect and tingling, his palms rolling them with an erotic expertise that had them pushing against the confines of her nightdress while his thighs were insinuating themselves between her own.

The throbbing contact of his own powerful erection moving against fine satin was so intensely arousing that her thighs widened even more in an effort to gain greater friction where she most needed it.

His mouth left hers and he laughed. It was a sound far distant from humour but held angry triumph. 'What a hot little thing you are when you let yourself go,' he taunted. 'No wonder you preferred me to that grotesque little man who was knocking sixty. He could not have given you half this much pleasure.'

'Your mind is a sewer,' she shot at him.

'My mind is that low?' he mocked, and grabbed hold of the edge of her nightdress, tugged it up around her hips and entered her. No foreplay, no compunction.

To her utter horror, Mia went wild beneath him. Just like the last time, she was overtaken by an instant orgasm that set her body writhing and her insides throbbing, the tiny muscles inside rippling over him and around him as her head fell back and her throat began to pant out little gasps of riotous intensity while her heart raced out of control.

It shocked him again, held him paralysed for the few stunning moments it took for him to accept just how spectacularly she responded to him. Then his mouth lowered to one tightly stinging nipple. Through the stretched tautness of her nightdress he sucked the pulsing tip deep into his mouth and began to move, thrusting his hips with short blunt stabs that kept her locked in that muscle-clenched storm of hectic climax, the strokes growing longer and deeper and harder as he drove her on and on with no let-up, no chance to make a mad grab at sanity.

She was out of her head and it dismayed her, but she couldn't seem to do a single thing about it. When he withdrew she should really have come tumbling back down to earth with a crash—but she didn't. She stayed up there, lost in that world of electric sensation.

He muttered something, which she couldn't make out. His body slid sideways, the nightgown coming off altogether before his mouth clamped on hers again and his fingers began to discover what his throbbing manhood already knew—what it was like to feel a woman in the throes of a multi-orgasm.

Those tormenting fingers stroked and incited her, his hungry tongue mimicking the action. One of her hands found his nape and clutched at it desperately, holding his mouth down on hers while her other hand went in agitated search of other parts of him.

He was so big, so hard and slick and potent—she wanted him back inside her. She wanted his mouth on her breasts but she wanted him to keep on kissing her mouth like this. In the end and on an impatient sigh her fingers clutched at a handful of his hair to tug his mouth from her so she could present him with her breast instead, and through it all her body was still rocketing through space on its own agenda.

He began to throb against her caressing hand. She felt it

happen and released a sigh of satisfaction that came out closer to a salacious growl. She snaked her body beneath him and guided him into her, two hands clutching at his lean, tight buttocks.

Holding him like that, with his dark head buried between her breasts, she let go of everything, driving him onward with the thrust of her hips. Her cries of anguished pleasure echoed around the darkened bedroom as she felt his own pending climax build, felt the muscles bunch all over him, heard his soft curse as his self-control began to crack wide open, and this time they leapt together, high—so high Mia felt lost and disembodied.

The next morning when she awoke the only sign that Alex had ever been there was his scent on the sheets and on her body—in her mouth and in the soft subtle pulse of her body where he had so effectively stamped his presence.

It was a struggle to make herself get up. She almost stumbled her way into the bathroom, felt hardly any better by the time she came out again, and began to fumble round for something to wear.

It was sunny outside, the heat of the day surprisingly strong for this time of year, she discovered when she pushed open the window in an effort to drag some air into her lungs that did not smell of him.

It didn't work. He was in her system, she knew. Knew the man and his scent were destined to be an innate part of her for ever now.

It was a wretched thought—the kind of thought that made her shiver, as if someone had just walked over her grave, because she knew that no matter how passionately she had affected him last night he would be despising her more for the way she'd responded than he would have done if she'd simply remained cold beneath him.

Oh, face it, Mia, she told herself grimly. You would be despising yourself less if you'd managed to stay aloof—

and that's what is really troubling you. You're disgusted with yourself for being so sexually vulnerable to a man you hold so little respect for.

And, for all you know about him, he probably has the same effect on every woman he takes to his bed.

The great lover, she mocked acidly. The Don Juan of the nineteen-nineties!

Did that mean his mistress was well used to losing her head whenever he deigned to bed her?

Did it matter? she asked herself angrily as a nasty poison called jealousy began to creep through her blood. The point is, you respond like that and it's shameful!

But it didn't alter the fact that she fell apart in his arms like that every night for the next fortnight. During the day she didn't see him. He was never lying beside her when she woke in the morning. She got used to hearing a helicopter arrive and take off again very early—taking him to his offices in Athens, she presumed, though she was never given the opportunity to ask. He came back by the same means, usually just as dusk was beginning to colour the sky.

Where he ate she did not know, but it was never with her. The only contact they ever had was in the hours of darkness when he would slide into bed beside her and drive them both out of their heads with the devastating power of their mutual sensuality. He never spoke unless it was to comment on what they were doing, and he showed no remorse in using her like the brood mare she had sold herself as to him.

When it was over he would lie on his back beside her and she would curl on her side as far away from him as she could get while she waited for the aftershocks to stop shaking her body. Aftershocks she knew he was keenly aware of, and she had a feeling that they were the reason he lingered in that bed with her afterwards—because he saw those tremors as part of his due. They fed his ego—

an ego she knew had been badly damaged by him giving in to this deal in the first place.

Perhaps he even hated himself a little for giving in to it. Certainly, sometimes in the darkness she had glimpsed a look in his eyes that had suggested self-contempt as he'd watched her go wild beneath him and had known—just as she had—that he'd been about to join her.

Whatever he did to her, she did to him. If he did acquire that depth of pleasure with every woman he bedded, then he did not like it happening with her.

But, then, neither did Mia like it. In fact, towards the end of that first fortnight she began hoping—praying—that Mother Nature would be kind to her and make her pregnant. If the potency of their intercourse had anything to do with it, she should be very pregnant. Then at least he would leave her alone.

But it was not to be. The morning she woke with those familiar symptoms that warned her period had arrived she wept.

That day Mia roamed about the big empty house in a sluggish state of deep depression. It didn't help that there was not a friendly face in the place from whom she could gain some light relief from her own sense of grim failure.

Now she had to find a moment to break the unfortunate news to Alex that he had not succeeded in his quest to make her pregnant and, more to the point, that her body was not available to him for the next five days.

But how did she tell anything to a man who only came to her in the dead of night? Leave a note, pinned to the door between his bedroom and hers? she mused bitterly.

The temptation to do just that was so strong that she almost gave in to it. In the end she did the only thing she really could do, and waited up for him to come to her. When eventually she heard the connecting door open she was standing by the window, covered from neck to toe in soft white towelling.

She turned to face him. 'I'm not pregnant,' she announced boldly, and watched him stop dead in his tracks.

He didn't move again for the space of thirty long seconds, his stance so taut that she gained the rather satisfying impression that she had disconcerted him so much that he just did not know what to do next.

It was wonderful, almost worth the disappointment to see him so utterly stumped like this. He was a big man, a man whose body she knew so well by now that she could even read the frustration in his beautiful muscle formation.

'I suggest you use your mistress for the next few days,' she added with icy relish. 'I will, of course, let you know when I am available again.'

Oh, she enjoyed saying that! He treated her like a whore and she was responding as a whore. His dark lashes fluttered, folding down over his eyes then back up again as the full brutal smack of her words hit him full in his arrogant face.

Because he was no fool he recognised that she was not only acknowledging herself as a whore but that he was no better in his treatment of her.

But he got his own back. Heavens, did he get his own back! 'Fine,' he agreed smoothly. 'I will do that.'

The door closed behind him, leaving her standing there where she had faced up to him with her chin high and her stance proud, while the tears trickled unchecked down her pale cheeks.

Why was she crying? She didn't know. What had she expected, after all? For him to show disappointment, concern for her health, a bit of human compassion for her lonely plight?

The man didn't give a damn about her as a living, breathing human being, and went on to prove it by not coming back to the island for the next seven days.

A week to the day later, she was just climbing out of the swimming pool when Sofia came out onto the terrace. 'The master wishes to speak to you on the telephone,' she informed her.

The *master*. Mia mocked the title acidly. The man with everything—*master* of all he surveyed! Except an island he coveted and a child he hadn't managed to conceive.

'Thank you.' She nodded coolly to Sofia, grabbed her beach robe and pulled it over her dripping body as she followed the maid into the house and to a telephone extension in the drawing room.

'A helicopter is on its way to you,' Alex announced. 'It will arrive in about thirty minutes. It has no time to linger so be ready to board as soon as it lands.'

'But—'

That was as far as she got for the line went dead. Frowning slightly and wondering what this new development could mean because she had not been out of the confines of the estate since she'd arrived, she hurried upstairs, showered, dried her hair, then quickly knotted the still slightly damp mass at her nape. She threw on a pale blue cotton sundress, added a white linen jacket and gathered a few things together in a large white linen beach bag because she didn't know if she was going to be away for an hour or two or for a week.

She was waiting when the helicopter touched down on the purpose-built pad situated a little way off from one side of the house. The pilot didn't stop the rotors while he waited for her to duck beneath them and climb on board.

An hour later she was being transported by a chauffeur-driven limousine into the centre of Athens.

The car drew to a stop outside a residential apartment block, the driver getting out to escort her inside. He led her to the lift, smiled politely but briefly as he pressed a button on the lift console then stepped back again, leaving her to travel upwards alone.

Was this where he usually met with his mistress? she wondered, and felt her stomach turn over—felt the usual surge of bitter self-contempt begin to burn at how she let him get away with it.

Was it the mistress's turn to be unavailable?

The doors slid open on a private foyer. Sucking in a deep breath of air, she forced her unwilling limbs to start moving. Chin up as usual and her eyes revealing no hint of what was eating away at her insides, she stepped out of the lift and heard the doors hiss as they closed behind her.

But it was the man propping up a doorframe directly across from her who really held her attention. He was dressed casually in pale chinos and a white polo shirt that clung to the taut contours of his muscle-tight body. His big arms were folded across his wide chest, and one neat ankle crossed over the other. His lean, dark, frighteningly ruthless face was shuttered, his eyes hooded by long lush lashes as he looked her over.

'The hair,' he said.

That was all. Just 'the hair'. As she reached up in mute obedience to loosen the heavy flow of red-gold she saw the intensity with which he watched her fiery tresses tumble around her arms and shoulders.

It was a look she knew well and could feel it touch deep, deep in the very essence of her womanhood.

Desire, unhidden and unwanted.

It was time to begin again.

CHAPTER FIVE

IT SET the pattern for the next two months. When commuting to and from the island to Athens, Alex came to Mia's bed every night without fail except at weekends when, she presumed, he went to his mistress.

Mia told herself stubbornly that she didn't care, that the five days when he did come to her meant she deserved a brief respite on Saturday and Sunday from his insatiable demands on her.

Anyway, she always rang Suzanna on a Saturday morning and spent long, precious minutes reassuring the poor child that she had not been forgotten.

Those telephones calls hurt as much as they made each passing week bearable. The little girl was lonely. Mia knew what it felt like because she had been there herself during her own loveless childhood. She would usually spend the rest of the weekend sunk in the kind of heavy mood that made Alex's absence a relief.

During the day she had formed her own quiet routine where she swam twenty lengths of the pool before breakfast and the same again late in the afternoon. In between she read a lot, silently grateful that his home possessed such a comprehensive library.

Over the next three weeks Alex had her transported out to him on two occasions when he was away on business— once to Milan and another time to Paris. Each time she found herself being taken to the penthouse suite of one of his own hotels for a night of wild and wanton bedding.

She couldn't call it loving—*wouldn't* call it loving because what they shared was about as far away from that emotion as any two people could get.

At least during those brief trips away from the island they ate together—they talked to each other, even if it was a rather wary and constrained kind of talking. And the sex was different because he would not wait until she was safely lying in the darkness before coming to join her. He would undress her himself, and had her undress him. And sometimes—just sometimes—it would seem as if he almost cared for her a little, the way he would stand there in the middle of a bedroom and caress her with hands that almost seemed to revere the smooth, silken flesh they were touching.

And once during one of these much more intimate beddings that took place away from his private villa—times when he was warmer, kinder, much more attentive towards her, yet still managed to drive her into that mindless state of sensual fervour—he stopped when his body was lost deep inside her, pushed the wild strands of hair away from her face then lay there on top of her, his expression sombre.

'Why do you let me do this to you?' he asked.

Why? The answer almost escaped her kiss-warmed lips but she managed to bite it back. After all, how much mocking mileage would he make out of her admitting that she couldn't help herself?

'I don't know,' she replied honestly enough because she really did not know or understand why this man of all men should be able to move her so dramatically. 'What's your excuse?'

He sighed, something like that old self-contempt, which she had not seen in his face for a week now, clouding his lean, taut features. 'Like you, I don't know,' he answered heavily. For a moment, for a horrible gut-twisting moment, she thought he was going to withdraw from her and leave her in this high state of sexual need, the conscious acknowledgement of what they were doing here enough to cool his ardour.

But, far from withdrawing, what he actually did was bury

himself all the deeper inside her, his mouth trembling slightly as it came down to her own mouth. 'Whatever it is,' he muttered huskily, 'we may as well enjoy because once you are pregnant it will be over.'

It was a statement of intent. A *re-statement* of that intent issued to her, it seemed, so long ago now that she could barely recall the moment in her father's study when he had first made it.

It made their loving all the more urgent that night, made him come back to her time after time after time. The next morning, when she awoke to find him gone from her as usual, she was grateful for his absence, the pride-lowering fact that he never so much as acknowledged her during daylight hours for once a relief because she felt so utterly bereft, though she did not understand why that particular morning should be any different from all the others when she had woken alone like this.

Then the inevitable happened. Three and a half months into this marriage that wasn't really a marriage she missed her period.

Oddly, she said nothing. Oddly, she let him go on making love to her throughout the next four weeks until her second period failed to show itself. Oddly, she felt so terribly depressed by this second missed period that she was glad Alex was in the States again and therefore too far away to send for her for his habitual single night of passion to break up a business trip. Instead, she could use the time to come to terms with her own odd reaction to the one thing this had been all about.

A baby. They had managed to make a baby. A baby that was to make all her most secret dreams come true and would give Alex what he coveted most.

His island, his special piece of rock that lay out there somewhere among that cluster of tiny islands she could see from her bedroom window.

Will it all have been worth it? Mia wondered dully. All

this isolation she had endured, all the nights of loveless passion?

Oh, yes, she told herself flatly, it will have been worth it, and she grimly dismissed the way her heart coiled up tightly then throbbed as if it were hurting for something it had never been given the right to hurt for.

He arrived back at the villa late one afternoon while she was taking her usual exercise in the pool. She watched the helicopter fly over then disappear behind a bank of trees that acted as a wind-break to the pool area. As its rotor blades slowed in the warm still air she grimly returned to her exercise, pounding steadily up and down the pool with a stubborn resolve, refusing point blank to acknowledge any of the fluttering sinking sensations that were crawling around her insides.

She was just pulling herself out of the water when she glanced up to find him standing there.

It was a break from habit, and the irony of that break, coming now, did not escape her. He was still dressed for business in iron-grey trousers and a crisp white shirt, though his jacket was missing and his tie had been tugged loose. He looked tired, she saw. His eyes were hooded as usual as he ran them over her slender figure, encased in white clinging wet Lycra.

Already she was aware of the changes in her body, the extra heaviness in her breasts and their new excruciating sensitivity. She knew her waist was slightly thicker simply because her clothes felt tighter, and she was aware of a swelling around her abdomen that must show under the clinging swimwear.

It was therefore a purely defensive action that made her reach for a towel to cover herself, her eyes dropping away from his with guilt, embarrassment and a multitude of other things that didn't bear thinking about.

One of them was causing disturbance in the deepest parts of her body. It was desire, pure and simple. No matter

who he was or what he was—or even why he was—she
had grown to need him. She needed what he could do to
her to make her lose her grip on the fierce self-control she
had spent the best part of her life maintaining for one
wretched reason or another.

Alexander Doumas, with his dynamic sensuality, had
somehow managed to find a chink in her otherwise impenetrable armour, and in doing so had unwittingly made himself so indispensable to her new need to break free from
her own constraints that she did not know how she was
going to go on without him now it was, in effect, over.

And the worst thing of all, she acknowledged as she carefully wrapped the towel around her, was that knowing she
felt like this about him had to be the most pride-lowering
effect of the whole rotten bargain.

'I'm pregnant,' she announced, just like that without any
preamble. It came blurting out because it had to be said
before he had a chance to say the words she knew were
about to come from him. She had seen the look in his eyes
and had recognised it. He had been away for longer than a
week, and if he had not been able to use the services of his
mistress in that time then he had come to search her out
like this because he needed her sexually.

If she'd hoped to jolt some kind of response from him
by boldly announcing it like that, she failed miserably.
Neither by stance nor expression did he hint at anything.

'Are you sure?' he asked quietly.

Her small chin lifted, her green eyes steady as they gazed
into his. 'Yes.'

'How far?'

She gave a shrug of one sun-kissed, slender shoulder,
and suddenly realised that she was going to have to admit
that she'd let him go on taking her while she'd already
suspected she could be pregnant. 'I missed my second period last week,' she told him with the usual defiant tilt to
her chin. 'I w-wanted to be sure before I told you.'

It was a weak excuse but he made no comment. He just stood there and gazed at her in total silence, his eyes and his expression telling her absolutely nothing.

Yet she sensed in him something—something that kept her very still in the warm sunshine, held in breathless waiting suspense for...

For what? she asked herself confusedly.

Then she knew exactly what because when his answer came it struck so deep that it actually felt as if it might have made her bleed somewhere.

'That's it, then,' he said, and turned and walked away, leaving her standing there feeling cold, cast-down and rejected—feeling empty inside when, physically at least, she wasn't.

An hour later she was standing in her bedroom when she heard the helicopter take off again. With white face, clenched teeth, closed eyes and hands coiled into two tight fists at her sides, she stood there in the middle of the room and listened until the very last whirr of those rotor blades had fluttered into silence.

'That's it, then.' Those cruelly flat words had not stopped lacerating her since he had spoken them. There had been no enquiry as to her health—nothing but those three words that showed his contempt for both herself and their baby. Showed that the man had feelings cast in steel—he wanted the family island and did not care what he was forfeiting to get it.

She had expected nothing more from him but still the words had managed to cut her.

Then, quite without warning, the connecting door to his bedroom swung open. Mia started in surprise, whirling jerkily on her heel to find him standing where he should not have been.

The shock and confusion she experienced was so great that it sent her head spinning and the blood rushing from her brain to her tingling feet. Without really knowing why, since it had never happened to her in her life before, she quietly and silently sank into a faint.

'What the hell happened?' Alex's voice was curt, gruff, grating at her eardrums as she came round again to find herself lying on the bed with him standing over her, his dark face a fascinating mix of anger and concern.

'I thought you'd gone,' she whispered frailly. 'It w-was a shock when you walked in here.'

'You thought I'd gone?' He sounded so incredulous that she almost laughed. 'I've only just arrived. Why the hell should I want to leave again so quickly?'

'Why the hell should you want to walk into my bedroom during daylight hours?' Mia countered waspishly.

He shifted uncomfortably, his expression becoming closed as he dropped down to seat himself on the edge of her bed. 'I may be ruthless,' he muttered gruffly, 'but I'm not that bloody ruthless.'

It was such a small concession, such a very insignificant gesture on his part, that it really did not deserve the response it actually received yet...

Her arm came up, and of its own volition seemed to hook itself over his shoulder and around his neck as her eyes filled with weak, burning tears. She raised herself up and buried her face in the back of his shoulder—and wept.

Which of them was more shocked was difficult to determine. Mia was shocked at herself because, even in her darkest hours, she had never let herself do anything like this! She'd never cried in front of anyone—hardly ever let herself cry even in private—so she was shocked to find the flood-gates opening as abruptly as they did.

Alex was so shocked that he went rigid. She felt his shoulders grow tense, and his neck. She felt his heart thud against his ribcage as though the shock had jolted it out of its usual steady beat.

Then, with an odd, short, constrained sigh he was twisting around and putting his arms around her, holding her, saying nothing but allowing her to do what she seemed to need to do—to weep in his arms as though her heart were broken.

But, as with all impulsive gestures, this one had to come to an eventual end. When it did, when the sobs changed to snuffles and she became aware of just what she had done and with whom she had done it embarrassment washed over her in a wave. It coloured her damp cheeks and made her shudder in horror. She pulled away from him, scrambled off the bed and made her way to her bathroom, leaving him sitting there with his dark eyes following her.

She didn't look back, didn't want to know what was going on in those eyes. She wanted privacy while she came to terms with what had just taken place in that sunny bedroom.

For the first time in too many years to count Mia had reached out to another human being for comfort. She despised herself for her weakness. She hated him for making her this vulnerable to him. And she hated this whole horrible situation that should never have started, but which now had to continue on its set course.

It was a course which settled her into the next stage of limbo. Surprisingly, Alex did not walk away and forget all about her now his part in the deal they had struck was done. If he was in Athens he came home to the villa every evening. He even began to eat his meals with her, talking, spending the evenings with her. He took her out—picnics to quiet bays in the afternoons, or into Skiathos town during the evenings to enjoy a stroll along the busy L-shaped quayside, now bustling with golden-skinned tourists.

But, true to his word, he never came to her bed again. At night she would lie there, aware that he was lying in his own bed on the other side of that connecting door, and know that he would never cross that threshold again.

Another month drifted by and then another, and a doctor was transported from Athens on a regular basis to check her over. Her weight gain was swift, so much so that she was certain that if she did not keep up her exercise, by swimming twice daily in the pool, she would blow up like a giant balloon.

She didn't see the bloom on her face that seemed to glow with a secret kind of vitality or the way the rich redness of her hair had deepened, having a glossy sheen that shimmered like living fire in the sunlight.

She could not see how voluptuously alluring she looked, with her new maternal shape moulding the front of her body while the rest of her remained incredibly slender in every other way.

In fact, the one and only plus point she could find to all of this was that she loved her baby already. Although she might not like what he was doing to the shape of her body, she did not resent him doing it.

'You grow, my darling,' she whispered softly one morning, as she stood in front of the full-length mirror, ruefully viewing the physical changes while her fingers ran a gentle caress over her swollen abdomen. 'You take whatever you want from your mama to become the strong little man I want you to be.'

And he did take a lot, she had to admit. Took enough to see her safely tucked up in bed before ten each evening and resting several times throughout the day.

Then, on a Wednesday afternoon, two weeks into her fifth month of pregnancy, she was lying on her bed, resting, when she received a telephone call that put the energy back into her with a vengeance. Sofia had answered the call, then came running to get her.

'A Mrs Leyton?' She said the name with difficulty. 'She say it is urgent.'

Mrs Leyton—Cissy, her father's housekeeper—ringing here? Alarm shot through Mia, the kind of alarm that sent her legs to the floor and had her rushing down the stairs to the nearest telephone.

There were only two reasons why her father's house-keeper would be calling here—either something had happened to her father or something had happened to Suzanna.

Pray to God it isn't Suzanna, she begged as she lifted the receiver to her ear with a trembling hand.

It was Suzanna.

Ten minutes after that she was rushing around her bedroom, packing a small case, in a state of high turmoil.

'Listen, Elena,' she snapped at the hovering housekeeper for the very first time since she had arrived here. 'I have to go to England. I don't care how I get there, even if I have to swim! But I do have to go!'

'But the master says you are not to leave the island without him.'

'I don't damn well care what *the master* has said!' she bit back, lifting a flushed face and wild eyes from what she was doing. 'You must have some way you can contact him in case of an emergency! So contact him!' she commanded.

'Contact me for what?' a cool voice enquired from the open doorway to her bedroom.

Mia straightened from what she was doing and spun around to face him. 'Oh, Alex!' she sighed in relief. 'Thank goodness…'

'*Prosehe!*' she heard him shout as sudden dizziness overcame her.

She landed in an ungainly huddle on the bed beside her open suitcase, not unconscious but sickeningly close to it. Beyond the dizziness she could hear him still cursing, and was vaguely aware of him pushing the housekeeper out of the way in his urgency to reach her.

'You stupid, thoughtless female!' he growled at her angrily as he came to stand over her. 'When are you going to learn that you cannot exert yourself like this?'

'I'm all right now,' she whispered, through lips gone strangely numb.

'Oh, you look it,' he mocked grimly, watching the struggle it cost her to sit up again. 'Go any whiter and I won't be able to tell you from the sheet!'

'Just listen!' she cut across him, impatiently ignoring the lingering dizziness, the cloying sense of sickness disturbing her stomach. 'Suzanna, my s-sister, has been taken ill with acute appendicitis. I have to go to England,' she told him. 'She needs me.'

'She needs her father,' Alexander inserted coolly. 'You need to rest and take care of yourself.'

Was that a refusal? Mia glanced up at him and saw that his face was wearing that familiar closed expression. She felt her heart sink when she realised she had a battle on her hands. Elena, she noticed, had disappeared out of the firing line.

'She needs me,' Mia insisted.

Alex walked off towards the bathroom as if she hadn't spoken.

Mia got up, panic beginning to join all the other fears that were flurrying through her. 'Alex…' She met him at the bathroom door, her limbs still shaking and her head still whirling so dizzily that she had to clutch at the doorframe to steady herself. 'Please…' she pleaded with him. 'She's only seven years old! She's in pain and frightened! She needs me there to reassure her! I've always been there for her when she's needed someone!'

'Well, this time it will have to be someone else,' he declared, 'because you are not going. Here…' He offered her the glass of water he had gone into the bathroom to collect.

'I don't want that,' she snapped, and tried to spin away from him, but he stopped her, his free hand closing around her wrist.

'You are amazing, do you know that?' he bit out angrily. 'You walk around this place as if you live on a different planet to the rest of us! You rarely show emotion. You rarely raise your voice or make a move that has not been carefully thought out beforehand! You drift through each day as though you are not really living it. Then some stupid damned phone call comes, and you are suddenly so out of control that you are actually a danger to yourself!'

'What are you talking about?' She frowned at the anger blazing in his eyes.

'You—and the way you live here as if you do not really exist!' he barked. 'You…' his dark face came closer '…almost fainting because you are suddenly doing everything so thoughtlessly that it makes a damned mockery of all that self-control you usually exert over yourself! You!' he said forcefully. 'Almost making the same move just now that sent you toppling on the bed a mere moment ago! And all because of what?' he demanded. 'A sister who has a father to look to her comfort! A sister who can damn well comfort herself because you are not moving off this island!'

'But, you *know* my father!' she cried. 'Do you honestly think he would make time to bother visiting a child he barely remembers exists? She needs me, Alex! Me! And I have to go to her!'

'No.'

It was that blunt—so unequivocal that Mia let out a stunned gasp of appalled disbelief. He ignored it, as he ignored her pale, pained shattered face. He let go of her wrist to walk around her.

'In case you hadn't noticed,' he went on grimly, 'I am back here earlier than usual today because I thought you might enjoy a change of scenery.'

He was back early? Mia blinked at her watch and then blinked back at him, wondering confusedly what the hell that had to do with Suzanna.

'So I have arranged for us to eat a picnic out on a secluded bay I know on the other side of the island,' he continued off-handedly. 'Sofia is preparing the food for us as I speak.'

'I'm not going to sit quietly and eat some damned picnic while Suzanna needs me!' she gasped.

'You will, Mia.' It was so unusual for him to say her name that hearing it now made her blink again and stare at him—made her see exactly why he was using it. He was using it as a don't-push-me-or-I'll-get-nasty warning. 'You will do exactly what I say you can do. Your sister is not your concern.' he said. 'The child you now carry in your womb is your concern. Get your priorities right and forget you even received that phone call for, I promise you, it will be the last one you will receive from this moment on!'

'Oh, I see,' she said, her mouth turning down in a derisive sneer. 'The prisoner has now been placed in solitary confinement—is that it? I am not allowed off this stupid island in case someone guesses the shape of my body may have something to do with you! I am not allowed to speak to anyone outside these grounds in case I stupidly let them know my connection with you! Now I am not to receive phone calls from my own family in case they get the foolish impression that I still have a mind of my own to use now and then!'

'That's it…' he nodded '…in a nutshell. Now, do you want to swim while we are there? If so, pack some swimming gear.'

'I am not going with you!' she shouted at him.

His eyes narrowed, his dark head lifting as if she had just reached out and struck him. 'Don't speak to me like that,' he said, actually sounding shocked.

As an answer to that she walked over to her half-packed suitcase, closed it and hauled it off the bed.

She was a fool to try it, she knew that even as she attempted it. The suitcase was wrenched from her, the hand that came around her swollen body careful of the pressure it applied but demonstrating its intent none the less.

'Now, listen to me,' he said though gritted teeth from behind her. 'You signed a contract whereby I have more rights over you than you have over yourself. You are carrying my child!'

'Your passport to your most coveted dream, you mean,' she tossed at him. 'Other than that, I am nothing to you but the damned loss leader you had to accept if you had any chance of getting your hands on that stupid dream!'

'Loss leader?' he seemed rather stunned at her choice of phrase. 'You see yourself as a loss leader? What the hell do you think I am?'

'A cruel and heartless swine, if you keep me from going to a sick and frightened child who needs me!' she threw at him, and pushed his arm away from her, rather surprised when he let her do it. 'But, unlike you, I can't treat a child's pain and distress as nothing so I'm going—whether you like it or not!'

Reaching out, she snatched up her handbag and began to walk towards the bedroom door. Blow the case, she told herself grimly. She didn't need it. She had money of her own. She could buy fresh clothes when she needed them. She didn't need Alex. She could pay for her own passage off this damned island.

'I will not let you go, you know,' he informed her grimly.

'I am not aware of asking your permission,' she replied, as cold as ice and shaking so badly her legs could barely support her.

'My men will detain you the moment you approach the gates of the villa.'

She was at the top of the landing now, her hand clutching the banister, so she felt reasonably safe in spinning to face him without risking tumbling down those stairs in another silly faint.

He was standing several feet away, but was eyeing her calculatingly, as if he was wondering what she would do if he made another dive for her.

'Are you saying they will physically stop me?' she demanded.

'No,' he conceded, 'but I certainly will. Come away from

the edge of those stairs,' he commanded tersely. 'Your face tells me you are struggling to stay upright.'

'And your face tells me you have no idea whatsoever of what it is like to love someone more than you love yourself.'

'Are you talking about your sister?' he countered.

If anything, she went even paler. 'Yes,' she confirmed. 'Suzanna needs me. I am the only m-mother she has known all her life, and she has a right to expect me to come to her when she's hurting.'

'Go to her without my permission and you break your contract with me.'

Just like that. She stood there and stared at him.

Oh, so clever, she was thinking bitterly. He was calling her bluff. He was reminding her of the one tiny clause she had shown no interest in among all those other clauses he had thrust upon her in that contract—the clause that stated she not leave Greece without his permission while carrying his child or she forfeited custody of the child.

At the time of signing she had seen no reason why she should want to leave Greece until this ordeal was over.

Her heart gave a painful thump, her stomach muscles coiling in sickening understanding. It was time to choose— Suzanna or the baby growing inside her. A baby she loved already and would go on loving far more than this cruel man would ever love it.

Could she do that to her baby—forfeit all control over his little life to this man?

The rest didn't matter. The rest would happen, no matter what she did now. She was putting nothing else at risk but her baby's future.

My God, she thought bleakly, why does fate like to test me like this? Her eyes closed, her throat moving in a constricted swallow. As she hovered there, at the top of those polished stairs, she saw Suzanna's wan little face, looking up at her. Suzanna, with the same solemn green eyes as her own, with the same copper-red hair as her own and with the naturally vibrant personality that went with green eyes and red hair crushed out of her, just as it had been crushed out of Mia.

And, yes, she accepted, with an ache inside that almost sent her doubling up in agony, that she could forfeit this baby for Suzanna. She could do it simply because Suzanna had endured enough misery in her seven short years, whereas at least this baby would be allowed to be himself— that was one distinction she felt she could make between Alex and her father. Both might be despots, both might be ruthless and heartless, but Alex would not punish his son for the sins of the mother.

Mia's eyes fluttered open and looked into those darkly watchful ones. 'I h-have to go,' she whispered. 'I'm sorry.'

With that, she turned and walked down the stairs. Her heart was bleeding and her eyes were blurred by wretched tears because it was like history repeating itself and she didn't think she could bear it.

'Wait.'

She was at the bottom of the stairs before his command hit her eardrums. She stopped, shaking, frozen by the horrible fear that she was going to completely break down and give in to him if he put any more pressure on her.

His soft tread on the stairs as he came down towards her sounded like thunder inside her head. She didn't turn this time. She couldn't bring herself to face him because she knew her own face was showing such a conflagration of emotion that he would probably not understand it.

'Why?' he demanded roughly as he reached her. 'Give me one good reason why this so important to you, why you would throw away all rights to your own unborn child, and I will let you go to your damned sister!'

Her eyes fluttered shut, her heart squeezing in her breast on a pang of agony that only she would ever understand. Give him one good reason, he had demanded.

One good reason.

Well, she had one. 'Suzanna is not my sister,' she informed him unsteadily. 'She is my daughter...'

For the first time in seven years she had let herself say it, and it felt so strange that she shuddered.

'Is that a good enough reason for you?' she said into the bone-crunching silence that echoed around her.

CHAPTER SIX

No ANSWER. Alex didn't say a single word and, after that, neither did she. Mia was trembling too badly to speak, anyway. She didn't know what kept Alex silent, and at that moment she didn't really care.

She was too shocked, dazed by her own admission and paralysed by the burning knowledge that, by saying what she had said, she had just lost Suzanna on a broken promise to another man.

Her father had warned her. It had been part of their bargain, written into that other contract they had signed between them. She was to tell no one of her true relationship to Suzanna before he had his precious grandson.

Now what had she got left? she asked herself starkly. She was standing here, ready to forfeit her claim over her unborn child, and had now, in effect, forfeited her claim over the one she had given birth to seven long years ago!

What did that make her? What kind of mother was she?

The hand was gentle on her wrist when it caught hold of her this time, but it was a mark of how badly she had shaken herself that she didn't even try to pull away from him.

'Come on,' he urged her huskily. 'It will take about an hour to get my plane to the airport here. Come and sit down while I make arrangements…'

He was treating her like someone would a highly volatile substance. She didn't really blame him. She felt very volatile, as though she might just explode with any more provocation.

It was a further mark of how weakened the ugly scene had left her that she allowed herself to lean against him a little as he guided her across the hall and into the sunny sitting room. He saw her seated on one of the pale blue sofas then seemed to hover over her, as though he was preparing to say something.

Mia kept her eyes lowered and bit deep into her trembling bottom lip, waiting tensely for the questions to come.

Yet they didn't come. In the end Alex let out a small sigh and moved away—right out of the room, in fact—leaving her sitting there, still tense, still locked in the appalling fall-out of her own shocking confession.

Later—she wasn't sure how much later—Sofia arrived with a tray of tea-things, which she placed on a table in front of Mia, and then disappeared without a word.

More minutes ticked by. Alex came back and paused when he saw her sitting there just as he had left her. It was he who poured out a cup of tea for her and gently placed the cup and saucer in her hand.

'Drink,' he commanded.

She drank like an automaton. He stood over her, and once again she could sense the questions, rattling around his head. He wasn't a fool. He would already have worked out that if Suzanna was seven years old and Mia twenty-five then Mia had to have been very young when she'd fallen pregnant.

Seventeen years old, in fact. A small grimace touched her bloodless mouth as she lifted the cup to it. Seventeen, and her mother barely cold in her grave after killing herself in a car accident that was her own fault because she had been drinking. Her husband had driven her to look for escape from his mental cruelty in an alcoholic haze—which was still no excuse for leaving Mia alone with a father who hated her and a brother who couldn't care less about her.

So she'd rebelled.

And what a rebellion it had been, she mocked herself now and as bitterly as she had done ever since those wild six months after her seventeenth birthday.

She'd skipped boarding school. Run away. Had got in with a crowd of young groupies who'd followed the current rock group of the time around the country. It had taken the lead singer two months to notice her, a month to take her virginity and a another month to tire of her and throw her out of his life.

So there she had been—seventeen, homeless, penniless and pregnant. By the time Suzanna was born she had hit an all-time low, but it was still a very last resort that had sent her begging to her father.

'Drink some more.'

She glanced up to find that Alex was sitting on the sofa opposite. Her eyes quickly dropped away again, but not before they had taken in the fact that he had changed his clothes somewhere along the line. The business suit he had arrived home in had been replaced by something more casual in a pale linen fabric and a plain white T-shirt.

A sound outside brought her head up again. It was a car, drawing up at the front door. Alex stood up, came over to her and bent to remove her cup. 'Sofia has packed for us,' he murmured flatly. 'All we need to do is go now. OK?'

OK? Why was he asking her if it was OK to leave when he had never bothered to ask her opinion on anything before?

It didn't really matter now, she told herself hollowly as she nodded her head with its neatly styled hair, which should have drawn his anger but was a small detail that seemed to have passed by him unnoticed.

He went to help her rise to her feet again, but she withdrew abruptly from his touch. He was the enemy, she grimly reminded herself. You do not lean weakly on the enemy.

The journey to the airport was carried out in silence. The transfer to his private jet was achieved with the minimum of fuss, and it was only as she sat there, feeling the jet's surge of power as it shot smoothly into the air, that it sank in that Alex was actually sitting beside her.

'You didn't need to come with me.' She found her voice at last, frail and constricted though it was. 'I will come back just as soon as Suzanna is feeling better.'

He didn't answer. His lean, dark face was a closed book as he sat there, gazing directly ahead. Not piloting the plane himself this time, she noted. Not doing anything but sitting here, lost deep within his own grim train of thought.

Tears filled her eyes. She didn't know why. They just did. Then almost directly out of the rubble in which her emotions lay, her chin rose in what had become a familiar habit to those who had been around her during the last few months. Her bloodless mouth straightened and her tear-washed eyes cleared.

'I am not a whore.'

Why she said that was just as big a surprise to her as the tears were that had preceded it.

'You announce yourself in those terms,' Alex quietly replied. 'I have never used the term to you.'

'You don't need to. I can hear it screaming at me every time you look at me.'

From the corner of her eye she saw his grim mouth twist. 'You are your own salesman,' he said. 'Don't blame others for believing what you place in front of them.'

Was that true? she wondered, then sighed because she decided it was most probably very true and that she did present herself as the kind of cool-headed mercenary who would have sold her body for the proverbial pot of gold.

'Well, just in case you're worrying that I might have passed on some dreadful social disease with my whoring ways, I think I had better reassure you that there have only been two men in my life who have used my body—Suzanna's father was one of them, and you the other.'

'If I had been worried about such a prospect I would have insisted on the relevant test to reassure myself. As it is...' his dark head turned to study her whitened profile '...I already knew most of what you have just told me. I had you thoroughly investigated, you see, before I agreed to any of this. The nun's life you have been leading since your wild rebellion eight years ago was easily discovered, which made the way you responded to me all the more intriguing...'

Her cheeks went red, and he lifted a finger to gently stroke that heated skin. 'Only the fact that you have given birth to a child escaped my investigators. Now that,' he added softly, 'was a surprise.'

'And one you are now going to use against me, I suppose.'

'Will I need to?'

It was a challenge. Mia shivered delicately and shifted her cheek so his finger had to drop away. 'I want my baby,' she murmured huskily, 'but I will not keep him at Suzanna's expense.'

'He doesn't warrant the same fierce feelings of love and protection your daughter ignites in you?'

'Yes,' she admitted, one of her hands moving to rest on that firm mound where her new baby lay. 'But Suzanna has paid long enough for the misfortune of having me as her mother. She deserves better and I am prepared to do anything to make sure I am in a position to give it to her.'

'Like sleeping with a man you hold in contempt?' he suggested. 'Like taking any flak he might wish to throw at you, without saying a thing in your own defence? Like allowing yourself to be sent into isolation while he punishes you for his own weaknesses?'

'So you acknowledge you have weaknesses?'

He smiled rather drily. 'I know myself quite well,' he answered flatly. 'I know my weaknesses—and my strengths. I am thirty-six years old, after all,' he added. 'If I have not learned them by now then I truly am in danger of becoming a man like your father. That is how you see me, is it not—as a man no better than your father?'

'You see a chunk of real estate as worth more than life itself so—yes,' she admitted. 'You are no better than him.'

'And you?' he challenged. 'What does that make you?'

Her green eyes flashed—the first sign of life they had shown since she'd walked away from him in that sunny bedroom back at the villa. 'I sold myself to you, not another's life.' She made the distinction. 'And you bought the use of me from my father, not from me. In return he gives you your precious island while he gets what he wants—a male heir to whom he can leave his filthy money. I get Suzanna and this child as payment. So the only thing I have sold to anyone is the use of my own body. You tell me what that makes me.' She threw the challenge right back at him.

His smile was cynical, to say the least. 'You seem to have conveniently forgotten the five million pounds your father is paying you on delivery of his male heir,' he drawled derisively.

Mia's heart-shaped upper lip clamped itself tightly to her much fuller bottom lip and she looked away from him out of the window at the clear blue stretch of sky through which they were flying.

The new silence pulled at the tiny muscles in her throat and around her heart, lining the wall of her tensely held ribcage.

'There is no money,' he bit out suddenly. 'You lied about the five million to throw me off the scent!'

'I have money of my own,' she countered defensively. 'I don't need money from my father.'

'Your mother's money.' He nodded, surprising her with just how deeply his investigators had dug into her life. 'She placed her money in a trust fund for you, which matured on your twenty-fifth birthday. A paltry two hundred thousand pounds,' he added with biting contempt.

Two hundred thousand was a small fortune to most people and more than Mia had ever had access to before. She could easily live off it with a bit of careful planning. She could bring her children up, know they would want for nothing materially.

'You know,' he muttered, 'you *are* a whore in a lot of ways.' With an angry movement he unfastened his seat belt and stood up. 'You sell yourself cheap and you see yourself as cheap!'

With that, he walked away, leaving her sitting there alone while she let the full thrust of his final angry words sink in.

It was getting quite late when they eventually landed, the August evening cool after the evenings Mia had grown used to back in Greece.

'Which hospital?' Alex asked her as they settled in the back of a chauffeur-driven Mercedes.

She told him, and he leaned forward to relay the information to their driver, who was separated from them by a tinted sheet of glass.

It was a small relief that he wasn't making a battle out of going directly to the hospital. She knew she was tired, and knew how that tiredness was showing on her pale, pinched face, along with the worry and strain she was experiencing for Suzanna's sake.

Suzanna. Her daughter. Her stomach flipped over, a frisson of anxiety shaking her system for that poor child she had never been able to claim as her own but who shared, none the less, the kind of bond with herself that really only a mother and child could share.

Mia might have been forced by circumstances to hand over her daughter to her father but he had never managed to break that bond, though he had tried—many times. 'She's my daughter now,' he had announced with grim satisfaction the day the adoption papers were signed. 'Ever be tempted to tell her who you really are and it will be the last time you will ever see her.'

Mia shivered as she sat there beside a silent Alex, remembering the choices she had been offered the day she went home to her father, frightened, desperate, destitute and carrying her new-born baby girl in her arms, to beg from the last man on earth she wanted to go crawling to.

'I won't have any gossip about my promiscuous daughter and her bastard child,' he'd warned her brutally. 'If you want my support, let me adopt her, though, God knows, I don't need another damned female hanging around me. You can be a sister to her,' he had decided, 'but as far as anyone is concerned she is my child, not yours, and don't you let yourself forget that.'

So she'd placed her own life on hold and had stayed living with her father so she could be close to her daughter. It was she who had brought Suzanna up since she was a baby, she who had seen to her needs throughout her young years, and she who had visited the child every weekend since her father had placed Suzanna in that dreadful boarding school. 'To toughen her up,' he'd announced heartlessly. 'The way you mollycoddle her, she will never learn to take care of herself if I don't split you up.'

But really he had sent Suzanna away to school because he knew how it would hurt the two of them to be separated like that. And because it placed Mia under yet more obligation to him. 'You can have her to yourself during the vacations,' he'd promised. 'So long as you remain living here with me, that is.'

Then Tony had been killed, and his whole attitude to both Mia and Suzanna had taken on a radical change. In Tony he had seen the continuance of himself. He hadn't needed to look any further for a male heir to his fortune. That was when Mia had become a tool for him to use for a different purpose—and Suzanna was the bait he had used to make Mia agree to everything he'd demanded.

'You get me a grandson and I'll let you have full custody of Suzanna. I'll choose the man. I'll discover the weak link that'll make him marry you. All you have to do is go to bed with him—not a problem for a whore like you.'

Not a problem. In the dimness of that luxury car she grimaced. Well, it hadn't been a problem in the end, had it? In fact, going to bed with Alex had turned out to be a pleasure! Which probably meant her father knew her better than she knew herself. Did he know she was already pregnant? Had Alex told him? She certainly hadn't. She'd had no contact whatsoever with her father since she'd got married. But Alex would have been eager to announce their success to Jack Frazier, she was sure.

In four more months or so her father would get the boy to whom he wanted to leave all his money, Alex would get his island and Mia would get custody of Suzanna.

All pacts with the devil, with this small baby growing inside her the unwitting champion for the three of them.

'Does she know you are her mother?'

The question made her jump, coming out of the blue as it did.

'No,' she replied. 'I am not allowed to tell her until this child is safely delivered.' Then her breasts heaved as she sucked in a tense breath of air and let it out again before she added huskily, 'I was not allowed to tell you either. If my father finds out that you know, he will say I have broken the contract I have with him and keep Suzanna, just for the hell of hurting me.'

The hospital came into view, its brightly lit windows announcing that time here had no real meaning. Work here went on twenty-fours a day.

Alex came with her, travelling through the corridors with a tight-lipped silence that kept his presence remote from Mia, who had become barely aware of him as her anxiety grew the closer they got to the ward to which they had been directed.

They came upon a nursing station first, with a pretty young nurse standing behind it who glanced up then smiled the warmest smile Mia had been offered in months. 'You must be Suzanna's sister,' she declared immediately. 'You look so much like her.'

'How is she?' Mia asked worriedly.

'Fine.' The nurse came around the station to touch her gently on the hand. 'The operation went off without a hitch. The appendix hadn't burst so she should have no complications. She's already out of Recovery and back on the ward here, though we do have her settled in a room off the main ward so we can keep a special eye on her.'

'Can I see her?' Mia's eyes were already darting off in the direction the nurse's hand had indicated.

'Of course. She's asleep,' the nurse warned as she moved off, with them following, 'but you can take a quick peek at her to reassure yourself. She has been asking for you constantly...'

The room was nothing more than a tiny annexe, with brightly painted pictures, done with childish hands, pinned all over the white-painted walls. But it was the little bed in the middle of the room that held Mia's attention. Her eyes darkened, her face losing what bit of colour it possessed as one trembling hand went up to cover the sudden quiver of her mouth while she stared at her daughter lying so pale and still.

Without taking her eyes off that sleeping face, Mia walked over to the bed, then gently stroked the child's pale cheek before she bent and replaced the hand with a kiss.

'She looks so vulnerable,' she whispered, worry-darkened eyes running over that little face with its shock of bright hair tied back to keep it tidy.

'She'll be sore for a few days,' the nurse said quietly, 'but she shouldn't feel too much discomfort. Her worst worry was that you wouldn't manage to come.'

Mia winced. Somewhere beyond the periphery of her own vision someone else winced also.

'Apparently, you were not in the country when she became ill.'

'I got here as soon as I could,' Mia said huskily. 'Has my father been in to see her?'

'No.' The nurse's tone cooled perceptibly. 'Only the lady who came in the ambulance with her. A Mrs Leyton—your father's housekeeper, I believe? She stayed until Suzanna was safely back up here again before she left.'

'Thank you,' Mia murmured. 'I'll sit here with her for a little while, if you don't mind.'

'Of course not,' the nurse said. 'There is a chair just behind you,' she added, and with a curious glance at the man who was standing in the far corner of the room, but who had contributed nothing to the conversation, she left them alone.

Mia didn't even notice. Her whole attention was fixed on Suzanna as one of her hands searched blindly behind her to find the chair so she could sit down on it.

Then she reached for and gently closed her fingers around Suzanna's small fingers, lifting them to her cheek and keeping them there. 'I'm here now, darling,' she murmured softly.

The child didn't move. She was still too heavily sedated to be aware of anything that was going on around her. But that didn't stop Mia talking gently to her, murmuring the kind of reassuring phrases a mother seemed to find instinctively.

Maybe the child did hear within the fluffy clouds of her own subconscious because something seemed to alter about her. Her slender limbs lost a tension that hadn't been apparent until it had eased away and her pale, rather thin face seemed to gain some colour.

As silently as he had observed everything, Alex observed the change in the child also, and just as silently he walked

out of the little room and left them to it, sensitive enough—
no matter how Mia believed the opposite about him—to
know he was intruding on something private.

He came back an hour later and, after pausing in the
doorway to frown at the look of exhaustion straining Mia's
features, he stepped forward and touched her shoulder. He
waited for and received the expected start that confirmed
to him that she had forgotten his presence.

'It's time to go,' he said quietly. 'We will return tomorrow, but you need to rest now if you don't want to end up
too tired to be of any use to her.'

A protest leapt to her lips—then hovered for a moment
before it was left unsaid. He was right, she conceded. She
was so utterly weary she could barely function. So, without
a word, she stood up, bent to the child's cheek then straightened, and without so much as a glance at him she turned
and walked out of the room.

As soon as she was settled in the car again her head went
back against the leather headrest and her tired eyes closed.

'You are very alike,' Alex remarked quietly. 'Does she
have your colour eyes, too?'

'Mmm.' Mia didn't want to talk—didn't even want to
think very much. Relief was, at this moment, playing the
biggest role in making her feel so exhausted. She had travelled from Greece to the hospital in a state of high nervous
tension, not knowing what she was going to find when she
got there. Now she had reassured herself that Suzanna was
going to be all right it seemed to make everything else
deflate inside her.

'Has no one ever made the natural connection between
the two of you?' Alex persisted. 'It seems impossible to
me not to consider a stronger bond than sisterhood when
the likeness is so strikingly obvious.'

'My brother had the same colouring,' she explained.
'People suspected Suzanna was my brother's child but not
mine because I was so young when I had her.'

'I thought you told me your father did not believe you were his daughter.' He frowned. 'But if you and your brother have the same colouring, surely he has to accept the blood connection somewhere?'

'We have the same mother,' she said. 'Exactly who it was that fathered us was a different thing entirely.'

'And a son was easier for your father to accept as his own than a mere daughter,' he concluded grimly, 'because it suited him to accept a son where, because of his bigotry, he didn't need to accept the daughter.'

'Now you're catching on,' Mia said very drily. 'If you want the full truth of it, I don't think my father is capable of fathering children,' she announced quite detachedly. 'More to the point, I think he knows it, which is why he set you and me up for this kind of deal when he could, at his age and with his money, have quite easily got himself another wife and produced a dozen more sons of his own. What's more,' she added, 'I think my mother was unfaithful to him from the day she married him.'

It was another confession that managed to shock her simply because she was actually telling it to Alex of all men.

'She came from a very socially acceptable family that had lost most of its money to inheritance tax. My father wanted to be accepted by that society so he bought himself into it, by marrying my mother. He wanted very socially acceptable sons to carry on his name for him, but when she didn't produce them he began to get nasty, calling her all those unpleasant names people can call women who don't have children easily. So she went out and got herself a lover. Conceived a child—though she was never absolutely sure whether either of her children belonged to her husband or her lover because she continued to sleep with both of them right up until the moment she managed to kill herself.'

'And the lover?'

'He died of cancer a couple of years ago,' Mia said, then

added reluctantly. 'He was Karl Dansing, the electronics magnate.'

There was a stifled gasp of shock from the man beside her. 'Are you trying to tell me,' he murmured gruffly, 'that you could be Karl Dansing's daughter?'

'Does that impress you?' Mia drawled. 'Well, don't go off the deep end about it,' she said mockingly before he could say anything further. 'As father figures go, neither impress me much. Karl Dansing must have known that Tony and I could have been his children but he never once owned up to it while he was alive, and didn't even give us a mention in his will.'

'But—.'

'Look—' She sighed wearily. 'Can we stop the inquisition, please? I'm too tired to deal with it and just too indifferent to want to talk about it! If you want to know anything else, put your investigators to work,' she suggested grimly. 'I'm sure they will come up with something juicy for you if you pay them well enough!'

With that, she closed her eyes firmly again, aware that she sounded embittered by her own sordid history. After all, who wanted to claim as parents the kind of people she had just described? She certainly didn't. Even spoiled, selfish, supremely avaricious Tony hadn't. 'I'll make do with what I've got,' he'd said to her once when Karl Dansing's name had come up. 'He may be worth a hell of a lot more than Jack but he has four other kids to share his money, whereas I'll be getting the whole lot from Jack one day.'

Only he hadn't got anything in the end, had he? Because Tony had died very much the same way their mother had died—in a car accident, while driving too fast with a skinful of booze and heaven alone knew what else.

She still missed him. Oddly and surprisingly, considering his selfish view of life. But they had shared a kind of affection for each other. And Tony had been good to Suzanna. In his own way she suspected he had even loved the child, which was enough for Mia to forgive him his other faults.

Suzanna…

Her mind drifted back to that poor, defenceless child she had left sleeping in her hospital bed. All at once depression swept over her. What was she going to do? she wondered fretfully. How was she going to bring herself to leave Suzanna again when Alex decided it was time to go back to Greece?

A more urgent question was how long he was going to let her stay here. A couple of days? A week? Maybe two, if she was lucky?

Whatever, it was not going to be long enough. Just seeing the little girl lying there had told Mia that Suzanna needed her to be closer to her!

It was the long vacation from school at the moment, which meant Suzanna would have to go back to her father's house when she was eventually discharged from hospital. The child couldn't cope with Jack Frazier on her own. She never had been able to. He only had to look at her to petrify her.

Cissy had told her during that hurried phone call today that her father had accused Suzanna of fabricating the pain in her side. He'd called it attention-seeking, and had told her that if she expected to get Mia back by playing on his sympathy then she was in for a disappointment because Mia was never coming back so she may as well get used to it.

Oh, God. How could one human being be so cruel to another? What had made Jack Frazier the cold hearted monster he was?

Her hand came up to rub at her eyes, where the ache behind them was beginning to drag at what was left of her severely depleted stamina.

Beside her, Alex moved. She went still, her nerve-ends beginning to sing beneath the surface of her skin because she had a horrible feeling he was going to reach out and touch her. If he did touch her, she was going to fall apart completely.

Then the car stopped and, bringing her hand away from her wary eyes, she found that his attention was fixed outside the car and not on her at all.

Which was a levelling experience, she discovered as she watched him open his door and climb out, impatiently waving the chauffeur away so he could come around the car and open Mia's door himself.

'You are almost dead on your feet,' he muttered, watching her sway slightly as she joined him on the pavement.

'I just need a good night's sleep,' she replied.

'What you need,' he grunted, as he helped her up the steps of a very exclusive white-painted town-house she presumed must be his home when he was in London, 'is to be yourself occasionally, and not all these other personalities you conjure up, depending on who it is you are having to deal with!'

'Oh, very cryptic,' she mocked.

'Not cryptic—tragic,' he corrected grimly. 'A good psychoanalyst could make a life study out of you,' he muttered, stabbing an angry finger at the front doorbell. 'Today alone I have met the vixen, the ruthless negotiator, the loving mother and the cynic,' he said, with tight-lipped sarcasm. 'As the old saying goes, would the real woman please stand and reveal herself?'

'Not for you she won't,' she tossed back frostily.

'Oh, I've already met her,' he insisted tightly. 'In her bed, in the darkness. And she is quite the most fascinating one of all, I assure you.'

'You're mistaken,' Mia replied. 'That was the whore you met there— Why are you ringing this bell, instead of using a key to get in the house?' she asked frowningly.

'Because—obviously—the house does not belong to me,' he replied sardonically.

The front door swung open, and she was suddenly faced with exactly whose house this was.

Oh, hell! she thought wearily. What now? Why this? What was it supposed to mean?

It was Alex's younger brother, Leon.

CHAPTER SEVEN

'AH,' LEON smiled politely enough. 'So you are here at last. We were beginning to give up on you.'

But Mia could see by the way his eyes barely touched her that he was no happier to see her standing on his doorstep than she was to be here. He obviously still resented her intrusion into Alex's life, and was not going to bother to hide it.

'Come on in,' he said.

Her shoulders drooped wearily, the long, long day spent enduring all the other stresses leaving her with nothing with which to fight this next ordeal.

An arm came warmly about her shoulders, and for once she huddled gratefully into it, going into retreat because it was the only thing she could do as Alex propelled her into a warmly lit hallway then paused to murmur something to his brother in his own language.

She didn't know what he'd said—didn't want to know—but she sensed the hint of a warning beneath the casual tone and the arm around her shoulders tightened briefly, as if to offer support.

With what she suspected was a forced lightness, Alex enquired rather drily, 'Where's the wicked witch?'

'I heard that,' a sharp female voice responded.

What now? Mia wondered, raising very wary eyes to see the most exquisite vision of blonde loveliness, dressed in tight faded jeans and a skinny white top, appear at the top of the stairway in front of her.

Very tall and incredibly slender, she had the bluest pair of eyes Mia had ever encountered but what was most disconcerting was that those eyes were smiling at her warmly—genuinely warmly.

'Hi,' she said pleasantly. Then, before Mia could answer, she went on, 'Oh, good grief, but you look dreadful! What's the matter with you, Alex?' She frowned at him. 'Trailing a pregnant woman all over the world, as if she's some piece of baggage! How is your sister?' she asked Mia, without waiting for Alex to answer either. 'Is she very poorly? Mia, isn't it?' She smiled that warm smile again. 'I'm Carol,' she announced. 'The lucky one because I got the nicer brother. You drew the short straw, I'm afraid, when you got Alex.'

'Mia is exhausted,' Alex interrupted rather irritably. 'She doesn't need all your crazy chatter right now. She needs her bed.'

'Oh, sorry,' Carol said, sounding rather disconcerted by his curt tone, 'This way, Mia. Gosh, you look done in. Will you let me help you? You can lean on me, if you want to. I don't mind.'

'I can manage, thank you,' Mia answered quietly.

'Yes. Right.' Carol nodded, and after a short pause, when she glanced from one brother to the other, she turned and began to lead the way up the stairs while Mia followed, having to draw on the very last dregs of her stamina

She was shown into a prettily decorated bedroom, with blue walls and apricot furnishings. There was a connecting bathroom, where Carol took it upon herself to run Mia a bath while all Mia could do was lower herself onto the side of the bed and wilt.

By the time Carol came back into the bedroom Mia knew all about Leon, the great love of Carol's life. How they met, where they met and where he had proposed to her. She now knew that they had been married for two years but were not going to start a family yet because Leon had insisted that his children were born in Greece and they couldn't go and live in Greece until the new hotel they had just bought and were refurbishing here in London was finished up and running.

'The bath's ready,' Carol announced. 'All you have to do is get undressed and sink into it. I'll be back in half an hour to make sure you're all right…'

Silence. At last a blessed, beautiful silence fell upon the room at her exit. Mia remained where she was for a few precious minutes and simply let that silence flow all around her, then made herself get up and trail her weary body into the bathroom.

By the time she had hauled herself in and out of the bath again she was so utterly worn out that she had to sit down on the bathroom stool to recover. Hell, she thought as her head began to swim, a quick shower would have been more sensible in your condition. You really should have known that!

'How are you doing in there?'

Carol was back already, Mia noted wryly.

'One moment,' she called back, hurriedly donning the short white silk slip-style nightdress Carol had thoughtfully hung behind the bathroom door for her. She ran a quick brush through her hair and, on a deep fortifying breath, let herself out of the bathroom.

'Wow!' the other woman gasped. 'Look at all that hair! You're gorgeous, aren't you? No wonder Alex has been walking around looking as though he doesn't know what's hit him! I hope my figure looks as good as yours does with a bump stuck on the front of it. Here, get into bed. You'll be more comfortable there…'

Without a word, Mia did as she was told. A tray landed across her lap. Her pillows were fluffed up.

'Now…' Standing back to view her ministrations, Carol frowned and then smiled when she realised she was frowning, as though she was trying very hard to make Mia feel wanted. 'I'm going to leave you—Alex's orders.' She grimaced. 'He's frightened I'll say something I shouldn't—

like I think its disgraceful the way he's been treating you, no matter what the circumstances. See?' She grinned. 'I've said it anyway!'

Not that she seemed to care!

At last she disappeared. Mia wilted again, and in the next second her mind switched off. As if it had taken more than enough for one day and was refusing to accept any more, it dropped her into a slumber from which she didn't even stir when the bedroom door opened again an hour later.

Alex stood on the threshold, staring at the way she had fallen asleep, half sitting up and with the untouched tray still lying across her lap.

With stealth he closed the door, then moved across the carpet to stand over her. She looked exhausted, even in sleep, the signs of stress evident in her washed-out face. Without disturbing her, he removed the tray and set it aside Then, after another brief grim study of her, he turned and walked into the bathroom.

Ten minutes later he was back, showered, shaved and wrapped in a thin black cotton bathrobe. Silently he moved around the room, switching off several lamps Carol had left burning. Then, with the darkness enfolding him, he came back to the bed, removed the bathrobe and slid his unashamedly naked body into the bed beside her.

Still she did not so much as move a muscle. He lay there on his side and watched her for ages before—on a grimace that said he didn't much fancy what he was about to do next—he leaned over her so he could slide an arm beneath her shoulders and lift her just enough to remove one of the pillows from behind her.

As he settled her back again in what he hoped was a more comfortable position her eyes flickered open, green homing directly onto guarded brown.

Mia blinked slowly, her sleep-sluggish mind taking its time to remember that it had been long months since she had woken to find him leaning over her in the darkness like this.

As she did remember, her eyes widened warily.

'It's OK,' Alex said softly. 'I was not about to seduce you while you were sleeping. I was simply trying to make you more comfortable.'

'What are you doing here?' she whispered, still staring owlishly into those rich, dark, slightly rueful eyes of his.

'Carol's idea,' he said. 'She naturally assumes we share a bed, and I was not up to one of her question-and-answer sessions, by informing her that we did not.'

Grimacing, he moved away from her, going to lie on his back and stare at the ceiling while Mia took a few moments to take in this totally unexpected new situation.

He intended to share her bed, she seemed to find it necessary to tell herself. They had been married for almost seven long months, and *never* shared the same bed as a married couple normally did.

Now this. It felt weird, like lying next to a stranger.

'Do you mind?' he asked quietly.

'Its a big enough bed.' She shrugged. 'I suppose we will manage.'

Silence fell, the kind of tight, stinging, uncomfortable silence that caught at the breath and increased the tension in the darkness of the room.

'Why did you bring me here to your brother's house?' Mia asked when she could stand it no longer.

'It is the *family* house,' he said. 'Leon and Carol are in residence right now because Leon is based here at the moment. They expect me to stay with them when I am in London. It would have been…awkward if I had taken you to a hotel.'

'I won't do or say anything that could embarrass you,' she assured him huskily.

His dark head turned. Mia felt his eyes on her. 'You have a very low opinion of me, don't you?' he said.

Mia's head turned so that their eyes clashed again. 'It's mutual,' she countered.

He didn't answer, those lush, long, coal-black lashes flickering slightly as he continued to lie there studying her in the darkness—a darkness they had always been more comfortable in. A darkness where most of their most intimate moments had taken place—their mutual passion, their ability to drown in each other.

Drown, as Mia could feel herself beginning to drown right now—drown in those deep, dark, sensually knowing eyes that could probe right inside her and touch places only this man had touched, ignite senses only this man could ignite.

'Go to sleep,' he ordered softly.

Sleep. Yes, she agreed, dragging her eyes away from his. Don't look at him, she told herself sternly as she turned her head on the pillow. Don't even think about him, lying here next to you.

And don't, for goodness' sake, remember what it feels like to have him make love to you!

The stern lecture made no difference because she did imagine him making love to her. She could feel his hands caress her body, feel his mouth move sensually on hers, could feel her breathing growing shallow as her heart picked up pace and that place between her thighs begin to pulse with a message so erotic that she had to lie very still with her muscles tightly clenched in an effort to subdue the feeling.

What made it all worse was that it was all happening under his steady gaze. She could sense him watching her, knew he was witnessing the increase in her breathing and the way her eyes couldn't close because she was holding herself so tense beside him. A tension that was fizzing in the air around them. Sexual tension.

'Go to sleep,' he repeated in a soft, silken voice that

utterly rejected every message her stupid body was sending him.

Dismayed, she threw herself onto her side and away from him, so agonised by her own weaknesses that it actually hurt like a physical pain.

It took her ages to relax and ages to drift back into a restless slumber—only to come blisteringly awake again the moment she felt him move beside her.

With her heart beginning to pound in her aching chest, she listened to him release a heavy sigh then carefully slide out of the bed. There was a rustling sound as he pulled a robe over his body. Even in the darkness, with her back towards him, she could feel his grimness and knew—just knew—that the grimness was there because he hated this situation so much.

Hated having to lie here beside her in this bed when he was probably wishing himself a million miles away.

With his mistress, most probably.

He threw himself down in one of the easy chairs by the curtained window. She heard him sigh again, then—nothing. Nothing for long minutes while she held herself still, listening until she could stand to listen no longer and turned over in the bed to gaze at the dark bulk by the window.

He was asleep, stretched out in the chair with his dark head thrown back and his face a mask of grim perseverance.

Tears began to burn at the back of her eyes. Weak tears. Wretched tears. Foolishly hurt tears! She fell asleep like that, with the tears still clinging to her lashes.

When she awoke next morning she was alone as usual. The knowledge that Alex had found it impossible to spend a whole night in the same bed with her lay like a lead weight across her chest.

Then she remembered Suzanna and got up, showered quickly and dressed herself in a pair of comfortable stretch white leggings and a pale blue overshirt, before taking a deep breath and letting herself out of that bedroom to go in search of the others.

She was just coming down the stairs when Alex walked out of one of the rooms off the hallway. He saw her and paused to watch her descent through those impenetrable brown eyes of his.

'You still look tired,' he observed huskily.

Still stinging from last night's humiliating rejection, she dropped her eyes from his and concentrated fiercely on the stairs in front of her. 'It's worry, not tiredness,' she contended. 'I would like to ring the hospital,' she went on coolly. 'Is there a telephone I could use?'

'Of course.'

Stepping back to the room he had just walked out of, he opened the door and gestured her through it. She found herself standing in a study that was very male in style—a lot of polished wood, walls lined with books and the more modern state-of-the-art communications hardware.

There was a desk by the window, with a telephone sitting on it. Mia thanked him quietly and walked over to pick up the receiver.

Her thanks had been a polite way of dismissing him but, to her annoyance, he didn't leave her to her privacy but came to lean on the desk beside her so he could watch her face while she spoke to the hospital.

Suzanna had spent a comfortable night, she was assured. She also knew that Mia had been in to see her late last night, and the fact that she was actually here in London had cheered the child up remarkably. 'She keeps on asking when you are coming in again,' the nurse told her.

'Later this morning,' Mia replied. 'Tell her I will be with her just as soon as I can be.'

'OK?' Alex asked quietly as she lowered the receiver.

Mia nodded, her lips pressed together to stop them from trembling, but it still hurt to think of that little girl spending the whole of yesterday sick and in pain and probably very frightened of what was happening to her.

'Then what is the matter?' he asked. 'You look almost—hunted.'

'I'm fine,' she lied. 'I n-need to ring my father next, that's all.'

'Ah,' he said, as if that explained everything. 'Would you prefer me to make that particular call for you?' he offered.

Instantly her chin lifted and her eyes met his with their usual defiance to give him his answer. He smiled wryly. 'You trust me about as much as you trust him, don't you?'

Mia didn't answer—didn't need to. He knew exactly how little she trusted him.

The housekeeper answered her call. The moment she heard Mia's voice she went off on a harried burst of speech that showed just how anxious she had been about Suzanna.

Mia listened with her eyes lowered and her fingers clenched. Her knuckles were white around the receiver as she strove to contain the black anger that was building inside her.

For three days Suzanna had been complaining of pain—and for three long, wretched days her father had cruelly dismissed the child's distress as a ploy to bring her precious Mia back.

Her eyes began to flash and her heart to pump on an adrenaline rush. Beside her, Alex shifted his position a little, catching her attention and bringing those green eyes flashing upwards to pierce him with enough burning venom to make his own blink.

'No—no, Cissy,' she murmured smoothly, in reply to whatever the housekeeper had said to her. 'I'm right here in London. I visited Suzanna last night, and I'm going back to the hospital this morning so you don't have to worry about her now.'

Another volley of words hit her burning eardrums and

Mia had difficulty containing what was screaming to be released inside her.

Alex brought a hand up to grab her chin, then tugged it around in his direction. His eyes were black, boring into hers with stunned fascination. 'My God,' he breathed. 'You're cracking up! The ice is beginning to melt at last!'

'Is my father there?' she asked the housekeeper in a voice as cool and calm as a mill pond on a winter's day, while her eyes spat murder into those probing black ones. 'Can I speak to him, please?'

Cissy told her that her father had meetings all day and that he had left the house very early, without even bothering to ask after Suzanna. Why? Because the child held no great importance in the real plan of things! She was simply a very small pawn he used to make Mia jump to his bidding.

Another loss leader.

It was cruel, it was sick and it was downright criminal. By the time Mia replaced the telephone she was shaking like a leaf and ready to hit out at the nearest person.

Alex.

Angrily she turned away from him, her slender arms wrapping around her own body in an effort to contain what was desperately clamouring to burst free.

'Mia—'

'Say one more word,' she bit out, 'and I am likely to spoil your handsome features!'

There was a choked gasp from behind her. 'What did she say to you?' he demanded roughly.

'Nothing you would find unacceptable,' she retorted. Then, because she knew she needed to calm down because she could feel the usual dizziness surging up to pay her back for allowing herself to get this agitated, she took a jerky step towards the door. 'I need to—'

'No!' The hand that closed around her wrist stopped her from going anywhere. 'I want to know what she said to make you so angry,' Alex insisted grimly.

Mia rounded on him like a virago. Her teeth bared and her eyes spitting green fire, she hit out at him with her free fist. It missed its target because he ducked out of its way—which in turn sent her off balance so she stumbled and would have fallen if he hadn't caught her to him.

'What the hell was that for?'

'Three days!' she choked out. 'She was ill for three whole days before my father condescended to let Cissy bring in a doctor!'

'And you think I could be that callous?' He looked white suddenly—white with anger. 'I am *not* your damned father!' he railed at her furiously.

No, she thought, you are just the man who is breaking my heart in two! 'Oh, God,' she said brokenly when she realised just what she was telling herself. 'Let go of me,' she whispered, feeling the all too ready tears beginning to build inside.

Maybe he sensed them threatening—certainly he could feel the way her body was trembling as he was holding her so close—because, on a driven sigh, he let go of her. 'You should not let yourself get upset like this,' he muttered. 'In your present condition it cannot be good for you.'

Ah, her present condition. Mia allowed herself a tight smile. 'I'm fine,' she said grimly, pulling herself together. 'It's my sister's health that worries me, not my own.'

'Your *daughter,*' he corrected.

'Sister,' she repeated. 'She will not be my daughter again until I have safely delivered this child I am carrying now.'

Alex came with her to the hospital that morning, though Mia wished he could have shown a bit of sensitivity and let her have this first very painful meeting with Suzanna alone.

As it was, the child took one look at her as she walked in the room and dissolved into a flood of tears. Mia just gathered her gently into her arms and held her there, struggling hard not to weep herself.

'Daddy said you wouldn't come,' the child sobbed as she clung to her. 'He said you didn't want me any more because I'm a nuisance.'

'That's not true, darling,' Mia murmured reassuringly. 'You will never be a nuisance to me and I will always come if you need me. Always. Didn't I promise you that the last time I saw you?'

'But he said you'd gone away to start your own family!' the child sobbed out accusingly. 'S-so I'd better get used to you not being around! But I missed you, Mia!'

It was a cry from the heart that cut so deep even Alex, a silent witness to this tragic overload of emotion, could not stay silent any longer.

'Hello,' he said, stopping Suzanna's tears as if he'd thrown a switch.

Her face came out of Mia's shoulder so she could look towards that deep, smooth, very male voice, first in surprise because she hadn't noticed him come in with her precious Mia and then with all the natural wariness of a child towards any total stranger.

A very tall, very dark, very handsome stranger, who was smiling the kind of smile that made Mia's heart flip because she recognised it as the same smile he had once used on her—before her father's bargain had effectively killed it.

'My name is Alex,' he introduced himself. 'Mia is my wife.'

Wife. Her heart flipped a second time. He had formally acknowledged her as his wife for the first time ever, and the word seemed to echo strangely inside her head.

Like a lie that wasn't quite a lie but still sounded like one nonetheless.

'And you are Suzanna...' With each gently spoken word he came closer, holding Suzanna's attention like a hovering hawk mesmerising a wary rabbit. He came down on his haunches beside the bed where Mia was holding the child against her. 'I am very pleased to meet you.'

He offered Suzanna his hand in greeting. Her tear-spiked lashes flickered to the hand, then uncertainly back to his face again—before finally looking to Mia in search of some hint as to how she should respond.

Don't ask me, Mia thought drily. I still haven't worked that one out and I've been living with him for months. She smiled reassuringly. 'It's OK. You can like him. He's nice.'

'Thank you,' Alex murmured in a dry undertone that said he'd caught the mocking intonation behind the remark.

By then Suzanna was cautiously placing her little hand in his, and Alex's full attention was back on the child.

It was a revelation, simply because Mia had never known he had it in him, but within minutes Suzanna had forgotten her tears, forgotten her woes. In fact, she seemed to have forgotten everything as, with amazing intuition, Alex breached the little girl's natural shyness with men in general by encouraging her to describe—in lurid detail—every stage of her emergency dash to the hospital in an ambulance and the ensuing course of events that had led to her waking up here in this bed with stitches in her tummy.

'They're horrid,' she confided. 'They hurt when I move.'

'Then try not to move too much,' advised the man, whose simple logic seemed to appeal to the child.

'Thank you,' Mia murmured gratefully an hour or so later, when Suzanna had drifted into a contented sleep.

'For diverting her mind from the horrors your father has fed into her?' He got up from the bed where somehow he had managed to swap places with Mia so she had ended up seated more comfortably on the bedside chair. 'That does not require thanks,' he stated grimly. 'It requires defending.'

He was right. It did. Mia didn't even take offence at the comment. 'He is not a nice man.' She sighed. 'He likes to control people. You, me, Suzanna—anyone he can gain power over.'

'Which does not justify her being treated to that kind of mental torture,' Alex countered harshly.

Mia went pale, but she nodded in agreement. 'Maybe now you can understand why I had to marry you. I had to do what was necessary so I can remove her from his influence.'

'An influence she should never have been exposed to in the first place!'

They had been talking in low voices by necessity in such close proximity to the sleeping Suzanna, but those words cut so deep into Mia's bones that she could not sit still and take them on the chin as she really knew she should do.

She got to her feet and walked right out of the room on legs that were shaking so badly they could barely support her.

When Alex eventually came looking for her he found her standing in the corridor, staring out of one of the windows that overlooked the hospital car park.

'I'm sorry,' he said heavily as he came up behind her. 'I did not mean to sound so critical of you. It was your father I was condemning.'

She didn't believe him. 'You think I am the lowest of the low for handing my child over to him,' she murmured unsteadily. 'And don't think that I don't know it!'

'That is your own guilty conscience talking,' he said with a sigh. 'I only wish you could have told me from the beginning why you had been forced to agree to this marriage!'

'What was I supposed to say?' she said cynically. 'Oh, by the way, I'm doing this because I had another child but I gave her away and this is the only way I can get her back again?' Her eyes flashed, her cheeks blooming with anger. 'That would really have made you respect me, wouldn't it?'

'And you want my respect?' he asked huskily.

Her heart hurt with the truthful answer to that question. 'I just want to get through these next few months without falling apart,' she answered shakily.

Silence greeted that, a grim kind of silence that held them both very still in that hospital corridor. Alex stood behind her, a dominating force as he stared over her shoulder at the car park beyond.

Mia felt like crying. Why, she didn't know—except maybe it had something to do with the need pounding away inside her breast that wanted her just to turn around and throw herself against the big, hard chest behind her.

'Do you have copies of the adoption documents?' Alex asked suddenly.

She steadied her lips and nodded. 'Yes,' she whispered.

'Where are they?'

Mia frowned at the question and turned to face him. 'I keep them with my other papers in my vanity case back at the villa in Skiathos,' she told him. 'Why?'

'Because I would like to see them, if you have no objection.'

No objection? Of course she had objections as a sudden fear drained her face of its colour. 'You want to use them against me, don't you?' she accused him shakily. 'You think that if I gave my child away once then a court of law would not give me custody of a second child! You—'

'You,' he cut in angrily, 'have a nasty, suspicious, insulting mind!' He was so very right!

'And that makes you feel very superior to me, doesn't it?' she flashed back hotly. 'Well, let me tell you something, Alex. I won't ever think you superior to me while you go on believing that a lump of rock somewhere in the Aegean is more important to you than your own DNA!'

CHAPTER EIGHT

ALEX rocked back on his heels as if Mia had struck him. He looked frighteningly angry and Mia couldn't breathe—she didn't dare to in case she released whatever it was she could see threatening to explode inside him. Her heart began to hammer, the world beyond his stone-like stance blurring at the edges. Then he moved, and so did she, sucking air into her starved lungs on a tension-packed gasp.

What she'd thought he'd been about to do to her she had no idea, but when he turned on his heel and strode away she stared after him with horror that verged on remorse.

Because it hit her—really hit her as she watched him go—that she had just inadvertently struck at the very heart of him, though she did not know how or with what!

When she was ready to leave Suzanna, after eating her tea with the little girl, it was Carol who appeared in the doorway to the little room.

'Oh, you have to be Mia's sister because you are like two peas from the same pod!' she declared, making Mia jump nervously and scan the empty space around Carol in the flesh-tingling fear that Alex would be there.

He wasn't. For the next ten minutes Carol talked Suzanna into a blank daze as she produced, during her mindless chatter, little presents from the capacious black canvas bag she'd had slung over her shoulder when she arrived.

A pocket computer game. 'From Alex,' she explained to Suzanna. 'He thought it may help to fill the time in when Mia has to rest. She's making a baby—did you know she's making a baby?'

Suzanna gave a nod about the baby, whispered a thank-you for the computer game and stared at the beautiful Carol with something close to star-struck idolisation as the other woman chatted on as if they'd known each other all their lives.

'Now, I've been ordered by Uncle Alex to take Mia home and make her rest,' Carol informed her latest conquest, 'so she can be fresh as a daisy when she comes back here tomorrow.'

'Will you come, too?'

Mia felt the wall around her heart crack, oozing a warm, sticky liquid called heartache for this child of hers who was so hungry for this kind of warm affection.

'I'll be coming to collect Mia after I've finished work.' Carol nodded.

When Mia bent down to receive her goodnight kiss the little girl clung to her neck. 'You will come back again, won't you?' she whispered anxiously.

'Tomorrow morning,' Mia promised.

'What did you say to put Alex in such a bad mood?' Carol asked the moment they were inside her car. 'He's been stomping around the hotel like a demolition man all afternoon.'

'You work there, too?' Mia asked in surprise.

'You think I'm a real blonde bimbo, don't you?' She grinned. 'I'm not, you know. I am an interior designer. I work on all the Doumas projects.'

She changed gear with a flourish and changed lanes with the deftness of someone who was used to taking on London rush-hour traffic.

'It's called keeping it in the family,' she explained. 'Leon is the construction expert, Alex the one who makes every new project pay. We are in a rush to get this one in London completed so we can start on the island project once you've had this baby. Only the island will be a private renovation,' she explained, oblivious or just completely indifferent to the way Mia had stiffened up at the fact Carol knew exactly why Alex had married her.

'The house has been left to decay while your father has been in possession. The land around it has turned back to scrubland that only goats find idyllic. Once it was a beautiful place…' she sighed wistfully '…and we intend to return it to its former glory. Now you know that I know exactly what goes on between you and Alex, will you tell me what you said to upset him?'

'None of your damned business,' Mia said abruptly, feeling angry, bitter and utterly, cruelly betrayed. And, worse than all that, feeling as if every rotten word she had thrown at Alex earlier had just been well and truly justified!

'Since you seem to know *all* my business,' she added angrily, 'do you think I could have a bedroom of my own, please? Knowing it all must surely mean that you also know that Alex never sleeps in my bed! So let's make life easier for him and give him his very own bed in his very own room so he doesn't have to spend the night stretched out in the chair in my room!'

'Oh my…' Carol drawled after a long taut silence. 'I think I've put my big mouth in it again! Did he really sleep in the chair?' She had the cheek to giggle. 'That'll teach him not to play mind games with his next of kin!'

'I don't know what you're talking about,' Mia said crossly.

'I know,' Carol laughed. 'That's what makes it all so amusing!' The car pulled to a stop outside the white townhouse. 'Are you sure you want a separate bedroom?' she goaded teasingly. 'He's supposed to be a dynamic lover— so rumour has it. Won't you miss him slipping between your sheets to have his evil way with you?'

Too angry to care any more, Mia retaliated spontaneously. 'You have it all wrong,' she snapped, grappling for the car door lock. 'He will still slip between my sheets when the mood takes him. He just does not approve of spending the whole damned night with a whore, that's all!'

As an exit line it was perfect, except she had nowhere to exit to. She hurled herself out of the car, certainly, but she had to stand by the closed front door and wait until Carol opened it with her key before she could make her real exit.

'I'm sorry,' Carol murmured as she stepped up beside her, and for once the other girl sound genuinely subdued. 'Believe it or not, I wasn't trying to offend you,'

No? Mia thought. Well, you could have fooled me!

'I was, in actual fact, teasing you at Alex's expense,' she admitted ruefully. 'He was the one who insisted that you share a bedroom, you see...'

Which meant—what? Mia wondered. That he was attempting to save face in front of his family? Well, if that was the case, he should have kept his mouth shut about the rest of their arrangements, shouldn't he?

'Do you have a key for this door or do we stand here until someone arrives who does?'

'I have a key.' Carol sighed, and fitted it into the lock, then pushed open the door. 'Mia—'

But Mia was already stalking towards the stairs and so furious she was barely managing to contain it.

'He's going to kill me if I have to confess what I've said to you!' Carol cried pleadingly after her.

'Good,' Mia said between gritted teeth. 'Do me a favour and kill each other—it will solve all my problems for me if you do!'

'This isn't a joke!' the other girl shouted.

Then Mia did explode, turning round at the base of the stairs to glare back down the hallway. 'You're right it's no joke!' she cried. 'I am seriously having his baby! And he seriously impregnated me to get it! So don't you dare make a mockery out of— Oh,' she groaned as the hall began to swim around dizzily.

The next thing she knew she was huddled on the floor, with Carol leaning over her, her lovely face chalk-white with shock. 'My God,' Carol gasped. 'What happened?'

'It's all right,' Leaning against Carol's shoulder, Mia closed her eyes and waited for the world to stop spinning. 'It happens sometimes,' she breathed. 'Nothing to worry about. I'll be fine in a moment or two.'

'But you fainted!' Carol gasped. 'That can't be normal, can it?'

'It is for me,' Mia said, a trifle ruefully. 'If you could help me get to my feet, I think I would be better lying down in bed now.'

'Of course.' Eager to help, but feeling guilty for bringing on the faint, Carol helped Mia to her feet. Together they mounted the stairs.

In the bedroom Mia dropped weakly onto the bed and lay there with her eyes closed while Carol hovered anxiously, uncertain what to do next.

'Can I get you a drink or something?' she offered in the end.

'Mmm.' Mia nodded carefully. 'That would be nice. Just a glass of water, please.'

Two minutes later Carol was back with the water and Mia was able to sit up and drink it, without feeling dizzy. 'Mia...,' Carol began cautiously. 'Please don't let Alex know what I said before,' she begged. 'He's always going on about my big mouth. If he finds out I've been baiting you with it my life isn't going to be worth living around here...'

Thinking about it now the anger had subsided, along with the dizziness, Mia supposed the other woman was right. What was the use in causing yet more friction in a situation that was already too full of it?

'If you don't tell him that I fainted just now,' she bargained. 'He knows it happens,' she quickly assured Carol at her immediate protest. 'But he'll stop me from visiting

Suzanna if he hears about it, and at the moment the little girl needs me.'

'OK,' Carol agreed, but she sounded reluctant, to say the least. 'I'll say nothing about you fainting if you'll not chuck him out of this room so he knows my mouth's been working overtime again. Deal?'

'Deal,' Mia agreed, then lay back again as the front door slammed and the sound of two male voices drifted up the stairs.

'I'll go and head him off,' Carol said, shifting quickly to the door. 'If he sees you looking this washed-out he'll know something's wrong with you.'

Then she was gone. Mia could hear their voices through the half-open door. 'Where's Mia?' Alex was demanding. 'Why is your bag lying on the floor with its contents tipped all over the place?'

'Mia is tired and has gone to bed,' Mia heard Carol answer. 'She said to tell you not to disturb her when you came up. And my bag is on the floor like that because I was so desperate for the loo when I got home that I just dropped it and ran. Any more questions?'

It was a challenge, and one issued with her usual flippancy that belied any hint of deceit. The voice changed and became the brother's, whose tones were warmer as he greeted his wife the way loving husbands did.

After that, all went quiet as the three of them disappeared into the kitchen and Mia dragged herself up, got herself undressed and into her nightdress then fell between the sheets.

She slept very heavily and woke the next morning feeling thick-headed and lethargic. By the imprint on the pillow beside her, Alex had shared her bed last night, though whether he'd stayed there all night or had spent half of it stretched out in the chair she didn't know or care.

She was still angry with him for discussing their private business with the rest of his family. It made her feel exposed, more the outsider than ever, even though, on the face of it, he had allowed her closer to his family here in London than he had done while they were living in Greece.

When she went downstairs she found Carol alone in the kitchen. The men had apparently already left for work, and it was Carol who drove her to the hospital. Mia spent the morning entertaining Suzanna, who was allowed out of bed today and was walking around although she found it sore to do so.

They had just finished lunch, and Suzanna was resting on her bed while Mia read a story to her, when Alex walked in. He sent Mia a fleeting glance and then directed his attention at Suzanna.

'You look much brighter today.' He smiled.

The child smiled, too, her face lighting up like a puppy starved of affection who saw the chance of some coming its way in the shape of this man.

'I've drawn you a picture,' she told Alex shyly, and asked Mia to pass her a new sketch pad Carol had given her yesterday. 'It's to say thank you for my computer game…'

Inside were three pictures, although there was another one, which Mia had already been given for herself, of a church with a bride and bridegroom standing outside it and a child standing beside them, her hand tucked in the groom's. It said such a lot about the child's secret wishes that Mia had had to fight the urge to weep when Suzanna had handed the picture to her. Now she had it safely tucked away in the carrier bag in which she had brought Suzanna's gift—the set of story books they had just started reading. One of the set, *The Lion, the Witch and the Wardrobe*, was Suzanna's favourite story.

Now the child was solemnly handing Alex his picture. It showed blue skies and a large sun, beaming down on a man, a woman, a little girl and a baby around a swimming pool with a pretty house in the background.

More secret wishes unwittingly portrayed for the discerning to read. Mia had told Suzanna all about Alex's villa on Skiathos, and she had drawn herself there with them because that was where she most wanted to be.

No, thought Mia, Alex was not a fool. The way his eyes were hooded as he studied the picture meant he was reading all the right messages.

'I have one for the other lady, too,' Suzanna told Alex shyly.

'Carol,' Mia said.

'Carol,' Suzanna obediently repeated. 'She brought me these felt tips and the sketch pad,' she explained to Alex. 'She wanted me to draw my operation so I have—do you think she'll like it?'

This picture was gory in the extreme. When Alex finally managed to drag his attention away from his own offering to look at Carol's picture, he couldn't help the rueful smile that touched his mouth. 'I should think she will love it.' he murmured very drily. 'Thank you for my picture.'

From being ready for a nap, Suzanna was suddenly so animated Mia felt something painful clutch at her heart as she watched the little girl hunt in the clutter on her bed to unearth her computer game, which she handed to Alex.

'Would you like to have a go?' she offered eagerly, switching it on for him. 'You press this button here, then—'

It was like watching a light go out. One moment all three of them seemed to be basking in the brilliance of Suzanna's excitement and in the next, darkness fell in the form of a metaphorical big black shadow. The child had glanced up, that was all—just glanced up distractedly—and, wham, she was a different person.

Mia was sitting on the side of the bed, with Alex seated in the chair on the other side. She looked up, too, and rose jerkily. Alex glanced up, saw who was standing in the doorway and frowned as his eyes flicked to the other two then back to the door again.

Jack Frazier was standing there, transfixed. His eyes were locked on Mia's body, greed glinting in their cold grey depths as he absorbed the obvious evidence of her pregnancy.

'So it is done,' he said with unmasked satisfaction. 'Why didn't you tell me?' The accusing words were flashed at Mia. 'When is it due?' He laughed, and turned to Alex, who was rising slowly to his feet. 'I can't damn well believe it! Well done, man. Well done!'

Not seeing or completely ignoring Alex's grim expression, Jack Frazier walked forward to grab his hand and began to pump it up and down.

'When do we close the deal, then?' he asked eagerly.

On the other side of the bed Mia was reaching for Suzanna's hand as the child's hand searched for hers. Neither smiled. Neither spoke. As far as Jack Frazier was concerned, they might as well not have been there for all they mattered. Mia only mattered as a vessel required to make him his so-called grandson and Suzanna didn't matter at all.

'We will let you know at the appropriate time,' Alex said coldly. 'As it is, Suzanna's health is the main concern in this room.'

As a pointed reminder of his duty, Jack took the hint and at last condescended to notice Suzanna. 'Got your Mia back, then?' he taunted drily. 'The lengths children will go to get their own way.'

'She didn't stage-manage appendicitis,' Mia said tightly, as the poor child lowered her head so she didn't have to look into those coldly indifferent eyes.

'No?' He sounded dubious. 'Well, never mind about that. I want to know about my grandson. Were you going to bother to tell me at all, or was I supposed to wait until the damned thing was over and done with before I found out anything?'

She didn't answer—she refused to. She had nothing whatsoever to say to him that he didn't already know.

'Like that, is it?' He grimaced. 'Well, at least you carried through. I did wonder with this long silence whether you'd chickened out at the last hurdle. But...' he glanced at Suzanna's lowered head again '...we all have our price, don't we, Mia? And your price almost became a non-runner. I wonder what you would have done then?'

It was such a cruel thing to suggest that Mia actually swayed in horror. Luckily, the child didn't understand what he was talking about—but Alex did. In one step he had hold of Jack Frazier's arm.

'Let's go for a walk,' he suggested grimly. 'We have a few things to say to each other, I think...'

He had them both out of the door before Mia could react. The dire threat in his words filled her with such a dark sense of impending horror that her legs went from beneath her. She slumped down beside Suzanna and pulled the little girl close to her breast.

He couldn't mean what she feared he'd meant, she told herself desperately. Alex wouldn't break a confidence and tell her father that he knew about Suzanna, would he?

Oh, please, she prayed as she held the little girl even closer. Please don't let him say anything stupid!

'Daddy hates me,' Suzanna whispered painfully.

'No, he doesn't, darling,' Mia said soothingly. 'He just doesn't know how to love anyone, that's all.'

It was the truth. Her father was incapable of loving anyone. The man was a single-minded egotist who measured his own strength in his ability to close his heart to others. He had done it with her mother, with his children and with all his competitors when he'd squeezed them dry without conscience. He saw himself as omnipotent, his only regret in life being the loss of his son to carry on his name even if he hadn't been his blood heir. To Jack Frazier that hadn't mattered so long as Tony bore his name.

Now he had to accept second best in a child who would bear the name of its father and not its grandfather, but it was written into the contract he had drawn up with Alex that the child Mia carried would be given the second name of Frazier. For Jack Frazier, that was going to be good enough for him to bequeath his millions.

He made her sick. The whole filthy situation made her sick! The sooner it was over the sooner she could begin to wash her life clean again.

Alex didn't come back. Mia spent the rest of the afternoon worrying about what he'd said to her father. By the time Carol arrived, with Leon in tow, she felt so tired and wretched she was more than ready to leave.

But Suzanna was still feeling the effects of Jack Frazier's visit, and at least Carol's bright chatter helped to lift the child's mood again. Leon was quiet but, then, he always was. He glanced often at Mia who had removed herself to the window and stood there, gazing out with a bleakness that isolated her from the rest of those present.

While Carol was sitting on the bed, drawing a bold picture in Suzanna's sketch book, Leon came over to stand beside Mia.

'Are you all right?' he asked quietly.

It surprised her enough to glance at him. 'Tired, that's all.' She tried a smile and almost made it happen before she was turning to stare out of the window again.

'Alex was coming back to get you himself, but something came up only he could deal with. He asked me to ask you if you would mind waiting until he gets in tonight before you retire because he has something important he wishes to discuss with you.'

Something to do with her father? Mia wondered fretfully, and gave a nod of acquiescence.

'Thank you.' Politely Leon moved away from her again. He didn't like her, Mia knew. He resented the pressure her father had used on his brother. He resented her presence in his brother's life.

Back at the house, Mia found enough energy from somewhere to help Carol prepare dinner, then sat and ate with them in the dining room, though she felt like an intruder. But it was either eat with them or go to her room and eat alone, which would have been rude in the extreme. By the time they had cleared away after the meal, and Alex still hadn't put in an appearance, Mia couldn't take the tension any longer and excused herself with an apology.

'I just can't keep awake any longer,' she explained. 'I'm so sorry.'

She had just climbed wearily into bed when the bedroom door opened. *Alex looks less than his usually immaculate self* was the first anxious thought to hit her. He needed a shave and his clothes looked decidedly the worse for wear. His hair was rumpled, as if he had been raking impatient fingers through it.

'I'm sorry I'm so late,' he said, when he saw she was awake, 'but this could not wait until the morning.'

He closed the door and continued to stand there for a few moments, his tired face brooding as he studied the pensive way she was sitting in bed, banked by snowy white pillows, waiting for him to say what he had to say.

Then he sighed—heavily. 'Look, do you mind if I take a quick shower before we talk?' he asked tiredly.

'N-no, of course not,' she replied, but she would have preferred him just to get on and say what he had to because she didn't like the grim mood he was in, and she needed to know what he had discussed with her father. But he had already walked off into the bathroom, leaving her sitting there trapped in an electric state of tension.

True to his word, though, he was back in minutes. He had showered and shaved and looked marginally less weary, though no less grim, wrapped in a blue towelling bathrobe that left too much naked golden flesh on show for her comfort because her imagination was suddenly conjuring up images that set her over-sensitive breasts tingling and made that place between her thighs begin to throb.

Her knees came up, her arms loosely wrapping around them in an instinctive act of defensive protection for those susceptible parts of her body. But her eyes never left him as he came over to the bed and sat down on it beside her, the tension seeming to sing loud in the quietness of the softly lit bedroom.

'What's wrong, Alex?' Mia asked anxiously, unable to hold the question back any longer.

His dark eyes flicked up and clashed with hers, then he smiled a rather rueful smile at her that did nothing for her equilibrium. 'Nothing,' he assured her, then went silent, those deceptively languid eyes of his studying her worried face for a few moments before he eventually went on, 'Nothing that you need worry about, anyway…'

He did a strange thing then. He reached up to touch her hair, gently combing it away from her cheek and one creamy shoulder. The electricity in the air sharpened, sprinkling that well-remembered static all around her. Her heart began to race, those two over-active parts of her body sending her another jolt that reminded her just how irresistible she found this man.

'I have to return to Greece,' he announced, making her blink and forcing her to come back from wherever she had flown off to—bringing reality tumbling back into perspective. 'I expect to be gone for about three weeks.'

His hand dropped away. She wanted to shiver, as if she'd just been shut out in the cold, and hated herself for being this vulnerable to him.

'I accept that you cannot leave Suzanna yet,' he continued while she struggled with her foolish emotions, 'so I have arranged with Carol and Leon for you to stay here for now.'

At least he wasn't making her return to Greece with him,

Mia noted with relief, although remaining under this roof
with his brother so clearly resenting her presence didn't
exactly fill her with joy. Still, she'd lived with worse, she
told herself bracingly. And she could spend most of her
time with Suzanna—keep herself as scarce around here as
possible.

'The other problem is Suzanna,' he went on, as if his
own train of thought was following the same lines as her
own. 'She is due to be discharged from hospital in a couple
of days.'

'I'll go with her to my father's house,' Mia offered instantly. 'It seems the best thing all round. I won't be putting
anyone here out.'

Alex was already shaking his head. 'No,' he said. 'I will
not have you exposed to your father in your condition so I
have done a deal with him.'

Mia stiffened instantly. 'You didn't tell him you knew
the truth about her, did you?' she asked tensely.

'Of course not!' he snapped. 'What do you take me for—
a monster? You think I was blind to the way that child
shrivelled up in his presence—the way you did the same
thing yourself? You think I enjoy watching any child react
to an adult like that?'

Mia lowered her lashes and said nothing—after all, it
wasn't that long ago that he'd enjoyed seeing her cringe
from him.

The air grew thick, laden with anger, then he sighed
heavily. 'You cannot bring yourself to trust me even a small
amount, can you?' he muttered. 'So, what do you suspect
I am about to say to you now? That I have sold you into
purdah for the duration of your pregnancy?'

'Why not?' she shot back. 'I was in purdah before we
came to London. Why not put me back there again?'

'I have offered to take Suzanna off your father's hands
for the next three weeks until she returns to her school,' he
cut in tightly. 'Your father has agreed, so long as you both

reside at this house and Suzanna is not taken out of the country!'

'He's agreed to that?' Mia couldn't believe it.

'He almost bit my damned hand off!' Alex rasped in disgust. 'Apparently, his housekeeper is about to take her annual vacation, which meant him having to hunt around for someone who could temporarily take charge of the child. So you being here fitted in very well with his own situation!'

'Oh,' she said, disconcerted by the amount of thought he had put into all of this. 'Thank you,' she mumbled belatedly.

'That is not all,' he continued, all that softness she had glimpsed in him a moment ago well and truly gone. 'I have my own provisos to add to your father's. The main one is that you promise me you will come back to Greece the day you take Suzanna back to school. The reason I demand this is because I will not be able to get back to London to collect you myself so I am going to have to take your word for it that you will come back to me.'

'I'll come back,' she promised, frowning because she had never so much as considered doing anything else. They had made a deal, one where she had agreed to give birth to his son on Greek soil. 'I will drive Suzanna back to school, then catch the next scheduled flight to—'

'My plane will be waiting for you at an airfield close to Suzanna's school,' he interrupted. 'And you will not drive yourself anywhere while you are here,' he went on grimly. 'One of my own drivers will be left at your disposal for the rest of your stay here.'

'But I have a car!' she protested. 'It's sitting, doing nothing, at my father's house! It would be nice to drive myself again while I'm here in London!'

'Not while you keep fainting,' he said.

'I do not keep fainting!' She hotly denied that.

'But those dizzy spells affect you too readily for you to

be safe behind the wheel of a car. I saw the way you barely managed to hold yourself upright in front of your father at lunchtime,' he added tightly when she opened her mouth to protest yet again. 'So you agree to my terms or I take you back to Greece with me now. The choice is yours.'

He was, after all, only protecting his investment! 'Yes, oh, master,' she said sarcastically.

He had been about to stand up when she'd said that, but now he stilled and Mia felt a frisson of warning shoot down her spine as he turned those dark eyes on her—she recognised the look, recognised it only too well.

'You know…' he said, super-light, super-soft, 'you are in real danger of baiting me once too often, *agape mou.* And, despite the delicacy of your condition or the fragility of that protective shell you like to hide behind, I am going to retaliate,' he warned her. 'And you're not going to like it because I know your secret.'

'I d-don't know what you're talking about,' she said warily.

'No?' he said quizzically—and his dark face was suddenly very close to her face. Her eyelashes began to quiver, and her fingers clutched nervously at the sheet. 'Well, let us see, shall we?' he suggested silkily, and his mouth covered her trembling one.

It was like being tossed into a burning furnace—she caught fire that quickly. Her mind caught fire, as well as her body, and she wasn't even aware of how spectacularly she had done it until he was having to use force to prise her clinging fingers from his nape before he could separate his mouth from her greedily clinging one.

'Now that…' he drawled, touching a punctuating fingertip to the pulsing fullness of her lips, 'is your secret. You may prefer to hate me, but you cannot damned well resist me!'

His words made her want to hit out at him, but he caught

the hand before it landed its blow and arrogantly pressed his warm lips to her palm.

That was the point where her sense of humiliation plumbed new depths because the moment she felt his tongue make a salacious lick of her palm she was lost again. Her eyes closed and her breathing ruptured as that lick sent its sensual message down her arm and through her body, arrowing directly at the very core of her.

'I can delay my departure for an hour or two, if you want me to...' he offered.

That stung a different part of her entirely. Her eyes opened, angry fire burning alongside the passion. 'Only an hour or two?' she said scathingly. 'Well, that just about puts your attitude to sex in a nutshell, doesn't it? One quick fix then you're off again before the sheets get warm!'

He should have been angry—she'd said it all to make him so angry that he would walk out! But he completely disconcerted her by arrogantly taking up the challenge.

'You want more than that? A whole night of wild passion, maybe?'

'You aren't capable of spending a whole night in the same bed as me!' she said scornfully.

His eyes darkened. Mia felt real alarm take a stinging dive down the length of her spine. 'That lousy opinion you have of me really does need amending,' he said curtly. Suddenly he was standing up, determined fingers already working on the knot to his robe.

'W-what are you doing?' she choked. 'No, Alex...' she protested huskily, not even trying to pretend that she didn't know exactly why he was stripping himself.

It didn't stop him. Her heart began to race, her tongue cleaving itself to the roof of her dry mouth as she watched in a paralysed mix of greedy fascination and mind-numbing horror that magnificent naked frame of his appear in front of her.

The air left her lungs on a short, sharp gasp at the un-

ashamed power of his pulsing arousal. Her eyes moved upwards to clash with the fierce flame in his as he bent to lift
the edge of the sheet.

At last she found the motivation to attempt an escape,
slithering like a snake to the other side of the bed. His arm
caught her before she could get away. It drew her back
across the smooth white linen, then turned her so she was
facing him.

'I'm pregnant,' she reminded him shakily, as if that
should be enough to stop him.

It wasn't. His arm slid beneath her shoulders then angled
downwards across her spine so his hand could arch her
slender hips towards him. The firm roundness of her stomach was pressed into the concaved wall of his taut stomach.
He sighed a little unsteadily, his darkened eyes closing as
if this first physical contact he was having with their unborn
child was moving him deeply.

Enthralled by his totally unexpected reaction, Mia released a soft gasp. He heard it—felt the warm rush of air
brush across his face—and opened eyes which had gone
pitch black and seemed to want to draw her deep inside
them.

Which is exactly what he did do. He didn't speak—he
didn't need to. That expression had said it all for him. It
was need. It was desire. It was hunger too long-standing
for him to fight it any longer.

The last conscious thought she had before he completely
took her over was that he'd been right. She can't resist him,
not when he looked at her like that, anyway.

Her eyes began to close, her soft mouth parting as it went
in blind search of his. They fused from mouth to breast to
hip. It was that easy to give in to it in the end.

For the next few hours they became lost in each other,
the world outside with all its complications shut right out.

'Why?' Mia asked a long time later when they were lying

in a heated tangle of sensually exhausted limbs. 'When you rejected me the first night we came here.'

'I promised you I would not touch you again once you were pregnant,' he replied.

'You made that promise to yourself, Alex,' Mia corrected him quietly. 'I never asked you for it.'

He was silent for a moment, then gave a small sigh. 'Well, it is now a broken promise,' he announced, 'and one I have no intention of reinstating.'

Then he kissed her again, slowly, languidly, drawing her back down into that deep, dark well of pleasure from where she eventually drifted into a sated sleep, her arms still holding him and his still wrapped around her. It felt wonderful—so different from anything they had shared before that it was like a statement of future intent.

Yet when she awoke the next morning he was gone—as usual.

Which meant—what? she wondered grimly. A return to the status quo, with the sex thrown back in to spice it all up a bit?

CHAPTER NINE

SUZANNA was discharged from hospital three days later, and the time that followed went by much too quickly. Time that turned out to be a lot pleasanter than Mia had expected it to be, mainly because Leon's manner towards her had softened remarkably—though forced to do so, she suspected, by a child who was so very eager to please that even Leon Doumas didn't seem to have the heart to be anything but pleasant around Suzanna.

And that meant he had to include Mia.

Everywhere the little girl went, her fluffy rabbit, her pens and paper and her computer game went with her. Every night she insisted Mia read a story from her set of books. When in their company, her wistful green eyes followed Leon and Carol around like a love-starved puppy, eagerly waiting to be noticed. When not in their company she talked about them constantly, starry-eyed and happy, so pathetically grateful to the couple for allowing her to come and stay with them that sometimes it brought tears to Mia's eyes to witness it.

With the resilience of childhood she recovered quickly from her operation, and with the vulnerability of childhood she worried constantly about the moment when she would have to go back to school because she knew that was also the time when Mia would be going back to Greece.

'You might forget all about me when you have the new baby to love,' she confided one evening as she lay in the bed Carol had allocated her in the room next to Mia's.

'New babies don't steal love from one person for themselves, darling,' Mia said gently. 'They only ask that you let them share it. Do you think you can do that? Share all the love I have for you with this new baby?'

'Will Alex let me come and visit sometimes, do you think?' she asked anxiously. 'Will he mind if I share you with the new baby?'

'Of course not,' Mia said. 'Who was it who convinced Daddy to let you come and stay here until you go back to school?'

'Carol said Alex likes children,' the child said, with that painfully familiar wistful expression. 'She said Alex likes me because I look so much like you.'

Well, that was a very kind thing to say, Mia acknowledged, and made a mental note to thank Carol when she next saw her.

Carol just shrugged her thanks aside. 'It was only the truth,' she said. 'Alex does like children and he's got himself so tied up in knots over you that he's bound to like Suzanna simply because she looks like you.'

Tied up in what kind of knots? she wondered. Sexual knots? 'You don't know what you're talking about,' she replied dismissively.

'No?' To her annoyance, Carol started grinning. 'Did Alex ever tell you about his mistress?' she asked. When Mia instantly stiffened up Carol nodded, 'I thought he would. I know how his mind works, you see, and he would have told you about her just to score points off you. But I bet he hasn't told you that within a week of marrying you he had sent her packing.

'No,' Carol continued drily at Mia's start of surprise, 'I didn't think he would. Too bad for his ego to admit that, having had you, he couldn't bring himself to touch another woman. But that's our dear Alex for you,' she went on. 'Committed. Totally committed to whatever he turns his attention to.'

'Like an island he wants to repossess,' Mia said derisively, refusing to believe a word Carol was saying because believing would make her start seeing Alex through different eyes, which in turn could make her weak.

And she couldn't afford to be weak where Alex was concerned. She was already vulnerable enough.

'Certainly, recovering the family island has been the goal that has driven him for the past ten years,' Carol agreed. 'But marry some strange woman and produce a child with her in the quest for that goal?' She shook her blonde head. 'Now that was going too far, even for Alex. Or so I thought,' she added sagely, 'until I met you. Then I began to wonder if half the trap wasn't of his own making.'

'It wasn't,' Mia said coolly. 'My father is a master tactician.' And then some, she added bitterly to herself.

'Your father knew why Alex wanted the island back so badly,' Carol acknowledged. 'A solemn promise to his dying father—you can't really get a bigger incentive than that for a Greek. But I still say—'

'His father?' Mia cut in sharply. 'Alex promised his dying father?'

'Didn't you know?' Carol looked surprised. 'Come on,' she said suddenly, taking hold of Mia's hand as she did so. 'It will be easier to show you,' she explained, pulling Mia into the hall and then into a room Carol used as a working studio. 'See,' she declared, bringing Mia to a halt in front of a large framed painting.

It was titled *Vision* and Mia's heart stilled as she recognised it as the original of the print she had seen in the lift at the Doumas office building.

'Their father had this painted when he knew he was going to have to sell the island,' Carol explained. 'Until then it had been in the family for ever. See the little graveyard.' She pointed it out. 'Every Doumas, except their father, is buried there, including their mother and their older brother. They were killed in a flying accident when Alex was a teenager and Leon a small child. The accident devastated their father. He adored his wife and worshipped his eldest son.

'With them gone, he felt he had nothing left to live for, hence the sudden drop in the Doumas fortunes. His own health suffered until he eventually died prematurely—but not before he had extracted a promise from Alex that he would get the island back and have his remains transferred there. Do you understand now?' she demanded finally.

'Understand?' Mia repeated. Oh, yes, she acknowledged heavily, she understood. Alex's island in the Aegean was not just a piece of rock for which he was willing to sell his soul. It was home. It was where his heart lay, right there with his mother and his brother and where his father needed to lay his own heart.

She finally did understand that the grip her own father had on Alex was easily as tight as the grip he had on herself. Blackmail—emotional blackmail. A far more powerful vice than mere financial blackmail.

Her hand came up to cover her mouth. 'I'm going to be sick,' she choked, and had to run to the nearest cloakroom.

It was ironic, really, that Alex should choose to call her that same evening. 'Are you all right?' he demanded the moment she announced herself on the phone. 'Carol said you were sick earlier.'

'Something I ate. I'm fine now,' she said dismissively, hoping Carol hadn't told him exactly why she had been sick.

And what had made her sick? Her own words coming back to haunt her. Cruel words, dreadful words, where she'd condemned him for selling himself for physical gain while she'd self-righteously seen herself as selling herself for love.

'You must not overdo it now that Suzanna is out of hospital,' he commanded rather curtly.

'I won't,' she said. 'She's quite an easy child to entertain.'

'I noticed,' he muttered. 'Too damned easy to please. Have you seen your father?'

Mia frowned at his sharpened tone. 'No,' she replied.

'Good,' Alex grunted. 'Let us hope it stays that way.'

'Is that why you're calling?' she asked. It was so unusual for him to bother. 'Because you're concerned about my father showing up here? He won't, you know,' she assured him. 'Having reassured himself that all is going to plan, he won't waste thinking time on me again until the baby is due.'

'Does that bother you?'

Bother me? Again she frowned at the strangely sharp question. 'No,' she said firmly. Her father's lack of interest in her as a person had stopped hurting her a long time ago.

'Good,' he said again. 'I have two reasons for calling you,' he went on, suddenly becoming all brisk and businesslike. 'You are due your monthly check-up with the doctor this week. Since it is not logical to transport you to Athens for a simple doctor's appointment, I have therefore arranged an appointment at a clinic in London for you.'

He went on to give her names, addresses, dates and times which she had to hurriedly write down.

'And the other reason I called,' he continued, 'is because I have just discovered that I have your passport here in Athens with me. I must have stashed it in my briefcase without thinking about it, when we travelled to London, and there it has stayed until I unearthed it this morning. I also happened to notice that it still bears your maiden name, which makes it invalid.'

'Oh,' she said. She hadn't given a single thought to either her passport or the fact that it was no longer valid. 'I suppose that means I will have to apply for a new one.'

'I am already arranging it,' he announced. 'Leon is seeing to the paperwork so we can get it rushed through before you leave for Greece. You will need to put your signature to the forms Leon is preparing and supply a new photograph. Can you see to that first thing in the morning?'

'Of course,' she said, 'but I could just as easily have seen to the rest as well. I'm pregnant, not an invalid, you know!'

'I never meant to imply you were.' He sighed. 'But I presumed you would prefer to devote your time in England to Suzanna,' he said, in a tone meant to remind her exactly where her priorities lay.

Which it did—irksomely. 'Is that it?' she said, sounding childishly uncivil even to her own ears.

She heard him mutter something that sounded very much like a profanity. 'Why do you have to turn every conversation into a battle?' he said wearily.

'Why do you have to be so damned arrogant?' she shot back, for want of something to toss at him.

'Because I'm trying to save you a lot of unnecessary hassle.'

'I don't like my life being organised for me!' she snapped.

'I am trying to help you, damn it!' he exploded. 'When are you going to stop being so damned bitter and realise that I am your ally, not your enemy!'

When you stop tying my emotions in so many knots that I just can't tell what you are any more! she thought wretchedly, and slammed down the phone before she actually yelled the words at him!

Then she stood, shaken to the very roots by her own anger, because she didn't know what she was angry about!

Yes, you do, a little voice inside her head told her. You want him to show you a little care and consideration, but when he does you get so frightened it isn't real that you simply go off the deep end!

Leon produced the relevant forms for her to sign the next evening—several of them, which made her frown.

'Copies in case I mess up,' he explained dismissively.

She shrugged and signed where he told her to sign, and handed over the requested photographs—four surprisingly good snaps, taken in a passport booth in the local high street. Carol had gone with her and so had Suzanna, and between them they had turned the excursion into a game.

Mia now had in her possession several photos of Suzanna pulling silly faces into the camera, and even a couple of Carol, doing the same thing.

She kept her appointment at the exclusive London clinic Alex had arranged for her. They gave her the full works, blood pressure, blood tests, physical examination and an ultrasound scan. No problems anywhere, she was relieved to hear. The dizzy spells were a sign of low blood sugar levels, easily remedied by keeping light snacks handy. Other than that, she was assured, they were nothing to worry about. She left the clinic feeling very relieved to have a clean bill of health—and a black and white photograph of her darling baby curled up inside her womb.

'Did it hurt?' Carol asked suspiciously as she studied the picture.

'What, the scan?' Mia asked. 'No,' she said. 'It just feels a bit strange, that's all—and they did prod and poke the poor thing a bit until they could get him to lie in a good position.'

Carol handed back the photograph, but there was an odd look in her eyes that Mia couldn't interpret—a look that bothered her for days afterwards, though she didn't know why.

Another week went by, and Alex didn't call again—not that she expected him to after the last row they'd had. But it hurt in some ways that he hadn't even bothered to call to see how her visit to the clinic had gone—though she would rather die that let him know that.

Then other, far more immediate concerns began to take precedence, not least the way Suzanna grew quieter and more withdrawn as their three weeks raced towards their imminent conclusion.

Carol found Mia one evening, weeping over Suzanna's school trunk which Mrs Leyton had had sent over to the house that day.

'Oh, Mia.' Carol sighed, and knelt to put her arms around her. 'Don't do this to yourself,' she murmured painfully.

'I can't bear to leave her,' Mia confided wretchedly. 'I don't know how I'm going to do it! She hates that school!' she sobbed. 'She hates being away from me! It's going to break her poor little heart and it's going to break mine, too!'

'Oh, dear God,' Carol groaned thickly. 'I can't cope with this. Mia, listen to me!' she pleaded. 'You—'

'Carol…'

It was the flatness in Leon's tone that stopped Carol from saying whatever she'd been about to say.

'Don't meddle,' he warned.

'But, Leon!' Carol cried. 'If Alex knew how—'

'I said, don't meddle,' he repeated.

He was standing in the open doorway to Mia's bedroom, and he sounded so formidable that when Mia glanced at him through tear-washed eyes she thought she could see Alex standing there. Alex, grim with resolve.

She shivered. They had a bargain, she and Alex, she reminded herself staunchly. A bargain that was too important to both of them for her to stumble at one of the very last hurdles.

'It's all right,' she said, pulling herself together so that by the time she had pulled herself to her feet all that cool dignity she had used to bring her this far was firmly back in place. 'I'm all right now.' She smiled a brittle smile at the tearful Carol as she also straightened. 'But thank you for caring.'

'We all care, Mia,' Carol murmured anxiously. 'Though I can well understand why you wouldn't believe that.'

The next day Suzanna's trunk left for the school by spe-

cial carrier. The morning after that, pale but composed—
they'd both been through this many times before, after all—
Mia and Suzanna came down the stairs together, the child
dressed in her dour black and grey school uniform and Mia
in a sober grey long-jacketed suit, prim high-collared white
blouse and with her hair neatly contained in a rather aus-
tere, if elegant, French pleat.

She expected to find Alex's chauffeur waiting for them,
but she had not expected to see both Leon and Carol standing there also.

'We're coming with you,' Carol explained. 'Alex's orders.'

Alex's orders. She almost smiled at the phrase, only she
couldn't smile.

The journey to Bedfordshire was utterly harrowing.
Suzanna sat between Mia and Carol in the back of the car
while Leon took the front seat next to the driver.

One of the little girl's hands was locked in Mia's and,
clicking into a sort of autopilot, Mia talked softly to the
child as they swept out of London onto the motorway and
kept on talking as the car ate up the miles far too quickly.

As they left the motorway Suzanna began to recognise
her surroundings and grew tense, her hand clinging all the
tighter to Mia's. A couple of miles away from the school
entrance the tears began to threaten. Carol muttered something very constricted, then reached out jerkily to grab at
Suzanna's other hand.

'Hey,' she said, with very forced lightness, 'this is an
adventure for me. I've never been this way before!'

'I hate it,' Suzanna whispered.

'But look!' Carol urged. 'There's a private airfield over
there! I can see a beautiful white plane sitting on the tar-
mac.'

Airfield.

Mia shivered. It ran through her like a dousing from an
ice-cold shower.

'You know,' Carol was saying brightly, 'Alex has a plane just like that one! Do you think he may have come to—?'

'What's going on?' Mia interrupted sharply as the car suddenly took a *sharp* right turn. She leaned forward, staring out of the car window. 'Why have we turned here?' she demanded.

To her confusion, Carol chuckled. 'A magical mystery tour,' she chanted excitedly.

The car stopped. Mia stared and her heart began to pound heavily in her chest for in front of them, just as Carol had indicated, stood a gleaming white Gulfstream jet, with its engines running.

'No,' she breathed. 'No!' she gasped more strongly as a horrified suspicion of what was actually happening here began to take a firm hold on her. 'Carol, this is—!'

But Carol was already clambering out of the car—and taking Suzanna with her!

'Leon!' Mia entreated jerkily.

'Trust us,' he said, then climbed out of the car—and that was when panic suddenly erupted.

'You can't do this!' she protested, scrambling out of the car in time to see Carol and Suzanna disappear onto the jet. 'No!' she shouted after them. 'Oh, God!' Leon's arm came round her shoulders. 'Leon, for the love of God, you don't understand!'

'Believe me,' he said soothingly, 'I do understand. It's OK…' He began urging her towards the plane. 'Alex has fixed everything. You have no need to worry. Trust him, Mia. He has your best interests at heart…'

Best interests at heart? Her blood pressure began to rise in a swirling red mist that almost completely engulfed her. She stumbled up the steps, dangerously out of control and near collapse. With her eyes she frantically searched out and found Suzanna—then saw the man who was squatting next to the child, talking to her.

'Alex,' she gasped in confusion.

His dark head came up, his eyes giving her a look of such grim determination that any small threads of pretence she might have been clinging to that this was not what she feared it was snapped at that moment.

As if in rehearsed confirmation, Suzanna's voice reached out towards her, shrill with rising excitement. 'I'm coming to Greece to live with you, Mia! I don't have to go back to that horrid school!'

'No,' she breathed in pulse-drumming horror. 'Alex, you just can't do this!'

'Go and sit next to Carol and fasten yourself in, Suzanna,' Alex urged the ecstatic child.

He straightened, lean and lithe and dauntingly real in a casually loose taupe linen jacket, black trousers and a black T-shirt that did nothing to disguise the tight contours of his body as he began striding towards her. Even in the midst of all this trauma Mia found herself in a tense state of suspended animation, her senses remembering the man's sensual might and not the might of his ruthless intellect.

'Be calm,' he was murmuring soothingly. 'There is no need to panic…'

No need to panic. The words rattled frantically around her. No need to panic? Of course there was a need to panic! This was wrong! This was crazy! It was going to ruin everything!

Behind her she heard the muffled thud of the plane's outer door sealing into its housing and the jet engines give a threatening roar. Her whole body quivered in violent reaction, the clammy heat of horror suddenly racing through her blood, and on a whimpering groan of pained accusation aimed at those compelling dark eyes that were coming ever closer she pitched dizzyingly forward into total oblivion.

She came round to find herself stretched out across two soft leather chairs, with a pillow tucked beneath her head and Alex squatting beside her, his fingers impatiently dealing with the tiny pearl buttons that held her blouse collar fastened at her throat.

He looked pale, grim-faced and extremely angry. 'I swear to God, with everything I have in me,' he railed at her the moment he saw her eyes flutter open, 'that you will spend the rest of this pregnancy locked away in a bloody stress-free environment!'

The blouse button sprang free. He sat back on his heels, his eyes flashing with rage when he saw her catch in a greedy breath of air.

'And the power dressing gets its walking orders as well!'

Still too dizzy to fight back, Mia lifted an arm to her face so she could cover her aching eyes with decidedly icy fingers. Almost instantly, the hand snapped away from her eyes again. They were already in the air! She could hear the aircraft's engines as nothing more than a faint purr as they flew them ever further away from England!

Shakily she pushed herself into a weak-limbed sitting position, her green eyes flicking urgently around the plush cream interior of the cabin.

They were alone. 'Where's Suzanna?' she demanded jerkily.

'In the galley with Carol, having the time of her life,' Alex said sardonically. 'We told her you were sleeping. She didn't see you swoon into my arms so she believed us.'

Is that what I did? Swooned right into the arms of the enemy?

So, what's new? she grimly mocked herself. You've been swooning into those arms from the very beginning! Knowing he was the enemy has never made any difference.

'Is anything else too tight on you?' Alex asked. His hands were already pushing the grey jacket down her arms.

'Will you stop doing that?' she snapped, trying to slap his hands away.

But the jacket came off, and his grim face did not unclench from the tension locking it as he angrily tossed the jacket away. Then he seemed to make a concerted effort to get a hold on his temper. A deep sigh ripped from him, his big shoulders flexed...

'I'm sorry about the cloak and dagger stuff,' he said heavily. 'I did not intend to frighten you so badly with it. I was afraid that if I had told you what I was going to do you would have panicked and warned your father.'

Which she would have done—Mia freely acknowledged that. 'But why, Alex?' she cried. 'Why are you doing this when you must know it will be Suzanna and me my father is going to punish for this bit of senseless defiance!'

'No defiance,' he said, shifting his long, lean frame into the chair directly opposite her own, where he leaned forward, placed his forearms on his spread knees and then, with the grimly controlled expression of a man who was about to drop a bombshell on the heads of the innocent, he announced impassively, 'I am calling the deal off.'

Mia just sat there, her blank, staring eyes telling him that she had not taken in what he was saying. He remained silent, waiting, watchful, noting the way her lips parted to aid the very frail thread of her breathing and the way her pale skin went even paler, the green of her eyes beginning to darken as the full import of his words finally began to sink in.

Her reaction, when it came, was not what he was expecting. 'Our deal?' she whispered tragically.

'No.' He frowned and shook his head. 'That is a completely separate issue, which I am not prepared to deal with right now. I am talking about my deal with your father. I am calling it off and, because I know that my decision is going to have a direct effect on you, I am placing both you and Suzanna under my protection. Which is why we are flying to Greece.'

'Protection?' she repeated. He was placing them under his protection when the very act of how he was doing it was effectively removing the only form of protection they had! 'How can you say that?' she cried. 'Legally, Suzanna is still his daughter! Legally, he can take her back whenever he wants to!'

'You *wanted* to leave her behind?' he challenged. 'You *wanted* to dump her at that school and walk away?'

No. 'But that's not the point,' she said with a sigh. 'My father—'

'Can do what the hell he likes,' Alex cut in grimly, throwing himself back in his seat in an act of indifference. 'But he will have to do it through legal channels because it is the only way he will get to see either of you again!'

Mia gasped, her mind burning up in horror at his cavalier attitude. 'But, Alex—this is abduction!' She pleaded with him to see the full import of what he was doing. 'You could be arrested for it! You could go to prison!'

'Try having a little faith,' he said.

Faith in what? she wondered deliriously. In him? In what he was doing? 'Suzanna doesn't even have a passport!' she told him shrilly.

His expression didn't alter by so much as a flicker as he reached into his jacket pocket and came out with something he tossed casually onto her lap.

Two passports. Two new British passports. Her stomach began to quiver, her icy fingers trembling as she made herself open both of them. She stared down at the two similar faces, which were staring right back at her.

One was an adult, the other a miniature version of that adult.

'H-how did you get this?' she whispered, picking up Suzanna's very own passport.

'With careful planning,' he replied drily.

'But…' Her eyes flickered downwards again, looking at the photograph of her daughter which was a match to the several sets she had tucked away in her bag.

Carol.

The full duplicity of what had been going on around her

for the last weeks finally hit her. 'You've all been very busy, it seems,' she managed to say at last.

'I am, by nature, very thorough,' Alex casually attested.

'Even to the point of getting my father's written permission for this?' she mocked,

'You authorised it.'

'What?' She stared at him blankly—only her eyes didn't remain blank because they were suddenly seeing that blur of forms Leon had got her to sign. 'Copies,' he'd called them, 'in case I mess up.'

'We will *all* end up in prison!' she said wretchedly.

To her absolute fury, he started to grin at her! Mia wanted to hit him! He never smiled at her—*never!* Yet he chose to do it now, in this dire situation.

'Oh, stop fretting,' he told her, leaning forward to take the two passports back and replace them in his jacket pocket before she had a chance to stop him. 'No one is going to question your connection with Suzanna when she looks so much like you!'

'It's still wrong, Alex!' she flashed back at him. 'And why go to all of this trouble, anyway?' she cried. 'It would all have been sorted out above board in a couple of months!'

To her utter confusion, his face closed up. 'I am not prepared to deal with that question at this present moment,' he said abruptly, and got up, his whole demeanour so grimly inflexible that she panicked.

'But, Alex!' she choked, jumping up to grab hold of his sleeve as he went to walk away from her. 'I need you to deal with it right now!'

'No,' he said, shook his arm free from her grasp then grimly walked away.

The rest of the long flight was achieved in an atmosphere of severely suppressed tension—suppressed because Suzanna was so clearly delighted with the whole wretched business that it would have been cruel to spoil it for her.

But it wasn't easy, and Mia retreated behind a cloak of cool repudiation where no one could reach her, except Suzanna.

They landed in Skiathos in the full heat of mid-afternoon, and Mia broke out in a cold sweat which didn't leave her until they were safely off the airport confines and driving away.

At every turn she had been expecting to see a group of officials bearing down on them to detain them—by order of her father.

But—no. She found herself safely ensconced in the passenger seat of the silver Mercedes, with Alex behind the wheel and Leon and Carol crushed into the back seat, with an excited Suzanna sitting between them.

The child chatted and bounced and asked question after question that, thankfully, the others answered because Mia couldn't lift her mood to fit the little girl's

She felt shut off, bricked in behind a wall of anger, stress and a terrible sense of betrayal. She had begun to let herself like these people—to trust them even, which was no mean feat for someone who had learned a long time ago that trusting anyone was a terrible weakness.

Suzanna trusted them—Mia's eyes began to water. Suzanna was opening up like a blossoming flower to the warmth of their affection!

The car turned in through familiar gates and swept down the driveway to pull to a halt outside the front veranda.

Car doors opened, and they all climbed out. The sun was hot, the sea was blue and the white-painted walls of the house stood framed by the dense greens of the hillside behind.

'Is this going to be my new home?' Suzanna trilled in breathless wonder. 'Is it truly—is it?'

Mia spun to face Alex across the gleaming bonnet of the Mercedes. 'If you hurt her with this, I will never forgive you!' she said thickly, then turned to run into the house.

CHAPTER TEN

ALEX caught Mia in the hall, one hand curling around her slender wrist while the other clamped itself to her waist.

'Let go of me!' she protested.

His grip only tightened as he guided her—almost frog-marched her—up the stairs and into her bedroom. The door shut with the aid of his foot. Then he was tugging her round until she was facing him, his arms anchoring her there while she glared through a mist of bright, angry tears into his set face.

'I am *not* going to let anyone hurt Suzanna!' he blasted at her furiously. 'I am *not* doing this to hurt you!'

'Then why are you doing it?' she spat right back at him.

'I told you!' he rasped. 'I am pulling out of my deal with your father!'

'But *why?*' she repeated. 'Why, Alex, why?'

He let out a string of rasping profanities, frustration and anger blazing out of his eyes. 'Because of this!' he muttered, and caught her mouth with a kiss that knocked her senseless.

When he eventually let her up again for air she could barely stand up straight.

'I want you, I want our child and I want Suzanna *more* than I want my island!' he growled fiercely. 'Does that answer your question?'

Answer it? It virtually consumed it! He wanted her, really wanted her that badly?

Her face went white, her eyelashes flickering as she started to tremble. Her deeply inbred sense of caution stopped her from believing what he was actually trying to tell her. What his eyes were telling her as they blazed pas-

sionately down at her. What her own senses were pleading
with her to believe!

'Don't faint on me!' she heard him mutter, and suddenly
she was being lifted into his arms. 'Why is it,' he rasped
as he strode towards the bed, 'that you either pass out or
take my head off whenever I try to hold a meaningful conversation with you!'

He sat her down on the edge of the bed.

'You are driving me out of my mind!' he growled, coming down on his haunches in front of her. 'I cannot get
close to you unless I use sex as a damned weapon!' he
ranted. 'I cannot talk to you without feeling as if I am
walking through a minefield of mistrust! And if I actually
do manage to get through to you, you do this!'

'I'm not doing anything,' she whispered.

'You are trembling all over!' He harshly discarded her
assurance.

'That's because you're shouting.'

'I'm not— Damn,' he grunted, as he caught himself
shouting out a denial.

He sighed, lowered his head to run impatient fingers
through his silky black hair, then sprang abruptly to his feet
and moved right away from her over to one of the windows.
He stood there with his hands thrust into his trouser pockets
while he stared grimly outside, as if he needed time to
recover his unexpected loss of composure.

'I want you to understand,' he muttered suddenly, 'that
I have done what I have done because I needed to be sure
that you and Suzanna were safe before I made a move on
your father.'

'But why bother going to all this trouble at all?' she
asked, still none the wiser as to why this had all been necessary. 'In a couple of months we could have had everything! You—your island, me—Suzanna, and my father his
precious grandson!'

'No.' He refuted her words.

'Yes!' she insisted, coming to her feet on shaky legs that did not want to support her. 'Deciding to renege on your side of the deal now is not going to change the fact that I am pregnant with your son, Alex—which is all my father ever wanted anyway!'

'No, you're not.'

Mia blinked. 'I'm not what?' she demanded, her bewildered eyes fixing on the bunched muscles of his back.

The big shoulders flexed, his expression when he slowly turned to face her so sombre that she was arming herself for a really bad shock even before she knew she was doing it.

'You are not carrying my son.' He spelled it out more clearly.

'I beg your pardon?' Mia choked, then released a shaky laugh. 'What do you think this is, Alex?' she said mockingly, indicating her swollen abdomen. 'A mirage?'

'It's my daughter,' he replied.

'What?'

'Sit down again!' he barked at her when the colour drained out of her face, his long legs bringing him back to her side so he could push her back on the bed. 'My God,' he breathed harshly, 'I never would have thought such a strong-willed and fiery woman could be this physically frail!'

'I'm not frail,' she said in a broken whisper. 'I'm just shocked that you could say such a thing!'

'It is the truth.' He sighed. 'The scan you had last week shows no male genitalia—'

'But...' She was frowning in utter bemusement. 'Your family only makes male babies!'

'Not this time, it seems.' He grimaced.

'No.' She shook her head. 'I d-don't believe you. You weren't even there to see the scan!'

'Your doctor faxed a photocopy to me.'

He did? She blinked up at him, surprised to learn that

Alex had taken that much interest in her pregnancy. Then she remembered that she had her own copy of that scan, and she was as sure as she could be that it had not given any indication *what* sex their baby was!

She began glancing around her urgently, looking for her bag so she could check for herself what Alex was claiming.

He beat her to it, by gently placing his own small black and white print into her shaking fingers. After that she didn't move— not a muscle or even an eyelash. This photocopy of her scan was different from her own copy. Her baby had moved—and was showing clearly that Alex was telling the truth.

'Oh, heavens,' she gasped. 'How did that happen?'

It was a stupid question in anyone's books, and he said sardonically, 'By the usual methods, I should imagine.' The comment was probably well deserved—except Mia was in no fit state to appreciate it.

It was all suddenly becoming so wretchedly clear to her. What he'd gambled and what he'd lost. What he'd ended up being saddled with when he hadn't wanted any of it in the first place!

'Oh, Alex,' she breathed. 'I'm so very sorry!'

'Why should you apologise?' he drawled. 'We both know who takes responsibility for the sex of any child.'

'But your precious island!' She was barely listening to him.

Suddenly he was squatting in front of her again. 'Do I look like a man in need of sympathy?' he demanded. 'Look at me, Mia,' he insisted, when she kept her burning eyes lowered to that damning picture, then made her look at him by placing a gentle hand under her chin and lifting it.

His eyes weren't smiling exactly, but they were not miserable either. And his mouth was relaxed—a bit rueful maybe, and incredibly—

She sucked in a sharp gulp of air, shocked as to where

her mind had suddenly shot off to—and at such a calami-
tous moment like this!

'I have to confess to being rather pleased to be the first
Doumas to father a daughter in over a hundred years,' he
admitted sheepishly. 'I am also pleased,' he added more
soberly, 'that this unexpected development has saved me
from having to find another way of getting your father out
of all our lives.'

'He's not out of mine and Suzanna's yet,' Mia shakily
reminded him.

'But he will be,' Alex pledged.

'He's going to come after her, you know.'

'I want him to.' He nodded gravely, then raised his hands
to her trembling shoulders. 'Trust me,' he urged. 'Suzanna
is safe here. He cannot touch her. I know this absolutely,'
he declared. 'and by the time he arrives here I will be in a
situation to make *him* know it also!'

Mia wished she could be so sure about that. She knew
her father, knew how he responded to insubordination of
any kind. She shuddered.

Outside, a sound drifted up from the garden. It was the
laughter of a happy child.

A sob broke from her, and the hands on her shoulders
tightened. 'I make you this solemn pledge,' Alex vowed
fiercely. 'No one—will ever—take that laughter away from
her again!'

Tears slid into Mia's eyes. Alex watched them come,
watched her soft mouth begin to quiver, and something
painful seemed to rip free inside him. He shuddered. 'You
are so damned vulnerable sometimes it makes my heart
ache just to look at you!'

So was he, she realised with a shock that stopped her
heart beating altogether. Alex was painfully vulnerable to
her vulnerability!

'Oh!' she choked—why, she didn't even know—but in
the next moment her arms were sliding up and around his

neck, and just as she had done once before without any warning, she buried her face in his throat and clung to him as if her very life depended on it.

How they got from there to kissing feverishly she didn't know either. Or how they ended up in a heated tangle of naked limbs on the bed. But she knew by the time she took him into her body that something very radical had changed in their relationship because there were no barriers, no resenting the way he made her lose control of herself.

'I adore you,' he murmured against her clinging mouth. 'You crept into my heart, without my even knowing how you did it. Now I cannot seem to take a breath without being made aware that you are there, right inside me.'

'I know,' she whispered in soft understanding because he had done the very same thing to her. 'I love you so much that it actually hurts me to think about it.'

He reacted like a man who had been shot in the chest. He stopped moving, stopped breathing. 'Say that again,' he commanded hoarsely.

His eyes were black, his skin pale, his beautiful bone structure taut under stress. Mia lifted gentle fingers to cover those taut cheeks and held those black eyes with her own earnest green ones. 'I love you,' she repeated.

He caught the words in his mouth, stole them, tasted them and made her repeat them over and over again until the whole thing carried them off into one of those wildly hot passionate interludes that had always managed to completely overpower them even when they'd thought they hated each other.

'This is it,' Alex murmured lazily when they were lying, limp-limbed and sated, in each other's arms. 'I will never let you go now.'

'Do you see me trying to get away?' She smiled.

'No.' He frowned. 'But—' A knock sounded at the closed bedroom door.

'Alex!' his brother's voice called out. 'Frazier is on the phone! You had better get down here!'

'Well?' Mia asked anxiously. She was hovering in the doorway of Alex's study where he stood, leaning against the desk behind her, his dark face lost in brooding thought.

He was dressed in the same clothes she had taken off him earlier, whereas she had delayed long enough to drag on a lightweight dress of cool blue cotton, before hurrying downstairs.

He glanced up and smiled, but it was a brief smile. 'He is on his way,' he told her. 'In flight as we speak.'

Mia shivered. 'W-when will he get here?'

'Tomorrow at the earliest.' he replied, then grimaced. 'The airport here does not accept incoming traffic after dark so he has no choice but to stop over in Thessalonika...'

'W-what if he brings the police with him?'

'He is not going to do that.' He sounded so absolutely certain about it that she was almost reassured.

Except that she knew her father. 'Alex...'

'No,' he cut in, and began to walk towards her, his lean face grimly set. 'You are not to worry about this,' he commanded. 'I know what I am doing.'

In other words, he was asking her to trust him.

But it was no longer Alex she didn't trust—it was her father. 'I'm going to find Suzanna,' she murmured, turning away.

He let her go—which only increased her anxiety. It took real effort to lift her mood to meet Suzanna's bubbling effervescence as they explored together this wonderful paradise Suzanna was now calling home.

'You've got to believe in him,' Carol said quietly when she caught Mia in a moment's white-faced introspection while Suzanna was enjoying her bath, before going to bed in the room she had picked out for herself. 'Alex is amazingly efficient when he sets his mind on something.'

'He lost his island.' Mia smiled bleakly at that.

'Ah, but that was because it came down to a straight choice between his old dream and his new one,' Carol explained. 'The new dream won, hand over fist. If it hadn't he wouldn't have given the island up, I can assure you,' she said. 'He has astonishing patience, you see. He would simply have kept you barefoot and pregnant until you produced the son he needed to stake his claim on the island.'

Suzanna interrupted them at that moment, dancing out of the bathroom wrapped in a towel and looking so blissfully happy that Mia firmly thrust her worries away so she could pretend that everything was as wonderful as the child seemed to think it was.

The call that Jack Frazier was on his way from Skiathos airport came very early the next morning while they were all sitting around the breakfast table, trying to look perfectly relaxed.

But, really, the waiting had got to everyone by then. No one ate, except Suzanna. No one spoke much, except Suzanna. In fact, it was all so very fraught that when Alex took the call on his mobile it was almost a relief to know the waiting would soon be over.

'Right,' he said briskly. 'This is it.' He sounded so invigorated that Mia suddenly wanted to hit him! 'Carol, you were going to show Mia and Suzanna your upstairs studio, I believe,' he prompted very smoothly.

'Oh! Yes!' Like a puppet pulled by its master's string, Carol jumped to her feet and turned towards Suzanna. 'Come on, poppet,' she said over-brightly. 'This is going to be fun! Wait until you see the size of the piece of paper we are going to paint a picture on!'

Eager to fall in with any plans, Suzanna scrambled down from her chair and was at Carol's side in a second.

'Mia?' the other woman prompted.

'I'll be there in a minute,' she said, turning anxiously

towards Alex as the other two walked away. 'Tell me what you are going to do!' she pleaded.

'Later,' he promised. 'For now I want you out of sight until your father has been and gone.'

'But—!'

It was as far as she got. 'No!' he exploded, turning angrily on her. 'I will not have you exposed in any way to that man!' he swore. 'So do as you are told, Mia, or, so help me, I will make you do it!'

Her chin came up, her green eyes coming alight with a defiance that showed the old Mia, whom he had spent the whole previous night loving into oblivion, had come rising up out of the ashes of all that time and effort. 'Back to purdah again, I take it!' she said cuttingly.

'He's at the gates.' Leon's voice came shiveringly flat-toned from just behind her.

'Damn and blast it, woman!' Alex rasped out frustrat-edly, and in the next moment Mia found herself cradled high in his arms and he was striding up the stairs with a face apparently carved from granite.

He dumped her on a chair in her bedroom. 'Stay!' he commanded. Then he strode angrily back out of the room, slamming the door shut behind him.

She stayed. She stayed exactly where she was as she listened to the sound of a car coming down the driveway, listened to it stop outside the house, heard a door slam—shuddered and closed her eyes on a wave of nausea when she heard her father's voice bark something very angry. She heard Leon's dark-toned level reply, heard footsteps sound-ing on the veranda floor...

Then nothing. The whole villa seemed to settle into an ominous silence. She tolerated it for a while, just sat there and let that silence wash over her for several long wretched, muscle-locking minutes.

But that was the limit of her endurance, and the next

moment she was up, stiff-limbed and shaking, walking out of the bedroom and to the head of the polished stairway.

As she moved downwards she could see the study door standing half-open, and hear the rasp of her father's voice as he blasted words at Alex.

As if drawn by something way beyond instinct, she walked silently towards that half-open doorway.

'I don't know what you think you're damned well playing at!' She heard her father's angry voice as she approached. 'But you won't get away with it!'

'Get away with what?' was Alex's bland reply.

'You know what I'm talking about!' Jack Frazier grated.

Mia saw him then, and went perfectly still. He was standing with his back to her, every inch of him pulsing with a blistering fury as he faced Alex across the width of the desk. Alex was seated, looking supremely at ease in the way he was lazing back in his chair, his dark eyes cool, his lean face arrogantly impassive.

But what really struck at the very heart of her was to see Leon, standing at his brother's shoulder.

Her breath stilled, her eyes widening as she instantly realised just what she was looking at. It was like being shot back to another scene like this—in another study, in another country altogether. Only here the roles had been reversed. This time it was her father who was pulsing with anger and frustration and Alex who was looking utterly unmoved by it all.

Leon's sole purpose was to stand silent witness, whereas in London it had been Mia who had played that role.

A deliberate set-up? she wondered, and suspected that it most probably was. Jack Frazier had humiliated Alex that day when he had made him surrender his pride in front of Mia. Now it was her father's turn to know just what that felt like.

She shivered, not sure that she liked to see Alex displaying this depth of ruthlessness.

'All I know,' she heard Alex reply, 'is that you have been standing here, throwing out a lot of threats and insults, but I am still no wiser as to exactly what it is you are actually angry about.'

'Don't play bloody games with me,' her father grated. 'You've reneged on our deal, you cheating bastard! And you've stolen my youngest daughter! I want her back right now—or I'll have you arrested for abduction!'

'The telephone sits right there. By all means,' Alex said invitingly, 'call the police if you feel this passionate about it. But I think I should warn you,' he added silkily, 'that the police will demand proof of your claim before they will act. You have brought that proof with you, I must presume?'

Silence. It suddenly consumed the very atmosphere. Mia's spine began to tingle, her breath lying suspended in her chest while her eyes fixed themselves on her father's back as she waited for him to produce the proof that she of all people knew he had.

Yet…he didn't do anything! He just stood there, unmoving, in that steadily thickening silence.

It was Alex who broke it. 'You have a problem with that?' he questioned smoothly.

'We don't need to get the police involved in this if you are sensible!' her father said irritably.

'Sensible,' Alex thoughtfully repeated. 'Yes,' he said agreeably, 'I think I can be *sensible* about this. You show *me* your proof of claim, and I will hand Suzanna over to you with no more argument.'

Mia felt the blood freeze in her veins, an excruciating sense of pained betrayal whitening her face as she took a jerky step forward. Then her pained eyes suddenly clashed head-on with a pair of burning black ones as Alex finally saw her there, and she went perfectly still.

No! those eyes seemed to be telling her. Wait! Trust me!

Trust him. Her hand reached out to clutch at the polished

doorframe. Trust him! her mind was screaming at her. If you don't, you will lose him! He will never forgive you!

Trust him. She swallowed thickly over the lump of fear that had formed in her throat and remained where she was.

'I keep that kind of stuff with my lawyers,' her father snapped out impatiently, 'not on my person!'

Mia lost Alex's attention as he fixed it back on Jack Frazier. 'I possess all the usual communication equipment,' he pointed out. 'Call up your lawyers, tell them to fax the relevant information here and all this unpleasantness could be over in minutes.'

He even rose to lift the telephone receiver off its hook and held it out to her father! His body was relaxed, his face utterly impassive, and he did not so much as flicker another glance in Mia's direction as a new silence began to stretch endlessly, along with Mia's nerve-ends as she stood there, clutching the wooden doorframe with fingers that had turned to ice.

Then she jumped, startled as Alex suddenly slammed the telephone back on its rest. 'No,' he said through gritted teeth. 'You cannot do it, can you, because there was no official adoption!'

His hand shot out, picking up something from the desk and then slapping it back down again in front of Jack Frazier.

'You conned Mia into believing she was signing away all rights to her baby,' he bit out, 'when in reality what she did sign was not worth the damned paper it was written on!'

Her father was staring down at whatever it was that Alex had slapped down in front of him. Mia's eyelashes fluttered as she, too, looked down at the desk where she could just see a corner of a sickeningly familiar document.

It was her own copy of what her father had made her sign seven years ago. It had to be. Alex must have gone through her private papers, without her knowing it.

'She did sign it, though!' Jack Frazier suddenly hit back jeeringly. 'In fact, she was only too bloody eager to hand over her bastard child to me!'

'Oh,' Mia gasped, having to push an icy fist up against her mouth to stop the sound from escaping.

He wasn't even bothering to deny it!

'Or be out on the streets, as you so charitably put it at the time!' Alex tagged on scathingly. 'You played on her youth, her naïvety, her desperation and her inability to tell a legal document from absolute garbage!' he went on. 'And you did it all with a cold-blooded heartless cruelty that must make her very happy that you are *not* her real father!'

'What's that supposed to mean?' Jack Frazier jerked out.

'This is what it means...' Another piece of paper landed on the desk. 'Your blood group,' he said curtly, then slapped another piece of paper on top of it. 'Karl Dansing's blood group.' Another piece of paper arrived the same way. 'And finally—thankfully—my wife's blood group!' Alex said with grim satisfaction. 'Note the odd one out?' he prompted bitingly.

'Any questions?' he then asked. 'No, I thought not, because you knew this already, didn't you? Which is why you have been punishing her all these bloody years. Well...' He leaned forward, his dark face a map of blistering contempt for the other man. 'It is now over,' he said. 'And you are no longer welcome here.'

'But what's the matter with you, man?' Jack Frazier blustered in angry frustration. Something had gone wrong with all his careful planning and he still had not worked out exactly what that something was. 'If I am prepared to accept Mia as my daughter, then the damned island is yours when she gives birth to my grandson!'

'But Mia is not carrying your grandson,' Alex coolly contradicted. 'She is carrying my daughter.'

'What? You mean she couldn't even get that right?'

Dark eyes suddenly began to look very dangerous.

'Watch what you say here,' Alex warned. 'This is my home—and my wife—you are maligning.'

'A wife you didn't damned well want in the first place!' Jack Frazier said scornfully. 'But if you've decided to keep her, there will be other children no doubt—sons!' he added covetously. 'All you have to do is give me back Suzanna, and Mia will be as compliant as a pussy cat, I promise you. Another year and you could still have your island!'

'You can keep the island,' Alex countered coldly. 'I have no wish to set foot on it again. In fact,' he added, 'you have nothing I want that I have not already taken away from you. Which makes you defunct as far as any of my family are concerned. So, as you once put it so eloquently to me—the door, Mr Frazier, is over there.'

'But—!'

'Get him out of here,' Alex grated at his brother, his face drawn into taut lines of utter disgust.

Leon moved, and so did Mia, jolting out of the stasis that had been holding her to move shakily back to the stairs. She had no wish to come face to face with Jack Frazier. She had no wish to set eyes on him ever again.

She was standing by the bedroom window when Alex came looking for her.

'I hope you are pleased with yourself,' he said in a clipped voice.

'Not really.' She turned to send him a wryly apologetic smile. He still looked angry, his beautiful olive skin paler than it should have been. 'I almost blew that for you,' she admitted. 'I'm sorry.'

'Why did you come down there when I specifically asked you not to?'

'I don't know.' She shrugged. 'It was a—compulsion. I couldn't see any way that you could make him give up Suzanna, without giving him what he wanted, you see.'

'And in return for your lack of trust in me you learned

a whole lot more about yourself than you actually wanted to know!'

That made her eyes flash. 'I learned that you had the bare-faced cheek to go through my private papers!' she hit back indignantly.

'Ah...' At least he had the grace to grimace guiltily at that one. The anger died out of him, his warm hands sliding around her body to draw her close. 'I was desperately in love with a woman who refused to trust me as far as she could throw me,' he murmured in his own defence. 'Men that desperate do desperate things. Forgive me?' he pleaded, bending his dark head so he could nuzzle her ear.

Mia wasn't ready to forgive anyone anything. Her head moved back, away from that diverting mouth. 'When did you go through my private papers?' she demanded to know.

He sighed, his smile at her stubbornness rueful. 'I came straight here after leaving you in London,' he told her. 'Initially, I wanted to see if there was any way we could reverse the adoption,' he explained, 'but the moment I read that damned thing I knew it was not legal!' His angry sigh brushed her face.

'But I needed to get that confirmed with my own lawyers before I dared take action. And you had signed it, *agape mou*,' he added gently. 'My lawyers were afraid that if I faced your father with what I had discovered while you were still in London, he could have used the fact you had signed away your right to Suzanna to make the child a ward of the British courts while we fought over her.'

'And thereby gain himself a different way of blackmailing us into doing what he wanted us to do.' Mia nodded understandingly.

'It was safer for me to get you both here to Greece before I faced him with what I knew.'

'So you kidnapped us.'

'Yes.' He sighed. 'I'm sorry if I frightened you.'

Frightened her? He'd put her through a hell of uncertainty over the last twenty-four hours! 'You are as under-hand and cunning as my father,' she said accusingly. 'Do you know that?'

'I love you madly,' he murmured coaxingly. 'I would not hurt a hair on your beautiful head.'

In answer to that blatant bit of seduction, Mia turned her back on him again—though she made no attempt to move out of those strong arms still holding her.

And Alex was not going to stop the verbal seduction. 'I adore you,' he whispered softly against her ear. 'I *ache* for you night and day I am so badly bitten.'

'Which is why you keep a mistress, I suppose.'

As a mood-killer it worked like a dream. His dark head lifted. 'Ah,' he said ruefully once more. 'The mistress. You are after your pound of flesh again, I think.'

I want more than a pound of your flesh, Alexander Doumas, Mia thought covetously I want it all! 'I apologise,' she said with deceptive contrition. 'I forgot for the moment that I am contracted not to mention the mistress.'

He laughed, not fooled at all by her tone, and the arms holding her tightened their grip. 'There is no mistress,' he informed her drily. 'And there never *was* a mistress.' His mouth was tasting her ear again. 'I have not looked at an-other woman since the first night I saw you across a crowded room and was instantly smitten—as I suspect you already know!'

Mia smiled a smile of feline satisfaction. 'Carol did imply something of the kind,' she confessed, and arched her neck to give him greater access to the ear lobe he was tasting. 'I just wanted to hear you say it.'

'I'm going to rip that crazy contract up...' he promised.

'Good,' she said approvingly.

'And make you sign another one that will tie you to me for life,' he added.

'What makes you think I will sign it?' she challenged.

His mouth moved to her throat, his tongue arrowing directly for a particular pulse point he knew all about. 'I have my ways,' he murmured against that exact spot—and laughed softly as she drew in a sharp, shaken gasp of air. Her body was already beginning to throb in his arms with pleasure when a sound outside caught her attention.

Glancing downwards, she saw Suzanna appear, with Carol and Leon in tow. They were dressed for swimming, with towels draped around their necks. Hand in hand, they walked off towards the swimming pool area.

'She has them wrapped around her little finger,' Mia drily remarked.

'I know the feeling,' Alex murmured. 'Her mama has me tied up the same way.'

Mia smiled and said nothing, her gaze following the trio until they disappeared out of sight, then she lifted her gaze to the larger view of this, her new home. Out beyond the gardens the sea was shimmering lazily, and beyond it stood the misted green-grey string of smaller islands.

'Which is your island?' she asked.

He didn't answer for a long moment, seemingly much more interested in tasting her. Then his dark head came up. 'The one you can see directly in front of us,' he said, 'with the two crescent-shaped patches of golden beach...'

Is that why he had bought this villa, she wondered, because it looked out on his true home?

'Your vision,' she sighed. 'I'm so sorry you lost it.'

'I'm not,' he replied, with no hint of regret. 'Visions can change. Mine has changed. All I want is right here with me, in my arms.'

'Still,' Mia said sadly, 'it seems so very unfair that you have to break a promise to your father because my so-called father is such a dreadful man.'

'I have you,' he said. 'I have my child, growing inside you.' His hands splayed across her abdomen in a gesture of warm possession. 'And I have a miniature version of you in Suzanna, who worships the very ground I walk upon because I rescued her from your father. I am very content, believe me.'

'Well, your contentment is going to fly right out of this window if you move your hands much lower,' she informed him quite pragmatically—then tilted her head, her green eyes twinkling wickedly up at him.

And he laughed, a deep, dark, very masculine sound that had her turning in his arms to face him. That was all it took. Their bodies fused...so did their mouths...and they were lost in each other.

Modern Romance™
...seduction and
passion guaranteed

Tender Romance™
...love affairs that
last a lifetime

Sensual Romance™
...sassy, sexy and
seductive

Blaze™
...sultry days and
steamy nights

Medical Romance™
...medical drama on
the pulse

Historical Romance™
...rich, vivid and
passionate

29 new titles every month.

*With all kinds of Romance for
every kind of mood...*

MILLS & BOON®
Makes any time special™

MAT4

1101/59/MB22

MILLS & BOON

Christmas
with a Latin Lover

Three brand-new stories

Lynne Graham
Penny Jordan
Lucy Gordon

Published 19th October

Available at most branches of WH Smith, Tesco,
Martins, Borders, Eason, Sainsbury's, Woolworths
and most good paperback bookshops.

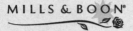